JUCHE

PART ONE

THE DEMON OF YODOK

ADRIA CARMICHAEL

To King Kim of Choson:

Please stop killing your people!

Cranes sang songs of joy from the mountain tops.

Double rainbows appeared in the sky.

The aggressors from the west were defeated. The invaders from the east were expunged. The traitors from the south were put at bay.

The people of Choson were finally free to create their own destiny, and so a hermit kingdom of people's rule rose from the ashes, and the doors to the enemies of the outside world were closed, never to be opened again.

The world around them moved on. Years passed. Decades passed. Peace and prosperity spread throughout the world, and nothing was heard from the secluded hermit paradise.

Then one day, people started emerging from its closed borders. The stories they brought with them were, however, not of a paradise on earth. Instead, what they depicted were horrors so vile and cruel that they almost exceeded human comprehension.

Little had the people of the kingdom known when they closed its doors to the outside world, that the vilest beast of all was still lurking among their midst, and as soon as the curtains had been drawn, the beast unleashed its reign of terror upon the people, not stopping until it had crushed and enslaved every soul within its reach.

The beast now rules the kingdom from a throne of human misery and agony.

No one alive has ever encountered this beast, but everybody knows its name.

JUCHE

"Hamhung"

"Hamhung"

"Hamhung"

My father's words echo in my head.

"Hamhung"

"Hamhung"

I'm standing in a long wide street. There are tall houses on both sides of me.

Where am I?

I don't recognize anything, but still, everything looks familiar.

Then I notice there is something on the ground around me. I try to focus, but my vision is blurry. There is something there. Some kind of objects.

Or…

Now the focus is getting clearer. They are bodies! They are everywhere. I jump in panic. I want to run away, but my feet are stuck to the ground.

I'm standing in a sea of sun-scorched, dried up corpses - as far as the eye can reach. Then I feel it. The stench of their decay stings my nose. I feel nauseous. I look down at the corpse closest to me. A man. He looks so strange. Like all his muscles and fat has been removed, and his skin tightly wrapped around his bare bones. All the corpses look the same.

All of a sudden, there is a movement in the corner of my eye. I turn my head.

Paralyzed with fear I watch one of the corpses rising until he stands before me a bit further down the street of death. He doesn't move, just looks at me with his dead silvery eyes. My blood is freezing to ice inside my veins. I look closer, squinting against the distant sun. The features of the man look strangely familiar. Then I suddenly see it. I gasp, and a flash of ice rushes down my spine.

"D-dad?" I utter below my breath. "Dad… what's going on… where are—?"

A loud screech in the sky interrupts me. I look up. A large black crow is circling high above us. Then another crow joins in. The screeching intensifies. Another one joins in, and then another. Before I know it, the whole sky has turned black with a swirling mass of crows, flying in a tornado-like circle right above us. I feel their beady eyes looking down at me.

The mass of crows now forms a funnel, spiraling downward toward us. I scream and put my hands up in defense. But the crows don't target me. The black moving mass instead completely consumes the living corpse of my dad.

"NOOO!" I scream as I helplessly witness the crows dismembering him piece by piece right before my eyes. They pull his eyeballs out from their sockets. They tear the skin from his arms and legs. I cry and scream. I want to run to him, to help him… but I still can't move.

Then it's all over, and the crows disperse and ascend back into the sky, bringing their ear-piercing screech and the pieces of my father's body with them. What was left of him is now again lying lifelessly on the ground. His face is still turned to me, but he had no more dead eyes to look at me with.

Another screech makes me look up to the sky again. The crows are circling ominously. Faster and faster. The screeching intensifies, cutting painfully into my ears, as they once more swirl down towards me like a tornado. I put my hands up in defense and scream as the first crow brushes against my hair. Another one grabs my arm with its claws. I try to break free, but my feet are still glued to the ground.

I now have crows all over my body, and as the one on my arm penetrates my skin with its beak, I…

Juche Year 83

-

May

CHAPTER 1

I woke up with a scream and the distinct feeling that I had just had a nightmare, but I couldn't remember anything - only the word *Hamhung* lingered at the back of my head.

Weird - I have never been to Hamhung… hardly even know where it is.

I lifted my head from my moist pillow and looked around me. Our bedroom was empty. I heard cluttering and voices from the kitchen down the hall, but no one was coming to see how I was or why I had screamed. Maybe they hadn't heard it. Or maybe they didn't care. Either way, I was relieved.

I let my head fall back on my pillow, and then I remembered which day it was. A smile spread across my face. I lied there a few moments more with my eyes closed, relishing the calm before the storm, and listening to the cheerful chirping of the spring birds outside my window. The morning sun felt good on my face. All bad feelings from whatever nightly misfortunes I had encountered in the dream realm were gone. Today was the day it was all going to change. Today was the day I was going to become free.

But first I have to get out of the apartment!

I sat up on my bed and looked at Nari's empty bed across the room. Usually, I'm more of an early bird than my younger sister, but remembering the many long hours of rolling around in my bed last night, I wasn't surprised to wake up later than her.

I knew it was a bit strange to call Nari my *younger* sister since she was only three minutes younger than me, but looking at us side by side, no one would have ever guessed we were twins. Nari was much shorter than me, and her slouching posture made her look even shorter. On top of that, she was probably the skinniest girl in school, and she wore thick glasses that made her eyes look big and weird under her too long bangs, which were just as flat as the rest of her hair. All in all, I would say that she still looked like an eleven-year-old girl.

I, on the other hand, was often told that I looked older than my fourteen years of age, and I always took pride in that, the same way I always secretly gloated when people treated Nari as a little girl. I even caught myself encouraging it sometimes.

Deep down, I did of course feel sorry for her. All those years of illness had really taken their toll on her and her body, and I knew she has suffered. A lot.

But so have I!

It was time to go. I rubbed my tired eyes with the palms of my hands and stretched my body back to life. I got dressed quickly and grabbed the bag I had prepared the night before. I could hear my sister and mother arguing in the kitchen - this was happening more and more lately.

I considered sneaking out without eating, but too much was at stake today, so not going to the kitchen was not an option. And Sun Hee would probably chase me all the way to school and make a scene if I did.

I can do this! Just in and out... don't engage!

I took a moment to compose myself. I grabbed my Great General pin from the dresser and rubbed it gently between my fingers - which I always did when I needed comfort or encouragement. Holding the smooth and warm metal firmly between my fingertips, I closed my eyes and took a deep breath… held it for a moment… then slowly exhaled. I repeated this two more times before reopening my eyes. I looked down at the radiating smile of my Father - the Great General on the pin in my hand and smiled back at him before attaching it over my heart on my school uniform.

I'm ready!

With my head down, I crossed the threshold into the kitchen and sank into my chair at the table.

The kitchen went quiet and tense, just like expected.

Don't engage!

I made a quick scan of the room just to see if Young Il had suddenly reappeared from wherever he was, but just like every other morning for the last month, his chair was empty.

My big, strong, fearless father! Working hard to save everybody - except his own family.

It was not unusual that he was away for long periods, but… *why didn't he tell us that he was going?*

Sun Hee was fiddling by the stove, apron tied around her back, her hair in an uneven knot at the back of her head. I wondered if this was how she pictured her life back in her glory days as a renowned theater actress. She didn't talk much about that anymore, but I sometimes caught her absentmindedly staring at her old posters that decorated our living room walls. Her face now was older and looked tired, but I could still see traces of her former beauty.

A bowl of rice and a bowl of pickled vegetables appeared in front of me by her hand. The sweet smell of the rice and the pungent smell of the vegetables tickled my senses. I felt Sun

Hee's judgmental and stern, but at the same time pleading, look burning on the side of my face. I bent my head forward to let the thick curtains of my long black hair shield her off. I didn't need to see her to know the look on her face. I knew it was the same look she had been giving me ever since my big news had struck down like a nuclear bomb a few months back.

I grabbed my metal chopsticks and started gulping down my rice, ready to endure the avalanche of pleads and prohibitions coming my way, but to my surprise, Sun Hee's attention was still on Nari.

"You need to set your priorities straight, Nari-ah," she said as she clanked away with the dishes.

Always using the endearing 'ah' with her favorite daughter, I rolled my eyes. *But for me - it's just plain 'Areum'.*

"I love your passion for learning," Sun Hee continued. "It's just that English is the language of our enemies… if you show too much interest in it… it might be dangerous.

"But they teach it in school, Mother," Nari said hesitantly.

I smiled to myself. Until not too long ago, Nari would never have contradicted our mother.

I guess even my mama's girl of a little sister is finally turning into a real teenager…

"I know they do, Nari-ah… but please understand what I'm saying to you - what's important in our society is to learn the teachings of the Great General. *That's* what you need to focus on. *That's* what you need to show interest in. What will people think if they see you hiding English texts inside the Great General's Memoir… his most sacred writing?"

Sun Hee turned away from the dishes to face Nari, kitchen towel on her shoulder, and both hands firmly on her waist - her go-to posture when reprimanding us or giving lectures.

I rolled my eyes again. I could never understand what was so fascinating about learning the language of our enemies. But

Nari had always been weird that way... *and who cares what she does or why she does it anyway. Soon she will be out of my life!*

"I'm sorry, Mother," Nari said in a low voice. "But..."

She hesitated for a while, but then drew courage to complete the sentence.

"But... I have already learned by heart all the passages by the Great General that the teacher has assigned to us. I have memorized the dates of his feats... all of his speeches... I get the highest marks on all the tests."

I observed with amusement how this poor little girl tried to defend herself against the towering beast of our mother. At least I was glad that Sun Hee's focus for once was not on me. I felt no pity for Nari.

What was she thinking? And also... why should I be the only one who gets reprimanded in this house?

"I'm just looking out for you, Nari-ah," Sun Hee continued. "I won't let the same thing happen to you as it did to... to *Mina*."

I felt like a bucket of icy water had been poured over my head and back.

Why does that girl keep haunting me? I can't escape her in my dreams, and I'm constantly reminded of her when I'm awake as well. If I could only go back in time and—

"Nobody knows what happened to Mina, and her... family," Nari's voice was breaking up.

"I'm sorry to bring her up all the time, Nari-ah... I know she was your best friend... I just want you to be careful... you know that people in our society who are not careful... sometimes... things happen to them."

"She didn't do anything!" Nari protested. "And she *wasn't* my best friend... she *is* my best friend!"

It was amusing to see Nari frown like that - it made her look like a little girl throwing a tantrum.

Sun Hee went over and squatted in front of her, putting her hands gently on Nari's arm.

"Oh, honey… it doesn't matter what she did or didn't do… what matters is what people *think* she did. What matters is what people *say* she did. That's why you can't go around like in a bubble, hiding controversial texts in the sacred writings of our Father - the Great General. Do you understand?"

Two tears rolled down Nari's cheeks.

"I understand, Mother," she said. "I'm sorry. I won't do it again."

"I know you won't," Sun Hee said, "because you're a smart girl." She gave Nari one of her radiating actress smiles and wiped the tears off her cheeks. "Always remember… there is nothing more dangerous than *appearing* disloyal."

"Yes, Mother."

Appearing disloyal, I scoffed to myself. Maybe *that* is the problem in our society. Maybe if people would just stop worrying about how they *appear*, and just be consumed by unconditional love for our immortal Father - the Great General like they're supposed to, our enemies wouldn't be able to pose a threat to us any longer. After all - only a weak and impure mind can be poisoned by the lies of our enemies. Everybody knows that. My eyes went to the picture of the Great General hanging on the wall over the kitchen table. He was young in this picture. And serious. He was a man - more than a man - who tirelessly was building this paradise… for all of us. I didn't need to look at the picture to see it before me - this was the same picture that hung in every room in every building in the country - even on buses and metro trains. I always found it comforting to see it, like he was always watching over us. Protecting us. Forever. And when I didn't have the picture before me, I could just close my eyes and rub the Great General pin over my heart to see it in my mind.

As Nari and Sun Hee's argument was coming to an end, I knew time was running out for me. I gobbled down the last grains of rice and pieces of pickled carrots, got up from my seat, and went for the door without saying anything. But as I was halfway across the threshold, Sun Hee's heavy voice stopped me dead in my tracks. Her tone of voice had changed completely from when she was talking to Nari.

"Areum," she said.

The kitchen went dead silent. Nari had stopped eating, and it seemed, even stopped breathing.

"Areum," my mother said again. "Don't go there today... after school... I beg you!"

Don't engage!

I finished my step and was now halfway out into the hallway. The front door was just a few steps away.

"Areum!"

This time Sun Hee's voice was harsher. I realized that my window was closing - it was now or never!

I made my move, determined.

Don't engage!

I grabbed my bag, which I had strategically placed by the front door, and put my hand on the handle. I could taste the freedom on the other side.

"Areum!"

Sun Hee was standing right behind me. She was so close I could feel her warm breath touching my neck. Her voice was still harsh, but this time broken with tears. Even though I was used to her crying over Nari, I was not used to her showing any emotions to me - apart from anger and disappointment - and I didn't know how to react to it.

"I forbid you to go!" Sun Hee continued pleading. "Do you hear me? I forbid it. You are not allowed to go."

Any moment now her hand would fly out and block the door, and part of me, to my surprise, wanted her to do it. But that didn't happen. For just a second I had the impulse to drop the bag and turn around and throw myself into her arms. But the bag remained in my firm grip, and I didn't move.

"I am your mother and you must obey me!"

The harsh command turned a switch inside me. I was once more filled with all the rage and resentment that had built up all these years. Towards her. Towards my father. And most of all - towards my sister. I pushed the handle and slammed the door open, hitting the side wall of the staircase. The deafening echo bounced around the body of our ten-story apartment building. I stopped for just an instant to make sure I wasn't being grabbed and pulled back into the apartment.

I wasn't.

Now there was nothing left to stop me, so I made a run for it. I rushed down the two flights of stairs, encompassing the empty space where an elevator originally was planned, but never built. I ran to freedom. Without looking back.

Sun Hee didn't follow me, but her continuous, and ever more desperate shouts, one by one growing closer to becoming screams, followed me, echoing from wall to wall in increasing intensity. By the time I reached the front entrance, they were completely overwhelming. It felt like an eternity before I managed to get the heavy metal door open enough to slip through. The screech from its rusty hinges merged painfully with the screams of my mother from inside. Then it closed with a bang, and there was nothing but silence.

The blinding sun hit my eyes. My brain struggled to process the contrast between the dark staircase filled with screams of desperation, and the warm sunlight silently caressing my face. My heart was still pounding, and my mother's desperate screams were still ringing in my ears.

Will she come after me?

Again, to my surprise, a part of me wanted her to.

I leaned back and rested my head against the withering, gray concrete wall of our apartment building. I closed my eyes - it was nicer than squinting against the sun. The cooling breeze brought with it the fresh smell of the river down the street. I took a deep, slow breath. Then another. And then another. Just like my gymnastics coach had taught me to do before a competition. The scene from just now, playing on the inside of my eyelids, was slowly being replaced by images of myself, tonight, at the stadium.

Finally, I will be free of this!

My anger and inner commotion started to fade. My emotions became centered. My body and mind became at peace.

Sun Hee was not coming for me. I had passed the first trial of today. Tonight will be the second trial - the trial that will change my life.

Failure is not an option!

As I opened my eyes, I noticed the birds chirping from one of the cherry blossom trees along the street again - or maybe they had been chirping all along. I was ready to move. I took a firm grip on my bag and stepped away from the wall. Then something caught my attention. There, in the dark shadows of the building right in front of ours, was a small red dot. It was barely visible, yet unmistakable. The red dot moved upwards. I squinted and held up my hand to shade my eyes from the sun. Something else was there in the dark. A figure. The figure of a man.

The red dot stopped mid-air, and as the man took a deep and slow drag on his cigarette, the intense red ember lit up his face, sending chills down my spine. The man's penetrating, ghostly white eyes were looking straight at me. More than looking - they were observing me.

In the split second that the moment lasted, I felt his gaze penetrating my soul, paralyzing me from head to toe. Then the ember faded, and the man's face disappeared in a dark cloud of smoke. I could move again, so I did.

I averted my eyes before he could take another drag on his cigarette and again paralyze me with his eyes, and started walking down the street. After roughly ten steps, I dared to turn around and throw a glance at the figure, but the red dot was gone. Left were only dark shadows, cast from the opposite twin of our apartment building.

I quickened my steps.

Get a hold of yourself, Areum! It's not like it's the first time you see a man staring at you!

I cleared the image from my head.

Today... there can be no distractions! Today... my mind must focus on one thing, and one thing only! And after school, my life will change for good!

The street was empty. No cars ever drove here, so, like always, I walked in the middle of the street. I followed my usual morning ritual of taking gymnastic leaps over the wide potholes. It was also a way to take my mind off things.

The ground was covered by the cherry blossom petals that, just until recently, had decorated the trees on the sides of the road in magnificent pink and white. Now the transient pink petals had given way to green leaves, signaling the end of spring and paving way for the summer. I wasn't sentimental, but spring, when the whole world comes to life in colorful splendor, gave me a lot of positive energy - and any source of energy was good.

As I reached the end of my street, I took a turn onto Tower of Juche Street, the grand avenue alongside Juche Park and the Taedong River. In this street, there were no potholes to be found, but still - no cars either. I saw some of my classmates walking to school in their usual groups, chatting cheerfully - probably about boys, like always - but I didn't pay them any attention. I always walked to school alone. Alone, or with Su Mi - if she hadn't overslept, which happened more often than not.

I stopped for a moment in front of the Tower of Juche. The strong sun reflecting in the still Taedong River behind it made it look like it rose from a sea of fire, and the same morning rays made the flame of Juche on the top come to life like a real fire, burning in magnificent red and gold.

Looking up into this flame of hope, I remembered the festivities on this very street five years ago, when I had only been nine. That day I had performed in front of the Great General himself. That day, *something* had awoken inside of me. And today, that *something* will set me free.

That hot summer day all those years ago, I had not awakened from birds chirping, but from a deafening noise from the streets outside my window. It was like the whole apartment, the whole building, the whole city was vibrating, shaking, pulsating. It was the first day of the 13th World Festival of Youth and Students, and the thousands of people who had flown in from every country in the world during the last couple of days were already out partying in the streets. There was music and shouting and singing and dancing. The usually so reserved and quiet city had virtually exploded with uninhibitedness and passion.

That day, I learned what the purpose of my life was.

I had prepared together with all the other performers for the past nine months, sometimes as much as twelve hours per day, through the ruthless cold of winter, through the constant rain of spring, and through the suffocating heat of summer. I had never been so exhausted in my life, but I didn't mind, because I had also never been so full of purpose and excitement. The spirit and the camaraderie of all the performers and instructors, together with the knowledge that we would soon perform before the Great General himself, was invigorating. And we knew we would help to show the whole world the superiority of our country that our eternal Father - the Great General had built for us. This was more than enough to keep us going month after month without a single word of complaint.

It had been the greatest day of my life - until today.

"Good morning, star gymnast!" Su Mi's cheerful greeting pulled me mercilessly back from the pulsating streets of that summer day into the present. "Wow, you seemed like you were miles away... thinking about *tonight,* I presume," Su Mi laughed.

"What have I told you about sneaking up on me like that," I snapped at her, but her cheerful smile softened me like always. Smelling her breath, however, I knew there was also something else contributing to her cheerful mood.

That's early... even for her!

But she hadn't overslept on my big day, and that made me happy.

"Ready for tonight?" Su Mi asked.

"I'm going to crush them," I smirked.

"Yeah, you are," Su Mi laughed. "Especially that painfully untalented Kyung Sook... I can't believe they're even letting her try out."

We then headed off to school, Su Mi telling me one exaggerated fantasy after the other about what amazing things will come my way after my mind-blowing success tonight. One of the reasons I liked to have Su Mi as my best friend was because she was also my biggest fan.

For myself, of course, I knew that Kyung Sook was far from being untalented… she might even turn out to be my toughest adversary tonight.

CHAPTER 2

"Areum!"

The authoritative voice of our history teacher, Mrs. Lee, pierced through the classroom and made me jump in my chair, harshly bringing me back to reality.

"Do the extraordinary achievements of our Father - the Great General bore you?" she asked. "All the hardships and struggles he went through for you to live a comfortable life in the most prosperous society in the world... without the oppression of our enemies... always having three meals a day... doesn't that mean anything to you, Areum?"

I looked at her, confused, and then at Ji Young, the extremely skinny girl who was reciting a passage from *On the Juche Philosophy,* written by the Great General's oldest son - the Minister of Culture and Propaganda - the one the rumors said is immortal, just like his father. I must have spaced out, staring blankly out the window again.

Live every second outside of home as if you're being watched by the Great General himself! One wrong word... or even one wrong look might be the end... for all of us!

Sun Hee's cautionary words that she had always sent us off to school with replayed in my head. Like a reflex, my mind immediately went to Mina. My old rival. The girl who was no longer here.

I quickly stood up from behind my desk and bowed down so deep I was facing my shoes, and with the deepest humility and regret I could muster in my voice - as if I was about to burst into tears any second - I yelled out the well-rehearsed apology I knew this situation called for.

"I am so deeply sorry, Mrs. Lee! I have profoundly dishonored the Great General, I am a disgrace, please accept my sincerest and deepest apology! I am so sorry, Mrs. Lee! I am sorry, my Father - the Great General! Please forgive my insolence! Please forgive me!"

As I kept my pose, awaiting the teacher's reaction, I felt the tear I had managed to squeeze out running down to my eyebrow and dripping down, hitting the floor with a tiny inaudible splash. The classroom was in complete silence. The seconds felt longer and longer.

Was my performance not good enough?

The uncomfortable position and my increasing anxiety made cold sweat pearl on my forehead, mixing with my fake tears, stinging my eyes.

Just as I gathered my strength to launch another, even more emotional and frantic apology that the teacher could not mistake for anything but the sincere remorse of a loyal subject of the Great General, Mrs. Lee said, "Fine, take your seat, Areum… but I expect to hear about this during the Meeting of Ideological Struggle this afternoon!" Her voice was still stern, but softer than before.

I straightened myself up and then bowed down again.

"Yes, Mrs. Lee! Thank you, Mrs. Lee! I will better my behavior for our Father - the Great General! I will be sure to bring this personal failure to the Meeting of Ideological Struggle today." My voice trembled with remorse and shame.

Acting had always come naturally to me - at least one positive thing I had gotten from my mother.

As I discreetly slid back into my chair, I looked over at Su Mi, who was sitting next to me in the back, and with a barely noticeable wink and a smile behind the curtain of my big black hair I signaled, *piece of cake!*

Su Mi laughed soundlessly into her hand - just for an instant - while Mrs. Lee was telling Ji Young to continue her recitation.

Facing forward again, my eyes met the stern eyes of the Great General in the picture on the wall above Ji Young. I felt his firm gaze judging me for what I had done. I felt guilty. Yes - my apology had been a well-rehearsed performance, but I truly did have the deepest reverence and gratitude for our Father - the Great General - our immortal leader who will live forever to take care of us and our children, and their children, until the end of days. For me, he was not only the father of our nation - he was *my* father… the father my *real* father never had been… and I would give my life for him in an instant. I gently caressed the Great General pin firmly attached over my heart. It felt warm and nice from being heated up by the morning sun seeping in from the row of windows to the left of me. It soothed me. It always did.

I started thinking about Young Il, my so-called *real* father, and my stomach turned. I didn't know what Nari and Sun Hee were so worried about - he always goes here and there on long business trips for his *precious* Ministry of Food Distribution, just like his father - our great and wonderful grandpa Kim Hyun Woo, a patriot of the highest rank and founder of the Universal Food Distribution System - had done before him. I guessed this time, Young Il just got so busy he forgot to tell us. It didn't surprise me at all. Sure - it was a bit weird that the Ministry wouldn't tell us where he was… but on the other hand, it was probably just classified… being important government business and all. Just like everything else he did. The Ministry was his real family - not us.

Ji Young continued her memorized recitation of *On the Juche idea*. Her low and weak voice sounded just as fragile as her body looked.

I swear… she must be even skinnier than Nari!

It was uncomfortable for me to look at her, so I stared at her clean but worn-out shoes instead.

"…It is more than a century since the days of Karl Marx, the great founder of the union of the international working classes and the author of the scientific communist theory. Karl Marx made a great contribution to the liberation cause of mankind, and because of his immortal exploits, his name is still enshrined in the hearts of the working class and peoples of all countries…"

A big yawn came upon me, and I struggled to not make it noticeable. Looking around, all my classmates were also struggling to stay awake, being helped only by the painfully uncomfortable wooden chairs we were forced to sit in. Mrs. Lee, on the other hand, was silently forming every syllable Ji Young was saying with her mouth where she stood next to the blackboard, nodding her head in enthusiastic agreement.

I threw another uncomfortable glance at Ji Young. She looked more than fragile - she looked sick. Her skin was all pale and flaky, and she had thick dark circles around her eyes and even some strange rash around her neck under her bright white school uniform shirt. I diverted my eyes again - I hated looking at sick people.

"…Karl Marx was the greatest thinker of the 19th century. His greatest contribution to mankind was that he created Marxism and gave the working class a powerful ideological weapon to help them to liberate themselves from oppression…"

I felt a nudge on my right arm. I knew the routine. I looked over at Mrs. Lee to make sure the coast was clear, and then extended my arm to receive the little note from Su Mi. This was an easy way of communicating during class since we always sat next to each other at the back, and without exchanging notes, most classes would be unbearable.

"…Thanks to Marx's outstanding contribution, the working class could finally see the road they should follow to attain class emancipation and to build a prosperous new society. He foresaw that the struggle of the working class against the capitalist class would inevitably bring about the dictatorship of the proletariat…"

I unfolded the note and read, *Hang out to celebrate after your tryouts?*

I smiled to myself. Su Mi was like the sister I always wished I had. She admired me. She praised me. She gave me full attention and required none in return - just like younger sisters should do. In our family it was the other way around - Nari was the one who got all the attention… her and her illness. I was truly grateful that they hadn't put me and Nari in the same class, although that probably had more to do with previous negative experiences having twins in the same classroom, than with my wellbeing.

"…At the beginning of the 20th century, in Russia, Vladimir Lenin continued Marx's work and created Leninism by creatively developing Marxism to suit the new historical conditions of the time and the local conditions in Russia. Thanks to Lenin and Leninism, the socialist October Revolution emerged victoriously, and the first state of proletarian dictatorship was born…"

I turned over the little piece of paper, and wrote on the backside, *Sorry, can't today,* and passed it back to her with a quick apologetic look.

I would of course rather spend the evening having a good time with Su Mi and her mother than being at home in my cold prison, but if all goes according to plan tonight, I wouldn't just go home to be a prisoner like always - I would go home to break free.

"...In a communist revolutionary movement, the leader plays the decisive role. If Marx had not founded Marxism, the international working class would have fumbled in darkness, not knowing their historic mission. If Lenin had not advanced Leninism, the first socialist state in the world would have never appeared..."

Only a few moments later there was another nudge, and I reached down to get the new note. It read, *Come on, you deserve some time to yourself to celebrate!*

I re-read the note a couple of times. Maybe coming home one hour later wouldn't make any difference... and she was right - I did deserve to celebrate!

"...Just like in the past, the same is true today. The communist revolutionary movement can only triumph under the guidance of a great leader. In our country, we are extremely fortunate to be under the wise and loving guidance of our eternal Father - the Great General, who for decades brilliantly walked us down the victorious path of national liberation under the banner of Marxism-Leninism..."

I had made up my mind - I will go with Su Mi. I could already savor the victory, and I knew how happy Su Mi's mother would be for me. Sun Hee and Nari could wait. They had no power over me anymore.

I turned around to Su Mi and gave her a nod and a smile. Su Mi formed, "yay" with her lips, and smiled back.

"...Since revolutionary movements take place in different historical backgrounds and places, the communists in each country must adapt the principles of Marxism-Leninism to the conditions of their reality and their needs. This was true also for our country - Choson - and so our eternal Father - the Great General, created the Juche ideology for us, on which everything in our country today is based. Juche means independence, and it is the Juche principle that lets us pursue our communist revolution independently from other

countries. With Juche as our leading star, we will never again let other countries influence our politics, our society, or our way of life…"

I started to half-listen to Ji Young's recitation. I liked the part about our independence and self-reliance - it resonated with me - but just then I was distracted by another note from Su Mi.

Can't go to my place today, Grandma's sick. The river?

I was disappointed. I liked to be at Su Mi's house. After her younger brother died, her mother kind of let me fill the void in her life. I was happy to be there for her. And it helped me fill my void as well. Su Mi's father, on the other hand, reacted differently to the death of his child - he drank himself to death. Su Mi was the one who found him in the bathroom one day three years later, the bottle still firm in his hand.

Either way, it was probably best not to go to her mother today - I didn't want her to feel like she was losing another child. And I wasn't good with goodbyes either. The river next to the stadium would do just fine - and there's a special atmosphere walking around in the pleasant fresh evening air, surrounded by the subtle shapes of the pitch-black city. It could be just what I needed to help me strengthen my mind for the confrontation to come.

I wrote, *Perfect!* And gave it back to her with a discrete thumbs up. She laughed, drawing a disapproving glance from Mrs. Lee.

"…The Juche ideology is a brilliant fruit of our Father - the Great General's ideological activities that cover more than half a century, and as such, it is the crystallization of the revolution in our country. Following the Juche-oriented leadership of our Father - the Great General, our people first heroically liberated our country from our enemies in the east after centuries of oppression, and then fought back the invasion of the imperialists from the West in the fierce Fatherland Liberation War…"

Thinking of Su Mi's loving mother made me remember that night six years ago. Nari was in the hospital. Again. I was supposed to be sleeping, but I was so worried about Nari that I sneaked out of bed to listen to my parents talking in the kitchen, hoping to hear something - anything - reassuring about her condition. I didn't. And that was the last night my home felt like a real home for me. That was the last night I had a family.

"…After the liberation of our country they continued to implement the Juche revolution under the wise leadership of our Father - the Great General, demolishing the old feudal society, and bringing the dictatorship of the proletariat to the northern half of Choson and converted it into a powerful base of the revolution in our nation. By applying the Juche idea we changed in a short time our once backward country into a powerful socialist state which is independent, self-supporting and self-reliant in—"

There was a loud thump. I looked up and saw Ji Young lying on the floor. Several of my classmates shrieked, and there was a commotion of desks moving and chairs falling to the ground as everybody rushed to the front of the classroom to see what had happened. Su Mi also rushed forward, but I stayed a bit in the background not to get involved - *there can be no distractions today!* - but still close enough to still my curiosity. Mrs. Lee was already down on her knees over Ji Young, softly slapping her cheeks.

"Ji Young! Ji Young! Wake up!" she shouted, but Ji Young didn't move. Mrs. Lee, now covered in a cold sweat, checked Ji Young's neck for a pulse with trembling fingers, after which she seemed to calm down a bit.

"Min Ji, go get the nurse! Jae Ho, bring me a glass of water and a cold wet cloth!" Mrs. Lee ordered a couple of my classmates, who immediately rushed out the door. Mrs. Lee continued to slap Ji Young's face and shake her body softly, calling her name. When Jae Ho came back, and Mrs. Lee applied the cold wet cloth on Ji Young's forehead, she started to move slightly. "Can you hear me?" Mrs. Lee asked. Ji Young's eyes opened slightly, but just for a second. Mrs. Lee lifted her head and put the water glass to her lips, and she drank a little.

Ji Young tried to say something, but nobody could hear it. Mrs. Lee put her ear against her trembling mouth.

"What do you need, dear?" she asked.

Ji Young whispered something in her ear.

"What did she say?" several people in the class asked.

"S-she said… *food*," Mrs. Lee mumbled. "Oh my poor girl, I'll get you something to—"

At that very moment, the bell rang, but nobody moved, looking nervously at each other and Ji Young. Then they turned to Mrs. Lee for direction, but her undivided attention was still on Ji Young.

I remained firm.

There can be no distractions today!

I got the stuff from my desk and grabbed Su Mi to do the same. Once the two of us had started moving it seemed that Mrs. Lee acknowledged that the bell had rung, so she told everybody, "Go on, go to your next class!" waving her hand, but keeping her eyes on Ji Young on the floor. "The nurse will be here any second, and there is nothing you can do anyway."

Su Mi was moving too slowly, her eyes fixed on Ji Young, so I grabbed her arm and said, "let's go!" dragging her with me out of the room.

"That was so crazy," I whispered to Su Mi as we walked under the half ceiling along the schoolyard. "What's wrong with her? Do you think it's some kind of virus?"

"I don't think she has eaten enough," Su Mi answered.

"Not eaten enough?" I said, surprised. "Why wouldn't you eat enough?" It didn't make any sense to me. I mean, I also had to limit what and how much I ate, but that was to improve my performance, and I would never eat so little it would make me faint in front of my whole class.

How will she come to school again after this? That was so embarrassing!

"I don't know," Su Mi said in a distant voice, "I've heard that some families have their food rations cut, so maybe that's what's happening to her... do you know anything about that? I mean, with your dad in—?"

I shook my head.

"Anyway, let's go to the bathroom, I need to fix my makeup. And so do you, by the way," she added with a wink.

Since the loss of her brother, Su Mi was not able to be serious for too long. I playfully pushed her shoulder, and we went laughing towards the bathroom. Of course, neither of us had much makeup to talk about, otherwise the fashion police - the groups of women who go around giving warnings and fines to people whose appearance doesn't fit the Juche lifestyle - would give us trouble. All we had was some foundation and subtle mascara. I would say that neither of us needed it, but for me, it gave me a sense of control over my life. It was the same for Su Mi. And of course - I did like the looks I attracted...at least most of the time.

Just as we were about to open the bathroom door, the door swung open from the inside, almost hitting my nose.

"Watch it!" I screamed in pure reflex, but then froze when I saw who was standing in the doorway in front of me.

Nari's eyes were puffy behind her thick glasses - she had been crying again. Su Mi looked at me, unsure of what my reaction would be. As soon as I unfroze, I diverted my eyes and passed around Nari to enter the bathroom without saying a word, and Su Mi followed my lead.

"Areum—" Nari said with a weak, broken voice, reminding me of Ji Young's recitation.

"What?" I sighed, rolling my eyes.

"Areum… can we talk?"

"What is there to talk about? I have to go to the bathroom and then hurry to my next class… so do you mind?"

For me, the conversation was over, but Nari continued blocking my way.

"Areum, please! Just give me a second! I need to talk to you!"

Nari seemed different today. Usually afraid of everything - even to look people in the eyes - now her determined eyes were fixed on mine. I rolled my eyes again.

"Fine!" I said and walked off towards the center of the schoolyard.

"You go ahead," I shouted to Su Mi over my shoulder. "I'll catch up with you in a second."

As we slowed our pace I felt the lump in my chest tightening and my shoulders tensing up. I crossed my arms and leaned against the lone cherry blossom tree in the middle of the large square cobblestone schoolyard. Its pretty pink petals formed an even circle on the ground around it. Their scent still lingered faintly in the air. A gray cloud blocked the sun and I felt a chill running through my body as I faced Nari with the most indifferent expression I could muster.

"So?" I said.

This time Nari had difficulty looking at me - she had not thought through what she was going to say.

"Areum… dad has been gone for a whole month today."

"And you think I don't know that?"

I sighed again, intensely regretting having accepted to talk to her.

"Of course, Areum, It's just… I don't know what to do. I mean… what does this mean? Where is he? When is he coming back? Why won't anyone tell us anything?"

Nari was speaking faster and faster, her face increasingly distorted in agony as two teardrops left her eyes simultaneously.

I sighed deeply.

"Nari... I don't know more than you do... I don't know more than I did yesterday."

I noticed my voice had softened. I knew that her whole life revolved around our parents and that our parents' whole lives revolved around her. Without each other - they were all lost. But at the same time, I was sick of that always ending up becoming my problem.

"What can I say, Nari? All we can do is wait. Anyway... it's not like it's the first time he's on a business trip, right? And it's not the first time he stays away longer than he had promised. He's usually away more than he is at home."

"But he has never gone without telling us before. Never! And he has never been gone this long before - *a whole month!*"

She was right - but how will talking about it make any difference?

"Nari, I don't know any more than you do! There is nothing I can say that will fix this! What do you want from me?" I was raising my voice as well.

"I want you to be my *sister*!" she shouted. "Why do you hate me so much? What have I ever done to you? Why can't we just be *sisters*?" Tears were now streaming uncontrollably down her cheeks.

With my cheeks burning like fire, I saw Su Mi coming back out from the bathroom.

There can be no distractions today! Stay focused!

"You are such an ungrateful little brat!" I snapped at her. "After all I have done for you... and for mom and dad... all those long years when you were sick... and you dare accuse me of being a *bad sister*!"

I turned around and started walking towards Su Mi, my heart was pounding through my chest. Then I stopped and turned around.

"You know what... I'm not a *bad* sister - I'm not your sister *at all!* So just leave me alone!"

My urge to get away from this situation - away from her - was overwhelming, so I ran the last distance until I reached Su Mi. Her face looked worried and scared as she watched me approach.

"Let's go," I told her and dragged her away towards the school building where we had the next class, not minding Nari's loud sobbing behind me.

"Areum... I'm sorry!" I heard Nari call after me, but I was done with her.

As we entered the building, Nari was out of sight... and soon she would be out of mind too.

There can be no distractions today!

CHAPTER 3

I started sweating as the hands of the clock moved closer to three. It was time for our weekly Meeting of Ideological Struggle.

Of course, it was only our teachers who called it that - the rest of us simply called it *self-criticism sessions*, because that was essentially what it was.

We go into a special room that has no decoration or furniture, except for the stern face of the young Great General on one wall observing us. One teacher is also there to keep us in order and take notes. We sit in a circle on the floor. One person - the Subject - stands up and confesses how he or she has failed the Great General and the principles of Juche this week, which is followed by the declaration of intent to do better in the future. After the self-criticism part has finished, the Subject has to endure rounds of criticism from the rest of us, which - in different variations - is just a repetition of what he or she had said in the first place. Once the Subject of the criticism has been sufficiently humiliated, it is the next person's turn, and like that it goes on until the whole circle is done and nobody can look each other in the eyes any longer. But as soon as we leave the room, all is forgotten. At least… most of the time.

Usually, our group talked about not having studied hard enough, which I think everybody in the school was guilty of every week - *except for Nari, of course.*

I never worried too much about the self-criticism sessions when I was younger. It was just part of normal life, like sitting for hours and listening to the boring lectures of our teachers at school. But a few years back, that changed. By then, I was already part of the school gymnastics team. And so was Mina. We had quickly learned to hate each other. At least - I hated her. In gymnastics, we were on almost the same level, which I was proud of, considering how much taller I was than her, but everybody liked her much more than me. She was the perfect girl - always smiling with her perky ponytail bouncing left and right on her shoulders as she walked, saying nice things to everybody, helping people, and she was always surrounded by a large group of friends who adored her. And to further twist the knife lodged in my back - her very best friend was my pathetic little sister… Nari.

Everybody thought Mina was as pure as the Great General himself. But I knew better. I knew it was all just an act. That deep down she was pure evil and was just using the people around her to get ahead - including my gullible sister. But whenever I pointed it out, suddenly I was the bad one.

But then one day in that self-criticism session around two years ago, her true nature surfaced. She blatantly accused me of distracting her during a gymnastics competition, causing her to lose. I, of course, lost my temper and called her a liar.

That I should not have done. If there is one sacred rule in the Meetings of Ideological Struggle, it is that you must accept all and any criticism that comes your way and say that you will try to do better in the future - for the Great General. *Defending* yourself - even the slightest - is a deadly sin. I was put on cleaning duty as punishment for a whole month after that.

I hated Mina before that incident, but after it I loathed her, and every self-criticism session that followed became our personal battleground where we attacked each other to such a degree that even the teacher had to ask us to take it easy on each other. Of course, we both knew the rules of war - whatever attack came our way, we promised to do better in the future - for the Great General. On the inside, however, we were plotting next week's counter-attack.

It went on like this for a couple of excruciating months. Nari also suffered, being torn between us. Then one day Mina was gone. Vanished. Her whole family too. Nobody knew where they had gone - but there were rumors. Rumors of hell-like places in the mountains where bad people go and are tormented by vicious demons until the end of their days. I didn't believe in demons, but I still found myself praying to the Great General that she was not in such a place. I couldn't deny that I wanted her to pay, but not even she would have deserved *that!*

Due to our rivalry, there were many rumors around school that I was involved in her disappearance... I even started thinking so myself.

Was it my fault? Could it be that it had something to do with... what I had done the week before?

I tried to ignore those malicious voices - including the ones in my head - as best I could, but it wasn't easy. This was another reason why I stayed away from people. Except for Su Mi, of course. She was always on my side... always had been.

The self-criticism sessions since Mina disappeared were calmer in general, but for me, they were filled with more anxiety than ever. Everybody who had loved Mina - which was *everybody* - stared at me... judged me, and when my turn came, everybody jumped at the chance to criticize me. They only talked about minor things - like the unofficial school rules dictated - but I could see in their eyes that they were thinking about Mina. Thinking about what I had done to her. I hated these sessions now, almost as much as I hated my so-called family.

With that thought in mind, I opened the door to the Meeting of Ideological Struggle and was met by thirty judgmental looks and one smile from the circle on the floor. The smile was from Su Mi, and I was late. That became my first topic of self-criticism.

The self-criticism session was harsh, as always, but I kept firm.

Today there can be no distractions!

As soon as I left the room, I blocked it out of my mind. I had become good at blocking things out since Mina disappeared.

There was, however, one thing that was becoming increasingly difficult to block out. Shortly after Mina had been taken out of the picture, I managed to make a new enemy that took her place - Yang Kyung Sook - and our hatred for each other quickly reached the same level. But the similarities with Mina ended there. In all other aspects, Kyung Sook was the exact opposite of her - she was arrogant and mean to anyone who didn't treat her like some kind of royalty of the old dark feudal days before the Great General liberated us. I guessed it was because her father was the Minister of National Defense - the same ministry my father always complained about, saying they all thought they were above everybody else.

I had to confess that I liked having Mina as an enemy better, because no matter how much I hated her, at least she was a worthy adversary, and I couldn't help but respect her. Kyung Sook, on the other hand, had no more worth than the flea-infested stray dogs sneaking around the Capital's numerous black markets.

She won't beat me today... I won't let her!

I also had an emergency plan in place… just in case it would come to that.

It was around five o'clock - just a few hours left before my tryouts - so Su Mi and I went to buy something to eat at the nearby black market. The normal stores didn't have much to offer lately, but the black markets always had plenty to choose from… if you had the money, that is. When I was at these - officially illegal, but in reality, condoned - black markets, I always thought of my Grandfather - the great Kim Hyun Woo, who in the early days of Choson created the Food Distribution System that now fed the whole country. I knew he always wanted to obliterate the black markets from the face of the earth but never succeeded. And now, they were an inevitable part of life in Choson. Why the normal stores couldn't be stocked with the same abundance and variation of food as the black markets, was a mystery to me.

I wonder if Young Il is working on that. Could that be why he's away?

Su Mi bought some steaming hot beef curly noodles to go, but I needed something lean, so I bought a small portion of kimchi with sticky rice and a bottle of non-flavored green tea.

"Wait here," I told her and went over to the stand that sold baby products. I looked around to make sure no one I knew was there, then I discretely bought a can of baby powder, hid it in my bag, and went back to Su Mi. She gave me a worried look.

"Are you sure about this?" she said.

"It's just as a last resort," I said. "I won't use it unless it's absolutely necessary."

Su Mi nodded.

We walked across the Okryu Bridge and took the Metro to travel the last distance to the Konsol station. The grandeur and luxury of the metro stations always took my breath away with their oversized chandeliers in the ornate ceiling, the massive marble pillars, and of course, the beautiful murals or mosaics of the Great General - sometimes alone on a mountain top, sometimes surrounded by hordes of smiling children bringing him flowers. It inspired me. It filled me with love.

Once we were above ground again, the air was fresh and the sky was clear. The sun was setting behind the gray block shapes of the city contour, painting them fiery red and orange. We went to our normal spot in front of the enormous concrete skeleton of what one day will be the Ryugyong Hotel, which was only a few minutes away from the Capital Arena where I, in about one hour's time, would have the greatest challenge of my life - the gymnastics tryouts for the Great General's National Gymnastics Team.

There was no doubt in my mind - *I will qualify for the team! And then I will be free… at long last.*

I pictured Sun Hee's face as I told her the news. I smiled.

We sat down on a patch of grass in front of the towering concrete skeleton and unpacked our meals. The spicy kimchi stung my mouth pleasantly and was wonderfully contrasted by the sweetness of the rice. I looked up at the enormous structure behind us. The Ryugyong Hotel was still by far my favorite place in the Capital. It will supposedly be the tallest building in the world, and it has been breath-taking to see it grow during all the years I had been coming here.The weathered billboard in front of us showed an illustration of how it would look when it's finished - a huge pyramid-shaped tower, completely covered in blue glass, with horns sticking up on the sides close to the bottom. It reached far up into the painted sky - into the clouds - with seven revolving restaurants stacked on top of each other at the top. From there you will be able to see the whole city - and probably beyond. I dreamed of sitting there one day, when I was famous and loved by everyone. Maybe Su Mi would be there with me, or maybe a boyfriend… or a husband… or maybe even…

Right now, however, no people or machines were working - it must have been a couple of years since I saw any progress - so it still looked like an enormous dark pyramid-shaped skeleton, ominously emerging from the ground and reaching up through the dark sky. That was why I preferred to sit facing the billboard, fantasizing about its future perfection and grandeur - a fitting symbol of the prosperity of our nation.

After we finished eating, we sat in the cool breeze in silence until it was time to go. Su Mi was normally very chatty - especially when she was on a buzz, which was most of the time nowadays - but she was also good at reading me, and understood that I needed to be in my own head now before the tryouts. When it was time, we got up and made the five-minute walk over to the entrance to the huge round concrete building of the Capital Arena - the biggest indoor arena in the country. Most of the gymnastics competitions were held there - even on elite level.

I bribed the guard to get Su Mi in, like usual - only coaches and family members were allowed - and entered. Before parting ways, Su Mi hugged me.

"I'll be ready if you need me," she said. "Just give me the signal… but I'm confident you can beat them!"

"Thank you," I said. Then we parted ways - me to go down to the locker room, and Su Mi to go up to the stands.

"Crush them!" Su Mi shouted after me laughingly before disappearing out of sight.

CHAPTER 4

The locker room was full of girls my own age, all wearing similar tight gymnastics outfits of varying colors. I knew most of them, but some were new - probably they had been brought in from other parts of the country by local hotshots who wished to gain favor with the Capital.

Country girls - there is nothing sadder!

Some coaches and trainers were there as well. It was very quiet, only a few words exchanged in low voices here and there. The atmosphere was tense.

As I stood in front of my locker in my silvery gymnastics uniform, I could feel my heart pounding inside my chest. I felt nauseous and my hands trembled. But I knew this would pass as soon as I set my foot on the mat - it always did. I took out my notebook from my bag and looked at the picture I had in it of my hero - Kim Gwang Suk - the best female gymnast who had ever represented Choson in international competitions. I visualized her perfect score on uneven bars during the Juche Year 80 World Championship. She was amazing. She had dazzled the whole world and brought great pride to our nation. I had gotten it on a video cassette from Coach Park and must have watched it more than a thousand times.

Today I must be like her! Nothing else will do!

Of course, I had my size against me. Gwang Suk was tiny - even for a gymnast.

But that won't matter… I know I can do this!

I took a deep breath and composed myself. Before I closed my locker, I threw one last glance at the warm smiling face of the Great General on the pin on my school uniform.

I won't let you down!

I closed the locker and walked out into the Great Hall, where I immediately found Coach Park and Coach Bu waiting for me.

All in all, we were around fifty girls there, and approximately twice as many adults - trainers, coaches, physical therapists, medical assistants, administrators, arena staff, and a bunch of others that I didn't know who they were or what they did. I also didn't care. What I *did* care about, were the people who had not arrived yet - the judges. They would be here any minute. We all waited for them patiently to give us the information we already knew. That ten of us would be picked. The rest would not. Ten lives would rise to the stars. Forty lives would be ruined forever.

My eyes wandered over the other gymnasts, assessing the competition. Most girls - and their coaches - looked just as nervous as I felt. Some of them were warming up, others were just standing with their eyes closed, probably meditating. Even though almost all of them looked like scared little girls, I didn't let the perception fool me - when the time came, they would all perform. I knew that. I knew they would all be a threat.

My eyes finally landed on Kyung Sook, who always stood out from the crowd. She didn't look nervous at all - she never did. With her usual arrogant expression she observed her competitors, assessing them, the same as I was doing. Our eyes almost crossed, but I averted mine just in time.

There can be no distractions! Stay focused!

Like me, Kyung Sook was taller than the other girls, which in gymnastics is a clear disadvantage, so we both knew that neither of us would finish in the top five. That meant we would fight to finish in the top ten. Just like me, her strongest discipline was uneven bars - which is just swinging like a monkey between two bars, one low and one high. That made her even more of a threat. Just like Mina had been. I looked over at the chalk bucket next to the uneven bars. It was right under the spotlights.

I found Su Mi over in the first row of the stands. She waved at me cheerfully, quickly hiding a bottle under her seat.

Today I can't worry about that! No distractions!

There were a few other people also sitting in the stands, but not too many. As my gaze hovered over the stands, something caught my attention in the dark unlit upper section. A single red glowing dot.

I suddenly got the chills, remembering the ghostly white eyes of the man from this morning. Watching me. Observing me.

Snap out of it, Areum! There can be no distractions - remember?

But somehow I couldn't look away. I strained my eyes to see the smoking man more clearly, but the area he was sitting in was too far away and too dark for me to see his face, even if it slightly lit up in red from time to time. I could not see his eyes, but I still had the uncomfortable feeling he was observing me. I used my hand to shield my eyes from the strong spotlights in the ceiling. The red spot suddenly disappeared. It was dark for a moment. And then a light flashed, and his face became clear - just for a second, as he lit a new cigarette. I could swear that the same two ghostly white eyes as I had seen this morning were looking directly at me. An increasingly uncomfortable feeling was creeping down my neck and down my spine. I felt cold. Then I noticed something else - was he wearing a soldier's uniform? I looked around the enormous room. No other soldiers seemed to be here.

And why would they be?

I turned away from the red dot. None of this mattered. It was just a soldier smoking a cigarette. A different soldier than this morning.

There can be no distractions today!

I turned around and waved at Su Mi again to get a boost of positive energy. She got to her feet and waved wildly with both hands, smiling radiantly. I laughed. But I could still not shake the feeling of having the burning gaze of the two ghostly white eyes of the smoking man in the back of my head.

The next moment, however, the five judges that would determine my future appeared, and everything else just disappeared from my mind.

The head judge - an elderly bald man with a gray beard and a wise face - gathered us around him. He smiled and welcomed us. His voice was kind but firm and methodical. In reality, I didn't hear a single word of what he was saying. I was visualizing my routines in my head. I visualized my name among the top ten on the scoreboard. I visualized breaking free. I visualized... *the chalk bucket.*

After the head judge was finished, we had fifteen minutes to warm up. I used a mix of taekwondo and tai chi like I always did. In the past, I had also competed in taekwondo - and I had even won numerous times - but as soon as it had become clear that gymnastics was my ticket out, there was no room for anything else.

Fifteen minutes later, one of the coordinators blew his whistle. It was time. And I was ready.

We would mainly be judged by our performance in our strongest discipline, the one we competed in - which in my case was uneven bars - but performance in the other disciplines also had a heavy impact on the final score.

We started with *the floor* - which is routines performed on a spring floor without any accessories. That was easy enough for everybody. The main challenge was the landing, like in most disciplines, and even though there were a couple who half stumbled on their finish, no one made a fool of themselves.

Last was Kyung Sook. She did well too, but she had chosen a very basic routine.

If she continues like this I won't have anything to worry about.

But my relief was cut short when the score was announced - Kyung Sook had received the same score as me - eight point four. I wanted to scream.

How could we get the same score when my routine was much more complex than hers?

Coach Park put his hand on my shoulder as if he had read my mind. *I need to be professional,* I told myself. *I need to stay calm! If I lose my temper, the judges will punish me with lower scores. Or worse - disqualify me altogether.*

With the coach's firm grip on my shoulder, I closed my eyes and took a couple of deep breaths. It helped. Temporarily.

When all the participants had finished, Kyung Sook was in tenth position… and I was in eleventh. I was burning up.

She's cheating! She must have bribed the judges!

But Coach Park held my shoulder firmly.

"It doesn't matter, Areum," he said. "You both have the same score, so the position on the board doesn't mean she's ahead of you. Just save your energy for the uneven bars. That's the part that matters."

I nodded that I understood. I closed my eyes again and took several deep breaths.

I need to stay focused!

The vault was by far my weakest discipline, but as I sprinted at full speed towards the Yurchenko vault horse, I knew I had it down. I jumped forward, put my hands onto the mat, did a round-off onto the springboard, and firmly made a back handspring onto the vault.

I'm nailing this!

I finished off with a double twist up in the air and then made a clean landing onto the finishing mat. My body was shaking with adrenaline, but my posture was impeccable. I smiled at the judges until they flashed the score - eight point nine. It was a personal best. I jumped into the air and screamed *yes!* Then I ran over and hugged my coaches.

My euphoria only increased as all but six girls scored lower than me.

I'm in the top ten!

Last was Kyung Sook. Her face was pure determination - like always - but now it only amused me.

She's a joke. She'll probably pull another basic routine like last time!

Kyung Sook got ready, then with full power, she sprinted forward and bounced up from the springboard, made a back handspring on the vault, and then finished off with a double twist and a solid - but not impeccable - landing.

I stood there with my mouth wide open.

That was a complete copy of my routine! That bitch!

As Kyung Sook stood there smiling, our eyes met and she winked. My face was burning up. Then the judges flashed their assessment - nine point zero. I completely lost it. I ran over to the judges - faster than my coaches had time to react - screaming and waving my arms.

"How can you give that a nine point zero? That was a complete rip-off of my routine... and I did it way better than her. How can you give her a higher score? This is an outrage!"

The judges looked at me in utter shock. My two coaches caught up with me instantly. Coach Park grabbed me, apologized to the judges, and dragged me away while Coach Bu started an elaborate deep bowing apology ritual. There was full commotion around us, people talking and pointing fingers. A lot of outraged faces.

"What are you doing, Areum?" Coach Park yelled at me when we had reached some distance. "Are you crazy? You will ruin everything! You are still number eight, and that's not even your main discipline… do you want to be disqualified and lose everything?"

I didn't say anything. I was just panting, gasping for air, burning up inside as I was staring at the smiling face of Kyung Sook. She winked at me again. I made another attempt to break free, but Coach Park caught me in time. He turned me around.

"Areum… she's doing it on purpose to provoke you, you see that right? She wants to get you disqualified! Your only option is to calm down. Remember the exercise… it's precisely for this kind of situation. Close your eyes… and breathe. A deep breath… hold it… and exhale, slowly."

I did what I was told, following the rhythm of Coach Park. With the first breath I still wanted to break away and kick Kyung Sook in the face, but already with the next breath, I felt my pulse dropping. Ten breaths later I opened my eyes. And then I started crying.

"I messed up… is it all over? Am I disqualified?"

"I think we can fix it," Coach Park said without too much conviction, "but you need to go and apologize to the judges… and to Kyung Sook."

My intestines were twisting into a painful tight knot inside me. I cried harder and buried my face in his soft jacket. But just for a moment. Then I raised my head, wiped my tears, and nodded.

"Good girl!" Coach Park gently massaged my shoulders. "If we're lucky they'll give you one more chance. But make no mistake, Areum… this is your last chance! You need to stay calm!"

"I understand," I said. "I'm sorry! It won't happen again."

Coach Bu came rushing up to us.

"I talked to the judges - you're not disqualified yet… but you must go and apologize… right now!"

It was a walk of shame back to the judges' table. I dragged my feet - every fiber of my body protested. Around me, everyone was staring, whispering, and pointing fingers as I passed them.

Kyung Sook stood next to the judges' table, her face serious and offended, but smug as ever, arms crossed over her chest.

She really has the judges wrapped around her fingers!

"Honored judges, honored co-athlete Yang Kyung Sook… please accept my deepest apologies!" I said with a trembling voice. "Please forgive me for my insolence! I was completely out of line. There is no excuse, but I will not let it happen again. I'm so sorry!" I bowed down so deep I could almost smell the wooden floor. Coach Park and Coach Bu bowed down as well.

"Please accept our sincerest apology!" Coach Park pleaded. "It was just a one-time slip… Miss Kim… she just broke under pressure. I swear on the Great General himself it will not happen again. I beg you, please forgive her… please forgive *us*!"

"Broke under pressure?" the elderly bearded judge said in his calm and methodical voice, then he scoffed. "Do you realize what kind of pressure she will be under if she were to compete for the Great General's National Gymnastics Team? You must be aware that there will be no room for weakness there?"

My heart almost stopped. Blood was flooding to my head, now only inches from the ground.

Is this the end? Did I blow it? Will I be stuck in that prison forever?

CHAPTER 5

"Miss Kim lost her temper - yes," Coach Park pleaded as he bowed up and down before the judges, "but believe me - she's not weak. I dare to say she's the strongest student that I have ever trained. I am certain... as certain as I am of the immortality of our Father - the Great General - that given the chance, she will bring nothing but honor to our great nation. I ensure you - this was just a one-time incident. And I beg you... please give her just one more chance! Allow her to bring honor to the Great General and to all of Choson!"

The judges whispered among themselves for a moment. I couldn't see their faces from my uncomfortable position. My head was getting dizzy, and my whole body was hurting. Every second felt like an hour.

Finally, the bearded judge cleared his throat.

"You say you want to bring honor to the Great General," he said in the same calm and methodical voice as before, "but there was no honor in the spectacle you just forced us to witness. However... in the spirit of our Father - the Great General and of Juche, we have agreed that Miss Kim will be given one more chance to prove herself. I advise that you use it well, Miss Kim. And I warn you... if we see even the slightest hint of unsportsmanlike behavior, you will not only be disqualified - you will be banned from competing in gymnastics for life. Have I made myself clear?"

I straightened myself. Tears streamed down my face.

"Thank you, Sir! Thank you! I won't let you down! I swear on the name of the Great General - I will bring honor to him. Thank you!"

All three of us bowed down to our feet again. And then again and again, repeating the same mantra over and over. Once the ritual was finished, I stood up and looked at Kyung Sook. She looked like she was about to explode - face scarlet red, eyes bulging out from their sockets. With tears streaming down my face, I bowed down to my feet again.

"I'm so sorry, Kyung Sook," I said in a broken voice. "I have dishonored and disgraced you... please accept my deepest apology."

Now I was certain that she was the one who wanted to kick me in the face, but the judges were observing us attentively, so she took a deep breath and cleared her throat.

"I won't deny that I'm deeply offended... but our Father - the Great General teaches us the importance of bestowing forgiveness upon those who admit to having strayed from the righteous path... so I do forgive you," she said politely, using words I recognized as stolen directly from one of the Great General's speeches on the Juche philosophy. She thanked the judges cordially and walked away without giving the three of us another glance.

As we stood up again, I didn't know what to do, but my coaches put their arms over my shoulders and pulled me away as fast as they could without appearing disrespectful.

"They still look pretty angry," I said once we were at a safe distance.

"They *are* angry," Coach Bu said, "but you have gotten your second chance now... your last chance. You need to listen to me, Areum... I need you to block all of this out of your mind now. You need to have a complete and unwavering focus on the next disciplines. You need to perform flawlessly... better than you have ever done in your entire life. That is your only chance. If you don't - all will be lost. Do you understand me?"

I nodded. Tears were still streaming down my cheeks, and I tried to wipe them away as quickly as I could. I could feel my freedom floating away and disintegrating in the distance.

I need to focus! I just need to focus! I NEED TO FOCUS!

I did the breathing exercise again, my eyes closed.

There is still a chance! I just need to focus!

But I still felt off. I had lost my confidence.

It was time for the third discipline - *the Balance Beam*. My body obeyed my mind and performed the right movements, but it felt stiff and rigid. I didn't feel like myself. Then, during the finale, the disaster happened. It was just a slight slip of my left hand when dismounting the beam, but it was completely noticeable, and my landing became anything but graceful. I felt like I was dying inside while I stood on the finishing mat with my fake smile plastered on my face.

The assessment from the judges was swift and merciless - five point zero.

That's it! I'm done for! It's all over!

I ran over to Coach Park and buried my face in his jacket again. He patted my back.

"It's okay... you still have the uneven bars. That's your strongest discipline - that's the one that counts. Just harness your inner strength and you will fly like Kim Gwang Suk in the World Championship. It's not over yet. Harness your strength. Focus!"

But I couldn't focus. As I watched all the girls do their routines on the balance beam better than me, my heart sank deeper and deeper. Then it was Kyung Sook's turn. I didn't breathe during her entire magnificent performance. As she stood on the finishing mat with her hands held high after a perfect landing, our eyes met once more. She smiled at me and winked. Nine point zero was her score - again. But I had no anger left in me. Only desperation.

I was now twentieth on the scoreboard, and only a miracle - meaning a perfect performance on uneven bars - could save me. And that was only if the judges would give me an unbiased score - which was unlikely. I felt my hopes crumbling.

But I refuse to give up. I won't! I must break free!

I repeated this mantra in my head as I went over to the chalk bucket and chalked my hands. Then I stepped onto the soft mat in front of the uneven bars, surrounded by angry and disapproving stares - everybody expecting me to fail... hoping that I would fail. I closed my eyes and took a deep breath. There was complete silence in the arena. I visualized the whole routine in my head, taking one deep breath after another. Everything else disappeared - the people's judgmental looks, my thoughts about Nari and my parents, of Kyung Sook... of Mina. Even the judges disappeared from my mind.

Left was only me and my routine... the visualization of Kim Gwang Suk flying through the air in the World Championship... and the spirit of the Great General inside of me.

I opened my eyes.

I'm ready!

I sprinted a few steps before I leaped up to the first bar and started swinging. It was almost like an out of body experience, where I saw myself lunging between the bars at the same time as I visualized the moves in my mind. I was in a perfect flow, and the bars were in perfect harmony with my body. Before I knew it, I landed on the finishing mat, raised my arms above my head and smiled like I had never smiled in my life. It was a pure and honest smile. A proud smile. I felt like the embodiment of my hero, Kim Gwang Suk. I *was* her in the World Championship, and she was me. My coaches smiled at me from the side. This was worth at least nine point five. *At least!*

I looked over at the judges. They were talking among themselves, looking at me with disgruntled faces. I felt my smile wearing off, but I forced it to stay on, like a mask. Every second felt like an eternity. The argument among the judges became increasingly animated.

This is unbearable!

Then the argument ended, and in front of them appeared my score - eight point eight. My heart dropped to my stomach. I hadn't gotten below nine point zero in a competition on uneven bars in years. And my routine had been perfect. For those ninety seconds I *had been* Kim Gwang Suk. I felt my eyes filling with tears again, so I quickly bowed towards the judges, still with my forced smile glued on my face, and then quickly walked off the mat. I saw Kyung Sook on the side. She looked worried. But I was even more worried.

Was eight point eight good enough? Will it save me?

I rushed over to Coach Park, who congratulated me, but instead of saying *thank you*, I looked him straight in the eyes and said, "What was that? That was as close to a perfect performance as there could be. That was not a fair score!" My lips were trembling.

Coach Park sighed deeply and put his hand on my shoulder.

"Areum... your routine was nearly flawless... you did extremely well... but considering your behavior before, you're lucky to get such a high score. And it *is* a high score - you're still in the game. You can make it!"

He pointed at the scoreboard. My name was taken from number twenty and moved to number eleven. My heart leaped.

I still have a chance! Uneven bars is most gymnasts' weakness… some of them are sure to drop from the list!

I felt that my freedom, which had almost been snatched away right before my eyes, was again within my grasp. I could feel it. Then I saw the name next to the number ten, just above my name. It was Yang Kyung Sook.

My heart, which had just leaped with hope, froze again. Uneven bars were her strongest discipline as well. She would be the last one to go up, and considering the scores the judges seemed to be giving her…

This can't be happening… she can't beat me! Not on uneven bars! She just can't!

I now clearly saw Kyung Sook standing between me and my freedom, embodying everything that was bad in my life. My mind went to the baby powder in my gym bag. I looked over at Su Mi in the stands.

Maybe this is the only way…

The tryouts continued, and every time a new girl stepped up to the bars, my heart all but stopped. I couldn't look, but I couldn't look away either, and as they stood on the finishing mat afterward, smiling, their arms in the air, I swore I was more tense waiting for the judges' verdict than they were. But every time the score was lower than eight point eight. I could breathe again - although it felt more like gasping for air. But then the next girl approached the bars, and the whole circle of torment repeated all over again. Names moved up and down on the scoreboard, but the name Kim Areum remained as number eleven. And the name Yang Kyung Sook remained as number ten. Some girls, for whom it was already over, broke down crying and left the arena. I could easily see on the faces of their coaches if the poor girls would be consoled or punished as soon as they were away from the public eye.

At last, it was Kyung Sook's turn, and then the tryouts would be over. All she had to do was to score eight point eight or higher, and she would join the Great General's National Gymnastics Team… and I would go home to my cold prison, where I would rot away for eternity. I looked over at her - the embodiment of everything that was wrong with the world - where she stood with closed eyes, surrounded by coaches who massaged her shoulders and helped her with breathing exercises. She looked just as focused and self-confident as I felt feeble and weak. I couldn't breathe. The time for hesitation was over… and I made a decision.

I quickly, but discretely, went over to my gym bag, which I strategically had put close to the chalk bucket. I took out a pocket mirror and pretended to check my hair, flashing it against the ceiling spotlights towards Su Mi in the stands. Then I waited.

Just a few moments later, there was a scream, sounding like it came from the depth of an abyss, at the side of the arena. There was a huge commotion as everybody rushed over to see what was going on. With my heart pounding through my chest, I quickly took out the can of baby powder and emptied it into the chalk bucket. I hid the can back in my gym bag and looked around in panic.

Nobody seemed to have noticed.

I ran over just in time to see a security guard carrying Su Mi kicking and screaming out of the arena, away from the poor girl - one from the top ten - who was sitting on the floor crying, surrounded by her coaches.

"That girl was drunk," I heard some people say.

"How did she even get in here?"

I was so nervous my whole body was shaking as I saw the guard whom I had bribed standing by the crying girl. But I was fairly sure that he wouldn't confess to having let her in.

Then I suddenly saw Kyung Sook. She was looking at me.

Had she recognized Su Mi? Did she know that we are friends?

I wanted to look away, but it was like I was paralyzed.

The whistle blew again and the judges announced that we would continue with the tryouts. Kyung Sook's suspicious eyes lingered on me for a moment longer, but then she turned around, walked over to chalk her hands, and then stepped onto the mat under the uneven bars.

Sweat pearled all over my body. I felt like everybody was looking at me. But of course, they weren't - they were looking at Kyung Sook.

Then, light as a feather, Kyung Sook left the ground and, defying gravity with her tall body, she started swinging her body round and round and lunging herself back and forth between the bars. It was splendid. It was magnificent. It was horrendous. I looked at the judges. They looked - impressed.

Oh no, oh no, oh no! This can't be happening! It's not working! IT'S NOT WORKING! Oh no! She will take everything away from me!

I had to look away. Panic was spreading all through my body - a level of desperation I had never experienced before in my life. I forced my head to turn back to the gracefully flying body in front of me.

Then I noticed it. It was barely perceivable, but I was certain I had seen it - a slight loss of grip on the high bar. I held my breath. Kyung Sook was now in the middle of her big finale - spinning through the air in a double mid-air flip. She flew down toward the low bar with tremendous speed. She grabbed it… and slipped, falling helplessly to the ground. It all happened in the blink of an eye. There was a loud thump and a crack. And then a scream. Then gasps and screams multiplied throughout the entire arena, but Kyung Sook's scream of unspeakable agony pierced through all other sounds.

Together with everyone else, I hurried over to see the injured athlete, but on the way I made sure to stumble over the chalk bucket, spreading white powder all over the floor.

"Her leg is broken… we need to get her to a hospital," somebody screamed from the middle. There was even more turmoil. I pushed through to the center of the circle. Kyung Sook lied wailing on the ground, holding her leg. It was twisted in an unnatural angle, and a sharp white and red object was sticking out from her skin. And there was blood… so much blood.

My whole body was frozen to ice. I was in shock.

H-how did this happen? I… I just wanted her to fail her routine… not to get her injured. I swear on the Great General, I didn't!

I looked around in panic. Had anyone else seen what had *actually* happened? Had anyone seen what I did? I looked over at the stands but remembered that Su Mi was no longer there. I looked around to see if anybody else was looking at me suspiciously, but everybody's focus was on Kyung Sook on the floor.

Then, far up in the darkness of the stands, I saw the burning red dot. I couldn't see anything else, but the eerie feeling returned that the man was still watching me, that he had seen what I had done, that he would tell everybody.

Stop it, Areum… it's all in your head! It's just a guy smoking!

Turning my attention back to Kyung Sook on the ground, I saw that the medical assistant had tied her injured leg with a rope to stop the bleeding. Her coaches put her arms around their shoulders, and lifted her from the floor. With her eyes pressed shut she screamed in agony. She opened them again and stared wildly around her. Then, suddenly, her eyes interlocked with mine. I saw her expression change. Her right hand twisted from around her coach's neck and pointed at me.

"It… it was her! She did this!" I could see her screaming, but her words drowned in the uproar of voices shouting from all around the arena, and when her coaches improved their grip around her, she interrupted herself with another agonized scream.

"Hurry… she needs to get to the hospital," people were screaming as the coaches, almost running, carried her towards the exit. Kyung Sook was hopelessly trying to resist, twisting her neck, screaming and looking furious with her distorted face. Some other people ran with them, carrying their bags and helping them to open doors. One ran in advance to get a car.

A moment later she was gone, and left was only the commotion and a big puddle of blood on the mat under the uneven bars.

Coach Park came over and put his arm around me.

"Are you okay?" he asked. "I know the two of you were fighting just now, but it must be traumatic to see a fellow athlete injured like that."

"I…I'm fine," I stuttered, "I'm just… just in a bit of… shock."

"It's perfectly normal," he said. "Just close your eyes for a moment. Do your breathing exercise. It's over now."

And so I did. I breathed. I blocked Kyung Sook out of my mind - and everything else as well - and when I opened my eyes again, there was only one thing on my mind - *am I in the top ten?*

The judges took the floor and urged everybody to settle down. We all formed a half-circle around them - the few of us who were still here.

The bearded bald judge with the wise face - the one who had questioned my ability to handle pressure - stepped forward and began to speak.

"What happened here today was a great tragedy, and I understand you are all in shock. But I need to tell you that these things do happen. They can happen to anyone… they can happen to you. Honestly speaking - it's even likely that it will happen to some of you." He looked at all of the young scared faces in front of him. "This… you need to accept. If you are truly serious about giving your heart and soul to train and compete as a member of the Great General's National Gymnastics Team, that will be part of your reality. And most importantly… if you are *not* willing to accept this risk as part of your reality, I urge you to find other ways to serve our Father - the Great General."

He let his calm gaze sweep over the half circle to see if there was any reaction - to see if anyone would just pick up their bag and leave. But of course, no one did.

"Very well then… with that, I hereby proclaim these tryouts for the Great General's National Gymnastics Team concluded. We will remove Miss Yang's name from the tenth position on the board, meaning that number eleven will be moved up one step. The rest of the positions remain unaffected"

In a state of amazement, I watched as the name Yang Kyung Sook was taken off the board, and my name put as number ten.

"If you meet Miss Yang, please give her our best wishes for her recovery. If she recovers well, she might have a chance again next year. But she might want to start thinking about a different way to serve the Great General. For all of you who made it to the top ten - congratulations! Please stay behind for some further information about your future."

My head felt thick - completely unable to process thoughts. All sounds around me seemed muffled. The perception of space and time was altered.

Was it...? Had I...? Was I dreaming?

Then suddenly I was lifted from the ground and swung high up in the air.

"You did it, Areum. YOU DID IT!"

Coach Park and Coach Bu caught me and threw me back up in the air. Again and again and again. I felt dizzy. Delirious. Then they put me down on the ground - they had to hold me so I didn't fall over. They hugged me and patted my back.

"Areum... now you are an *elite gymnast* in the Great General's National Gymnastics Team. Can you believe it? Congratulations! How do you feel?" Both coaches' radiating smiles made me even dizzier. I felt nauseous. I thought about Kyung Sook.

"I... I... I can't believe it... I..." I stuttered.

"Well, you'd better believe it!" Coach Bu said, messing up my hair with his hand. "You will be a star, Areum... you will bring great honor to the Great General. I'm sure of it! And we will be with you every step of the way. You'll be winning the biggest competitions as easy as *that*!"

He snapped his fingers, and with that, my mental paralysis broke. Tears flooded from my eyes.

"I... I don't know if I—"

But Coach Park and Coach Bu grabbed me and laughingly flung me back up in the air.

Then the realization finally dawned upon me.

I have done it! I am free! I actually did it! A whole new life starts today... and I will finally have a real family!

Being flung up in the air over and over, I smiled. And then I laughed. And then I cried and laughed again. Soon my coaches became tired and let me down, so I grabbed both of them and hugged them with all my might through an eternity of bliss. Tears flooded from my eyes - but they were tears of joy.

I'm free! There's no stopping me now!

The arena was almost empty - only the ten of us who qualified and our coaches remained. The arena staff was cleaning up around us, dismantling the bars, putting away the vaults and sweeping up the blood, as the judges gathered us around them and gave us the information I felt like I had waited for my whole life. They told us that we in just a few weeks would leave our families and be taken to the Great General's National Gymnastics Team training facility outside of the Capital. There they would start preparing us for the next Olympics.

In my delirious state, I was only able to pick up on some keywords and phrases here and there... but it didn't matter. Nothing else mattered anymore!

Once it was all over, I headed back to the locker rooms to change, but just before I left the arena, in the corner of my eye something high up in the stands suddenly caught my attention. It was a small glowing red dot in the darkness, and for just a moment I felt the burning gaze of the two ghostly white eyes on me.

Then I looked away, and it disappeared from my mind.

I did it!

CHAPTER 6

When I came outside into the cool night air as one of the last girls after showers, I still had the same ridiculous smile glued on my face. It wouldn't go away. I waved goodbye to my coaches and then spotted the contour of Su Mi standing hidden in the darkness by an unlit streetlamp - the lights illuminating the facade of the Capital Arena were the only electric lights around here. As soon as my coaches were at a safe distance, I went over to her.

"Wow, Areum… I can't believe it's actually over. You did it… for real!" Su Mi's face lit up like the sun. "How do you feel? Do you feel amazing? Are you floating on clouds?"

I didn't have to reply to this - my face did the talking for me. My cheeks hurt a little - I wasn't used to smiling this much, or for such long periods. But I loved it.

We started walking in the direction of the Potong River. The light from the Capital Arena faded softly behind us and was gradually replaced by the lights illuminating the enormous Monument to the Victorious Fatherland Liberation War next to the river.

"Have you rehearsed how you will break the news to your family?" Su Mi asked.

Suddenly the full implication of me qualifying for the team hit me like a sledgehammer.

I'm going to leave my family and go to live with the Great General's National Gymnastics Team... somewhere... at an undisclosed location. That will be it. I might never see them again... ever.

To my surprise, I felt scared. It wasn't an understatement to say that this had been my only goal in life since my performance in front of the Great General five years ago - but now it all became very real. Uncomfortably real.

Will it be as good as it has been in my dreams?

I had to fight off the anxiety that was spreading in my mind. *Yes,* I told myself - *it's for the best. For all of us. I will no longer be a nuisance for them either.*

"You okay?" Su Mi gave me a worried look.

"Perfect," I assured her, putting the smile back on my face. "This is the greatest day of my life! I can't even describe it. It's like... it's like I still can't believe this is happening."

Su Mi smiled and leaned her head against my shoulder.

As we stood before the massive monument - which in reality was several huge monuments next to each other, depicting our brave bronze soldiers fighting off our vicious bronze enemies at the front, all of them abundantly illuminated by strong spotlights from all sides - my family left my mind. I liked coming here before competitions. The fierce bronze struggle inspired me... gave me energy and focus. My favorite was the center piece with the soldiers raising the Choson flag on the battlefield in furious refusal to surrender against the superior invading force that outnumbered them ten to one. I identified with that somehow.

The monument had been unveiled only a year ago to mark the fortieth anniversary of our victory in the Fatherland

Liberation War. I remembered fondly how I had performed in the perfectly synchronized parade leading up to the unveiling, and how impressive it had been when we finally got to see it after all those months of practice when it had been shielded from our curious eyes by a huge solid fence all around it.

I felt Su Mi pulling my sleeve.

"I don't want to look at war and death," she said and dragged me away. We passed the monuments and started walking along the concrete-paved river bank. Apart from the illumination of important monuments and government buildings that we could see seeping up into the air here and there around the city, everything was veiled in pressing darkness, only alleviated by the cold reflection of the full moon on the still surface of the Potong River. The cool evening breeze felt good on my face, still burning from exhaustion and excitement.

"Look what I have!" Su Mi sang playfully and took out a half-full curvy bottle from her backpack, which I in the moonlight immediately recognized as pomegranate liquor - no doubt stolen from her mother's liquor cabinet. This wasn't the first time. "I knew we were either going to celebrate or mourn, so I prepared for either occasion," she laughed.

"Thanks, Su Mi-ah, but only a little… remember I haven't had a drink in over ten months because of my training, and I'm exhausted… and you know… I would prefer to get home in one piece tonight."

"No worries… I'll pull the biggest weight… as always," Su Mi smiled. And it was true - she always did.

We sat down on the rough concrete ledge with our feet dangling down over the water. Su Mi poured the pomegranate liquor into two paper cups she had brought with her and handed one of them to me.

"Here's to you! You were awesome back there," Su Mi said as our cups soundlessly touched in the air between us. "It would have been a *scandal* if you wouldn't have been picked."

Su Mi emptied her cup, and as she poured herself another one, a pressing silence fell over us.

"I really didn't want it to go like that," I finally said.

"I know, Areum-ah," Su Mi said. "But there is no way you could have known... right?"

I shook my head, but without looking up at her.

"I mean... you have fallen hundreds... maybe even thousands of times, right?" she continued. "And nothing like that has ever happened to you. It was just... a freak accident, that's all... it's not your fault... you were just trying to even the score. I mean... it was so obvious that her parents had bribed the judges... anyone could see that."

"You really think so?" I asked hesitantly.

"Definitely," Su Mi said and emptied her second cup as well. "I mean... just take your second routines... they were identical... and you did it better than her... and still, they gave her a higher score... there is no other explanation."

I took a small sip of my pomegranate liqueur.

"Thank you," I said.

I turned my head and shyly met her eyes.

"I can never repay you for what you did for me today."

"Don't mention it," Su Mi winked. "It was fun."

Then her eyes turned serious as she emptied her third cup.

"Just... don't forget about me... you know... when you're a big superstar and all," she said.

I put my arms around her.

"I promise... you will always be my sister," I whispered in her ear.

Su Mi poured herself another cup. My euphoria was wearing off and the cool breeze now made me shiver.

"Do you think she will be alright?" I asked.

"Definitely," Su Mi said. "I mean… I don't know if she will ever become a star gymnast, but she's the only daughter of the Minister of National Defense, so… it's not like she will live a life of poverty."

I nodded in silence.

"And besides," Su Mi continued. "She's a cheater… her whole family are cheaters… she doesn't deserve this… but you do!"

"I hope you're right," I said.

"I am right," Su Mi said. "Now put that out of your mind and just enjoy your victory!"

We sat in silence, listening to the slow flow of the water below our feet, feeling the familiar smell of algae occasionally brought to us by the breeze. I looked at the barely distinguishable silvery skyline against the dark sky on the other side of the river, taking small sips from my cup. The smooth oily substance tasted sweet and pungent at the same time. I had missed drinking it with Su Mi. It felt nice to sit here, absorbing the atmosphere of the Capital, feeling her warm arm around my back.

"How did you know it would work, by the way?" Su Mi suddenly asked. "I mean… with the baby powder."

"I… er… babysat the neighbor's baby last year… my parents made me… and when I changed the diaper and put on baby powder, I got some on my hands and noticed that it looked and felt exactly like the chalk we use for the bars and beams… but it was much more slippery… I never thought I would use it in this way, though… not until…"

I didn't finish my sentence. Instead, I took another sip from my cup. Even after only half a cup, I started feeling a slight tingling in the front of my head.

"We really live in a beautiful city," I said, changing the subject.

Su Mi sat up. She was now sipping her drink like me instead of emptying the cups in one gulp.

"So… still no news about your dad?" she asked.

"No… nothing."

"But he must be on a business trip, right?" she said hesitantly. "I mean, where else could he be?"

The night air became tense again.

Why did she have to bring him up?

"I don't know," I replied. "That's probably what it is… it's just that he always lets us know before he leaves."

Saying that made me feel like Nari, which made me shudder.

"I've heard him telling Sun Hee they are having some problems at the Ministry… something about food supply… I don't know… and when there are problems, apparently it always has to be *him* who has to go around the whole country solving them. Or maybe it's just an excuse for him to get away… you know… from us… from all the problems. He has been traveling more and more the last couple of years, and when he's home, he's still somewhere else in his mind."

After Su Mi had finished her fourth cup, the bottle was empty. She threw it into the river together with her cup, and we watched them slowly float away. I gave her my cup - it was still half full, but I already felt woozy and I didn't want to get sick tonight.

Su Mi emptied my cup as well and threw it into the river, then we got up and continued walking. My head was spinning, so I moved away from the ledge. I had forgotten what that felt like. I remembered the buzz I had gotten when Su Mi had introduced me to my first drink two years ago. She had stolen her mother's pomegranate liqueur that time as well. That night,

I ended up hugging the toilet, which was one of the most horrible experiences of my life. Luckily, Sun Hee and Young Il were with Nari at the hospital, so that has remained my little secret. The next day, I swore never to repeat that experience... and after that, I have never had more than one cup per night. Su Mi, on the other hand, didn't seem affected at all, despite having drunk almost half a bottle. Unfortunately, I was not surprised.

We continued walking in silence for a while, just being together side by side. It was getting colder now, but thankfully there was almost no wind. I heard a lone car in the distance. For a moment, I wondered if it was Young Il being driven back in a Ministry car, but this sounded heavier - more like a tractor or a truck.

We passed the USS Pueblo, a tiny spy ship that we had captured during the Fatherland Liberation War forty years ago - a success that was still celebrated today. I asked Su Mi if we could sit down on the bench in front of it.

"My head is spinning... it's been ten months, you know."

Su Mi was understanding.

As we sat down, I couldn't help yawning.

Maybe I don't have to tell my parents tonight. Maybe it can wait until tomorrow.

"I'm sure he's fine," Su Mi said, finally. "Your dad, I mean... I'm sure he's fine. He'll call or turn up any day now... you'll see."

I nodded, but I knew where her mind was going - I could see it on her face - and I didn't like it. My mind had been going there more than often as well during this past month, and the more I thought about it, the clearer I saw before me people being tormented by vile fiery demons high up in the mountains. Inevitably, my mind also went to Mina. I knew Su

Mi thought about her too, even though we never talked about it.

But then I just wanted to slap myself in the face - *there are no such things as demons!* And besides, in the stories, it was only traitors - the enemies of the Great General - that ended up in the beastly claws of the demons. That didn't apply to my father… or Mina.

Since my thoughts had now reached an unbearable level of discomfort, I did what I always did.

"So how about your dream boy Jae Bong?" I asked, nudging her side with my elbow.

"Oh My God, Areum… he's so hot!" Su Mi moaned. "He took me to the park last Sunday and we made out in the grass for like an hour. Of course, I had to make the first move. Otherwise, we would have continued just holding hands for another two months," she laughed.

We managed to stay on this safe topic until it was time to go home. We completed the circle back to the Konsol Metro Station just in time to catch the last train of the day. Entering the brightly lit station from the dead dark of night was a shock to my senses. It took the entire escalator ride down to the marble and chandelier-decorated depths of the earth before the pain in my eyes stopped and I could see clearly again. It was a good thing I wasn't claustrophobic - our Metro was said to be the deepest one in the whole world since the stations were designed to also be used as bomb shelters in case of another war.

After we had resurfaced at our home station around ten o'clock, we walked together back to the Tower of Juche.

"Areum… do you think the Great General really is immortal?" Su Mi asked.

"What? Where did that come from?" I asked, surprised.

"I don't know," she said. "I mean… can a person truly live forever?"

I shook my head.

"No… a person can't live forever," I said. "But the Great General is more than a person… he was put here on this earth to watch over us so that no harm will ever come our way… until the end of time… so stop with those silly questions."

I smiled at Su Mi's silliness in the dark.

We stopped as we reached the brightly illuminated Tower of Juche, and stood there for a while looking at each other in nervous silence, not sure exactly how to say goodbye. I looked up at the flame of Juche - it looked very different from this morning when it had been bathing in an ocean of fire and light from the rising sun. Now it glowed white and cold from the naked moonlight and the spotlights on the ground. Then Su Mi took a step forward and hugged me. Long and hard.

"You're like the sister I always wanted," she whispered in my ear.

"Thank you, Su Mi… you're like a sister to me, too," I hugged her back. When we finally let go, Su Mi grabbed my shoulders with both hands and stared at me with her watery eyes.

"I'm really, *really* happy for you, Areum-ah… you deserve *everything* that's coming to you… now go home and break up with your family!"

I laughed and nodded, but my insides were again twisted into a painful knot.

"And don't forget… we'll still be sisters when you're a superstar, okay?"

"Always," I said. My eyes were moist too.

We parted ways, and I started walking the last distance along the dark silent streets towards my home, guided only by the light of the pale moon above me.

I couldn't get a grip on how I was feeling. I had expected to be ecstatic and euphoric - and I was - but many more feelings were storming around inside of me. Conflicting feelings.

Get a grip, Areum! You're free now... that's all that matters. You're free... and so are they!

I suddenly felt all alone where I walked along the big carless avenue. Sadness crept into my heart. I thought back on that winter night six years ago when my world had collapsed. The night when I had lost my family.

The Capital had been hit hard by a snowstorm that December, almost paralyzing the whole city. But despite the weather, mom and dad managed to visit Nari every day at the hospital where she had been for the past three weeks after her heart condition had gotten worse. She was born with a congenital heart defect three minutes after I had been born completely healthy. The doctors didn't expect her to survive - but she did. She needed surgery, but the doctors said that we had to wait until she was strong enough. If she made it to ten, then she might have the surgery... then she might have a chance. But it was a big *if*. Now, that didn't seem very likely. It started with her having fits - her whole body shaking in convulsions. That was not unusual, but this time they were more intense and happened more frequently. On top of the fits, she vomited a lot - sometimes several times a day. Other times she was coughing her lungs out and had difficulties breathing. The scariest part of all was that her skin was turning blue. We didn't know when she would be able to come home from the hospital. We didn't know if she would come home at all.

Mom had long since given up her demanding acting career at the Capital Theater - to the great joy of her understudies - to take care of Nari. She hated her new job as a low-level secretary at the Ministry of Agriculture, but since the Minister of

Agriculture was a personal friend of dads, she had full flexibility to take time off for Nari as much as she needed. Therefore, she could spend almost every day these past weeks sitting by Nari's side at the hospital, stroking her hair, reading the Great General's Memoir out loud for her.

Dad was at that time already very busy at the Ministry of Food Distribution, working for Grandpa Hyun Woo, who was the Minister at that time. Grandpa Hyun Woo had certainly not been a family man - for him, a man is married to the work he does for the Great General… one's *actual* family comes second. But for these occasions he let dad leave work for a while, here and there. I guessed that even for a hardened patriot like Grandpa Hyun Woo - family did have some importance. After work and visiting Nari, there was not much time left of the day - and not much energy either - so mom and dad usually came home just to sleep.

I also wanted to visit Nari after school, but mom and dad didn't have time to come and get me, and they told me that I needed to take care of my schoolwork and extracurricular activities - and also to keep the house clean. Now I thought that maybe they just didn't want me there. But at least they brought me to see her at the weekend. I remembered thinking that no one should have that color on their skin. It scared me. Nari slept a lot, emitting one excruciatingly long wheeze after the other. It hurt me to see her like that - maybe we had some kind of twin connection after all.

There was an uncomfortable tension in the room. Mom and dad sat on chairs beside her bed. My usually strong dad - nothing could ever get him down - sat with a hollow look on his face, like he was miles away, unable to bear the harsh reality of the hospital room. Mom sobbed quietly to herself almost the entire time I was there. None of us talked much.

Once in a while, Nari had to rush to the toilet to vomit. Or she had a fit. Then the silent tension in the room turned into a panic with dad running out to get help, my mom's sobbing turning into desperate screaming as she with all her strength fought to keep Nari from falling off her bed, doctors and nurses rushing in and injecting her with something. After the convulsions had passed, the room went back to tense silence again, waiting for the next one.

In a way, I was glad I couldn't go and visit her on weekdays. It was just too uncomfortable… too scary. But I wished I could have more time with mom and dad at home.

One night, mom and dad came home especially late. I was already lying in my bed, but I couldn't sleep. I was prepared to pretend to sleep if they came to check on me - I couldn't take seeing my parents' faces filled with agony and distress one more time. But my preparedness was not necessary - they didn't even peek through the door to see if I was okay… or if I was even there.

I heard them sit down in the kitchen, and then there was silence. Not even the stove was turned on to make a cup of tea. They just sat there without talking. The more silent it became, the louder I could hearthe beating of my own heart. I wished to the Great General that Nari was okay. When I couldn't bear it any longer, I decided to go join them in the kitchen. I could be the good girl I always was and make them a cup of tea - maybe even comfort them with some hugs.

I got up and tiptoed out of my room. As I passed the front door in the hallway, the silence from the kitchen suddenly broke.

"There is still hope," dad said. "It's not over yet… there is still hope."

I stopped dead in my tracks. It sounded like he was trying to convince himself more than mom.

Mom didn't answer, but now I heard her silent sobbing.

I couldn't move. I wanted to go in and hug my mother, to comfort her, to say that everything will be fine... but I was afraid... afraid of what they might tell me.

"I don't know what I would do if she died," mom finally said. "I don't think I could go on living."

The silent sobbing continued for a while longer.

"Don't even think about that," dad said in a low voice. "She won't die. I refuse to believe it... she's strong, she will pull through. *We* will pull through... as a family. Doctors are wrong all the time—"

"I just couldn't live without her," mom shrieked as she gasped for air between the sobs, making me jump. "She means everything to me. *Everything!* Without her, there is no life... no meaning... no nothing... I can't go on living without her..."

My dad didn't say anything.

I remained paralyzed in the dark cold hallway, tears running down my face. The snowstorm howled on the other side of the windows.

Is this really it? Will my twin sister die? Will I be left alone here?

It all became so real. Nari's condition had always been there, around me, in me... but it never felt like she could actually die. She had always been there, like an inseparable part of me... of us.

How will we be if she's not here anymore? I suddenly asked myself. *How will I be?"*

Mom's words repeated in my head and hit me like a hammer. "*She* means everything to me," she had said. "*Nari* means everything to me".

Then what about me? If Nari means everything, does that mean that... that I don't mean anything?

My head started to spin.

What will happen if Nari dies? Will my parents die too? Will I be left alone? Will they... resent me for her death... wishing that I would have died instead of their favorite daughter?

Mom's crying in the kitchen continued, but mine had stopped. My whole body was damp from cold sweat. I could hardly breathe and I had a pain in my chest that was so intense that I was afraid I was going to drop dead right there and then. I couldn't help wondering if this was how Nari was feeling most of the time.

I was suddenly able to move again. My heart was pushing me to run into the kitchen and embrace my crying mother, to tell her how much I loved her... that I would always be her devoted daughter. But instead, I went back to bed. Silently, so that no one would hear that I was there.

I lay in bed with my eyes wide open, listening to the wind and snow batting against the windows.

What is my purpose here if mom and dad only care about... if they only love... their other daughter? Does it even matter that I'm here?

I don't know how long I lay in bed like that, but at one point I must have fallen asleep. When I woke up, the pain in my chest was gone. And so was everything else. Left was only a void - a void where my family's love had once been.

As I walked down the empty avenue, further and further away from the bright Tower of Juche, I gently stroked the cold metal of the Great General pin over my heart.

That stormy December night had been the end. This night was the beginning... and I could finally put this false existence behind me.

It's time to join my real family. It's time to join my real Father - the Great General.

Still, I could not help but feel a deep sadness inside me. I saw before me the faces of my dad and my mom... and my sister. I had been dreaming about this moment for so long... to finally be able to tell them that I'm free from their clutches - *and that they finally are free from me*. The victory would be complete. I had won.

But... is victory supposed to feel like this?

With conflicting feelings and thoughts storming and swirling around in my mind and body, I turned right into my street without noticing that something was off. Only when I had come halfway to my building did I notice the big truck that was parked diagonally across the sidewalk in front of my door.

Strange - I can't remember the last time I saw any kind of car here.

Looking closer, its shape was unmistakable - it was an army truck with a tent-like cover over the cargo area. I knew the type very well - it's the same uncomfortable monsters they use to bring us, students, to the annual harvest outside the city, leaving our bodies beaten blue and purple.

As I walked closer, I saw something else in the darkness in front of the truck, and a strong chill rushed down my spine.

A single red dot glowed intensely in the dark.

CHAPTER 7

I forced my body to move forward.

Why is the military here? Has something happened? Does it have anything to do with Young Il?

The truck was parked right in front of the entrance door to our building, leaving barely enough space for a person to pass, and I would have to pass the smoking man to get through. I swallowed as I looked at the red dot in the darkness, moving up, intensifying its glow, and then moving down again. I felt that I couldn't walk normally. My whole body was stiff.

Is it because I'm afraid or because of the tension from the tryouts?

As I neared the front of the truck, the red dot dropped to the ground and disappeared. I slowed my steps. Suddenly there was a flash of light almost blinding me as the soldier lit another cigarette, showing me his face up close for the first time. His white ghostly eyes were looking right at me, although up close they didn't look that ghostly. The light went out as the soldier flipped the lid of the lighter, and left was only a new red dot in front of his dark contour. In my mind there was no doubt - these were the eyes that had been observing me the whole day.

But why?

A horrible thought appeared in my mind.

Are they here because of Kyung Sook? Because of what I did to her? But... then why would he have been here already this morning watching me? They couldn't have known what I was going to do... I didn't even know myself.

I forced my body to continue moving forward but was unable to take my eyes off the spot where the soldier's eyes had been. I was very close to the red dot now. The soldier suddenly broke the silence, startling me.

"Lovely evening isn't it," he said through a cloud of smoke that stung my nose and eyes. His voice was deep but soft... young, but manly. For a split second, I wondered if I had to answer him, but instead, I hurried past him, squeezed myself in between the truck and the wall, and rushed to the front door of my building. Something in my body screamed to me that I should get far away from this man as quickly as possible. Throwing a glance back I noticed that he was not alone - in the driver's seat of the truck sat another man, but he appeared to be sleeping. I quickly opened the heavy door and slipped through inside.

In the tomblike stairwell, which was only dimly lit by gas lamps on the walls, there was complete silence, making my shoes sound disproportionately loud as they hit the concrete floor.

Then I heard the thumps of things falling to the ground from upstairs, followed by voices. First, a strong male voice echoed down the stairs. It sounded angry. After that, I heard a pleading female voice.

Mom?

I started to slowly walk up the first flight of stairs. The voices became louder and louder... and then they disappeared.

There was another thump, but this time it was behind me. With a gasp, I turned around. There, leaning against the entrance door of the building, stood the soldier, still with the cigarette in his mouth. He didn't move, but he was looking straight at me. And he was… smiling.

I started running up the stairs. I looked over my shoulder to see if he was following me, but he wasn't.

When I reached the top of the first floor I heard the male voices again. I heard the woman also, but now she wasn't talking - she was crying.

Mom?

I continued climbing the stairs until I reached my floor. The soldier was still not following me. A lump tightened in my chest as I slowly walked towards my door.

As I grabbed the handle and started turning it, I noticed a movement in the corner of my eye. I turned my head and saw the smoking soldier standing completely still at the top of the staircase.

How did he manage to climb the stairs without making any sound?

But before I could finish my thought, the door was forcibly opened from inside, hitting me painfully in the forehead. My eyes teared up from the pain and I stumbled backward.

"I thought I heard something out here," a man said from the doorway as he grabbed my arm, preventing me from falling. I shrieked.

The man dragged me into our apartment and yelled to someone in another room.

"Hey… the second daughter is back!"

He then told me to sit down, but before I had time to react, he forcefully pushed me down to the floor. My mind raced as I desperately tried to understand what was happening. I noticed that the smoking soldier now stood in the doorway, and so did the man who had pushed me.

"Corporal Lee… get in here!" he told the smoking man.

"Good evening, Lieutenant Sun," Corporal Lee said respectfully.

"You made us wait," Lieutenant Sun said factually, without any hint of anger in his voice. "Did you run into any problems?"

Corporal Lee shook his head. With a cigarette still in the corner of his mouth, he entered the light of our hallway and removed his military cap, clearly revealing his features for the first time. He was tall, almost a head taller than Lieutenant Sun, but not tall and skinny like the few other tall guys I had seen in my life - he had a solid build… muscular. Now, in the bright light of the hallway, his eyes didn't look ghostly white anymore. In fact, I was astounded by how handsome he was. He had a mane of thick black hair combed to the back, which he ran his hand through to loosen it up from the shape of his cap. He had the body of a fully-grown man but still retained boyish features in his face. I guessed he was around twenty, but it was difficult to tell. Normally, an attractive man like that would have made me blush, but now, all I felt was panic from the bizarre situation I had stumbled into.

Seeing the panic in my eyes, Corporal Lee gave a smug smirk, confirming to me that we indeed had spent the whole day together.

I felt nauseous.

I looked around at the messy hallway. Our belongings were lying on the floor everywhere, but Nari and mom were nowhere to be seen.

Who are these men? What are they doing here? What have they done to my family?

I shifted my eyes from Corporal Lee to Lieutenant Sun and noted he was wearing a strange kind of uniform, different from that of Corporal Lee. The Capital was virtually crawling with soldiers of all ranks, so I thought I had seen them all, but that kind of intimidating pitch-black attire, including a pitch-black overcoat, reaching from top to toe, and a pitch-black cap, I had never seen before in my life.

Is he really a soldier?

I wanted to speak… to protest… but my mouth seemed to have lost the ability to articulate words. Instead, I got up.

I have to find them! I have to find mom… and Nari.

But before I had gotten to my feet, Lieutenant Sun pushed me back down to the ground and yelled, "Stay down!" I barely managed to extend my arms to protect my head from hitting the floor. After the pain in my hands and elbows had passed, I cautiously sat back up on the floor. My heart was pounding, my vision blurred from tears and the hair glued to my face. Finally, my verbal paralysis broke and I managed to squeeze out a few trembling words.

"W-where's my family? W-what have you done with them?"

My words went ignored. The men were too busy going through our belongings.

I removed the hair stuck to my face, wiped the tears out of my eyes, and started looking around me for any indication to where they could be. Suddenly I heard my mother's crying from the living room.

Mom!

I tried to get up again but was again pushed back onto the floor. Then a third man came into the hallway. He was older and was wearing the same kind of pitch-black uniform as Lieutenant Sun, but he had stripes on his shoulders.

"Good… now you're all here," he said calmly, then turned to Corporal Lee. "We started to worry you weren't going to show… was this little girl too much for you to handle?"

Corporal Lee lost the smirk on his face. He threw the cigarette butt on our floor and put it out with the thick sole of his army boot.

"This one decided to go partying by the river after her tryouts, Captain Pan," he said.

"So why didn't you bring her home?" Captain Pan asked without taking his stern eyes off Corporal Lee. "Did this fourteen-year-old girl intimidate you?"

Corporal Lee fiddled with his cigarette carton. His face was taking on a hint of red.

"There was no point creating a scene out in public… this way she came home quietly by herself, and didn't cause any problems," he said.

Captain Pan didn't look convinced.

"WHAT HAVE YOU DONE WITH MY MOTHER AND MY SISTER?" I screamed.

All eyes were now on me where I sat panting on the floor.

"Who are you? What do you want from us? Mom! MOM! Are you there?"

I could hardly remember the last time I had called my mother *mom*, but at that moment, all of that had disappeared from my mind.

Suddenly, I heard my mother's broken voice from my parents' bedroom.

"Areum-ah… honey… please stay quiet! Everything will be okay… just stay quiet and do what they say… we'll sort all this out."

All this what? What is happening?

Nothing made any sense, but at least hearing my mother's voice… knowing that she was just in the other room, calmed me down a bit.

"You'd better listen to your mother if you know what's good for you," Captain Pan said. "Now stay there and be quiet!"

The three soldiers went back to ignoring me. They walked around the apartment, looking through our things. I could hear them throwing our books to the living room floor, going through our clothes in the closets and drawers, clinking our fine china and silverware in the kitchen. I saw Corporal Lee carrying my mother's jewelry case from the bedroom into the living room. Dad's gold watch was on his wrist.

Dad!

Corporal Lee and Lieutenant Sun seemed to be quite close - they were talking, making jokes and laughing, which annoyed Captain Pan, who was also moving from room to room, making notes in his notepad and muttering curse words at Corporal Lee.

After a while, I saw Captain Pan close his notepad. He nodded at Lieutenant Sun, who grabbed my arm and pulled me to my feet. Pain shot through my shoulder.

"Come on, let's go," he said. His grip around my arm was so tight that I immediately felt my arm becoming numb.

He dragged me down the hall and into my parents' bedroom. There, on the bed sat my mother, holding Nari tightly in her arms, stroking her hair. Nari was crying. Mom's eyes were puffy and red. When she saw me she gave me a feeble smile.

Despite the situation, my heart leapt. I wanted to run over to them and join them in hugs and tears, but Corporal Lee dragged me across the room and pushed me down into the armchair in front of the makeup table instead.

I looked at mom in hope of some explanation, but she just met my eyes for an instant and continued staring at the floor in front of her, leaning her head against my sobbing sister, her arms tightly wrapped around her in a futile attempt to comfort her.

Corporal Lee watched us in silence as he lit another cigarette. The two other men were now in the hallway, arguing. After a while, Corporal Lee became restless and peeked out into the hallway. I took my chance and whispered to my mother.

"Mom… what's going on? Who are those people?"

My mother threw a scared glance at Corporal Lee's back, then she just shook her head and diverted her eyes.

"Come on, tell me what's going on!"

My fear was turning into anger - *I need some answers… anything!*

As the argument in the hallway intensified, Corporal Lee told us not to move and left the room to join in. I couldn't catch every word, but it seemed like they were discussing how to divide our belongings among themselves, and how much would go to the *department*. I had no idea about which department they were talking about.

Mom threw another scared look at the doorway, then she leaned over to me.

"Areum… I'm sorry! I'm so sorry! But please, just do what they say… don't make it worse, I beg you—"

"Sorry for *what*?" I asked. "Make *what* worse? Who are these people?"

Mom sighed deeply.

"I don't know exactly what's going on either, but these men will take us somewhere… they will take us to where your father is."

I started to look around the room as if I expected to see Young Il having appeared from nowhere, but he hadn't.

"So he isn't on a business trip… where is he?"

"I… I don't know… I'm sorry…"

"Mom… you must know something… talk to me!" I implored, but she didn't say any more, throwing scared glances at the empty doorway.

"Nari?" I looked over at my sister, hoping in vain that she by some kind of miracle would have an explanation for me, but she just kept crying in her curled-up position in my mother's arms.

Suddenly, I noticed the argument in the hallway had finished, and then all three men gathered back in the bedroom, standing in front of us. From the looks of Corporal Lee and Lieutenant Sun, the outcome had not been in their favor.

"Mrs. Kim Sun Hee," Captain Pan said without any visible expression on his gray leathery face. He pointed at a paper I just noticed was lying on the bed next to my mother. "The truck is leaving in fifteen minutes. I strongly advise you to sign that paper… if not, you will be on it as well."

"What about my children?" mom asked.

"Your children are going… but you don't have to. All you need to do is to sign that paper."

The writing on the paper was too small for me to read, but I distinguished the word *divorce* in the headline. *What is this? What is going on?* Everything seemed so surreal - like I was in a dream.

Could that be it… could I be dreaming?

I closed my eyes hard and wished it was so.

Mom scoffed.

"What kind of mother would I be if I stayed and let them go?"

"They will be taken care of… they will be together with their father," Captain Pan said.

"Where is my husband?" my mother cried, but the only answer from Captain Pan was a blank stare.

"I will not sign it," my mother finally said. "Wherever you're taking them, I'm going, too."

"And you understand the implications of your decision?" Captain Pan asked.

"Of course not! What implications? You haven't told us anything," mom yelled with a voice full of desperation. "But it doesn't matter… my mind is made up. Where they go… I go. So just get this paper out of my sight."

There was no doubting my mother's firmness, despite the trembling of her voice.

"Very well… then it's decided," Captain Pan said indifferently as he took the unsigned paper from the bed and returned it to his folder. "You now have thirteen minutes until the truck leaves. You can gather some clothes, kitchen utensils, food and other things you might need and bring it with you… but only as much as the three of you can carry by yourselves… no more. Corporal Lee… you stay with them."

When none of us moved, Captain Pan went over to my mother and sighed.

"I ensure you, Mrs. Kim… you don't want to leave on that truck in thirteen minutes without bringing as much as you possibly can with you… but it's up to you, of course." He looked at his wristwatch. "You now have twelve minutes."

This time, my mom reacted immediately. She grabbed both me and Nari and dragged us into the kitchen. Corporal Lee followed us and observed us from the doorway.

As my mother tried to take some of our fine China plates, Corporal Lee cleared his throat.

"Not those!" he said.

Mom nodded that she understood - those they would keep for themselves… or give them to the *department*. She went to another cabinet and took out our plain everyday bowls made of wood instead.

As we stood in a small circle, packing all the bags of rice we had left into our backpacks, I saw another opportunity.

"Mom… please tell me something… anything… there must be something that you know," I whispered. "What was that paper? Are you going to divorce dad?"

"I'm not going to divorce your father, Areum," she whispered, flustered, throwing a worried glance at Corporal Lee in the doorway. "I don't know any more than you do… but

I do know that if we don't take food and clothes, things will become very difficult for us. So please… just help pack, okay! There will be plenty of time to talk about this later… but right now we only have a few minutes, and our lives depend on it. Do you understand?"

I looked at her incredulously. I couldn't believe what I was hearing. What did she mean by *our lives depend on it?* Nonetheless, I started to grasp the severity of the situation, so I didn't say anything more, just nodded.

Mom let me go and started shooting rapid commands at me and Nari. During the remaining minutes, we gathered all the rice, pots and pans, our emergency oil lamp, and all the durable clothes for all seasons that we could carry.

"It's time… get them ready," Captain Pan ordered from the hallway, and Corporal Lee nodded at us to get moving. Mom and I took the heaviest bags with rice and kitchen utensils, and also the biggest bags with our winter clothes and quilts. Nari took the lighter bags with our summer clothes and underwear.

With a growing pain in my chest and stomach, I followed the men out of our apartment and down the stairs. Some of the neighbors who had been peeking out from their apartments to see what was going on quickly closed and locked their doors as soon as they saw us coming. When we came out into the cold night air, the driver, who had been asleep when I came, was now smoking next to the truck. He didn't pay us any attention, just opened the door and got back into the driver's seat, still with the cigarette in his mouth.

The three soldiers observed us while we loaded all the belongings we had left into the cargo area of the truck. I helped Nari and mom to get up before jumping up myself. There was nowhere to sit but on the dirty wooden floor of the cargo area, so mom unpacked a few quilts for us to sit on. We put the soft bags against the sides of the truck to lean against, and the rest of our belongings between us.

Corporal Lee also got up and sat at the end of the cargo area.

I guess it's my fate to spend the entire day with this creepy guy… but at least now I'm aware of it.

"We'll send you your share next week… Lieutenant Sun will see to it," Captain Pan muttered to Corporal Lee before disappearing back into our building. The engine made a couple of strained attempts to come to life, then ignited with a roar, and the truck started moving immediately.

I guess it's only the four of us on this trip to… to…

Suddenly I caught myself picturing a black pit with hideous demons stringing people up and skinning them alive.

No… that can't be where we're going… it can't be!

CHAPTER 8

The image of the demons stringing people up and skinning them alive made me panic, so I quickly blocked it out of my mind. Instead, I pictured Captain Pan and Lieutenant Sun back in our apartment dividing up all our precious belongings between them… and the department.

Were the men in black uniforms working for this secretive department?

Either way, I had the sad feeling that I would never see our apartment and our things again. Ironically, that was exactly what I had wanted for so many years. But of course… *not like this!*

The night was cold but clear. I noticed a tear in the cargo area tent cloth right next to me. Through it, I saw that the truck was driving on a wide, straight road, with the moonlit contours of almost identical tall buildings of the Capital swooshing by. There were no other cars on the road. The lights of our truck were the only lights to be seen, and the sound of our engine was the only sound to be heard. We were completely alone.

I looked over at Corporal Lee, who was observing us with a tired indifferent face. The gleeful smirk he had shown in the apartment was gone. He lit yet another cigarette. I wondered how many packets he smoked each day. The red dot was back… and so was the ghost-like appearance of his eyes, barely visible in the moonlight.

I looked over at my mother and Nari. Nari was lying on mom's lap with her eyes closed, but I knew she wasn't sleeping. Mom was just looking down at the floor, while rhythmically stroking Nari's hair. I still had the same urge to ask my mother what was going on, but I knew I would get the same answer again. I fought my craving to get more information, but at last, I couldn't retain myself any longer, so I turned hesitantly to Corporal Lee.

"Sir… we're already in the truck… can't you please tell us where we're going?"

Mom looked up at me with a scared expression and then quickly looked over at the smoking guard.

"You will see soon enough," he answered in his deep casual voice. "But don't worry… it's not a bad place. And your father is there… you'll be together again."

"I-is he… alright?" mom asked.

"He's fine," he said. "I've seen him myself."

Corporal Lee's sudden shift in tone surprised me, but he still hadn't answered my question. I knew, however, that there was no point in asking again. In my anxious state, I stroked the Great General pin firmly attached over my heart, but it didn't comfort me in the way it usually did. I closed my eyes and prayed that the Great General would come and rescue me… save me from… whatever this was. I opened my eyes, but the Great General had not magically appeared before me. I tried again… and again.

The truck continued its journey along the empty highway through the Capital. The only thing I could see through the tear in the cloth was the moonlit shapes of buildings and monuments that we passed on the side of the road. The buildings were changing, becoming smaller and farther apart. And in worse condition. It seemed like we were leaving the city.

Soon, we passed an enormous white arch that was lit up by spotlights. I had seen it only once before, on a school trip outside the city. It had the shape of two giant ladies in beautiful traditional dresses standing on opposite sides of the road with their hands meeting in the middle, holding up a sphere with a picture of Choson on it - the whole of Choson, united, symbolizing the reunification of our war-torn country, which today was mercilessly severed in half, with our poor countrymen in the south suffering under the brutal puppet regime controlled by our enemies. The arch filled me with such wonder and amazement when I had seen it as a ten-year-old, but now it just looked monstrous where it towered up in the darkness, like an enormous gate with the warm safety of the Capital and our home on the other side, while on this side was… the unknown… veiled in ominous darkness.

As the night deepened, the air got even colder, and not even my jacket, scarf, and hat could prevent me from shivering where I sat on the bumpy floor. Corporal Lee didn't seem bothered - he just continued smoking his cigarettes, leaned up against the cloth tent of the truck. I considered crawling over to my mother and Nari to get some warmth from them, but I couldn't bring myself to do it. Instead, I found some more quilts in our bags to cover myself with. Under it, I breathed into my palms and rubbed them together. It helped a little. But not completely.

In the cold darkness, my thoughts involuntarily went to Mina…

I must have fallen asleep because suddenly I woke up by bumping my head against the hard floor of the truck. The pain was acute, and the cold I had been fortunate enough not to feel while I was sleeping hit me with full force. Looking over at mom and Nari, they seemed to have just woken up in the same way as well. They sat up in front of me, hugging each other, pulling their quilt tightly around them. Neither of them said anything. Neither of them asked how I was doing. My old resentment sparked to life again.

Things never change!

I took my eyes away from them and suddenly noticed that we no longer were alone in the truck - a man and a woman, and what appeared to be their young son, were sittingbetween us and Corporal Lee. They must have been picked up from somewhere while I was sleeping. The woman's sad blank gaze met with mine for just a moment before she looked away. I looked away too.

In the distance, I could see the sun shooting its first brave rays of light over the horizon, and for the first time since we got on the truck - which seemed like an eternity ago - I was able to get a glimpse of the surroundings through the tear in the cloth. We were driving on a bumpy dirt road on a desolate plain, with very little vegetation in sight. In the distance ahead of us was a tall mountain range. That's where we were headed.

We're going up into the mountains… we're going to where the demons are!

I pressed my fingers against my temples so hard it hurt. I needed to rid my mind of these ridiculous thoughts.

Around midday, my whole body was hurting from being tossed around on the uneven dirt road. I was getting hungry. I was reluctant to ask mom for food, but luckily, I didn't have to - Nari asked instead. Mom took out some rice balls wrapped in seaweed and gave them to us. The sweet sticky rice and the crispy salty seaweed tasted wonderful in my mouth. The other family looked jealously at us. I noticed that they only had one small bag with them.

Were they not allowed to bring more… or didn't they have anything else to bring?

I suddenly noticed that Nari was pressing her hand against her chest.

"Are you okay, honey?" mom asked.

Nari nodded, but we all knew what it was… the same symptoms she had had her whole life. Soon, the nausea would start… and the fits would follow.

But she hasn't had any symptoms since her surgery four years ago…

The bumpy ride continued, but now the sun was up in the cloudless sky, so at least I wasn't as cold anymore. Nobody spoke, but the rattling engine and crashing and squealing of the truck hitting every pothole on the uneven road more than filled the silence.

I discretely looked over at our new travel companions. The woman met my eyes again. I didn't know if I was allowed to talk, but it seemed like Corporal Lee had dozed off, so I gave it a try.

"Hey," I whispered as I leaned over, "where are you from?"

"Areum!" I heard the worried voice of my mother from the side, but I ignored it.

"Changrim," the woman answered. I had never heard of that place in my life, but that was also not my main concern.

"Do you know where we are going?" I asked.

"No talking!" Corporal Lee shouted at us - apparently, he had not been as sound asleep as he looked. The woman shrugged her shoulders and shook her head before she turned back to her family.

They're in the same situation as us.

A few hours later the truck stopped in a small village with a few worn-down three-story concrete buildings on the side of the road. They looked really out of place where they stood surrounded by nothing but farmland and nature. We started gathering our things, but Corporal Lee stopped us.

"This is not your destination," he said.

I didn't understand at first, but soon an elderly couple, gray, around sixty-five, boarded the truck to join our growing group. The space in the cargo area was getting tighter, and the rest of us had to squeeze together to make room for the couple and their belongings - they had one large bag each.

I noticed that the woman from Changrim started whispering with the older woman when Corporal Lee was looking in the other direction - maybe he didn't have the energy to bother about it anymore. I saw the old woman utter one single word before turning back to her husband. The face of the woman from Changrim had, in an instant, been completely drained of blood, and I could read pure horror in her eyes. As she leaned over and told her husband, he had the exact same reaction, making them look like two horrified ghosts. The woman started crying and pulled the boy sleeping in her arms tightly against her chest, kissing his head, over and over.

I couldn't endure it any longer - I needed to find out what was so horrifying. I started moving closer to the woman from Changrim, but my mother stopped me with her hand. At first, I was angry, but then she opened her bag and took out a rice ball. She showed them to Corporal Lee, indicating that she would like to share it with the poor family who hadn't brought anything. Corporal Lee nodded indifferently.

"Thank you so much," the woman from Changrim said through her sobs. "Thank Great General there are still some good people left in this world." She signaled to her husband to come over to us and receive our generous offer. As my mother handed him the large rice ball, she whispered, "What did they tell you?"

The husband, again with horror on his face, threw a quick glance at Corporal Lee, who was observing us from the end of the truck. He leaned over to us and whispered in a barely audible voice.

"Yodok… she said we are going to Yodok."

He then quickly took the rice ball back to his family, where he split it into three equal pieces. Within a couple of seconds, they were gone.

Yodok… another place I've never heard of…

My mind suddenly went to the word *Hamhung* and my father… and a vague recollection of the dream I had woken up screaming from yesterday. I looked over at my mother and saw she now had tears in her bloodshot eyes, and her hand looked like it was trying to prevent her mouth from screaming. Her face scared me.

"Mom… what is Yodok?"

She didn't respond. She just sat in the same position with her distorted face, holding Nari, who was sleeping again, tightly in her arms.

What is this? I need answers… NOW!

I bit my lip and forced myself to wait for my mother to calm down a bit before asking her again. Being the only one on the truck who didn't know about Yodok was killing me, especially after seeing everybody's reaction, and it scared me to my core. I considered that maybe it would be better not to know.

No… I need to know!

I envied Nari for being able to sleep so innocently through all of this, even though she looked very pale on mom's lap… exactly how I had seen her so many times in the hospital.

The road was becoming steeper and bumpier as we drove deeper into the mountains. Despite that, I must have dozed off again, because I woke up by being tossed up in the air, this time hitting my head on the side of the truck. I grabbed my head and felt a single stream of blood running down around my left ear as the pain blended with the excruciating pain in the rest of my body.

Shortly after that, we stopped - the family we had shared our rice with had requested a toilet break for their son, so we all got to stretch our legs and relieve ourselves while Corporal Lee pointed his machine gun at us.

The short break made it even more painful to sit on the bumpy truck as we continued our path up into the mountain.

It was evening again. I saw the red sun slowly setting behind the mountain range to the west, but above us, heavy raindrops started falling on the cloth covering the cargo area. Soon, we were in a full-blown storm with ferocious winds and thundering rain whipping the truck from all sides, spraying us with icy water through the cloth.

Seeing our scared faces, Corporal Lee shouted that we're getting closer to our destination.

My mother still didn't say anything - she just stared down at the floor, trying her best to shield Nari from the rain. I was completely exhausted from hunger and my aching body, so I didn't have the energy to engage with her again. Especially since it would mean I had to scream to drown out the storm. More than anything I just wanted to get off this truck. No matter how bad that Yodok place might be… right now I didn't care… my only wish was to stand on firm soil again… to stretch out my sore legs and back, even if it meant being soaked by the cold rain. All the rest I could worry about later.

Just then, a couple of words carried through the drumming of the rain from the old couple sitting next to us made my blood freeze. At first, I wasn't sure if I had heard it right, but after replaying it in my head, there was no doubt about it. They had said the *Demon of Yodok*.

My whole existence transformed into pure panic. I sat there, petrified, not moving an inch.

Oh, Great General… that means they weren't just stories… the demons are real… and one of them resides there, where we're going… in Yodok!

I was still in a frantic state when the truck entered a narrow passage a few hours later. The high rugged cliffs on both sides threw our truck into darkness. The massive rain that had accompanied us up the mountain had all but stopped, but I could hear the truck struggling to get traction in the wet mud. After we left the passage, we emerged before an enormous concrete wall stretching from one mountain ridge to the other. On the top of the wall were twenty or so guards, all dressed like Corporal Lee and armed with machine guns. In the middle of the wall was an equally tall solid iron gate, and in front of it were more armed guards.

Nari threw herself into her mothers' arms. In my mind, there were no doubts left. This was the place from the stories… this was where the demons resided. I felt every single hair on my body stand on end. I looked up at the wall again through the tear in the cloth, expecting to see some kind of black horrendous monster climbing over the top with large sharp fangs sticking out from its mouth and fire instead of eyes… but all I could see were stern human faces and machine guns. However, that didn't make me feel relieved. Not in the slightest.

I looked at mom, but she was still just looking down at the floor with her bulging red eyes. Her breathing was shallow and fast. I looked at Nari. She was looking for answers in my face, but there were none to be found.

As the truck stopped in front of the gate, the guards first approached the driver and then came back to inspect the cargo. Their faces were grim under their rain-soaked caps, which was further emphasized by the intimidating machine guns firm in their grips.

"Hey, Kang Min… Beom Seok… how's it going?" Corporal Lee greeted them. The smirk reappeared on his face.

"Hey, Chang Min," the closest of them replied. "Finished your vacation in the Capital, I see… I hope you haven't gone soft on us."

"Never," Corporal Lee laughed. "So… are you going to let us in or what?"

"That depends… did you bring us something fancy from the big city?"

"I've got something I think you'll like," Corporal Lee winked.

The guard tapped the back of the truck twice with his hand and signaled with a loud whistle to the people on top of the wall. There was a long and uninterrupted metallic screech that painfully pierced my ears until the gate had completely opened.

The truck started moving again. All guns and eyes were aimed at us as we passed yet another gateway into the unknown. It was difficult to breathe.

As I witnessed the enormous black iron gate closing behind us, I had the feeling that I would never see the other side of it ever again. I looked over at Nari, and her face looked exactly the way I was feeling. Mom's face was buried in her hands.

I looked outside through the tear in the cloth. There was still enough light to be able to see the surroundings. The valley that we entered was enormous and stretched far into the distance, encompassed by a tall and vast mountain ridge, closing us in from all directions. At first glance, it looked like the mountain ridge had spikes sticking out from it, but I concluded it was my tired eyes playing tricks on me.

The truck continued up the uneven dirt road, its wheels fighting not to get stuck in the wet mud after the rain. At first, there were no signs of life anywhere around - only some trees and bushes up on the hills - but after a short while, we arrived at what looked like an enormous bizarre village consisting of thousands of identical one-story boxlike wooden houses in perfect rows along smaller side roads as far as the eye could reach. There was a big hand-painted sign in front of the village that read *The Rose Garden*. The sign also had a poorly painted rose in the upper right corner. I looked around, but there were no roses in sight.

The truck continued its path through the village. It was getting dark. Soon, the truck stopped in front of a part of the village where the houses were smaller and completely square-shaped. In front of them was another hand-painted sign that read *The Orchid Garden*. That one also had a picture up in the right-hand corner of something that in no way resembled an orchid.

"Get off!" Corporal Lee ordered us and was the first one to jump down.

I was both scared and relieved as we gathered all of our belongings and climbed down on the muddy road. Once we were all off, the truck ignited with a roar again and drove off further into the heart of the valley. Corporal Lee lit another cigarette.

"It'll just be a moment," he said.

We stood there in the mud like a bewildered pack of stray dogs looking around at our intimidating new surroundings. Further up the road, I could see a constellation of larger buildings, which were the only ones I could see that had electric light emerging from them. The roads were almost deserted, but

I saw a few people walking around. At least, I think they were people. In reality, they looked more like animals. They all wore the same dirt-gray patched up rags, and their faces were equally dirty, as was their short messy hair. It was impossible to distinguish the men from the women in the dim twilight. Some of them had worn-out shoes, but most of them just wore rags wrapped around their feet. Their features were just skin and bone with pale, flaky skin, which made me remember Ji Young from school.

Was it just yesterday that she passed out in front of our entire class?

The people stared at us shamelessly where we stood in our fashionable, clean clothes from the Capital. We stared shamelessly back at them as well. In their eyes, I could see nothing but tiredness and hopelessness. They scared me.

I suddenly noticed Nari. She looked as pale as a ghost and was holding her stomach. I knew that look all too well, and just a moment later she vomited where she stood.

"Oh, my poor baby," mom cried and lifted her hair like she always did. She stroked her back gently. The others shrugged back with disgust on their faces, and Corporal Lee just watched us with his cigarette in his mouth, doing nothing… not even asking if she was okay.

Nari vomited once more, and then, shivering, hid her face in mom's chest.

Mom was crying, and I understood why - this was the first time she had vomited since the operation.

I also felt the same helplessness that I had felt my whole life sweeping over my body.

What will we do if she has a fit?

Shortly after, the truck came back and stopped in front of us, leaving a short skinny boy in an oversized uniform, and then left again in the direction of the iron gate.

"Hi, Chang Min," he said to Corporal Lee with a tender, almost feminine voice that perfectly matched his face. "I'm glad you made it back safely."

"Hey, Chul… were you worried?" Corporal Lee laughed. "It wasn't exactly a mission across enemy lines."

Chul seemed slightly offended by Corporal Lee's arrogant reply but didn't comment.

"Are these the new prisoners?" Chul asked, looking at us.

"There's no fooling you," Corporal Lee scoffed.

Chul again ignored his remark, but for me, it wasn't their strange interaction that concerned me. My mind was instead preoccupied with the word *prisoner*, which had struck me like a sledgehammer.

We can't be prisoners. We're not traitors. We haven't done anything wrong. I'm a gymnast in the Great General's National Gymnastics Team. I shouldn't be here!

Chul looked down at his note.

"Okay, so who belongs to the Kim family?" he asked.

The three of us raised our hands.

"Great… so you're assigned to a family house here in the Orchid Garden… and I see one family member is already here… good… so, you guys can come with me. The rest of you are assigned to the barracks over there in the Rose Garden… Corporal Lee here will take you there."

As we went with Chul, Corporal Lee lit another cigarette and indicated to the others to follow him, and soon they were consumed by the darkness, and I felt a great relief being away from him for the first time since yesterday.

I looked over at Nari. She seemed slightly less pale now, and I hoped that this had only been a one-time thing and that her heart condition was not worsening again.

"I'm Private Gang, by the way," Chul said as we walked along the dark street.

"Where is my father?" I suddenly blurted out without thinking, but then immediately got terrified of the consequences.

"You'll see him soon," Chul said. I thought I heard a hint of compassion in his voice, which surprised me. When we came to the middle of the street he stopped.

"Here… house number hundred and twenty-four is yours," he said and opened the unlocked door. "You're lucky… very few families get these. Now go and get installed! I'll be back for you tomorrow morning to take you to the orientation meeting. All your questions will be answered then. Stay inside until I come back… but if you need to use the toilet, it's over there at the end of the street."

I froze.

We don't have our own toilet? We have to share with… those animals?

But then I realized that the toilets probably were the least of our problems right now.

Chul went back toward the main road, and the three of us went into the dark house. Mom lit the oil lamp we had brought from our apartment, and a soft light spread across our new home. The room - which was the only room in the small house - was almost empty. There was no furniture, no beds… not even any windows. There were only three things in the room - a small stack of firewood by one of the walls, a tripod stand for teakettles and cooking pots in the middle of the room standing over a round concrete section with a large black spot where it had been permanently scorched by fire, and a bare light bulb hanging from the ceiling. I found the light switch on the wall, but it didn't work. I looked around at the walls and noticed that there was no picture of the Great General anywhere. I couldn't remember ever having been in a room without his calm gaze watching over me. It was unsettling.

We moved our belongings to the furthest corner of the room, putting the rice at the back, so it was hidden by the rest. Mom took out three quilts and rolled them out around the cooking place. Those would be our beds tonight.

For how many nights?

I was extremely tired, but I couldn't sit down. After sitting uncomfortably on the bumpy truck for almost twenty-four hours, it felt good to stand up and be able to extend my legs and my back and to be able to walk around a bit. I also knew that sitting down right now would be more painful than standing. I realized I needed to go to the bathroom, but I didn't dare to go outside, so I endured it.

I haven't drunk anything since yesterday, so maybe it will go away!

We waited in the house for what seemed like an eternity. Nobody talked. Nari was again lying in my mother's lap. I suddenly became aware that I hadn't heard her speaking once since last night. I remembered her many nights and days at the hospital when she didn't utter a single word either. At least now her skin color looked better. Maybe it had only been the stress of this last day that had affected her... it wouldn't be strange if it had.

It started to rain outside again. At first, the rain was light, then it became strong and heavy, rhythmically battering the wooden roof. Despite being loud, the sound was soothing. But then water started to drip from the ceiling. We hurried to move our quilts away from the emerging puddles. It was getting colder, so I wrapped myself in my quilt and finally sat down on one of the soft bags with our clothes. It hurt terribly, but it was nice to sit on something that didn't move. My mother took out another rice ball wrapped in seaweed and split it into three parts. I hadn't noticed how hungry I was until the rice touched my lips. It seemed completely unreal that it was just last night that I had qualified to the Great General's National Gymnastics Team… that I had made Kyung Sook break her leg… that I had celebrated my victory by the Potong River with my best friend. Now I was sitting in this cold damp room in…

… a hellish place, waiting to be tormented by the Demon of Yodok?

We didn't know what time it was, but outside was completely dark and the heavy rain continued to methodically batter against the roof.

"Mom…" I started but was interrupted by a lightning bolt that lit up the sky, immediately followed by deafening roaring thunder. More flashes of lighting followed. The storm - our second one today - intensified, and soon nothing could be heard except for the violent whipping of the rain and the never-ending roaring thunder all around us.

Suddenly, in the flashing light of yet another lightning, I saw that the front door was open, and in the doorway stood a huge dark shape. Both Nari and I screamed in panic, but our screams were drowned out by the following roaring thunder.

I pressed myself against the back wall. Fear consumed my whole body.

This is it… the Demon of Yodok is here… he has come to torment us!

But my mother reacted differently.

"Young Il," she said. "Is that you?"

CHAPTER 9

"No," said a soft, feminine voice, barely audible over the battering of the rain. From another bolt of lightning behind the silhouette, I could see that it wasn't a demon at all… unless the demon would look like a small skinny teenage boy wearing a uniform and a cap, with a face looking no older than my own.

My tired eyes must have played a trick on me again…

"I'm the one who brought you here when you had just arrived," the boy said. "My name is Gang Chul. You can call me Chul… I prefer that, but… just be sure to call me Private Gang when other people are around… not to get you into trouble."

Even though he had a man's name, his silky soft high-pitched voice made my brain want to think that it was a girl standing in front of us.

"Colonel Wan would like to welcome you to the camp, so I will take you to the Center of Ideological Struggle… it's not far from here."

"I thought the orientation was tomorrow morning," mom said hesitantly.

"It is… but Colonel Wan wants to say a few words already tonight… he does that sometimes. I don't know any more than that… I'm just following orders."

"When will I see my husband?" mom asked.

"He will be home as soon as he has filled his quota for today… you will see him then."

All of us looked at each other, thinking the same thing.

He's still working… at this hour?

Unlike the always smirking Corporal Lee, Chul sounded kind, even compassionate… or maybe it was just his feminine voice that made him sound that way. Either way, he didn't intimidate me… so I took a chance.

"Private Gang," I started respectfully, but then changed tactics. "*Chul*… this must all be some kind of terrible mistake. We're not supposed to be here… *I'm* not supposed to be here." I felt I was losing control over my emotions. "You can check the records. I'm Kim Areum. I'm a member of the Great General's National Gymnastics Team… they're like… like… the Great General's own family. And I… and I have performed in front of the Great General himself… you must see that I'm not supposed to be here, right? This is all a huge mistake." I looked at Chul frantically as he looked back at me with great sadness.

"I'm sorry," Chul said in his silky voice, "but I can't do anything about that. You'll have to talk to Colonel Wan, or maybe even General Roh, but—"

"But what?" I retorted. "You… you can't go around putting innocent people in prison—"

"Areum… that's enough!" mom said. "Private Gang… please forgive her… she's just a child."

"Please… don't worry about it, Mrs. Kim… it's perfectly alright. But…" he turned back to me, "unfortunately there's nothing I can do about that… I'm just a Private… and we get a lot of new prisoners who come with one explanation better than the other of how they were forced to confess, or that they were wrongfully put here in some other way. I just have to be honest with you… so far, I haven't seen *anyone* being sent back home as a result. In fact… it might even be somewhat dangerous to say things like that, so I would advise you to be very careful about that." He paused for a while, looking at the growing desperation in my face. "But don't worry… Areum was it? The work is hard, but you can have a decent life here… as long as you follow the rules. And not all the guards are as bad as… well—"

"BUT I'M INNOCENT!" I screamed. "THIS IS A MISTAKE!"

I took a few steps towards Chul, making him shrug back. Nari and mom intervened instantly, grabbing my shoulders to hold me back.

"Areum… you must stop it right now. You will get us all into trouble. If not for me… at least think about your sister," mom said. That comment made my already hot blood boil.

Chul looked at me… and then at Nari, with compassionate eyes.

"I'm sorry," he said, "but you have to come with me now. Colonel Wan will not be happy if you're late, and there are more people I have to gather on the way. You have one minute to get ready." He then exited through the door.

"But we're innocent," I pleaded to mom and Nari. "They must take us back home… they *have to…*"

Mom put both me and Nari in front of her and looked at us with a serious expression.

"Listen to me, both of you…they *will not* take us back home. Do you understand? They *will not* take us back home. Okay?" Her eyes shifted rapidly between us. Nari started sobbing. "I don't know exactly what's going to happen, but I know two things… they will not take us back… and if you continue saying that we're innocent, they *will* hurt us… so you must stop that at once, Areum. Tell me that you understand!"

"I understand, mother," Nari whimpered.

I glared at mom angrily.

"So how will we get out of here?" I asked.

Mom sighed deeply.

"I'm not sure we can… I don't know… but right now we have to focus on making it through *tonight*… okay? We have to make sure your dad is okay. So please… until we know more, please don't say anything that could be perceived as provocative, Areum… please!"

I nodded, but I was burning up on the inside.

"I know I can count on you," she said, stroking my cheek with her hand, making me twitch. She forced a feeble smile on her trembling lips. "Now come on, put on your coats… it's chilly outside… and it's still raining… things will be worse if we're late."

I knew it was pointless to try to convince mom, but I was horrified that she was so weak.

What doesn't she understand? This is a horrendous mistake… they must recognize that and correct it… there is no time to lose! I will talk to this Colonel Wan that we're being taken to. He will understand. And when they realize what a fatal mistake they have made, they will not only take us back home… they will apologize! I'm a professional gymnast in the Great General's National Gymnastics Team! And why does it always have to be me who does the heavy lifting to keep this family on its feet?

As we were heading out the door in our fashionable Capital-style evening coats, mom gently put her hand on my arm and leaned toward my ear.

"I know this is not the right time, but I'm proud of you for qualifying for the team yesterday… I never doubted you."

"I'm really proud of you, too, Areum-ah," Nari said and made a failed attempt to smile. In a normal situation, I would have given anything for these words of appraisal, but in my current state, I could only think one thing.

They're lying… like I would believe that they didn't want me to fail… they have always wanted me to fail… they have always been… AGAINST ME!

"Thank you," I said, trying hard not to let my anger seep into my voice. Like mom said - *this was not the right time!*

Before we closed the door, mom threw a worried glance at the last of our belongings, stacked against the back wall of the room. Seeing her face, I was suddenly struck by the same fear.

Will they still be here when we come back? In this house without a lock? We have several months of rice there. What happens if we lose it?

"Let's go," mom said. "It'll be okay… we won't be long." She looked at us unconvincingly for just a moment and then closed the door.

Once outside in the rain, we could see a large group of people gathering, many more than had come in our truck.

Did they have several trucks bringing people here?

From another lightning streak, however, I saw that some of them had machine guns.

They're not all prisoners… we're surrounded by armed guards!

My anger was again replaced by fear.

Chul took the lead and the rest of us followed. We stopped at a few more houses on the way. Chul then signaled for us to go towards a spot of light in the distance.

The grassless ground had turned into deep watery mud, reaching up to my ankles. I was afraid to lose my shoes, so I took them off and carried them in my hand instead, praying that I wouldn't step on anything sharp. We walked in total wet darkness for about ten minutes. The spots of light become slowly clearer and stronger before I could finally hint a larger structure in front of us. When we got close enough, the spots of light turned into weak lamps hanging on each side of a door. Over the door was a sign that read *Center of Ideological Struggle*.

Chul opened the door and let all of us in before entering himself, followed by the group of armed guards. We came into a large room that reminded me of the locker room at the Capital Arena. Chul ordered us to remove our shoes and to clean our feet with the water buckets lined up on the floor. As soon as we had finished, we were taken into a huge corridor with many identical doors. My bare feet felt strange against the oiled wooden floor. Chul lead us through the first door on the right.

The room we entered was large, bare, and dimly lit, without windows, and only one other door in front of us. It was almost identical to the room of ideological struggle in my school back in the Capital, and I assumed that there was an identical room behind every door in that long corridor. Again my mind went to Mina and the many battles we had fought in that room. There was no furniture or decoration, apart from the mandatory picture of the stern-looking young Great General on the wall to our right. I felt strangely comforted by seeing the familiar picture again, even under these horrible circumstances - it assured me that we were still in our society - where rules and order applied - and where we were under the loving protection of our nation's Father.

All of us confused and scared newcomers gathered in the middle of the room while the grim-looking soldiers with machine guns spread out to what seemed like predetermined positions along the walls, holding their weapons ready in their hands. All except for Corporal Lee, who left his machine gun hanging from the shoulder strap, as he casually leaned against the wall and lit a cigarette.

Are they really allowed to smoke in this sacred room?

From the door in front of us, another man suddenly appeared. His broad smile stood in stark contrast to the stern face of the young Great General in the picture on the wall. All the soldiers stood to attention - even Corporal Lee leaned away from the wall but kept the cigarette in his mouth. There was no doubt that this new man was Colonel Wan. Instead of the gray outfit and cap that all the guards were wearing, he wore a long, dark-green coat with golden stripes on the collar, each with two red lines and three stars in between, and a large bowl-shaped hat with a black visor, over which was a golden emblem with a bright red star in the middle. Over his heart, he wore the same Great General pin as I wore over my heart under my coat. This was a good sign. I put my hand inside my coat and caressed the pin. It was finally doing its job and calmed me down.

Colonel Wan was slim but muscular, and even though he was smiling, he had a face that demanded respect. But there was also something about his smile that felt off. It made me uneasy. In his hand, he held an ornate sword, which he let swing back and forth by his legs like a large pendant.

This is a man of integrity… a man who is devoting his life to the Great General's cause, I told myself. *He will recognize that I'm here by mistake. I just need to wait for the right moment to approach him.*

I continued caressing my Great General pin as if it would summon the spirit of the Great General to confirm my assessment.

Colonel Wan let his gaze sweep over me and the other twenty-five or so people who stood nervously in a half-circle before him. His smile suddenly disappeared, and his face was distorted by an expression of pure disgust.

"ON YOUR KNEES!" he roared, and immediately the other soldiers in the room started to ram the handles of their rifles into the back of the knees of anyone who had not reacted immediately, which was most of us. A flashing pain in my calf thrust me onto the hard wooden floor and was quickly replaced by a numbing pain in my knees and the palms of my hands as they broke the fall.

After a couple of seconds of immense commotion, Colonel Wan shouted, "QUIET!" and this time everybody reacted at once. A deafening silence took control over the room, and Colonel Wan had everybody's full attention.

"We live in the greatest country in the world," he said in a deep solemn voice. "Our eternal Father - the Great General fought off our enemies who attacked us on all fronts. He fought back the cowardly attack by the enemy-controlled puppet government in the south, which still today holds half of the population of Choson hostage." He made an artistic pause before continuing. "As if all that was not enough, the Great General then dedicated his whole life after the wars to build this paradise on earth that we can all proudly call *home.* We are safe from our enemies around the world, who are still looking at us with beady eyes, just waiting for us to show the slightest sign of weakness. We have plenty of food on the table. We have walls around us and roofs over our heads… and every day we have a place to go to where we can pay back our debt… where we continue making this - the greatest of nations - even greater… always guided by the spirit of Juche and the Great General. *We* are the most fortunate people on earth. *We* are the envy of all other nations in the world."

Colonel Wan paused his passionate speech for a while as he paced back and forth in front of us, playing with the sword in his hand, without paying us much attention.

This man is filled with the spirit of the Great General, I thought to myself. *He will listen to reason.*

I felt hopeful. I looked over at mom and Nari. They were both looking down at the floor with anything but hope expressed on their faces.

"However," Colonel Wan continued, "despite all the sacrifices our Father - the Great General has done for *all of us,* there are some people who for some reason don't recognize how fortunate they are. Can you believe that? How blind they must be." He shook his head theatrically. "As I said - all of our enemies are just sitting there, waiting for us to show any sign of weakness. And what do they find? That's right... they find these blind people. And these blind people, weak and susceptible, start to listen to the malevolent messages of hatred that our enemies relentlessly continue to spread, even within our very borders... and they become an extension of our enemies, festering within our society, spreading the disease, killing their neighbors, killing the revolution... killing our Juche way of living... like a plague."

In his next pause, I heard the roar of thunder in the far distance and again noticed the heavy battering of the rain against the roof. I realized that I had become completely mesmerized by this heartfelt speech, and I became more and more convinced that this was the man who would set me free.

Colonel Wan continued talking in his captivating voice.

"Fortunately... we are not defenseless against this disease... this plague. Fortunately... the self-sacrificing people of the State Security Department - our first and last line of defense against the enemies within our borders - have eyes and ears everywhere, and always find out when the disease starts to spread in a new place. Then they surgically remove it from our society before it has time to do too much damage."

The State Security Department!

I suddenly realized which *department* the men in our apartment had been talking about.

No wonder I had never seen their uniforms before... you don't exactly see the secret police of Choson walking around openly in the streets of the Capital...

He stopped pacing and turned around to face us, placing the blade of the sword in his left hand. The eerie smile had returned to his face. I felt more comfortable when he looked serious.

"Then… they send these infected people, who have strayed from the righteous path, here to us so we can cure them." He took a step closer to use, his sword still firm in his hand. "And as you probably have guessed… this is why all of you have joined our little community here today. Our mission here is to cure you. If you're worthy… you'll survive the treatment and find the righteous path. You will then be given a second chance to rejoin society, where you will continue to repay your debt to our Father - the Great General. If you're not worthy… you will perish together with the disease you're carrying. Either way, we will have done our duty to stop the disease from reentering society."

He smacked the blade of the sword forcefully against his left hand, making us all jump where we sat on the floor.

"So with no further ado, I would like to bid you all welcome to Penal Labor Camp No. 15! You have all come here with the disease, but I assure you… you will not leave with it."

CHAPTER 10

A soft gasp from the crowd filled the silence of Colonel Wan's pause. I could hear my sister breaking into quiet sobs. Colonel Wan's smile had once again returned to his face as he observed our reactions.

"Now… I know that the name *Penal Labor Camp No. 15* is a bit of a tongue twister… so for simplicity, everybody usually just calls it *Yodok*. Why? Because we're only twenty minutes from the lovely village of *Yodok* to the south of here. I would recommend a visit, but unfortunately… you will never see it."

He continued pacing back and forth in front of us, looking at our reactions, seeing if anybody would protest, but all of us sat as quietly as mice. I could feel the fear building up in the room. I couldn't deny that his words scared me as well, but they also gave me hope.

This is a man who shares my own beliefs and my love for the Great General… he will see that I don't have the disease in me!

"In short," Colonel Wan continued, "Yodok is a re-education camp, and you, *the Strayed* - the ones who have strayed from the righteous path - are here to be re-educated through hard labor… with emphasis on *hard*. To make your transition from your previous life - whatever it was - as smooth as possible, you need to accept one very simple truth." Colonel Wan's smile was again gone and replaced with disgust. "As long as you are here, you are no longer citizens of the great nation of Choson. You are *not* part of this great society. You are *not* under the loving care of our Father - the Great General. You have *no* rights. You have *no* worth."

Nari's sobbing intensified next to me.

"In fact… if you see a pig out by our farms… be sure to know that that pig has more worth than you do. The pig rolls around in the mud, and in the mud live maggots. Be sure to know that those maggots are worth more than you. Even the droppings of those maggots have more worth than you do… are you starting to see the picture?" He smiled at us again.

Every time his facial expression changed, I felt chills running down through my back. I started to get worried.

What if he saw me no different than all the real traitors in the room?

"Like I said," Colonel Wan continued, "that is a very simple truth… and accepting that is the first step in your re-education here at Yodok. Is that clear?"

There was an indistinct murmur around the room.

"I said, *IS THAT CLEAR?*" he roared.

This time, without delay, all of us shouted in completely unsynchronized panic.

"YES, SIR… ALL CLEAR SIR!"

Colonel Wan laughed.

"You there," he said and pointed at Nari with his sword. The whole back of my neck froze to ice. Nari looked up at the sword, then at his face, her whole body trembling.

"Tell me… who has more value - you, or the droppings of a filthy pig?"

"The… the… the droppings of a… filthy pig, Sir," Nari stuttered.

Colonel Wan laughed again.

"That's right... good that you were paying attention."

He moved away from Nari, and I could breathe again. I saw mom panting next to her.

"Very good... that is the first step," he continued. His smile was gone again. "Here... your re-education will require that every ounce of energy in your mind and body will be applied to hard work for the Great General. Now, if you ask for my personal opinion... the atonement for your crimes can, and *should,* only be completed by your death. Why? Because there *is no* atonement for the heinous crimes of treason you have committed. When you started colluding with our enemies - in my view - you renounced your life and the life of your families. That is my firm belief."

He smiled at us again.

"However... since the compassion of our Father - the Great General is so great... you will have the possibility to repent your crimes through sweat, blood, and tears. Isn't that astonishing?"

I was suddenly struck by fear.

Was this a rhetorical question, or did he expect us to answer it?

I looked around and saw the same thought on all the terrified faces surrounding me. Then to my surprise, mom was the first one to compose herself and said, "Yes, Sir! That is truly astonishing, Sir!" Everybody else then followed suit.

Colonel Wan looked directly at mom's face, which, for the first time since we sat down, was not bent forward. As he looked at her, a third expression appeared on his face. I couldn't make out exactly what it was, but it kind of looked like... surprise. Or... disbelief... almost like he recognized her. But then he quickly composed himself and looked away.

"It *is* astonishing!" he confirmed emphatically. To everybody's relief, he didn't punish anyone for answering late.

"It's so astonishing that I can't help but marvel at the… at least for me… excessive compassion of our Father - the Great General… but that only makes me love and revere him even more."

I couldn't help but agree with him.

But I'm not one of them!

"But," he continued. "Regardless of how compassionate the Great General is… until the time has come when you have proven yourselves to be cured… *if* that time comes… you are all mine!"

Saying this he stopped pacing and instead stood with a wide stance and looked right at us.

"And as you will see… I… am *not* compassionate. And I… am *not* forgiving."

As he went back to pacing before us, he briefly stopped to put his sword on the left shoulder of every person he passed. As he passed me, the cold metal made me shiver. Afterward, he went back to the middle and thrust the tip of the sword into the floorboards beneath him. His smile was back, scarier than ever.

"So these two things I would strongly recommend for you to bring with you now that you return to your new homes. First - in here you have no worth… and you will be treated accordingly. And second - your disease *will* be eradicated… and even if you have been here thirty years, if even the slightest suspicion remains that you still harbor it within you, I will personally make sure that you don't bring it back into society. That means that most of you will never leave here again. Reconcile yourselves with this fact!"

He let his inquisitive gaze wander over our scared faces. I suddenly noticed Chul, who stood in the corner to the right. He didn't seem to be too pleased by Colonel Wan's speech, which somewhat reassured me.

"Good!" Colonel Wan concluded with his broad eerie smile. "Now… some of you might think that since there is no hope for you, that you can just give up… that it won't make a difference whatever you do. Well… here I will be clear again - those of you who think that are sorely mistaken. If you think your life will be a living hell working hard for your atonement… that is nothing compared to what kind of hell you will end up in if you decide to give up… if you slack off… if you disobey orders… or if we in even the slightest way see that you are not giving your absolute *everything* to pay off your debt to our Father - the Great General. DO I MAKE MYSELF CLEAR?" he suddenly roared with insanely bulging eyes and flaring nostrils.

"YES, SIR!" all of us chanted without a moment's hesitation.

"Good!" he smiled. He continued to pace back and forth in front of us in silence for a while, waving his sword along his side. He nodded at one of the guards behind him who gave him a folder.

He opened it and said, "Ga Jae Eun?"

I heard a low whimpering *Yes, Sir* from one of the women behind me.

"Come to the front, if you please," he said in a low but firm voice. The woman, whom I had not noticed before, walked on her knees into the space between Nari and me. She looked about the same age as my teacher back in the Capital, Mrs. Lee, but taller, much skinnier, and with long greasy black hair with streaks of white in it glued to her cheeks and neck. Her face, filled with bruises and a cracked lip, was distorted by pain and panic. She was following the movements of Colonel Wan and his sword attentively, but never looked at him above his shoulders.

"Ga Jae Eun," he said without dignifying her with a look, "you are a prime example of the horrific crimes that the guests of our humble facility have committed."

He started reading from the binder.

"Openly criticizing our Father - the Great General... Spreading dangerous religious propaganda... Conspiring with the illegitimate puppet state in the annexed southern part of Choson to overthrow our one and only legitimate regime."

He continued pacing while reading this. He then stopped to look down at her with his eyebrows lifted, like he was waiting for her to answer a question that he hadn't posed. Jae Eun noticed this and started to say, "Eeehhh..." her brain racing to come up with something that wouldn't get her into trouble.

"Tell us, Mrs. Ga... how did you intend to overthrow the regime of our great nation?"

Jae Eun didn't find any words to answer him, but I could see the panic growing in her face.

"And just how many of your fellow countrymen were you planning on killing in the process?"

"I wasn't..." Jae Eun blurted out as a reflex, but then immediately constrained herself, her face turning dark red.

"You weren't *what*?" Colonel Wan asked inquisitively. "You didn't think anybody would get hurt while you overthrew the government? Or... what are you saying?"

"I... I..." Jae Eun stuttered, desperately looking around her for salvation.

"Or are you trying to say that you didn't commit these crimes? Because I have here a written confession, signed by *you*, describing in great detail the horrendous crimes you have committed... and the horrendous crimes you were planning on committing against the unsuspecting people of Choson... as well as against the Great General himself."

"I... I didn't—"

"We also have signed testimonials from neighbors and co-workers quoting you criticizing the Great General in public, and quoting you saying that you would like to leave our country to join the ranks of the puppet regime in the south," Colonel Wan continued.

"Those are lies!" Jae Eun suddenly burst out. She looked at Colonel Wan and the armed guards along the walls in pure desperation. "M-my neighbor... s-she just wanted my apartment... for her niece—"

Colonel Wan closed the binder with a snap and handed it back to the guard behind him.

"It truly never ceases to amaze me... all these people who come here after having committed terrible crimes... crimes they have confessed to... *in writing*... and yet they somehow continue to claim that it's not true... that they're all lies that people, for one reason or another, are telling about them... that they are here by some kind of *mistake*—"

"BUT THEY *ARE* LIES!" Jae Eun screamed, having lost all self-control. "I... I didn't do what they are saying... it wasn't me who wrote that... and... and... and I was forced to sign—"

Before she could finish, Colonel Wan had wielded his sword and pierced it through her throat. The blood-dripping tip of the sword was sticking out from her greasy hair in the back. Her eyes were almost falling out of her sockets and she tried to grab the blade with her hands, making more blood run down her arms.

As Jae Eun sat there, motionlessly, with unnatural gurgling sounds coming from her throat, as in a delayed reaction, people gasped and screamed and backed away from the bloody scene.

"SIT BACK DOWN!" Colonel Wan screamed.

We all looked at each other, then at Jae Eun and Colonel Wan. Then we slowly moved back into our original positions, although with a little more distance to Jae Eun. I saw Nari lying in mom's arms, her hand covering her mouth. I looked over at Jae Eun next to me. The unpleasant sound was still escaping from her throat, but her grip of the blade was becoming weaker, and her eyes were moving back into her sockets. Colonel Wan then retracted the sword in a swift movement, leaving Jae Eun falling to the floor. Deep red blood gushed from between her fingers that were desperately clasping her neck. Her body was twitching in convulsions. Colonel Wan received a white cloth to clean his sword from one of the guards. He then put it back into the sheath in his belt. Jae Eun's convulsions became weaker and weaker. Finally, she stopped twitching altogether, and just lay there with her eyes half-open in the ever-growing puddle of dark red blood.

I didn't move, but my whole body shivered from disgust when the warm sticky liquid reached my legs. My teeth were chattering so hard that I bit my tongue, and now I had the taste of blood in my mouth as well. It made me nauseous.

I can't get sick now… I'll be the next one with a sword through my throat! And he doesn't know that I'm innocent yet!

I closed my eyes, took a deep breath, and tried to compose myself.

Yes - I just witnessed a person being executed… but she was a traitor… she had plotted against the Great General… against… against all of us… she deserved what she got… right? I mean… traitors deserve to die… that's how it must be to keep the rest of us safe… right?

"So… do we have any more innocent people in this group?" Colonel Wan asked with a broad smile. "Anyone else who has *neighbors* making up *stories* to get your *apartment*? Or maybe they wanted your clothes… or your food… hah?"

There was nothing but silence in reply to Colonel Wan's question.

My heart was racing as I sat there, trying not to look at Jae Eun's blood-soaked corpse. I closed my eyes, but the image was still there, as well as the feeling of the warm blood against the skin on my legs. Then suddenly, another image popped into my head - the image of Kyung Sook on the mat under the uneven bars, holding her bloody leg with a piece of bone sticking out of it. I opened my eyes again and blocked that second image out of my head.

After Colonel Wan had stopped pacing back and forth in the silent room, he once again stood before us with his broad eerie smile.

"Very well then… I'm glad we got this chance to get to know each other," he said. "Again… I bid you welcome to Yodok. If you want to atone your sins, the first step is to know your place. And if any of you don't think you belong here… well, you can rest assured that you will *not* end up like Mrs. Ga here. She got off very easy. I assure you that you will *not*."

Unbearable silence once again spread throughout the room, and in the silence, a realization suddenly hit me - the stories about the hell-like places were true, but the stories were not about *real* demons… they were about people who are *like* demons… people like Colonel Wan here… he must be the *Demon of Yodok* that the man had talked about in the back of the army truck… and now, I was in the group of traitors he will torment.

No! That will not happen! If he is truly a patriot who protects our people from the disease within… he will see that I'm innocent. He has to! I just need to approach him the right way… at the right time…

As soon as I had finished that thought, a second voice appeared in my head.

No… don't be stupid, Areum… he will kill you, just like he killed poor Jae Eun… no… he will torture you instead… don't approach him!

"With that, I wish you all a good night," Colonel Wan said. "Gather your strength… for tomorrow you will need it. Private Gang and the other guards will escort you back to your quarters."

He turned around and marched out of the same door from which he had entered. In a moment of panic, I got the urge to stand up and call him back... to explain to him that I'm innocent - but Jae Eun's bloody corpse in the corner of my eye reminded me not to.

Now is not the time. Tomorrow we'll sort this whole mess out. Tomorrow I'll go back to my real life... and join the Great General's National Gymnastics Team!

"GET UP! MOVE!" the soldiers yelled, and this time all of us reacted immediately.

Chul walked up to me, Nari and mom from the corner where he had been standing.

"It's okay... everything's going to be fine... just come with me," he said in his soft feminine voice.

We followed him out of the door, avoiding the bloody puddle of Jae Eun and the hostile guards with machine guns around us.

Outside it was pitch black and still raining, and I had no idea where we were or where we had come from. If Chul hadn't been with us, there would be no chance for us to find our way back.

We walked through the thick mud without saying anything - but even if we would have tried to talk, our voices would just have drowned in the deafening battering of the rain.

Our numbers decreased slowly as families and lone prisoners found their lodgings. Chul finally opened the door to our house and lead us in. Mom found the oil lamp and lit it. Chul looked at us compassionately in the soft light and whispered, "I know that was a terrible thing to witness... but trust me... not everything is that bad here. Colonel Wan only wanted to establish his authority, and now he's done it. Don't worry... I will help you settle in."

"Thank you, Private Gang… *Chul*," mom said.

In the doorway, he turned around and said, "I'll be back tomorrow at six to take you to the orientation, so be ready by then. There you will meet General Roh. He is the camp director here at Yodok. He is different than Colonel Wan… you'll see." Then he left the house to guide the rest of the group to their houses.

Mom put a couple of pieces of firewood on the black mark on the floor in the middle of the room and lit it with the oil lamp before turning it off. The slow fire filled the room with warm light. I watched the smoke make its way up to the covered opening in the ceiling. Dad was still not here.

"Why do you think Chul said that?" I asked.

Mom sat down on the floor in front of the fire, extending her hands to warm them. Nari followed suit.

"Maybe he likes us," mom said. "Or maybe it's just their way of controlling us. One shocks us with fear… the other with kindness, leaving us afraid and hopeful at the same time."

"He seemed kind," Nari said. "Almost… like a girl."

In that precise moment, the door swung open with a bang, and another dark figure appeared in the entrance.

I don't know if I can take any more scares like this today!

The figure hesitated like he was trying to get a grasp of the situation. Then he took a few steps into the room and closed the door behind him. He looked completely different from the last time I had seen him. He was just skin and bones. His face was all covered in dirt… he even looked shorter. But there was no doubt about who it was.

"DAD!" Nari screamed and flew into his arms.

"Nari?" he said in a feeble voice, as if he wasn't sure this was happening, or if he was hallucinating. He touched her back, and then her hair. After that he looked over at mom and me.

Something changed in his face, and he fell to the ground, almost pulling Nari down with him.

"Oh no… oh no… I'm sorry… I'm so sorry!" he cried.

Mom rushed over to him.

"Young Il… honey… are you alright?"

Dad looked at her. His tears created white lines in his mud-covered face. I didn't move. I couldn't.

"I'm so sorry," Young Il said again between his sobs. "I wished… I prayed you wouldn't come here… I begged them not to bring you here… I'm so sorry."

Mom took his face in her hands. "Young Il, why are we here? What has happened?"

Dad's crying intensified. Mom stayed in her position, her eyes fixed on dad without blinking.

"I… I… I…" he started stuttering between the sobs. "I messed up… I'm… I'm so sorry! I never… thought… it would come to this. I never thought… they would do *this*. I was just trying to… trying to save us… all of us. People are dying… I had to stop it… I had to…"

His sobbing then took over and he fell into mom's arms. She stopped the interrogation and instead comforted her husband, stroking his muddy wet hair… what was left of it. Nari also joined in.

I couldn't.

I looked at them from where I sat by the fire. Another feeling had started to compete with the relief I felt to see my father alive. This other feeling grew stronger inside me. Intensified. Soon it had consumed me… all of me.

He did this! He just confessed to us… he did it! He is the reason why I'm here and not at home preparing to join the Great General's National Gymnastics Team at the luxurious gymnastics village outside the Capital. He is the reason I just witnessed a woman bleeding to death with a sword through her throat! He is the reason I'm here! HE DID THIS TO ME!

Tears streamed down my cheeks.

"What did you do?" I wheezed.

All three pairs of eyes turned to me.

"Areum— " mom started, but I didn't let her finish.

"No… tell me! Tell *us*! Why are we here?"

"Areum," mom said in a stern voice. "We'll have plenty of time to talk about all this tomorrow… the important thing right now is that we are all together again. Let's just cherish that tonight—"

"CHERISH WHAT?" I screamed. "Cherish that we're *together* in this hellhole? Cherish that we just witnessed a woman being executed? Cherish that Colonel Wan more or less promised that we'd never leave this place alive? I'm a professional gymnast in the Great General's National Gymnastics Team… I DON'T BELONG HERE!"

Tears were flooding uncontrollably from my eyes.

"But I *am* here," I continued. "I *am* here… so I just want to know *why*… why am I here? What have you done, Young Il? What did you do that… RUINED MY LIFE?"

I was panting. Young Il continued sobbing in mom's arms, whimpering from time to time, "I'm sorry! I'm sorry! I'm so sorry!"

"Areum, that's enough!" mom said harshly. "We'll deal with all of this in the morning, but right now… leave your father alone!"

"He's not my father," I said under my breath, but still so that everybody could hear it.

I took my quilt and a bag with underwear to use as a pillow, and lay down by the wall farthest away from the rest, turning my back to them.

For a long while, I listened to their quiet talking and sobbing. Eventually, my adrenaline started to wear off and was gradually replaced by exhaustion. A million thoughts swirled around in my head.

I thought of Su Mi.

I could be there with her right now… by the river… with a bottle of pomegranate liqueur… just celebrating… being together…

I felt overwhelmingly sorry for myself, but I knew that allowing this spiral of negative thoughts to continue wouldn't help me in the slightest, so I used every ounce of willpower I could muster to focus my thoughts away from my self-pity.

I have to get out of here. I WILL GET OUT OF HERE! Tomorrow I will talk to Colonel Wan. Today he was just establishing his authority… just like Chul said. He will recognize that I don't belong here. He will apologize to me and… and he will put me on a truck home before noon. Maybe he'll even let mom and Nari come with me. After all… they are just as innocent as I am.

But then my thoughts darkened again.

One of us is not innocent… one of us does indeed carry the disease. How could I have lived under the same roof as a traitor all these years without knowing it? How could I have failed my real Father - the Great General by not seeing the truth? I could have stopped him… I could have…

With these thoughts spinning around in my mind with increasing speed, I fell into a shallow restless sleep. My dreams shifted from the euphoria of seeing myself on the podiums at all the gymnastics competitions that I now might never compete in… to the bloody convulsing body of Jae Eun… and finally to the screaming Kyung Sook holding her broken leg with the bone sticking out from the skin.

Then suddenly I was back on that long unfamiliar street amid the sea of sun-scorched corpses with screeching crows ominously swirling down towards me to end my existence.

CHAPTER 11

"Areum!"

Mom's voice woke me from a dream, and just for a second I was blissfully unaware of where I was. Then I opened my eyes and the nightmare of my new reality dawned upon me.

My whole body was in pain - I had never slept directly on a hard wooden floor before, and the thin quilt I used as a bed didn't help much. My neck was so stiff I couldn't turn my head to the left at all.

There was a commotion around me - talking, unpacking, and the clanking of breakfast preparation. The fire was again burning in the middle of the room, and the lingering smoke that hadn't found its way up through the ventilation hole in the ceiling made me cough. Nari noticed I was awake.

"Good morning, big sister," she greeted in an unbecomingly cheerful way.

"Good morning," I muttered.

"Areum… help Nari with breakfast!" mom commanded from over by the pile of our belongings in the corner. Young Il was sitting on the ground with a cup of tea. It was his favorite porcelain cup from back home. On it, was a picture of the radiantly smiling face of the Great General. I guessed mom had been thoughtful enough to bring it for him.

Always playing the part of the devoted and loving wife...

A pleasant warm feeling spread throughout my body, as it always did when I saw the familiar image of my Father - the Great General - but at the same time, I couldn't help but feel nauseous.

How can a condemned traitor sit there and sip tea from a cup decorated with the most sacred of faces? Has he no shame?

My eyes moved from the warm and pleasant face on the cup to Young Il's starkly contrasting face right above it. His face was now clean from dirt - I guessed mom or Nari had helped him wash it thoroughly. But clean, it looked even scarier than when it had been all gray and muddy. His puffy cheeks and the hint of a second chin were gone, and instead, it looked like his bare skull had been tightly wrapped with a thin layer of leathery skin, making his cheekbones stand out unnaturally. His eyes looked frighteningly hollow - like they had sunk deep into his head. Around them were big, black circles - but not from being beaten... it was the same black circles I had seen around Ji Young's eyes the other day as she recited 'On the Juche Idea' before the class. The day she collapsed from hunger...

I swallowed as I continued exploring Young Il's gruesome face with growing discomfort inside my chest. His upper lip was broken in several places and had dried blood left in the cracks - it looked fresh. His beautiful, thick hair - which he always kept neatly combed to the back with gel - was all but gone, and his now unevenly cut short hair had several bald patches. He had large scars on his cheeks from what looked like burn marks, and a thick red line across his throat, which I could only assume was from being strangled with a rope.

Young Il noticed me staring at him and our eyes met. His face twitched as he blinked self-consciously a couple of times, then he looked away. I lowered my eyes, feeling ashamed I had made him uncomfortable, but I couldn't avert my eyes completely. Looking again at the cup with the Great General's warm smiling face on it, I suddenly noticed Young Il's hands and had to cover my mouth to prevent myself from screaming. All the fingernails were missing and in their place was nothing but ugly lumpy scar tissue. I suddenly felt a sharp stab through the base of my own fingernails. In a desperate attempt to rid myself of this all-too-real phantom pain, I started compulsively rubbing my fingertips as my eyes continued their undesired journey across the desecrated landscape of my father's mutilated body.

The rest of Young Il's hands and arms were also covered with scars from cuts and burns, which made me shudder, but it didn't affect me nearly as much as the absence of his fingernails. The rest of his body was fortunately covered by the dirt-crusted rags he wore, but I couldn't prevent my brain from picturing those parts of him in the same wretched state. I also noticed he had shrunk - he barely looked half the man I sat in front of at the breakfast table only a month ago.

The massive wall of resentment and hatred that had fortified my heart for so long suddenly cracked, and I was instantly overtaken by a flood of empathy and pity.

"What did they do to you?" I asked, surprised to hear the long-gone voice of their once concerned and caring daughter.

Young Il looked up at me with blinking watery eyes but then had to look away before he spoke.

"Don't worry about me, it's fine... really... it's just... I was stupid. I should have just confessed and signed whatever they wanted right away... but I was stubborn... *stupid*..." Young Il choked up again.

"D-dad… can you tell us what happened?" Nari asked. "I mean… from the beginning?"

Young Il sighed deeply but then nodded without looking up from his cup.

"I… was on the way to work… they were waiting for me there… three men from the State Security Department… they asked me to come with them, so I did… I mean… what could I do? As I was getting into their car, they hit me on the back of the head and all went black. When I woke up, I was tied up in the backseat, my mouth gagged, and with a black bag over my head. I don't know how far we went, but we must have traveled for several hours… to somewhere outside the city. They then started… *working*… on me…"

He took a sip of his tea with shivering hands, then put the cup down on the ground so he wouldn't drop it.

"When they finally broke me and I signed the confession they had prepared, they put me back in the car and brought me here." Young Il shook his head as he continued staring at the cup on the ground. "I was stupid, but I thought that maybe… just *maybe*… here they would listen to me. I told them it was a matter of life and death… that those people… millions of people… would lose their lives… not only in Hamhung but *everywhere*… that I had to get back to the Capital… to *fix* it—"

He let out another deep sigh.

All of a sudden, the image from my dream of the street filled with sun-scorched corpses appeared in my mind.

Again this 'Hamhung'… what does that city have to do with anything?

"But of course, they didn't listen to me here either," Young Il continued. "Instead, they locked me up down in the dungeons of the *Center of Truth*, and… and—"

With trembling hands, he again picked up his tea cup, ornate with the Great General's warm smiling face, and took a sip.

"W-what… what's the *Center of Truth*?" Nari asked. "What did they do to you there?"

Young Il shook his head again, pressing his eyes shut like he was trying to erase something vivid and agonizing from his memories.

"It's… it's an underground prison… they take people there to… *interrogate* them." He suddenly raised his eyes and looked right into mine. Meeting his penetrating gaze, I finally recognized the face I had always known - my father's face, full of power and determination. "Areum… all of you… you must stay away from the *Center of Truth*! Whatever you do… make sure you don't end up there… you must promise me that!"

The three of us looked nervously at each other as his desperate stare turned more and more frantic.

"We promise, dear," mom said in the same soothing voice she always used when he came home upset from work, vehemently complaining about all the idiots he was surrounded by there. "Just calm down… everything will be fine."

All of a sudden, Young Il gasped as if he remembered something ghastly, and then looked back down at the floor, hugging his legs that were tightly pressed against his chest. I wanted to ask how we could stay away from the *Center of Truth*, but I realized now was not the right moment. Nari went over and gently hugged him from behind.

"Do you want some more tea, dad?" she asked.

He nodded without looking up. The tears on his cheeks glistened in the flickering light of the fire.

As Nari went over to prepare another cup, Young Il composed himself enough to continue his story.

"I begged them… I begged the guards to at least tell me if my family was safe… if you were all okay. But they just… *laughed* at me… and continued to… to…"

His throat choked up again. Nari put the fresh cup of tea in front of him and returned to hug him from the side. Mom also went over to him and started softly stroking his back.

"Just take it easy, dear… don't talk… we're here with you… your family is here…"

"I failed him," Young Il mumbled. "I failed my father… I failed Hyun Woo…"

"Shhh…" Mom leaned over and gently kissed his cheek.

CHAPTER 12

As the warm sweet scent of the freshly made rice filled the room, Nari and I went over to prepare the breakfast bowls. I couldn't stop my eyes from wandering back to Young Il as I sprinkled the dry seaweed on top of the small steaming portions. His scarred, broken body frightened me, and I felt sorry for him.

But he's a traitor… he ruined your life, Areum! And he has confessed to his crimes!

After mom and Young Il had been served, I sat down with my bowl, and first then I realized how small the portion was. My stomach growled in pain as I gave mom a worried look.

"Your father says there is not much food here, so we have to make our stock last," she avoided my glance.

I couldn't imagine how I would make it through the day with this amount - the entire content of the pot for all of us was the normal portion of rice just for me back home in the Capital.

Anyway, it doesn't matter… I will be back there by tomorrow. Then I will have all the rice I can eat!

Thinking of the Capital, I had a sudden and intense urge to see Su Mi… and her mother, who always treated me like a daughter.

Will I ever see them again? Have they even realized I'm gone?

"Tonight, we'll make some dried vegetables as well," Nari tried to cheer me up. "And we have the daily cabbage and corn ration that dad gets from the camp."

I didn't reply.

"It's ten to six," mom said, looking at her pocket watch. "Private Gang will be here soon, so let's eat up."

I grabbed my old stainless steel chopsticks mom had brought for me. They were ornate with fierce-looking dragons of the ancient times, and holding them, strangely made me feel like I was at home... but the moment quickly passed.

As I started gulping down my food, barely acknowledging the sweet and salty sensation in my palates, I remained captivated by the scarred face and hands of Young Il. His mind, however, was entirely occupied by the feast he held in his hands. As the first grains of rice passed his lips, I saw his whole body shivering with deep satisfaction as his eyes flickered behind the closed eyelids.

"I haven't eaten rice in over... I don't even know how long," he exhaled as a couple of teardrops escaped from the sides of his eyes. "This is just... *divine*... there is no other word for it, and I don't give a damn that it's considered profane. I could die now a happy man."

Mom gave him a worried look as he put another small lump of rice with seaweed into his mouth and savored it for a long time before swallowing.

Traitor! You don't deserve dried seaweed... let alone rice! I thought to myself.

Halfway through the bowl, however, he opened his eyes, brought the bowl up right under his nose and gave it a long and deep whiff. He then handed it over to Nari.

"You eat the rest, Nari-ah... it's your first day, you'll need your strength... your *heart* needs it."

Nari didn't want to accept it, but he insisted.

"My stomach can't handle more anyway," he pushed the bowl into her hands. "This is more than I have eaten in a whole day since I was arrested." He stood up. "I have to go to the construction site. If I'm late, I'll be punished... and so will you if you're late for orientation."

"Be safe," mom said and gave him a peck on the cheek. Young Il went to the door and started tying his mud-crusted rags onto his red swollen feet.

"Dear... what happened to your shoes?" mom gasped.

"Somebody... took them," Young Il mumbled, embarrassed.

"But... you can't work like—"

"It's fine... really... don't worry," Young Il interrupted her. "Most people go like this... and I don't have a choice."

"If I had known, I would have brought the others from—"

"Really... don't worry about it... it's perfectly fine," Young Il mustered a fake smile, but not for long.

Mom didn't say anything else, and she didn't need to - it was all written on her face. Young Il knew better than to look at her... to *engage*.

"How is he?" I asked hesitantly while Young Il was working on his second foot. "I mean... General Roh... how is he? Is he the same as... Colonel Wan?"

Young Il shook his head.

"No, he's... different." He hesitated before continuing. "Just... whatever you do, don't cross him! Don't disobey him, don't even hesitate... whatever he says, just do it... and do it immediately. And most importantly... General Roh is all about redemption... he... er... *supervised* my interrogation here... he will give you a fair chance as long as you repent your crimes... but if you try to convince him you're innocent... he'll make your life here a living hell. I made that mistake... whatever you do, don't try to reason with him."

I almost choked on the rice I was chewing in my mouth. Again, my plans seemed to crumble before my eyes.

"But… we *are* innocent," I burst out. "*I'm* innocent. They need to know we're here by mistake." My blood started boiling in my veins. The hatred from yesterday re-emerged. "I don't know what crimes you have committed, Young Il… but I'm a member of the Great General's National Gymnastics Team... I need to be back with my team, bringing honor to the Great General and Choson… I haven't done anything wrong… I DON'T BELONG HERE!"

I panted, struggling to get air into my lungs.

"None of that matters," Young Il's voice was low and sorrowful. "You're not here because they think *you* did something wrong. They brought you here to pay for what *I* have done." He sighed deeply. "I don't know if they have taught you that in school yet, but the law of our country stipulates that guilt extends across three generations… at least when it comes to political crimes—"

"*Political crimes?* What are you talking about?" I panted.

"Well… anything that can be interpreted as a threat to the Regime is considered a political crime… and the law says that if one person has been corrupted, his children and parents - and sometimes even his brothers and sisters - have most likely been corrupted as well… and they're all sent to a place like this."

"That's… *ridiculous!*" I looked over at mom and Nari, who both looked at me with sad eyes. "Did you know about this?"

"It *is* ridiculous," Young Il confirmed, "but that is the way our country functions." I saw another tear escaping his eye. "I'm so sorry I did this to you… I didn't think it would come to this…"

"BUT WHAT DID YOU DO?" I screamed at the top of my lungs. "YOU STILL HAVEN'T TOLD US WHAT YOU HAVE DONE!"

Young Il looked at me but didn't say anything.

"That's enough, Areum," mom said firmly. "Stop attacking your father… he did what he thought was best… he is not at fault here. What's important now is that we stick together as a *family* and figure this out together."

Nari nodded and gave her father a sad but supportive smile.

"He's *not* my father," I wheezed. "I refuse to have a traitor as a father… I only have *one* father, and that is the Great General… and you took me away from him… I HATE YOU!"

There was a knock on the door and we all froze.

"That's Private Gang," mom gasped. "Young Il, just go… I'll talk to Areum… don't worry about us, we'll be fine."

Young Il kissed her forehead, and then Nari's. He threw one last glance at me with his teary eyes before opening the door and disappearing into the bright sunlight.

"Are you ready? It's time to go," I heard the soft feminine voice of Chul from outside.

"Good morning, Private Gang… we'll be right out," mom replied.

She gave me her all-too-familiar look, filled with a mix of anger, sadness, and disappointment. But she didn't say anything. She didn't have to.

We hurried to put on our clothes and shoes and met up with Chul outside, carefully closing our unlockable door behind us. Despite the fight we had just had, I knew we were all thinking the same thing.

Are our belongings safe here? Can people here be trusted?

The blinding sunlight hurt my eyes, and it took a while before I could see anything, but once my vision was back, I noticed we were surrounded by the same group of people as last night… except for one, of course. A sudden wave of nausea flushed over me. I took a deep breath and let my eyes scan my surroundings, trying to shake the etched image of Jae Eun's blood-soaked corpse and the feeling of her warm blood against my legs. Looking at the vast mass of houses in the *Orchid Garden*, I realized we must have been surrounded by houses almost the whole way we walked last night, even though it felt like we were walking through the heavy rain in a big black emptiness.

I guess there is no electricity anywhere in the prisoners' village...

It was easier to walk today. The heavy rain, which last night had turned the roads into rivers of mud, was now gone, and the road surface had turned into a fragile crust under the emerging warm late May sun and was cracking under the weight of our feet.

I looked over at Chul. He looked worried. More than he had looked last night when we went to meet Colonel Wan.

But Young Il said General Roh was different...

Corporal Lee was also there, flanking us from the side. He looked at us with his usual smirk, and as always, he had a cigarette hanging from the corner of his mouth. His gaze made my skin crawl, and the clouds of smoke the wind carried right to my face made me cough. I slowed down to get further away from him.

While we waited for Chul to get the next family from a house further down the street, I went out into the crossroad where our street intersected with the main road and I could see the entire camp surroundings clearly for the first time. Beyond the sea of box-like wooden houses of the *Rose Garden* and the *Orchid Garden* - my new, but very temporary home - there were some larger concrete buildings further up the road. Beyond them lay an enormous green valley that stretched as far as the eye could reach, and around it, rising from the ground like enormous walls built by giants, was a massive mountain ridge that locked us in from all sides. The only small crack in the mountain ridge was the pass beyond the main gate behind us, from where we had arrived last night.

Last night? Did we really just come last night? It feels like we passed that gate an eternity ago...

The scenery was astounding - or at least it would have been under different circumstances. It didn't even look real. Until now, I had only seen landscapes like this in paintings depicting the Great General, dressed in his traditional plain gray uniform, smiling in the foreground. I always wondered where those magnificent places were, and if maybe only the Great General was allowed to go there. In real life, however, I had never seen anything outside of the completely flat Capital, where I had lived my entire life, except for a few occasions when we went on field trips with school, or for the annual rice sowing or harvest days just outside the city. There, everything had also been flat as far as the eye could see. I had often dreamed of one day visiting mountains like the ones the Great General visited in the paintings. Now, I was in such a place, but not in the way I had envisioned it in my daydreams.

I followed the top of the mountain ridge with my eyes, and this time I was sure there was something that broke the otherwise smooth skyline, looking almost like the pins of a cactus sticking up from the rocky surface in regular intervals all the way around.

"They're guard towers."

Chul's voice from behind my back startled me. I looked around and saw that the entire group was gathered now.

"Come on, let's go, you don't want to be late," he signaled us to follow him and marched off along the main road toward the large concrete buildings at a fast pace.

"That's right," Corporal Lee said through a cloud of smoke, coming up right next to me. "Tall guard towers... all the way around, two hundred yards apart... except for in some parts where the mountain is too steep to climb anyway."

I tried to pick up the pace to get away from him, but he remained steady by my side.

"First day and already looking for a way out, eh?" he smirked at me.

I didn't answer.

"Well... I wouldn't recommend you to go that way. Each tower has guards armed with machine guns, and at night they have spotlights so they could see a mouse moving from miles away. And even if they couldn't *see* you, they have dog patrols day and night, and those beasts would *smell* you from a mile away. But if you make it past all of that, the rest is a piece of cake... you just have to get past a couple of rows of electrified barbed wire fence that would tear your skin and electrocute you at the same time...."

I looked up at him in terror.

Why is he telling me all this?

Corporal Lee noticed my reaction and laughed. Since he had gotten what he wanted, he moved up and started talking to Chul instead. I was left with a mix of hatred and fear boiling inside me.

Walking along the main road, we passed row after row of identical wooden barracks, from which people were emerging in the hundreds... or even thousands. They all looked the same to me - just skin and bones, covered in gray mud-stained rags, and with gray mud-stained hollow faces, many with the same strange black circles around their eyes and necks as Young Il had. Most had short hair, but for those who had long hair, the strands were uneven, twisted, and full of ugly lumps. But nobody seemed to care. Nobody seemed to be bothered by their horrendous stench either, but I prayed for a breeze of fresh air whenever one passed too close to me. Some of them wore shoes, but most of them only had rags on their feet, tied at their ankles by a rope, same as Young Il. All of them looked at us like we were from another planet. I also felt like I *was* on another planet. Or not even on another planet… it was more like I was in a… *living nightmare.*

I looked down at my trendy black polished leather shoes and school uniform, which was still surprisingly clean after the long bumpy truck ride and the midnight walk through the rain and mud. Observing the other people in our group of newcomers, it was clear that we were the only ones who came from the Capital. The rest had come from other parts of the country. I shuddered slightly. I'd never imagined I'd be lumped together with countryside people, but here we were - a distinct little group, being the only ones with normal clothes, shoes, and hairstyles.

I looked over at Nari, who was walking next to me, holding hands with mom. As she saw me, she stretched out her other hand for me to take.

I ignored it.

Corporal Lee was now again by my side, lighting a new cigarette.

"You know… there actually *was* an escape attempt last year," he said with his usual amused look. "A teenage girl, about the same age as you guys… she was on duty up in the mountains, gathering firewood and herbs and stuff… then one day she just disappeared, didn't come back at the end of her shift. We sent search parties with dogs to find her, but she managed to stay hidden for two whole days. We started believing she had actually managed to escape. Either that or fallen to her death in the treacherous mountains… which, to be honest, was more likely." Corporal Lee blew another big cloud of smoke that again ended up in my face and made me cough. I noticed that more of the newcomers had started walking closer to us as we progressed down the main road, and listened attentively to Corporal Lee's story. "On the third day, however, in the middle of the night, there was a power surge from the electric fence. We sent a dog patrol to check it out… and what did they find there if not the missing girl, electrocuted and blood-drenched from all the cuts on the barbed wire." Corporal Lee scoffed. "You know… she had thrown a piece of cloth over the bottom wire, thinking it would keep her safe from the current… stupid kid." I peered over at Nari and mom. Nari was crying, her left, free hand covering her mouth. Mom stared into the vast distance with a blank expression. "The thing was… when we dragged her out from the fence, we noticed she wasn't actually dead… scared the hell out of us, to tell the truth," he blew another puff of smoke. "The humane thing would, of course, have been to put her out of her misery right then and there, but we knew they wanted to make an example out of her, so we brought her to Doctor Death, who tended to her wounds so she wouldn't bleed out—"

"Doctor Death?" I blurted out by reflex.

Corporal Lee laughed.

"Yeah… that's what we call the camp doctor… I think you can guess why."

I indeed could guess why, and that caused chills to run down my spine.

"Anyway," Corporal Lee continued. "Once she was out of the woods, Colonel Wan ordered her to be brought down to the *Center of Truth*… two weeks later, she was tied up in *the Bloodyard*… which is where we're headed now, by the way. I remember the moment they removed the bag from over her head… she hardly resembled a human being anymore… and that was the end of it."

Corporal Lee threw the cigarette butt on the ground and lit another one. To my surprise, I thought I could detect a hint of compassion and sadness in his eyes.

"That hadn't been the first escape attempt, of course," he continued. "Many had tried before her... tried and *failed*... at least in recent times. But there was one that made it out and was on the loose for a couple of days... it was about ten years ago... long before my time. But his fate was worse than anybody else's in here... you can trust me on that. So if you don't want to meet the same fate, I advise you to take all of those ideas that are forming in your heads, bundle them up, and kick them right out. However... if you *do* want to try your luck... by all means, go for it."

He spun around and smiled at his entire audience.

"Cut it out, Chang Min," Chul shouted from the front of the group with his soft feminine voice. "There is no need to make them more scared than they already are."

"I disagree," Corporal Lee walked over and put his arm around Chul's neck. "I think it's good for them to get the lay of the land as quickly as possible... makes things easier... for everybody."

Chul shook his head but didn't say anything.

A moment later, we arrived in *the Bloodyard*.

CHAPTER 13

What Corporal Lee had referred to as *the Bloodyard* was, in fact, an enormous courtyard enclosed by three standalone concrete buildings - four stories high - forming the shape of a U. In the middle of the yard was a concrete wall about twice the height of a man that wasn't connected to the buildings in the U constellation. The concrete was damaged by what looked like bullet holes. In front of the wall was a slightly elevated platform - about two feet high - that almost looked like a narrow theater stage, but with four thick wooden poles sticking up from it.

"That's where we do the executions," Corporal Lee commented from another cloud of smoke. "Don't worry, I'm sure you'll see one soon, we have them quite frequently... maybe you'll even have a front-row seat, facing the execution squad." He laughed, savoring the reactions we gave him.

"Chang Min, please!" Chul pleaded.

"Relax, buddy," Corporal Lee winked. "Again... I'm just showing them the lay of the land... they'll thank me later."

Chul turned to us.

"Really... Corporal Lee is exaggerating... it's not *that* bad here," he comforted us. "And the executions are rare."

"You're such a big softy," Corporal Lee threw his arm around Chul's shoulder again. Chul didn't resist, it almost seemed he liked it.

Our group stopped in front of the concrete wall and the stage with the four poles.

"Wait here," Chul ordered. "I'll go and get the General. And Chang Min... please, no more stories!"

"We'll see," Corporal Lee smirked.

Chul sighed, but I could hint an almost childish smile appearing on his face. It made me think of that love-hate relationship Nari and I had when we were younger and how she couldn't help giving me that same childish smile when I was messing with her. But that was before... when we were still a *family*.

Then a thought occurred to me.

Could those two be brothers?

I discarded that idea immediately, however - they looked nothing alike.

But neither do Nari and I... and we're twins!

As Chul disappeared into the main building, I looked at Corporal Lee to see if he would continue his scare tactics, but instead he leaned against one of the execution poles and lit yet another cigarette, disinterested in the anxious group in front of him.

By the time Corporal Lee had finished his cigarette, Chul returned with four more people. I could immediately see who was in charge.

The tall authoritative man marching towards us was almost a head taller than Chul and very robustly built, which was further emphasized by his impeccable green general's coat. I had never seen anyone walk with such a perfectly erect posture before, and even though he was quite old - probably around fifty-five or so - his features displayed remnants of a striking handsomeness in his youth. He had a well-defined jaw and his hair was perfectly combed back to the side - not a single strand was out of place. The contrast between him and Chul - who looked even more insecure where he slouched next to him, shoulders to the front, hands in pockets, and with flickering eyes - was almost comical… at least it would have been in different circumstances. I couldn't help but notice that Chul looked much more nervous now, and I could understand why, considering the disapproving scowl on the General's face whenever he looked at him.

To Chul's right was Colonel Wan with his fiery smug eyes, contrasting the General's cold and emotionless gaze. The other two looked like any other officers I had seen in my life - just two blank stone faces in gray-green uniforms. They were the same kind of posse you could always see surrounding the Great General in the newspaper or on TV from his many visits to the factories and farms around the country.

The General walked past us without dignifying us with a look and stopped in front of the execution poles with his subordinates behind him.

"Form a half-circle, you maggots! MOVE IT!" Corporal Lee barked at us.

The General let his gaze sweep over the people standing in front of him, and when our eyes met, I was startled. His right eye was completely white - or rather silvery - giving his face almost a demonic appearance. His left eye was a normal hazel-brown color, but together with the silvery ghost eye, I felt like he was piercing into my bare soul. I looked around the half circle and saw I was not the only one startled by his appearance. Nari, to the right of me, was once more seeking comfort in mom's arms. As the silence fell, the General started speaking in an authoritative, fatherly tone that was in perfect harmony with his face and posture.

"I am General Roh, the director here at Penal Labor Camp No. 15. You are all here because you have strayed from the righteous path, and are guilty of betraying your country and our Father - the Great General."

His words delivered together with his ironclad gaze and emotionless tone, hit me like an armored truck.

I'm innocent! I haven't done anything! I wanted to scream at the top of my lungs, but instead, I just clenched my fists behind my back.

"Some of you have committed these treasonous acts yourselves. Some of you are related to the person who has committed them… a husband, a wife, a son or a daughter… or a parent. Just to be clear - it is of absolutely no consequence which scenario is true for you. Guilt is guilt."

I felt like he was looking specifically at me when he said the word *parent*, and his ghostlike silvery eye sent a chill down my spine.

"I am aware a lot of people feel it is unfair that relatives must be punished for something they haven't done. I can understand that sentiment. But we - as a nation - know very well from history that the sickness spread by our enemies is seldom isolated to just one person… it spreads… like smallpox… it spreads instantly throughout the entire family, to all its members, and it spreads… through *love*. Not unifying love, like the one us loyal subjects feel for our eternal Father - the Great General. It spreads through disruptive love… one that is transformed into *hatred* for everything that is treasured in our society."

I felt my heart burning painfully in my chest.

It spreads through love… another proof I'm here by mistake.

I examined the strong features of General Roh.

This is a man of reason - a man with a righteous mind. He will see that I don't belong here. He will set me free!

But Young Il's words lingered at the back of my mind.

'Don't try to convince him of your innocence!'

"Therefore," General Roh continued, "by decree of the Workers Party of Choson and our eternal Father - the Great General… to protect all his loyal subjects and this great nation he has built for us, it is stipulated that guilt of treason extends three generations. Since your guilt in the eyes of the law is undeniable and unquestionable, this topic will *not* be addressed ever again from this moment on… is that understood?"

"YES, SIR," we all replied in chorus after just a split second of hesitation. My mind, however, was already fully occupied with trying to find a way.

I have to risk it… it's the only way! He said it himself - the sickness spreads like smallpox, and it spreads through 'love'… but if there is no love - there is no spread. And if there's no spread - that means I don't have it. He must see that. He will see that!

I looked over at Nari. She watched me with a worried expression, shaking her head at me as if she was reading my mind and tried to convince me not to do it.

Does she really know? Can she feel what I'm thinking through some kind of twin connectedness that everybody keeps talking about? But if so… how come I never feel anything?

Either way, I couldn't help getting a certain satisfaction from going against her will… no matter what it's about.

"Now that we have concluded that first topic, here is the other message I want to convey to you all," General Roh continued, squinting both his hazel brown eye and ghostlike eye against the sun. The people who are brought here to us - yourselves included - are not *prisoners*… you are *Strayed*. You are people who have *strayed* from the righteous path. Therefore, you will not be *punished*… you will be *re-educated*. Hence, Penal Labor Camp No. 15 is not a *prison camp*… it is a *re-education camp for the Strayed*." His cold gaze swept over us once more.

"We here believe in redemption. *Yes*, you have strayed from the righteous path… *yes*, you are guilty of treason… but you are here because you have been given a second chance… a chance to redeem yourselves and atone for your crimes against our Father - the Great General. This is because he himself believes in forgiveness and the value of giving second chances, a virtue all of us, his mortal subjects, must learn from. But redemption will not come easy. From this day forward, you will have to prove your commitment to your ideological re-education through hard labor… every day… until the time comes when you have proven to have been reformed."

As I listened to General Roh's speech, I couldn't help but wonder if he could see with his silvery eye or if it was blind.

"I'm not going to lie to you - this will not be an easy journey. That time will not come tomorrow, or next week, or next year… but believe me - the righteous heart will, in the end, be rewarded with the forgiveness of our Father - the Great General. In a sense, this is the true essence of Juche - to bestow upon you the freedom *and* the responsibility to determine your own destiny. That is the principle on which this country is built."

At these words, he smiled with his mouth, but his penetrating eyes remained unchanged.

"So until the time comes for you to re-join society, you will be expected to work hard in any work assignment you are given… you will fulfill your quotas every day… and you will share the progress of expunging this sickness from your mind in the weekly Meetings of Ideological Struggle."

Immediately, I was transported back to the self-criticism room of last night, looking down into Jae Eun's wide-open lifeless eyes as she lay in the ever-growing puddle of her own blood on the floor. I shuddered, then tensed every muscle in my body and forced myself back into the present.

General Roh again let his powerful gaze sweep over us, but halfway through, something caught his attention and his face changed instantly. His jaw dropped slightly and his eyes widened. He just stood there, dumbfounded, staring at…

I followed his gaze into the crowd next to me.

No… it can't be…

But there was no doubt what he was looking at.

Mom? Why is he staring at mom? What's going on?

Just then I remembered the same reaction from Colonel Wan the night before.

Why are these people reacting to my mother like that?

Mom was clearly asking herself the same question as she stood there, her wide-open eyes fixed at the ground before her, face red and her teeth grinding, like she does when feeling uncomfortable.

"It… I…" General Roh stuttered without taking his eyes off mom.

Really… what is going on? What is this?

Everybody looked at each other, at General Roh, and my mother. The tension rose with every second of this awkward silence.

"Ahem…" Colonel Wan cleared his throat from behind, breaking mom's involuntary spell over General Roh. Flustered, he cleared his throat and quickly recomposed himself.

"As I said," he continued. "This is a place for redemption and re-education… your destiny lies in *your* hands, and in your hands only. Our job here is simply to help you on that journey." I could see that his eyes tried to return to my mother's face, but he forced them to stay away. "Now, the questions to all of you is - are you willing to *commit* to your redemption?"

"YES, SIR," we replied in chorus.

"Good!" he said, and this time he mustered a genuine smile. "With that, I welcome you to the first day of your re-education in our care. I wish you the best of luck. And now, I hand the word over to Colonel Wan, whom I believe you have already met. He will go over the ten Sacred Rules that will govern your life from now on, so please pay close attention." Colonel Wan gave us all an eerie smile from behind, squinting against the sun. "And again… good luck to all of you!"

"Thank you, Sir," we chanted.

"Thank you, General Roh!" Colonel Wan bowed reverently at the General as they changed places.

I continued discretely observing General Roh, and just as I had suspected, his gaze continued going back to my mother. I saw him leaning over and whispering something to the officer next to him, who also looked at mom, nodding and whispering something in reply. I had an ominous feeling in my stomach about this.

But I can't lose focus… all that matters is that I get out of here!

CHAPTER 14

Colonel Wan cleared his throat and smiled at us.

"So, ladies and gentlemen… as General Roh said, there are ten rules every resident of this camp has to abide by - ten *Sacred Rules* - but before I go into them, I see that several of you are still wearing your Great General pins." By reflex, my hand went to the familiar place over my heart, which I felt beating hard deep under my clothes. "As you surely understand, it's *very* offensive that you - the people who have betrayed our Father - the Great General - wear pins supposedly showing your allegiance to him. Corporal Lee… please collect them."

"Yes, Sir," Corporal Lee took off his cap for us to put the pins in.

Several people around me detached their pins from their chests, but mom and Nari didn't react, and I knew why - they hadn't worn theirs since we arrived. I, however, was wearing mine. As I held my hand over my beating heart, I felt the pleasantly cold metal against my skin. But my hand didn't move. I tried to force it, but it no longer obeyed me. My whole body was frozen stiff.

"Areum," I heard Nari whisper. "You have to take it off. Hurry!"

Corporal Lee was only a few steps away from me, but I still couldn't force my hand to move. I felt cold sweat pearl on my forehead.

"Hurry!" Nari whispered again with a growing panic in her voice.

A few seconds later, Corporal Lee stood right in front of me, looking at my right hand.

"Got something under there for me?" he asked with his usual smirk.

I opened my mouth but no sounds came out, and my hand was fixed in its place over the pin.

You have to do it, Areum! The only thing's that matters is to get out of here… after that you can get ten other Great General pins… or even twenty!

"What's the holdup, Corporal?" Colonel Wan asked impatiently.

Corporal Lee raised his right eyebrow at me.

As soon as I'm free I'll get another one… I promise! My brain screamed at my hand and finally managed to break the paralysis. As I removed the pin from my shirt with trembling hands, I felt like a piece of my heart was being ripped from inside my chest. I had to look away not to see the pin leave my hand and fall into Corporal Lee's cap, clinking softly against the others.

"Much obliged," Corporal Lee smiled and moved on to the next unfortunate soul.

I opened my eyes again and another pair of tears fell. I kept my hand over my heart. It wasn't beating as hard anymore but every beat was painful and heavy.

Corporal Lee nodded to Colonel Wan that he had finished.

"Good… now let's talk about the rules that will define your life for the foreseeable future," Colonel Wan smiled. "These *Sacred Rules* will help you stay on the right path, and you *will* obey them. Because if you don't… well, it will be the last thing you ever do." He smiled at us again with his eerie smile. "I will go through all of them now, but as you have probably already noticed, you will find them in every room of every building in this camp. Study them. Memorize them. *Live* by them!"

His face turned stern and hard, and so did his voice.

"*Rule Number One - Do not try to escape!* Anyone caught escaping, or anyone witnessing an escape without reporting it, will be executed."

His eyes landed on an old woman in the crowd.

"You there… what will happen if you try to escape?"

"I… I will be e-executed," the woman gasped almost in a whisper.

"I CAN'T HEAR YOU!" Colonel Wan screamed at the top of his lungs.

"I will b-be executed, Sir," the woman shrieked in panic.

"That's right! And don't you forget it!"

The woman sighed in relief.

"*Rule Number Two - Do not gather in groups!* If more than two prisoners gather outside of their living quarters, they will be executed. Work-related gatherings, authorized by the supervising guard, are the only exceptions to the rule.

"*Rule Number Three - Do not steal!* Any prisoner caught stealing, or helping another prisoner steal, will be executed.

"*Rule Number Four - Re-education officers must be obeyed and revered!* Any prisoner who fails to bow in respect when meeting a guard, or fails to comply with a re-education officer's instructions, or is disrespectful in any way, will be executed."

I felt my insides twisting tighter and tighter into a knot for every time he said the word *executed*. I was also confused by Colonel Wan calling us *prisoners*. General Roh had just a few minutes ago said we weren't prisoners - we were *the Strayed*.

"Rule Number Five - Report all and any suspicious behavior! You must watch your fellow prisoners vigilantly. Failure to report suspicious behavior will lead to execution.

"Rule Number Six - You must attend Meetings of Ideological Struggle every week! Failure to attend, or failure to sincerely criticize oneself or others, will result in execution."

Again, I couldn't stop myself from thinking of Mina and the battles we fought. I wondered if she also had to continue enduring self-criticism sessions wherever she was now.

"Rule Number Seven - You must fulfill your work quota every day! Failure to fulfill your work quota will lead to execution. To fulfill your work quota is to wash away your sins, as well as to compensate the Regime and our Father - the Great General - for the forgiveness he has shown.

"Rule Number Eight - There shall be no intermingling between the sexes outside the workplace! Conversations or touching between the sexes will lead to execution.

An indistinct murmur was heard around me at this rule but Colonel Wan ignored it and moved on to the next.

"Rule Number Nine - You must genuinely repent your errors! Failure to acknowledge your sins and instead denying them will lead to execution."

The knot inside me twisted so hard I almost squealed in pain. I couldn't breathe.

Get it together, Areum… he's not talking about you… this only concerns the real traitors!

"And finally," he continued, again with his eerie smile. *"Rule Number Ten - You must know these rules by heart and comply with them!* Failure to be able to recite these rules upon request by a re-education officer, as well as failure to comply with any of them, will lead to execution."

He observed our faces, content at the reaction he had evoked. At times like this, I really envied Nari, who could memorize anything without any effort whatsoever, for which she was always raised to the skies by our parents and teachers. The old flame of resentment sparked anew inside me as I caught the devastated face of Nari in the corner of my eye, her arms wrapped around mom, trembling like a fragile little flower. Mom had her arms around her, like always protecting the one daughter she really cared about.

I turned my eyes to the front and blocked my weak little sister out of my mind.

Let them praise her fantastic brain… soon, none of it will matter… by tomorrow morning, I will be long gone!

"In addition to these ten *Sacred Rules*, we also have a curfew," Colonel Wan added. "That means any prisoner who is outside their accommodation after sunset will be executed." He let his eerie gaze sweep over us to see if anyone dared a question. No one did, so he continued. "This is basically all you need to know while residing here. Memorize these rules and live by them… and we won't have any problems. Break them… and your journey to redemption ends there and then. IS THAT CLEAR?"

"YES, SIR," we all chanted.

"Very good… then I wish you good luck on your journey! Corporal Lee… take it from here."

General Roh and Colonel Wan turned around and went back to the building they had come from together with the other officers, but before General Roh disappeared through the door, he threw one last glance at my mother. Even though he was far away, I could tell his face was a mix of sadness and astonishment. I couldn't understand why my mother had this strange effect on him, but at least now I knew where his office was.

As soon as school finishes, I'll go and talk to him… then this nightmare will finally be over!

"Okay then," Corporal Lee said, taking the cigarette from his mouth. "You will now be divided into two groups. All adults - meaning all those fifteen years or older - will be given work assignments. These work assignments will start immediately, so we will show you where to go. This group will gather around me. All the children… that is you who have not had your fifteenth birthday yet… you will go to school. Private Gang will take you there." Chul raised his hand and casually waved for us to come, but Corporal Lee didn't have his level of patience, and immediately barked, "What are you waiting for, maggots? Divide into two groups…. MOVE IT!"

I rushed over to Chul, who gave me a shy smile. Two more girls joined our little group. Both looked like they were around fourteen, like Nari and I. One of them had two long braids on the sides and was nervously looking down at the ground. The other girl had short hair and a confident - almost provocative - expression on her face. Shortly after, three young boys stumbled over reluctantly after having been pushed by their respective parents. I couldn't tell how old they were, but the oldest couldn't have been more than eight.

So young! How could these children be considered traitors?

My mind jumped to when I was that age. How I had loved my family back then. How I had believed they loved me back. I was happy. It was also around that time I was picked by the school's gymnastics team… and I had the unwavering belief that my life would only continue to be better and better. Obviously, it didn't turn out that way. My heart went out to these children. Maybe yesterday, they were at home with their families, happy and unsuspecting, thinking *their* lives would only get better and better. Now, they were here - condemned by the crimes of their parents, just like me - and nothing would get better for them ever again.

But I will get out of here! I will!

I suddenly noticed Nari was not with us. I looked over at the adult group, and there I saw her with her arms tightly wrapped around our mother, tears streaming down her cheeks. Mom tried to get her to loosen her grip, whispering something in her ear.

Oh, come on… have some dignity! I rolled my eyes. *Now is not the time to be a scared mama's girl… what is she trying to do, get herself shot? And mom too?*

"HEY!" Corporal Lee took a couple of menacing steps towards Nari. "Are you deaf? All children gather over there… NOW MOVE IT!"

But Nari didn't let go. I saw the desperation growing on mom's face as she unsuccessfully tried to unlock her arms.

"SEPARATE!" Corporal Lee barked again, taking yet another step forward. "I'm warning you."

But Nari still didn't let go.

Come on… don't be a baby right now… just let go of mom and come over here! I wanted to shout at her, but I knew I couldn't. *Do I have to go over there and get her?*

"Please!" mom pleaded to Corporal Lee. "She's just a little girl. She's sick. She has never been apart from me before." But Corporal Lee didn't pay attention to her. Having lost his patience, he marched over and yanked Nari with enormous force away from mom.

"NOOOO…" Nari's cry of desperation pierced my ears. She was twisting violently in Corporal Lee's strong grip, reaching her arms out towards mom, trying to grab hold of something - *anything* - but it was useless.

"Please… please don't hurt her… she's not being disrespectful… she's just afraid, that's all!" mom pleaded, but Corporal Lee still didn't pay her any attention. He dragged Nari, kicking and sobbing, over to us and thrust her down to the ground.

"This one seems to be yours," he winked at Chul.

"Thanks, Chang Min… you're such a gentleman," Chul sighed as he tried to help Nari up, but she was sobbing inconsolably on the ground, stretching her hands out towards mom, who was standing frozen by the adult group, tears streaming from her eyes and one hand clasped over her mouth.

"Hey… it's going to be okay," Chul tried to calm Nari down.

She suddenly noticed me, and without any warning got onto her feet and threw herself into my arms where she continued sobbing.

I felt blood rushing up to my face. I grabbed her shoulders hard and dislodged her grip from around me.

"Stop it!" I whispered to her seriously, trying to make eye contact. "You have got to pull yourself together, Nari! This is no place for weakness… you'll get us all into trouble. Just stop being a baby and pull yourself together!"

Nari stopped crying for a moment and looked at me with bewildered eyes. She swallowed. Her whole body trembled. But then her tense muscles relaxed slightly, and she nodded.

"Good," I nodded back, but I noticed from the corner of my eye that Corporal Lee had marched over to mom and told her to get down on her knees. I felt Nari starting to rush over there, so I grabbed her arm and held her back.

"You're only going to make things worse," I whispered to her, but I still had to struggle to keep her in place.

"I think it's time for some repetition," Corporal Lee towered over mom, who was on her knees on the ground. He lit another cigarette. "Recite me rule number four!"

"I… I…" Mom was at a loss for words.

"ARE YOU DEAF?" he screamed and bent over so his face was only inches from hers. He took a deep drag on the cigarette and then made her whole head disappear in a thick cloud of smoke. I expected her to have a cough attack, but not a sound came out from the cloud. "I said recite me rule number four!" Corporal Lee repeated.

"I'm deeply sorry, Sir... I thought we had until tomorrow morning to memorize them," she said in a trembling voice.

All of us, including Chul, watched the scene in tense silence, which was further intensified by the total absence of any other sounds around us. Not even the wind was blowing.

"First day, and already coming with excuses," Corporal Lee straightened himself up. The smoke cloud was now gone and I could again see mom's face. "It sounds to me like you didn't even bother to pay attention when Colonel Wan generously sacrificed some of his very precious time to help you all get settled in. That is quite disrespectful, don't you think?"

"Yes, Sir... you're absolutely right, Sir... I'm ashamed... and I'm deeply sorry, Sir... but please, punish me... she's just a girl... she will learn... I swear on the Great General himself," mom pleaded as she threw herself forward and pressed her forehead against the drying dirt. "I... I... I do remember some of them... er... just not exactly in which order... er... one was that we need to learn all the rules... that was the last one, and... er... one was not to steal. Then there was one about fulfilling the work quota... er... and another one about... obeying the guards— "

"That's the one!" Corporal Lee exclaimed triumphantly, taking a step back from mom to address the entire group. "*Rule number four - guards must be obeyed and revered at all times*. Very good... you *were* paying attention," he smiled. "So tell me... what does rule number four say will happen if a prisoner fails to comply with a guard's instructions? Do you remember that... or had you stopped listening by then?"

Mom swallowed loudly.

"H-he... he will be executed," she stuttered.

"That's right!" Corporal Lee nodded gleefully. "He... or *she*... will be executed. That's absolutely right. So tell me, Mrs. Kim... what happened just now? What would you say your daughter just did?"

"P-please... I beg you!" mom pleaded and again threw herself forward and pressed her forehead hard against the ground. "She was just upset... punish me instead... please, I beg you—"

"Upset or not, the rules are very clear," Corporal Lee insisted. "So, in your view, what do you suggest I do about it?" He grabbed his machine gun with both hands and pointed it at Nari, but without taking his eyes off mom. Nari made another attempt to break free, but I kept her in place, not knowing if that was the right thing to do. At this moment, I didn't know anything.

Corporal Lee raised his eyebrows, indicating to mom that he was still waiting for an answer.

"Please... please..." mom sobbed from the ground.

"Come on, Chang Min... that's enough!" Chul suddenly shouted from right next to me. His voice was this time neither soft nor feminine. It was firm and hard... but still that of a boy.

"They have gotten the message, okay... now, can we please get on with it?" Chul's words sounded half like a plea, half like a command.

Corporal Lee still didn't take his eyes off mom. I suddenly felt a strong burning in my eyes and noticed my whole face was covered in sweat. I blinked rapidly not to miss a second of what was happening, but that only increased the burning sensation.

"Is that true?" Corporal Lee asked. "Have you *gotten the message*? Has your daughter also gotten the message?"

"Yes, Sir... we are very, very deeply sorry," mom pleaded, her forehead still firmly pressed against the ground. "I swear on the Great General, it will never happen again. Right, Nari-ah… it will never happen again… tell them!" She threw a pleading look at Nari who was now standing frozen in my arms. She was not crying anymore.

"Yes," she said in a feeble voice. "I won't do it again… I promise… I'm sorry… I'm really sorry…"

Corporal Lee looked at Nari. Then at mom. Then at Chul. Then he laughed loudly and put the machine gun back on his shoulder.

"Okay then… since Private Gang seems to believe you, I guess I have to believe you, too," he winked at Chul with a wry smile. Chul just rolled his eyes and sighed.

The situation was defused.

"Today… and only today," Corporal Lee continued, "you will be shown leniency. But starting tomorrow, all rules will be enforced in full and there will be no exceptions. You will live by these rules… or you will die breaking them. IS THAT CLEAR?"

"YES, SIR," we all chanted.

"Excellent!" Corporal Lee beamed. "Now take those kids away from here, Private Gang! We adults have serious business to attend to." He winked again at Chul, who turned around and signaled for us to follow him.

"So… now I will give you your work assignments…" I heard Corporal Lee's voice fading behind me. I threw one last glance at mom as I half-dragged Nari with me away from the execution place and out from *the Bloodyard*.

"Be strong!" mom mouthed at us before turning away.

We turned away as well and followed Chul in the direction of the main road.

Now we were alone.

Completely alone.

CHAPTER 15

As we came back to the main road, Chul stopped and turned to the seven of us in his group.

"Alright, I know it seemed pretty harsh what you just heard from Colonel Wan, but trust me... as long as you learn the *Sacred Rules* and follow them, you will be fine. I promise."

He talked to all of us but looked especially at Nari, who was still shivering. He put his hand on her shoulder.

"Okay?"

"Okay," Nari whimpered, but I could see she was far from okay.

My heart suddenly softened.

How will she last even a week here... let alone several months? Will mom and Young Il really be able to take care of her?

"And also," Chul continued hesitantly. "I know Chang Min... I mean, *Corporal Lee*... can seem somewhat harsh, but he's actually a wonderful guy... you will see... he just gets a bit carried away sometimes."

I looked at Chul astonished. That was the last thing I expected to hear from him. And I knew Corporal Lee well enough now to know nothing could have been further from the truth.

"Anyway… I will take you to your school now," Chul averted his eyes away from the disbelief written on our faces. "We only have two teachers, so they are teaching all the children we have here in the camp… which, thank the Great General, are not too many… but still enough to make the classrooms quite crowded. You will be divided into two groups based on your age. Corporal Bun is the teacher for all the children who have not turned ten yet, and Miss Ae is teaching all of you who are between ten and fifteen."

He gave us a thorough top to toe exam with his eyes.

"I'm guessing the three of you will be in the first group… younger than ten, right?" he looked at the scared-looking boys standing next to me. They nodded nervously.

My heart sank to my stomach - watching them now, they looked even younger than they had a moment ago. The youngest didn't look older than six.

How could they have brought a six-year-old to this place? How could he be guilty of anything?

"Great," Chul continued. "That means the four of you will go to Miss Ae's class."

Nari, I, and the two other girls nodded.

"Miss Ae is really nice, so you don't have anything to worry about," Chul smiled at us, but then gave the three scared boys a more concerned look. "Corporal Bun might be a bit intimidating at first, but as long as you follow the rules… I'm sure you'll be fine."

I noticed the lower lip of the youngest boy started to tremble. The boy next to him - maybe his brother - comforted him by putting an arm around his shoulder.

"So… I will escort you to school this once," Chul gave us a meaningful look. "That means from now on you'll be on your own, so you need to learn how to find your way around the camp without getting lost… and you need to learn it quickly. Is that clear?"

We nodded.

"Good! Now, before we go, I'll explain the main things to you, so pay attention!"

I found it cute that he tried to make his voice deeper and more authoritative when he talked to us. I wondered if the other guards made fun of him. Or disliked him… like General Roh seemed to do.

Chul pointed with his hand down the road we had come from this morning.

"You all live over there in the *Village of the Strayed*… we call it that because - as General Roh said - you're not *prisoners*… you're *the Strayed*."

You can call it whatever you want, I scoffed to myself. *It doesn't change what it is*

"Last I heard, around seventeen thousand people are living there, so you can consider it a large village. It's divided into two parts. The biggest one is the *Rose Garden*, which is where the majority of *the Strayed* lives. It consists of long barracks, and each of them houses around fifty people. They are either all male or all female… no mixed ones. The only exception is if a mother has a baby son to take care of, but only until he turns six, then he's moved over to a male barrack."

I looked over at the six-year-old boy in our group. He was crying now. Chul noticed it and quickly moved on.

"The smaller part of the village is a collection of chain houses where families are allowed to live together. That is called the *Orchid Garden*. They are very few, so only the families of the most privileged prisoners are allowed to reside there. And we have two of those privileged people right here in our little group," he smiled at Nari and me. "You are truly fortunate."

What is he trying to do… get us killed?

With burning cheeks I tried to ignore the hateful glares of the less fortunate boys and girls next to me.

And also… 'lucky'? That's not the word I would use for my current situation.

Nari raised her shivering hand next to me and I got ready to intervene if she started crying for our mother again. But instead, she asked a question.

"Why do you call them the *Rose Garden* and the *Orchid Garden*? I didn't see any flowers there…"

I sighed with relief. And I had to admit - I was quite curious about that myself.

"Right," Chul tapped his chin with his index finger. "Actually… I've never thought about it, but… maybe they just wanted it to feel more like home… I mean, if you think about going home to the *Rose Garden*… it kind of gives you a nice feeling inside, don't you think?"

Nari lowered her hand without answering.

I remembered the times we went to the botanical garden of the Capital - as a whole family. There had been plenty of roses and orchids of all colors, and indeed - when thinking about it, I felt a wave of warmth spreading throughout my body. But of course, I didn't know if it was because of the flowers… or because it was one of those rare happy moments I had spent together with my… *family*. Either way, this *Orchid Garden* and the house that we had spent last night in had neither of those things.

"The house just in front of the *Rose Garden*, which you see to the right, is the canteen where you get your daily food rations after the school day or workday has finished. Usually, each person is served his ready-made ration and eats it there, but those of you who live in the *Orchid Garden* are allowed to pick up the rations for the entire household and you cook it at home."

Since there were no questions, Chul turned around and pointed at the enormous U-shaped building formation we had just come from.

"That constellation is the *Oversight Office for the Re-education of the Strayed*... because just like General Roh said, the main purpose of this camp... and others like it... is to re-educate the ones who have strayed... so you no longer pose a threat to society once you re-join it. That's where all the senior officers and the camp administration is. For short, however, we just call it *the Oversight*. Please note that you're not allowed to go in there without written permission from a re-education officer... which is us - the guards."

Chul then pointed at a small run-down house next to the large U-shaped buildings, which I at first hadn't noticed since it was almost completely consumed by the surrounding vegetation.

"That building over there is the hospital. You're not allowed to stay home from school or work without written permission from the doctor..."

I shivered.

Written permission from Doctor Death?

"...and I'm going to be completely honest with you - he doesn't give permission very often."

Chul turned around and pointed at the mountain range towering up at the end of the main road.

"Up there in the mountains are the mines. We mostly extract coal, but there is gold and some other valuable metals and minerals as well. A lot of our residents work there, and... some of your parents probably will too." He flushed, realizing he once again had made everybody uncomfortable. Eager to leave that sensitive subject, he quickly lowered his arm and instead pointed at the fields on both sides of the road. "Over there is where we grow all our food - corn and cabbage for the prisoners and the guards alike, and rice for the officers... although, us guards also get rice on national holidays, like the Day of the Sun - the Great General's birthday. Truth to be told, though, we don't keep much of the food here... most of it is shipped away to other parts of the country. Now, I know it will be rough to have a diet consisting solely of small portions of corn and cabbage, and you *will* be tempted to grab some food that is just growing freely around you, but please remember rule number three - if you're caught stealing, you *will* be executed. So please fight the temptation."

He gave us a very serious look, which again created a comical contrast to his soft feminine voice. Luckily, none of us were in a laughing mood.

"Beyond the fields is the granary where we keep the harvested crops... you can't see it from here, but it's right next to the village where us guards live. Our village is, by the way, called the *Lotus Garden*, but... same as you, we don't have any lotuses growing there either," he smiled. "Oh, and by the way... be sure never to go in there without permission... trespassers are shot on sight. Okay?"

"Yes, Sir," we gasped.

"Good... and over there by the river," he pointed to the right, "is the watermill where we peel the rice and grind the corn. I'm actually the supervisor of that facility."

He let his insecure eyes sweep over our blank faces as he pondered what to say next.

"Well... that's about it, I think... and your school is right over there, just across the road from *the Oversight*. I will take you there now and then you will be under the custody of your new teachers. And remember - your teachers are also re-education officers, so rule number four applies to them as well. In short, just follow the rules and everything will be fine. Okay?

"Yes, Sir."

"Good. I'm sure you'll all be fine. Let's go!"

We followed the main road under the rising morning sun a bit further until we reached the intersecting road leading to the school building. It was a small worn-down wooden building - only one story high - but still significantly larger than the hospital, which was well on its way to be reclaimed by nature. There were a few windows on the side, covered with thick iron bars.

Why do they need bars on a school that's in the middle of a prison camp?

Over the entrance door was a sign that read '*School of Juche*'. Apart from that, there was nothing indicating it was a school - no yard or play park in front, no benches to sit on - it was just another anonymous wooden building surrounded by some trees and some patches of grass. I wondered what Su Mi would have said if she saw this - she couldn't stand things that were old and ugly.

We followed Chul through the door into a long corridor with four doors on the left side.

"Like I said… right now we only have two teachers, so two of the rooms are empty," Chul explained.

We stopped in front of the first door. We could hear a strong male voice from inside. Maybe it was only my anxiety speaking, but he sounded angry.

"This classroom is for you guys," Chul told the three scared little boys with pity in his voice and knocked softly on the door.

"WHAT?" barked the angry voice from inside.

Chul opened the door carefully and said, "Excuse me, Corporal Bun, but I have some new students here for you."

"THE HELL YOU DO!" Corporal Bun roared. "I haven't been informed about this… and what do you expect me to do with all these IDIOTS that I already have here? They're sitting in each other's laps as it is!"

I could not see into the classroom, but I was imagining Corporal Bun's enormous figure and scarlet red face steaming as he screamed at poor Chul in the doorway.

"I'm sorry, Sir… but my orders are to hand them over into your care," Chul said with a slight tremble in his feminine voice.

He really doesn't handle conflicts with authoritative figures very well. Maybe that's why General Roh doesn't like him.

"If those DIMWITS want to overcrowd my class, they can come down here and tell it to my face… then I will show them what they can do with their *newcomers*."

"I'm terribly sorry, Sir," Chul's voice trembled even more than before. "But… you know I can't do that. My orders are to leave them with you. Please… you must understand I can't disobey a direct order—"

"And how about the new teachers they have been promising for two years now? When are *they* coming? This is RIDICULOUS! Those clowns across the street have NO IDEA what the hell they are doing!"

Chul was at a loss for words and large sweat drops started to accumulate all over his face and neck.

"So, what are you waiting for then?" Corporal Bun finally grunted. "Send the new idiots in… does it look like I have the whole day to just wait around for you?"

Chul reacted immediately and opened the door to let the three scared boys in. They gave Chul one last pleading look, but he quickly shoved them into the classroom.

With the door open, I finally got a clear view of the angry Corporal Bun, and fortunately, I managed to keep myself from laughing. That deep-voiced angry bellowing that almost made the windows tremble had come from a tiny little man, almost a full head shorter than me, a bit chubby, and fully dressed in a spotless ceremonial uniform. But his plump little face was just as red as I had imagined it.

"Thank you, Sir!" Chul said and quickly closed the door behind the boys just as Corporal Bun's deep voice pierced through the door.

"THREE? For Juche's sake... HOW THE HELL AM I SUPPOSED TO FIT *THREE* MORE OF YOU WORTHLESS VERMIN OFFSPRING IN HERE? Just go and sit on the floor against the wall! MOVE IT!"

The scurried steps and loud screaming from the other side of the door quickly faded as we reached the second door.

"Like I said, these two rooms are empty," Chul didn't slow down. "Miss Ae's classroom is over there at the end.

We continued down the long dark hallway, which, apart from sudden outbursts from Corporal Bun's classroom and the sound of our shoes, was perfectly still. I felt a tightness growing in my throat as I imagined Miss Ae as a horrifying female version of the red little man we had just seen. I'd had my fair share of old and angry women teachers, and in my experience, they could be even *worse* than Corporal Bun. Walking towards the terrifying unknown behind door number four, the sizzling hatred for my father - for whatever he had done to make us end up here - once again spread through my body.

But I'm getting out of here. None of this will matter, because by tonight I will be far away from here.

I swallowed painfully.

But what if I'm not?

I threw the voice of doubt mercilessly out of my head as we approached Miss Ae's classroom.

Whatever is on the other side of that door, I can handle it!

My right hand went mechanically to the place over my furiously pounding heart where the Great General pin used to be, and instead of being able to caress the soft surface of the pin for comfort and courage, I resorted to grabbing the cloth of my shirt instead… hard. It didn't have the desired effect, and the tightness and pain in my throat only intensified.

Chul knocked gently on the door.

"Excuse me, Miss Ae… it's Private Gang."

Whatever is on the other side of that door, I can handle it… I will handle it!

CHAPTER 16

As I heard the ominous footsteps approaching on the other side of the door, my eyes fell on Chul. To my surprise, I noticed a complete change in his posture - even though still tense and uncomfortable, he didn't seem at all afraid. That made the tension in my throat lessen slightly. But only slightly.

The door opened and from the other side came a voice that for the second time today reminded me of pleasantly warm spring days in the botanical garden with my family.

"Ah, Chul… how delightful to see you!"

I still couldn't see her face, but I was immediately convinced the woman on the other side of the door must be the most beautiful girl in our vast country… nothing less would match that voice.

"Eh… yeah… it's really nice to see you too… as always, Miss Ae… but unfortunately, I'm here on official business. I… eh… have some new students for you." He flinched as if he expected this divine being to strike him down for his insolence. But since she didn't, he opened the door fully to display the four frightened girls in the hallway.

At first, her face was veiled in darkness, but then she took a step forward into the light. Before me appeared a young woman - she didn't look a day over twenty, but I assumed she must have been - with a radiant smile on her slim face. She was far from being the most beautiful woman I had ever seen, but her face, which glowed with nothing but pure kindness and inherent goodness, matched her voice perfectly.

Am I dreaming? Can such a person exist in a place like this?

"Well... we are a bit crowded here, as you know, but we can always make room for more," she said with her unwavering smile. "Come on in, girls!"

"I'm really sorry about this," Chul excused himself. "I don't know why you weren't informed... I have never seen Corporal Bun *that* angry..."

"Don't worry about it, Chul," Miss Ae chuckled. "I've been here long enough to know how things work... it's alright... really."

Chul muttered another apology at Miss Ae's shoes, but her focus was no longer on him.

"Come on now, girls... go find yourselves a seat," she clapped her hands. "Today will be easier since one girl is home sick... got the flu, poor thing... is really contagious. Thank the Great General, no one else has contracted it."

The classroom was large and filled with around fifty or so boys and girls of different ages. I had the feeling Nari and I were among the oldest, but it was difficult to say for sure. It was also impossible to tell them apart since they all were equally dirty and wearing the same kind of gray rags and short hair. Like all the people I had seen so far around the camp, they were all sickly skinny. All except for one.

The boy in the back of the room, who had drawn my attention, stood out from the rest in many ways, the first being his leaned-back posture. He wore similar clothes as the rest of the class, but they were not as worn out and dirty. He also wore shoes - *real* shoes. His hair was untidy, but almost in a deliberate way, and he had firm and kind eyes. As they met with mine, I blushed and hurried off to find a seat.

"I hope they'll behave," Chul smiled nervously at Miss Ae.

"They always do," she beamed back. "Take care now, Chul!"

"You too, Miss Ae!"

Chul closed the door softly and I could hear his footsteps fading down the hall.

The nerdy boy in love with the pretty school teacher… classic! She's so out of his league!

The classroom looked completely different from the ones I had back in the Capital, where everything was kept in perfect condition - clean, fresh, and with new comfortable desks… one per student! This classroom was old, dirty, and smelled of mold. The few remaining flakes of dry green paint on the walls revealed that the room had been painted at one point, but now they were nothing more than specks on the uneven wooden boards that constituted the walls. I could feel the floor was also made of wood, but it was impossible to see through the many layers of dried mud and dirt. We cleaned the classrooms in the Capital every day, but I was quite certain this room had never been cleaned.

The students sat on long lumpy wooden benches without back support - most had five per bench - in five rows on each side of the middle aisle. In front of them were equally long and lumpy tables. I didn't know if the tables had been painted black or if they were just so old they had turned black. There was no blackboard. Instead, somebody - probably Miss Ae or her predecessor - had painted part of the wall in front of the class black and used it to write on. There was no other decoration in the room. No maps of the united Choson. No posters with revolutionary slogans. Not even a portrait of the Great General.

It's a miracle she has crayons to write with!

I went over to the middle bench on the left and waited until the disgruntled students sitting there had squeezed together to give me room. Nari came up next to me, looking insecure with her big pleading eyes behind her dirty glasses.

"Go and find another seat!" I whispered to her, annoyed. "Here is full."

Nari frowned, but went and sat down at a bench two rows behind me. I felt sorry for her, but at the same time relieved - having to sit next to Nari would have made this situation even more unbearable. Either way, she needed to learn not to be so dependent on others.

The other two girls went to sit on different benches where the students squeezed together equally reluctantly.

"So," Miss Ae addressed us four newcomers once we had settled in. "Welcome to my class! You can call me Miss Ae and I will be your teacher until the day you turn fifteen. I know it might feel a bit inappropriate to use the word *welcome* given the circumstances, but I truly am happy to have you join my little flock. I want you to consider this classroom a *safe place* for learning and developing... as well as preparing for life in the camp after you turn fifteen and are assigned a work detail. I will do my best to help you make the transition as painless as possible." She beamed at us again with her smile of infinite kindness and compassion. "I know you are not here because of something *you* have done, and I know it doesn't feel fair... but as you know, this is a *re-education camp*, which means you have a good chance of being released back into society before you are too old. That means you will still have a long life ahead of you on the outside. So, *welcome* to your first step on your journey back to freedom." She beamed at us once more. "Now... let's get to know your new classmates. What's your name and how old are you?" she looked at me.

"Eh... my name is Kim Areum... I'm fourteen," I replied, my heart pounding. "But I will turn fifteen in a couple of months, on the eighth of July... well... my sister and I will."

"Your sister?"

I looked back at Nari who had raised her hand behind me. Miss Ae looked at her surprised.

"You have the same birthday?"

"We're... eh... *twins*," I felt my cheeks blush.

Miss Ae pondered for a while if we were serious or not - but she then accepted it as the truth and gave us a friendly nod.

"Of course... it's very nice to have you both here. Would you mind telling us your name too?"

"Kim Nari," she said with a slight tremble in her voice.

"Such beautiful names! Welcome, Kim Areum and Kim Nari! I was going to ask you where you're from, but I hear clearly on your accent that you're from our magnificent Capital."

Miss Ae winked at us and then turned her attention to the shy girl with the long braids who came in with us.

"And what is your name, dear?"

"So Won... Namgung So Won," the girl answered without looking up. "I'm also fourteen years old."

"*So Won*... that's also a beautiful name. And where are you from, Miss Namgung?"

"Hamhung," the girl answered.

I got a chill running down my spine at the mentioning of the place from my nightmares.

"Ah... such a wonderful city," Miss Ae beamed. "That's where I got my teacher's degree... at the Hamhung University of Education. It really is beautiful... and not to forget - it's the home to the largest vinylon cloth factory in the world. Did you know the Great General's uniforms are made there?"

So Won shook her head, again without looking up.

"Anyway, a really great city... I have many fond memories from there, but haven't been there in... oh, it must be five years already... time really flies... is it still the same?"

So Won's face turned red, but she didn't react at first. Then, barely noticeably, she shook her head.

"It... it has changed quite a lot in the last couple of years," she mumbled. "There's not enough food... almost no food at all, and... people are... they are..." So Won suddenly raised her head and started to frantically look around the room, her face in panic. "I... I mean... I don't know if... I mean... I'm sorry... it's —"

"I'm sorry to hear that," Miss Ae interrupted her rambling before she could incriminate herself beyond repair. "But I'm certain things will get back to normal soon... our Father - the Great General - would *never* leave his subjects in harm's way... wouldn't you agree, Miss Namgung?"

"Of course, Miss Ae... our eternal Father - the Great General - is always there to protect us... he would never let anything happen to us... I didn't mean to—"

"Of course you didn't," Miss Ae put the smile back on her face. "It's a difficult adjustment to come here, that's all... I think *everybody* understands that... right, class?" She glared at us all imploringly.

"Yes, Miss Ae," everybody chanted.

I didn't understand what was going on - apart from this new girl getting very close to committing treason by criticizing our nation's Father - but in an instant, the image of the street from my dream, filled with starved sun-scorched bodies, flashed before my eyes and completely derailed my thoughts.

"Good... and *no one* should have to pay for having a difficult time adjusting," she continued with her smile again beaming like the sun. "How old are you, Miss Namgung?"

"Thirteen."

"Then we'll have plenty of time to get to know each other and share memories from your wonderful home town. Good to have you here. And, by the way… I really like your braids," she winked.

So Won looked back down at her desk without answering, her face still deep scarlet red. I felt sorry for her, but at the same time I was in shock over her blatant transgression.

Miss Ae then turned to the last girl who came with us - the one with short messy hair and confident eyes.

"And how about you, dear?"

"My name is Min Ji… Noi Min Ji. I'm twelve years old, from Changrim. I have *never* done anything wrong in my life, but still… here I am." Min Ji stared challengingly straight into Miss Ae's eyes.

"Well… a big welcome to you too, Miss Noi." She placed her hands on the Great General pin over her heart. "And I really do sympathize with your fate… with *all* of your fates… and if there was anything I could do to change it, trust me, I would… but, unfortunately, there isn't." She let her eyes full of sympathy sweep over the class. "What I *can* do… and what I *will* do, however… is my very best to help you accept your new reality and to help you to make your life here as bearable as possible."

Miss Ae took a step back before continuing, pointing at the word written on the wall, which I hadn't noticed until then.

Juche

"That actually brings us to the topic we were discussing before you came. I know you're all familiar with the sacred principles of Juche, but what we were discussing before you came was what Juche means in the context of this place you're in now… in the context of a re-education camp… and how it can help guide you to make your lives here easier. So, let's continue on that topic."

I felt confused.

How could the Great General's sacred principles of how to build a prosperous society be applied here in this vile blemish on the otherwise perfect splendor of Choson?

"Jun Ha," she addressed the handsome boy with the wild hair in the back. "In your own words... how would you describe the essence of Juche?"

Jun Ha cleared his throat and leaned forward, his gaze firm and eyebrows arched. This boy intrigued me.

"Well... the Great General designed the principles of Juche - which very simply put means *self-reliance* - for us to be in control of our own lives, and to understand that we can't rely on others to solve our problems... Juche gives us the wisdom and ingenuity to solve our problems better than anyone else could ever do."

"Very good, Jun Ha. You're absolutely right... the principles of Juche teaches us to be *self-reliant*, to become better at solving any problem we might encounter... and if we can solve our problems ourselves, we will also have a better quality of life... both outside in normal society and here in the camp. So you see, class... you have probably been taught in school that Juche saves us from being slaves under foreign influence, which is what happened to our poor brothers and sisters down south, who are forced to live under the oppression of our enemies' cruel puppet regime... but that is more of an end-result... what Juche teaches us is that each citizen of our society needs to be *self-reliant* in contributing to our joint society."

Miss Ae made a pause to let the message sink in and looked at each one of us with ceremonious gravity before continuing.

"Jun Ha… could you give us an example from your own experience of how Juche helped you improve the quality of *your* life in here?"

"Of course, Miss Ae," Jun Ha nodded, but went silent for a moment trying to think of a suitable example to share.

"Well… when I first came here with my parents, I had a hard time accepting my situation, and I also got bullied by some of the older kids. My parents couldn't do anything, and none of the guards, nor my teacher - Corporal Bun - showed any interest in helping me… I was all alone. As the weeks and months passed, it only got worse, and I really thought I was done for… but then something happened… and it made me understand the *true* meaning of Juche… I realized that only *I* had the power to change my situation." He shrugged his shoulders as he leaned back against the wall behind him. "So… I found a way to save myself from the older bullies… I did what I had to do… and after that, nobody bothered me again. Eventually, I found other people who also had understood this true meaning of Juche… and together we became stronger… kind of like a society within the camp… doing what we needed to do… being *self-reliant*." Jun Ha averted his eyes from Miss Ae for the first time since he started talking and put his hands in his pockets. "Anyway… that's my experience. Life goes on… and now my life isn't that bad."

Miss Ae's proud smile was radiant.

"Thank you, Jun Ha, for that inspirational story. I believe we can all learn from it… right, class?"

"Yes, Miss Ae," we chanted.

At that moment, a bell rang from somewhere far away.

"Okay, class… time for lunch," Miss Ae clapped her hands. "Bring your bowls outside and get some fresh air and some sun on your cheeks. It's really nice outside now that spring has finally arrived… even to our altitudes. Areum and the rest of you who are here for the first time... I will arrange bowls and chopsticks for you today, but from tomorrow you need to bring your own from home." She then turned to a pair of students behind me. "Miss Gwan and Mr. Yang... I believe it's your turn to bring the soup rations today."

Outside, it was truly pleasant - just like Miss Ae had said - but, of course, my head was preoccupied with other matters.

Everybody spread out and sat in small clusters of one, two, or three students. Nari and I sat in the shade of a tree a bit further away from the rest. My eyes were automatically drawn to Jun Ha, who sat casually leaning against the school building wall with his eyes closed and face directed up towards the sun.

How can he be so relaxed in a place like this? Has Juche really helped him make a good life here? Is that even possible?

Miss Ae came out and brought the four of us dented tin bowls with matching crooked tin chopsticks, and shortly after, Miss Gwan and Mr. Yang came back carrying a big pot between them.

We lined up to be served, but when the repulsive sludge filled my bowl, I had to turn my head away in disgust.

"I guess you don't get fine cuisine like this on the outside," Jun Ha laughed behind me. I blushed and almost dropped my bowl... which actually might have been preferable. "Don't worry... it doesn't taste as bad as it looks. Truth to be told... it doesn't taste anything at all... it's basically just water and cabbage... and not the freshest one at that."

Without replying, I hurried back to my place under the tree with my cheeks burning, soon to be accompanied again by Nari.

We ate in silence. I couldn't help but wonder what Grandpa Kim Hyun Woo would have said if he saw these kinds of rations.

Did places like this exist when he was Minister of Food Distribution?

Either way, Jun Ha had been right... it really didn't taste anything, and as long as I didn't look at it, it went down without a problem. By the time I was finished, my stomach was screaming for more.

The rest of the school day continued in the same fashion and I was fascinated by Miss Ae's unrelenting enthusiasm. At the end of the day, the bell rang again.

"Okay, class... that's it for today. As homework for tomorrow... think about how you can apply Juche to improve your life here in the camp. Okay?"

"Yes, Miss Ae," everyone nodded.

"Wonderful! Class dismissed. But Jun Ha... and the four of you who are new... please stay behind for just a moment."

Miss Ae's smile didn't cease for a second as she greeted each student that streamed past her and out through the door, leaving the six of us alone in the room.

"Girls... this is An Jun Ha. He has been in the camp five years already, so he knows it like the back of his hand." Jun Ha smiled at us and nodded. "And I must say... he's also the nicest student I have ever taught," she added with another radiating smile.

"You're making me blush, Miss Ae," he smiled without blushing in the slightest.

"I'm just telling them the truth," Miss Ae beamed. "Anyway, I'm sure you have already learned a lot during orientation, and from Private Gang... he's an absolute darling, by the way, a really sweet boy... but I think it's a good idea to hear about the ins and outs of the camp from a fellow... well... *student*... who is in the same shoes as you... you know, to get the right survival skills. I can count on you for that, right Jun Ha?"

"Of course, Miss Ae… I'll take care of them, no worries," he winked at her and I noticed she blushed slightly.

"Thank you, Jun Ha," she again turned to us. "Girls, I will try to get hold of some extra pencils and papers for you for tomorrow… I will take care of that right away… it shouldn't be a problem, but… let's see… for now, just take your time to get familiar with the camp."

We nodded.

"And Jun Ha… here's a note so you won't get into trouble."

"Thank you, Miss Ae!"

"Girls… be safe!" Miss Ae concluded with a big smile. "Listen to Jun Ha. Apply Juche… and your lives here won't be that bad. Okay?"

"Yes, Miss Ae," we replied in chorus.

"Wonderful… see you tomorrow then."

She gave us a final smile, letting her eyes linger just for a second on Jun Ha, and then stayed to clean the writing off the black wall as we followed our newly appointed tour guide into the desolate hallway.

CHAPTER 17

We shortly came out on the patch of grass in front of the *School of Juche* and gathered around Jun Ha. The sun was still high up in the sky and I felt its warm rays stroking my hair. It felt good. Nari and So Won's eyes were shyly wandering the space around the tall boy in front of us. I wondered if it was for the same reason I couldn't help blushing when looking at him. It wasn't the first time I reacted like this to a boy, but it seemed silly - to say the least - considering the situation we were in. Min Ji, on the other hand, looked straight at his face with her arms crossed.

"Well then," Jun Ha observed Min Ji's challenging gaze with amusement. "Welcome to the first day of the rest of your lives! First of all… I don't want to hear how innocent you are, how you haven't done anything wrong, and that you shouldn't be here, or anything like that, alright? We're *all* innocent! You guys… me… every single kid in this school. And… as a matter of fact, most of the adults here are innocent as well. That's just how it is, and talking about it will only get you into trouble. Everybody clear on that?"

"You don't look like you've been here five years," Min Ji said without blinking.

"Thank you," Jun Ha laughed. "As Miss Ae said… life here doesn't have to be all bad, and I have found a way that works for me. You'll have to find your way. Either that, or your life here will be *very* difficult. And probably also short." He looked over at Min Ji, who continued with her crossed arms and unwavering gaze. "Just a tip, young lady… what was your name again?"

"Min Ji."

"Just a tip for you, Min Ji… you might be able to pull off that attitude with me… and maybe even with Miss Ae - that lady has the patience of an angel. However, *Outside* our classroom, you need to humble it down a notch. One wrong look at the wrong guard… or another prisoner, for that matter… and you're done for." Min Ji finally blinked but didn't look convinced. "Think of it like theater… like *acting*. You don't have to mean it. You can curse them and fantasize about beating them up or killing them in your head. But outwardly, you need to be as humble as a dove. And keep your eyes down… no eye contact with the guards. Clear?"

Everybody nodded. Even Min Ji uncrossed her arms and lowered her now flickering eyes.

"And you… with the braids… you should consider yourself extremely fortunate to be in Miss Ae's class. If you were in Corporal Bun's class, or in any other place in the camp, you'd had thirty or so people informing on you right now for what you said."

So Won looked up at him in horror.

"Don't worry… they have too much respect for Miss Ae to act against her wishes… but she won't always be there to protect you. Clear?"

"Yes, Sir… thank you, Sir!" So Won bowed down deeply.

Jun Ha laughed.

"I'm Jun Ha… not *Sir*… you'll get me into trouble if you call me stuff like that."

"I'm sorry, S… *Jun Ha*," So Won bowed down again.

"And don't bow to me, that will also get me into trouble," he winked. "Alright, so let's start the tour. Remember… no eye contact, and bow when you pass a guard… them you *have to* bow to."

He headed off towards the main road and we followed.

"First of all, I hope you all realize you could be *much* worse off. Yodok may not be a paradise on Earth, but compared to many other camps in our fair country - at least from what I hear - it's quite survivable. And I mean that literally. If you end up in any of the so-called total-control camps, you *will* die there. Here, however, you have a chance to get out. It doesn't happen to everybody, not even many… but it does happen. So we have the luxury of living with *hope*."

We reached the main road and stopped there.

"So, you already know the school, and I guess you're familiar with the *Village of the Strayed*. Any of you in family residents in the *Orchid Garden*?"

Nari and I uncomfortably raised our hands. So Won and Min Ji didn't.

"Wow, good for you. That is a rare privilege… I guess your mom or dad was a party hotshot?"

Flushed, neither of us answered.

"Well, consider yourselves lucky. The barracks are no fun. I don't know which is worse - the smell or the tension. But I guess the smell doesn't get you killed, and eventually… you get used to it."

He laughed, but nobody else joined in.

"Alright, I know you had your orientation in front of *the Oversight*, so you're familiar with that." We nodded. "But how about that building… right next to *the Oversight*?"

He pointed at something to the right of the enormous building complex, and I had to squint before I could distinguish that there actually was a building there… if you could even call it a building. It didn't look much more than a door that strangely appeared to be sticking out of the ground.

"That door leads to the underground detention center. It's like a prison within the prison… a bunker buried deep in the ground. They call it *the Center of Truth*, but *the Center of Pain* would be a more accurate description. If you think this here is as bad as it gets… think again. Fortunately, I can't give you a first-hand account of what goes on down there… I just heard stories. But whatever you do… don't end up there! That should be your personal *Sacred Rule* number one." Young Il's cautionary words from last night echoed in my head… and my father *had* first-hand experience. "If you just follow the actual *Sacred Rules* to the letter and don't stay out after curfew, you should be safe, though," Jun Ha added.

He waved his hand to indicate for us to follow him along the main road in the opposite direction of the *Village of the Strayed*. As we left the gray concrete buildings of *the Oversight* behind us, for as far as the eye could see until the mountain ridge rose in the distance, there was mostly brown or green farmland, disrupted by a couple of hundred identical gray dots that were working the soil. I could barely distinguish some clusters of buildings scattered around the fields far in the distance, but the only other structure nearby was a one-story house a few hundred yards down the road.

"Here we have the machine that feeds us… and feeds this country," Jun Ha extended his hand to the fields. "Of course, we are allowed to keep some of it for ourselves, but most of it is shipped off to cities around Choson… mainly the Capital, I would guess."

To my surprise, I forgot to blush.

"Wait… are you saying some of the food we ate came from… *here*?"

"Right… I forgot you're from the Capital," Jun Ha chuckled. "We don't get too many of you guys here… that's why I didn't recognize your accent. But hearing you now, it really *is* true what they say… people from the Capital sound more *arrogant* when they speak," he winked. "And yes, I would say that a lot of the food you used to eat came from here or one of the other camps. The rest comes from cooperative farms controlled by the Regime. I grew up on one of those farms down south, close to the border, and I can tell you… there isn't much difference between here and there. You might not be surrounded by guard towers and electric fences there, but you're just as much a prisoner on the outside as you are in here."

He looked far into the distance like he was reminiscing about his childhood.

"What are you talking about?" I started to get annoyed. "This is a place for *traitors*. It has nothing to do with the rest of the country."

"I see," Jun Ha calmly raised his eyebrows. "And how many parts of the country have you visited, Miss Capital? How many cooperative farms have you seen? How many farmers have you talked to?"

My cheeks were again burning, but this time not from infatuation.

"Our school went to help farms with the harvest outside the city every year… and the people there were happy and *free*."

"I see," Jun Ha chuckled again. "So the Regime sent you to a farm of *their* choosing in the Capital area… and it was nothing short of a paradise… is that right?" I was steaming. "Look… you can believe whatever you want, but I lived my first nine years out there, on a *real* farm, and the last five years in here, and I'm telling you... it's not a huge difference. It's worse here, I will not argue that... but it's not a *huge* difference."

"So what you're claiming," I panted, "is that our Regime... our eternal Father - the Great General... is treating our farmers - the people who put food on our tables - in the same way as these lowlife traitors?" I noticed my voice was too loud, but I couldn't help it. "Do you even hear how ridiculous that sounds?"

Jun Ha sighed.

"As I said, Miss Capital— "

"My name is *Areum*!"

"Right... as I said, *Areum*, you can believe whatever you want. But I know for a fact that whether you're inside these walls or on the outside... if you're not part of the Capital elite, then you're a slave *feeding* the Capital elite. It's as simple as that."

"*Nobody* is a slave in Choson! Our society is the freest in the world!"

"Yes... that's what I was taught in school as well," Jun Ha smirked. "Okay... I say we leave this interesting discussion at that before we attract unnecessary attention from the guards. If you want to continue believing that everybody in Choson lives in freedom and abundance, be my guest... but I bet you'll change your views after having spent some more time here in this charming place."

"I won't be here long enough," I muttered.

Jun Ha gave me a worried look, and so did Nari.

"Don't worry, I heard your warning... I'm not going to try to escape or anything. But I am a professional gymnast in the Great General's National Gymnastics Team... and as soon as they notice their mistake they'll send me home."

"Areum..." Nari gasped but didn't say anything else.

Jun Ha now looked even more worried, and So Won and Min Ji's faces were full of surprise. I crossed my arms and looked away.

"It's good to have hope and to be true to yourself," Jun Ha was now deadly serious. "Just don't do anything stupid, okay?"

I replied with a grunt.

"Anyway... let's continue," he said, but his worried eyes still lingered on me.

We continued our walk along the main road up through the fields. I looked at all the hunched-over gray remnants of people observing us.

"Many of you will probably get work assignments out here when you finish school. Probably me as well, I think." He pointed beyond the fields to the right and said, "Over there is the Ipsok River. It helps us with three things. *One* - it provides us with fresh water, both for drinking and irrigating the fields. *Two* - in the summer you can use it to wash clothes, and yourselves if you're not shy... and after a while here, you won't be." The thought of bathing in front of other people in the river made my face blush and I pulled my jacket tighter over my chest. "And *three* - it powers the watermill over there where the husk of the rice is removed and where we grind the corn for our daily rations. I hope you like corn, because that's all you'll get to eat around here. That, and cabbage." He spat on the ground. "Yep, not much diversity... but if you want to add some more items to your diet, you can do what many others do and try to catch frogs and rats to eat."

"What?" Min Ji shrieked in disgust.

I also felt a wave of nausea unsettling my stomach.

Do people actually eat frogs and rats here? I wouldn't do that in a million years... not even if I was starving to death... NEVER!

"I can see you're not quite there yet... but it will come," Jun Ha smiled. "Anyway... lately, I hear it's getting harder to find small animals around here... too many hungry mouths, I guess."

I looked over at the distant watermill while I half-listened to Jun Ha. With its large rotating waterwheel, slowly moved by the gentle flow of the river, it was the only sophisticated construction I had seen so far in the camp.

"I would stay away from there if I were you," Jun Ha said from right next to me. "The supervisor there is that girly boy who brought you to school today... he's bad news... you'd better keep your distance."

Before giving me time to react, he again turned to the group.

"I think we have gone far enough... the building over there is the guardhouse where all the guards supervising the food production gather... a bit further up is the tent where all the rice seedlings are growing, waiting to be transplanted into the fields... it's heavily guarded, so don't go near it. After that, you have the animal farm, the granary, and the villages where the guards and officers live. Beyond that is just more farmland until you reach the foot of the mountain where the mines are. I hope none of us - myself included - ever end up working there. People die there every day... cave-ins, toxic gases, the air runs out and people suffocate... you name it. They say there's no map of all the mining tunnels either, so people are known to get lost in the enormous network of abandoned tunnels and are never seen again. So that is my advice - do whatever it takes to stay out of the mines!"

"But... won't they just assign us to whatever they feel like?" Min Ji asked.

"Sure... but the mines are usually considered by the guards to be a form of punishment. If you stay on the guards' good side, your chances for preferential treatment improve."

"And how do we stay on their good side?"

"Mainly follow the *Sacred Rules*... there are some more tricks, but that's a talk for another time. For now, just remember - always be respectful to the guards. And speaking of which... here comes one now - your first lesson."

A sturdy man with mean eyes approached us. We all bowed like Jun Ha had instructed us, but Jun Ha just nodded and said, "Hey, Private On."

"Hey, Jun Ha. What are you up to? You know you can't gather more than two people at a time out in public."

"I'm on assignment from Miss Ae... need to show these newcomers around," he showed the note she had given him in the classroom.

"I see," Private On read the note and then scanned the four of us from top to toe. "You should really do something about those clothes," he shook his head. "You'd do best to blend in as quickly as possible... everybody in here is a thief... just a tip." He then turned back to Jun Ha. "You have been low on information lately... it's making me look bad."

"I'm on it, Private On... I promise... it's just been a slow week, that's all... but I'll have something soon," Jun Ha said with unwavering confidence.

"Give me something by the end of the day," Private On glared at him, then turned around and headed back towards the guardhouse up the road.

Jun Ha swallowed as he turned back to us without commenting on what just occurred.

"Okay, guys... there are a few more places I need to show you," he took the lead in the opposite direction of Private On.

As I walked next to him, curiosity brewed inside me, and after only a few minutes, I couldn't resist any longer.

"What was that guard talking about?" I asked as we once again passed the school. "What kind of information do you need to give him?"

"That's a talk for another time," Jun Ha avoided looking me in the eyes, and I reluctantly refrained from inquiring further.

We continued walking until we passed *the Oversight*.

"That abandoned-looking building over there," he said pointing to the right, "just in front of the forest... that's the camp hospital."

"Private Gang already showed us that," Min Ji said.

"That's good," Jun Ha smiled. "Did he also tell you the nickname of the doctor there?"

"D-Doctor Death?" Nari stuttered.

"Good, so you're already informed. And you have probably understood this already, but I want to stress it anyway... whatever you do, *stay away* from him and from that place! Okay? It's not only because he doesn't have any medical equipment to treat you with, or because he is drunk most of the time... he got his nickname because he's conducting sadistic experiments on the poor people who go to him for help. *Nobody* leaves that house alive... they just call the undertakers when there's a new body to be buried up on Cemetery Hill."

He pointed up at a large green hill in front of the mountain behind *the Oversight* that I hadn't noticed until now.

That whole hill is a cemetery? It must hold thousands of graves!

"B-but... why would he do that?" Nari whimpered.

"Who knows... he's probably just a sick, twisted old man... or maybe the camp made him that way... doesn't really matter why... what's important is that you stay far away from his murderous clutches."

"B-but... what if we're too sick to work?" So Won asked. "Private Gang said we need written permission from the doctor to stay home."

"Well, just to be clear... the guards will usually push you to work regardless of how sick or injured you are... they'll have you work until you drop dead, and then they'll just leave your body until the undertakers come for you... so don't expect to stay home whenever you have a runny nose. *But*... there is one exception, and that is when you have contracted a *contagious* disease, such as the flu... like the girl who wasn't in class today. A contagious disease could take out the whole camp in a matter of weeks, and not even the guards are safe from that... so if you get something contagious, they'll be completely terrified of you and let you stay home. Honestly speaking, they would probably prefer to just kill you and burn your body... but then they would have to get close to you, and they just won't risk it. Either way, in those cases you *will* need a note from the doctor. But a word of advice - don't go there alone. Go with your parents, or even better, with a guard if you have befriended one... and don't go inside, never cross the threshold!"

I looked over at Nari and saw the terror in her pale white face. I knew what she was thinking.

"T-there... there's no medicine... *at all*?" she asked with a tremble in her voice.

"Sorry... you just have to stay healthy," Jun Ha shrugged his shoulders.

Nari suddenly burst into tears, burying her face in her hands.

"Oh... I'm sorry, I didn't mean to scare you... I just want to help you stay safe," Jun Ha rushed to say. "But you don't have to worry... there are other ways to get better here. Some people go up into the mountains and bring medicinal herbs... and there's a doctor... a *real* doctor... among the prisoners... a lady. She helps people who need it... so it's not as bad as I made it seem, okay? I'm sorry!"

Nari continued crying, and Jun Ha seemed genuinely distressed by her reaction.

"She was born with a congenital heart defect," I explained. "She has been in and out of hospitals her whole life."

"Oh…" Jun Ha looked at her as if he expected her to drop dead right then and there. Nari continued standing there with her face buried in her hands.

"She's not on regular medication right now," I continued. "Not since her surgery two years ago… but she has been going to check-ups every month, and if her values are a bit off, they usually give her something."

"I'm so sorry," Jun Ha repeated. "But hey… don't worry. We prisoners stick together - the ones that can be trusted, at least - and we find ways to compensate for what the camp can't provide for us. If you want, I can take you to see that doctor lady one of these days, okay?"

He put his hand on her shoulder to comfort her. It made her flinch, but she quickly recomposed herself and removed her hands from her face, wet from tears.

"Okay," she mumbled. "Thank you."

"Of course," Jun Ha said. "Now… you probably have to wait a couple of days, because the doctor is the mother of the girl who is home sick today, so it's best not to visit her right now… but *soon*, I promise."

"Thank you," Nari whimpered again.

"Okay then… I think that might be it," Jun Ha pondered. "Oh… I forgot one important thing… I believe you have met the camp director - General Roh, and his deputy camp director - Colonel Wan. Stay as far away from them as you possibly can! They are vicious and cruel, and to them, your lives are worth even less than that of a worm in the ground. Do whatever you can to stay off their radar."

"But…" So Won looked up at Jun Ha for the first time since we started our tour. "Colonel Wan is terrifying… he killed a woman in cold blood in front of us yesterday. But General Roh seems reasonable… he says his job is to re-educate us and to help us re-join society… he says all of us can redeem ourselves through hard work…"

"Yes, that is what he says… and he probably believes it too," Jun Ha scoffed. "But General Roh has a dark side. There are stories… from long before I came here. I mean… there's a reason why he got the nickname the *Demon of Yodok.*" He said the last part in a whisper. "But never repeat that to anyone… that's something that for sure will get you sent down to the *Center of Truth.*"

CHAPTER 18

"What?" I blurted out incredulously, but then quickly lowered my voice to a whisper. "If anyone's the *Demon of Yodok*, it must be Colonel Wan! I mean… that man's a ruthless monster."

Jun Ha shook his head.

"I know it might seem that way, but trust me… Colonel Wan is just an extension of General Roh's viciousness. Long ago… long before my family and I ended up here… this was a straightforward labor camp… you had to work long hours, but you had enough to eat, nobody hurt you, and in the end, you could return to society as a free man… or at least as free as you can be in Choson."

I frowned at this last part, but Jun Ha ignored it.

"Colonel Wan was here back then as well, but General Roh kept him on a tight leash. Then the incident happened. I don't know exactly what went down, but from what I hear, General Roh just snapped… went completely berserk and launched into a killing rampage, slaying prisoners left and right… some say with his sword, others say with his bare hands. At first, people either stood paralyzed and just watched it happen, or panicked and ran away… but as the paralysis broke, some prisoners started to defend themselves… to fight back. Someone got hold of a knife - maybe it was the General's - and in the struggle punctured General Roh's left eye, leaving it permanently blind and looking all dead and creepy, as you have probably seen... gives me the chills every time I see it." He shrugged. "Anyway... once the prisoners started to fight back, the guards - who until then had only watched idly from the sidelines - intervened immediately. They dragged the General to the doctor... I think it was Doctor Death back then as well... who patched him up and drove him to the hospital in Hamhung, about four hours away from here... the rest of the guards arrested the man who had punctured his eye and rounded up all the prisoners who had fought back - or just had the misfortune to be nearby - and locked them up in the *Center of Truth* that we passed before. But they didn't beat them up or torture them or anything... they just left them there, even fed them full rations... until General Roh was well enough to return from the hospital around two weeks later with a huge band-aid covering his left eye, and a crazed look in his right. Like I said... all this happened long before I came here, but this is what I've been told. He went down into the dungeons of the *Center of Truth*, and he didn't come up for an entire month. Day and night, non-stop screams could be heard all the way up to *the Bloodyard*... until one day when they finally went silent and General Roh re-emerged from the depths. The band-aid was gone and his left eye was silvery and dead... making him look like a demon... hence the nickname. But it wasn't just his eye... his personality had changed completely as well... it was like he had lost his *soul* down there."

I felt my right hand being drawn to the place where the Great General pin used to be over my heart, and when I once again didn't find it, my anxiety rose.

"After that, everything changed in the camp," Jun Ha continued. "They increased the number of guards, food rations were cut, and they established the ten *Sacred Rules* with zero tolerance if they were broken. Everybody was forced to inform on each other, and prisoners started being detained in broad daylight from their work details... others disappeared during the night. Then one day, the concrete wall and the four poles were built in *the Bloodyard*... which at that time, of course, didn't have that nickname... and the very next day, the executions started. At first, only once in a while... but then more frequently. Colonel Wan became General Roh's right-hand man and he had no restraints in unleashing his sadism onto anyone unlucky enough to cross his path. Gradually, a reign of absolute terror paralyzed the whole camp. Nobody could trust anyone... parents informed on their children, children on their parents, brothers on their sisters, and so on. This camp became nothing short of a living hell on earth, meticulously designed by the twisted mind of General Roh, and ever since, the horrifying deeds of the *Demon of Yodok* have become entrenched in myths and legends whispered throughout the camp... even though no one would dare to utter them openly."

Jun Ha watched our expressions of terror with amusement, and then chuckled, breaking his spell over us.

"Anyway," he continued in a lighter tone. "As I said before, this country is depending on the food we harvest, army uniforms we produce, and the gold, coal, and minerals we mine here... so when the output started decreasing at the peak of his reign of terror, his superiors in the Capital started complaining... in the end, all that matters to *them* is how much food, clothes, and other stuff we can produce for them. After that, the situation became slightly better, but things never returned to the way they had been before... and the *Demon of Yodok* continued to rule his kingdom with an iron fist and with the bloodthirsty Colonel Wan by his side, spending his nights down in the dungeons of the *Center of Truth*, tormenting the daily harvest of unlucky souls. So, as I said... my advice is to stay as far away from both of them as is humanly possible."

As Jun Ha's voice was replaced by the soft spring breeze caressing my ears, I felt my last glimmer of hope die. General Roh was supposed to be the key to my salvation. He was supposed to be the reasonable man in this place who would recognize that a mistake had been made and that I wasn't supposed to be here.

Would I also end up in Colonel Wan's dungeon if I approached General Roh?

"So, now you know," Jun Ha broke the tense silence. "And again... I'm not telling you this to scare you... I'm just trying to help you stay safe."

He threw another worried glance at Nari.

"Thank you," I said, and the rest followed suit. Jun Ha's story had affected us all. Nari's eyes were moist and her lower lip was trembling. Even Min Ji looked startled.

"No problem," Jun Ha nodded guiltily. "And if you have any questions or worries... *anything*... just come to me. I will do my best to help you."

I nodded in agreement, but in my mind, I had already made a decision.

I don't care if General Roh is the Demon of Yodok... I don't care what he did all those years ago... I have to trust my instincts, and my instincts tell me he is my only chance. I have to take the risk. I have to get out of here... I have to take a chance!

"Good," Jun Ha clapped his hands. "Then I'll—"

Suddenly, a man walking towards us caught his attention. It was a prisoner - just skin, bones, and dirt like the rest of them - but there was something else off about him as well. Maybe it was his posture or the way he swung his arms. Or maybe it was the way he limped. When he came closer, I saw his face full of scar tissue, which made him look almost like a walking corpse.

"Shit… come on, let's go," Jun Ha turned around, but it was too late - the strange man had already caught up with us and shouted in an unnaturally high-pitched voice.

"Mister Aaaan… Mister Aaan!"

Jun Ha looked at us, frantically pondering which the best course of action would be.

"Mister Aaa-an!" the man almost sang.

Jun Ha reluctantly turned around to him and smiled.

"Hi, Lucky!"

"Ahhh… such clean, clean *clothes*… on such clean, clean *girls*," Lucky mumbled incoherently looking straight at me, as he came closer and closer.

"Hey, Lucky, we're kind of in the middle— "

"…how long it has it been… we don't get many like you anymore… clean, *beautiful* girls from our shiny Capital…"

As he limped closer to me I took a step back and gave Jun Ha a silent scream for help.

"…to see such clean hair… beautiful… it looks like… it looks like… like…"

He extended a hand to touch my hair, but I pulled away just in time. Then tears started streaming from his eyes. My heart pounded hard in my chest and I felt panic growing inside me. I didn't feel physically threatened by him - he looked like his body would break if I just touched him - but crazy people scared me.

I got ready to push him away from me, but before I had time to react, Jun Ha grabbed his arm.

"Lucky, that's enough! Stop it right now!"

It sounded like he was talking to a child. Not angry, but firm.

Lucky shifted his attention to Jun Ha, looking at him with his face distorted by his many scars, tears streaming from his bulging red eyes with black circles around them. Jun Ha looked back at him calmly.

In the blink of an eye, Lucky's face changed. It filled with rage and hatred. He pulled his arm away from Jun Ha's grip. His body started shaking. The vein on his forehead throbbed under the emerging sweat pearls on his uneven skin. He glared at Jun Ha and started grinding his teeth.

"Easy now, Luck— "

But before he could finish the sentence, Lucky charged at him with an unearthly scream and pushed him to the ground. Lucky climbed on top of Jun Ha - drool dripping down from his mouth onto Jun Ha's face - and he started scratching him and hitting him like a feral creature, with a strength that was completely disproportionate to his scrawny body.

"Stop… stop it, Lucky… what are you doing?" Jun Ha shrieked from underneath as he tried to protect his face from Lucky's wild claws and saliva. In an instant, my paralysis broke. I rushed over and grabbed the feral beast by his arms. In one motion I pulled him up and thrust him to the ground next to our shocked tour guide.

Both Jun Ha and Lucky lay panting on the ground, looking astonished at me, not believing what I had just done. Jun Ha then quickly composed himself, jumped to his feet and brushed the dust off his clothes.

"You okay?" I asked.

"Yeah… thanks, but I had it… he just caught me off guard, that's all," his voice was full of shame.

I guess he has never been saved by a girl before…

I looked over at Lucky, who was still lying on the ground. His face now looked more scared than enraged, but his body was still tense, ready to attack. I got ready to push him back down if he came at me, but there was no need. In the next moment, he rolled over to the side, crawled up into a fetal position, and started sobbing loudly.

"I'm sorry... I'm so sorry... I didn't mean to... you just looked too much like... like..."

Lucky's words became unintelligible in his spastic sobbing. We all stood at a safe distance in a circle around him.

"Should we... do something?" Nari asked. "Is he... okay?"

Lucky suddenly stopped crying. He sat up and burst into hysterical laughter, tears running from his anguished eyes as he clapped his hands and gasped for air between the outbursts.

"Come on, let's just go," Jun Ha said. "There's nothing we can do for him."

The three of them turned around and started walking away, but I didn't move.

"Who... who did you say I looked like?" I asked the crazy man on the ground.

Lucky's hysterical laugher stopped and he looked at me.

"No... no no no no no no... no no no... not like you, not like you," he stuttered. "But your *hair*... she had your hair, such loooong beautiful hair... at least at first when she came... also from our shiny Capital. But then... no more hair... no more beauty... no more person... no more—"

Lucky started crying again and fell back down into the fetal position, with his thumb in his mouth like a baby.

I looked around. Some people in the fields who was observing the spectacle quickly looked away and returned to their work.

I jumped as I suddenly felt Jun Ha's hand on my shoulder.

"Come on," he said. "That's just the way he is. Usually, he's harmless... don't know what got into him today."

I turned around and let Jun Ha lead me back towards the *Village of the Strayed*. Lucky's outbursts of sobbing slowly faded behind me.

"Who is he?" I asked.

"That… is the only guy who has ever managed to escape from here," Jun Ha said. "At least for a few days."

I looked at Jun Ha, astonished.

"But I thought that—"

"I know… but he's the exception. And like I said… he was only out for a short while before they caught him and dragged him back to the camp and down to the *Center of Truth*. It must have been around ten years ago, from what I've heard… it's a wonder he's still alive. Poor guy… every month the guards place bets on whether this is the month he'll die… sometimes some of the prisoners bet as well… but he never dies. At least so far. And nobody is allowed to touch him… that's the unspoken rule. Personally, I think it would be more humane to just put him out of his misery. People say it was the torture he endured in the *Center of Truth* that drove him mad, but me… I think it's because of what happened to his wife… and his son."

I walked beside Jun Ha in silence while I tried to process his story. I had many questions, but only one came out.

"But… why do people call him Lucky?"

"Well… for a very short while, that's what he was… the luckiest person in the camp… the only one who ever managed to escape. From what I hear, it was the only thing people talked about. But then, his luck changed. It was important for General Roh and Colonel Wan to send a message, to crush the tiny glimmer of hope he had sparked before it had time to spread. That's why they didn't kill him. Instead, they broke him… broke him to the core of his soul, and then released him. Since then, he's wandered the camp like a ghost… reminding people that it actually *can* get worse… *a lot* worse."

Jun Ha sighed deeply.

"Either way... the nickname just kind of stuck. For the past ten years, he's been *Lucky*... the unluckiest bastard in the whole camp."

I threw a glance over my shoulder. Lucky was no longer sitting on the road. After scanning to the left and right, I found him on the cornfield, making large gestures to one of the workers who did his or her best to ignore him.

"Come on," Jun Ha said. "I'll take you to the canteen. That's where everybody eats their dinner rations. Everybody, except for you who live in the *Orchid Garden*, that is. You will instead collect your rations to cook at home."

I couldn't shake the story of Lucky as we walked towards the long wooden building in front of the *Village of the Strayed*.

"How did he escape?" I finally couldn't restrain myself.

Jun Ha shook his head.

"That is a forbidden topic in here... better you don't get any ideas."

We arrived at the canteen, which in reality was nothing more than an ordinary house about the size of one of the barracks in the *Rose Garden*. It had a large opening in the wall facing the road. Behind it, ten or so enormous cauldrons simmered quietly, their steam slowly escaping from a couple of chimneys on the roof.

"We call it the *canteen*, but it might be somewhat of an overstatement," Jun Ha commented. "Basically you're served your soup over the counter and then go and eat on the ground somewhere. In winter, it's more common that people bring it back to their barracks, but it can become quite messy... and it has caused more than one fight that I have seen."

I looked around, but couldn't see a single person eating soup on the ground.

"It's still early… the adult prisoners still have many hours left on their shifts," Jun Ha saw my question coming.

Behind the counter, veiled in the darkness next to one of the cauldrons, stood a grim-looking prisoner with his arms crossed in front of him. As he saw us, he stepped out into the light. I immediately noticed the barbed wire tattoo around his left eye. My jaw dropped, but I closed it again and looked away, embarrassed by my reaction. I had heard stories in school about people in prisons getting tattoos, but I had never thought the stories were true… and I had never imagined people would get tattoos on their *faces*!

"Hi, Moon," Jun Ha greeted him. "How's it going?"

Moon shrugged his shoulders without changing the indifferent expression on his face.

"Got some first-time customers here for you. Also have the Kim family here to pick up their first family ration… they live in the *Orchid Garden*, house…?" he looked at me with raised eyebrows.

"124," I said, throwing another shy glance at the barbed wire around Moon's eye.

"Exactly… *house 124*," Jun Ha repeated. "So maybe you can start with them?"

Moon went to the backroom without saying anything and came back after a while with a couple of pieces of cabbage and a small dented bucket. He put them on the counter.

"This bucket is for you… it contains ground corn," Jun Ha explained. "You need to bring it every day when you come for your ration. Keep it safe… if you lose it, you won't get a new one."

I hesitantly took the food from the counter. The corn sludge in the bucket looked disgusting and the cabbage had spots of mold on it. The mere thought of eating it made my stomach turn.

"Don't worry about it," Jun Ha smiled at my reaction. "Just scrape it a bit to get rid of the worst parts… it's not harmful."

He then turned to the other two girls.

"If you state your names and barrack numbers, Moon here will give you your bowls with soup.

"Noi Min Ji… barrack 46," Min Ji stared shamelessly at his tattoo.

"Namgung So Won… barrack 32," So Won mumbled.

After they been served their hot soup - which was exactly the same as we had gotten for lunch - we all sat down together until they had finished it, which didn't take long. Jun Ha thanked Moon - who answered with a barely noticeable nod - and then took the lead into the *Rose Garden*. After we had dropped off So Won and Min Ji at their respective barracks, we continued to the *Orchid Garden*.

"You're pretty strong," Jun Ha commented after a moment of silence without looking at me. "You can handle yourself."

"I'm a professional gymnast," I replied, but as soon as the words had passed my lips, I felt a piercing pain shooting through my heart.

I need to get out of here… NOW!

"Besides, that guy was just skin and bones… weighed almost nothing." I looked over to see Jun Ha again blush with shame.

"This is where we… er… live," I said hesitantly when we had reached our street in the *Orchid Garden*.

"Good," Jun Ha said. "Any other questions before we part ways?"

We both shook our heads.

"In that case, I'll see you tomorrow in school," he winked before turning around and heading back towards the *Rose Garden*. Then, just as Nari and I had set off down our street, he shouted over his shoulder.

"And don't forget to memorize the *Sacred Rules*… it's extremely important!"

"Okay! Thank you!" we shouted back at him.

Nari and I walked in silence along the endless row of identical wooden houses. At this moment, in my mind, there was only one thought swirling around, over and over, and over.

I won't need to learn the Sacred Rules… tomorrow I will no longer be here!

CHAPTER 19

Our house was dark and empty. Nari lit a fire to make dinner while I lay down on my so-called bed and rested my eyes.

"Have you learned the rules?" Nari asked me.

"Of course not… when would I have had time for that?" I sighed. "But I presume you have?"

"I can help you memorize them… if you want," Nari looked at me nervously.

"Pass."

"Okay… I just don't want you to get into trou— "

"I was there, Nari… I heard everything you heard… no need to repeat it."

"I know… I just meant—"

"For Juche's sake!" I grunted and jumped to my feet. I put my shoes back on and headed for the door.

"I need to get some air."

"Areum… please don't go! I'm sorry…"

"I need to be alone for a while… I'll be back soon… don't follow me."

Nari stood up and looked at me with distress. I ignored it and barged out the door, slamming it behind me.

Great General, she gets on my nerves! I thought to myself as I shrugged her pathetic face out of my mind.

In reality, I wouldn't have had any problem containing my annoyance, but throwing a tantrum fit perfectly as an excuse to get out of the house by myself.

Mission accomplished! Another great performance, if I may say so myself!

I walked down the road with my mind determined. The sun was setting in the distance and the wind was getting colder and stronger. I wished I had brought a jacket, but I couldn't go back now. This was my chance. General Roh would listen to reason.

He will set me free!

Our street was virtually empty - everybody was still at work. The crust of the mud was now hard and no longer broke under my feet. In my head, I played out different scenarios of how the encounter with General Roh could go.

He may have been the Demon of Yodok back then, but that's not who I saw when I looked into his eyes... at least not his healthy eye. Anyway... those kinds of rumors always lose touch with reality as the years go by. Who knows how much truth is left in them by now... if any at all...

Suddenly, I saw a group of guards appearing in front of me on the main road. I panicked.

Am I allowed to wander around the camp freely? Technically it's not curfew yet since the sun hasn't set, but what would they do if they saw me and asked me what my business was?

I quickly jumped into the space between two of the houses to my right and waited for the guards to pass. I decided it wasn't safe to walk on the main road, but the houses were all connected, so I couldn't sneak through the village in that way.

When the coast was clear, I walked back towards our house, but then continued until the end of the road. There, behind the common toilets, to my relief, I found a small passageway between the last house and the tall concrete wall with barbed wire on top that separated the *Village of the Strayed* from the Ipsok River on the other side. It was very narrow and filled with garbage, dead tree branches, and left-over barbed wire, but I managed to squeeze through... barely. When I made it to the other side, I peeked around the corner to see if any guards were in sight, but the street was deserted. I continued on the same path. After all - *better safe than sorry!*

The next passageway was even more difficult to squeeze through, and I felt my clothes and skin being ripped by the sharp rolls of rusted barbed wire leftovers. I had to force myself not to scream from the pain and press forward. Then came the next one... and then the next. In the end, I couldn't keep track of how many rows of houses I had passed, but it felt like they were never-ending.

When I finally emerged from behind the last house of the *Rose Garden*, I sighed with relief and paused to catch my breath. I looked at the cuts bleeding on my arms and legs and prayed to the Great General they wouldn't get infected. My formerly white knee socks were now a mix of brown mud stains and red blood, but there was no time to worry about that now.

I sneaked over to the canteen and peeked around the corner. Between me and *the Oversight* was the *School of Juche*. I made sure the coast was clear once more and ran as silently as I could to hide behind the now hopefully empty school building, where I just a few hours earlier had sat and listened to the always smiling Miss Ae. As much as I liked her, I didn't feel the least sorry I would never see her again. And I was outright glad I would never have to hear the tiny Corporal Bun's angry screaming again.

I looked around the corner over at *the Oversight* building complex. That place was livelier than the *Village of the Strayed* with guards and officers walking between buildings across *the*

Bloodyard, or just standing around in the shade of one of the buildings or a tree, talking over a cigarette. It would be impossible to walk across the yard unnoticed - I had to go around.

Fortunately, there was vegetation along the houses on this side of the *Rose Garden*, so I calculated I could reach the main road hidden from sight that way. I ran back a bit to put some more distance between me and the guards and then crossed over into the line of untrimmed tall bushes. From there, I slowly but steadily crawled forward on my hands and knees until I reached the end.

Nobody had spotted me so far, but people were walking around, and there was a guard smoking right in front of me on the other side of the road. Staring at him from behind the dense leaves I suddenly got the impression he was looking right at me, and in a panic I got ready to run. Shortly after, however, he threw his cigarette butt on the ground and started walking up the road towards the fields. I sighed with relief, but there were still a lot of other people around, so I had to patiently continue waiting crouched down in the bushes.

After about fifteen excruciating minutes, the area around the main road finally became deserted enough for me to dare to cross.

I went out from the bushes and peeked to the left around the house corner to make sure no one was coming my way, then I sprinted with my most silent gymnastics steps across the road and continued until I was safe in the shadow of the left-most building of *the Oversight* complex. My heart was racing, but more from fear than from the sprint. There were no people around, so I sneaked silently through the uncut grass to the end of the building, passing the so-called hospital where it lay partially hidden under its thick layer of vegetation. Up close, it looked even worse than from afar - like it would collapse at any moment. I remembered Jun Ha's story and couldn't help but wonder if Doctor Death was in there right now, conducting sadistic experiments on some poor soul, and if the ones he called *the undertakers* were waiting for his call to come and bring the mutilated body up to *Cemetery Hill*. Then I thought of Nari and her still weak heart. I hoped the other doctor - the lady Jun Ha talked about - would be able to help her… and prayed that the flu wouldn't kill her or her daughter.

I reached the end of the massive concrete building of *the Oversight* and looked around the corner. The entrance to the center building General Roh had disappeared into this morning was just a few yards away. No guards were in sight - I could easily reach the door in a few steps. But instead of moving, I started to panic.

And then what?

I realized I hadn't thought this through.

Where will I go after I have entered the building? How will I find General Roh's office? How will I hide from people inside the building?

I crouched down on my knees to think, my heart pounding through my chest.

Come on, Areum… you can do this!

Then it came to me. General Roh is the most important person in the camp - he must be on the top floor. That's where Grandpa Hyun Woo used to have his office in the Ministry of Food Distribution, since he, apart from being its founder, had also served as the *Minister* of Food Distribution until his old age got the best of him. The top floor was also where Young Il had his office after his last promotion. When I was younger, I visited him there a few times together with mom. That was when I still considered him my *real* father.

A spark of hatred towards him once again ignited in my chest, and that gave me the courage and resolve I needed.

I checked around the corner again - the coast was still clear.

Just go for it, Areum… you can figure out the rest along the way!

I got on my feet, and without thinking twice, I spurted silently over and opened the heavy wooden door just enough so I could slip inside.

I'm in!

I stood in a large entrance hall, similar to the one we had in our apartment building back in the Capital.

Remembering the place I grew up, a violent stream of thoughts suddenly invaded my mind.

What has happened to our apartment? Have the guys from the State Security Department looted everything? Has somebody else moved in to live there now? Will we get it back once we are released from here… or won't we have a home to go back to?

I quickly forced those thoughts out of my head.

One problem at a time!

There were still no people to be seen anywhere. In front of me was the main staircase. I threw a quick glance through the open door to the right, which led to a long corridor with many doors on each side. It was also empty.

I walked slowly toward the staircase in front of me, listening attentively in all directions. I took a first cautious step up the stairs. Then another.

Suddenly, voices shot down from the floor above, followed by quick-paced footsteps coming down the stairs.

I panicked, and rushed back down, looking frantically around me for a place to hide. This time I wasn't a graceful and soundless gymnast - I felt like my footsteps echoed like elephant steps throughout the entire building.

Great General, they must have heard me!

In my frenzy, I noticed there was a space under the stairs behind a large plant, so I ran behind it and hid just in time as the footsteps and voices approached right over my head. Even though my body was screaming for me to gasp for air, I held my breath.

"I'm telling you… I'm really glad to be here at Yodok now," I heard a female voice say. "It's crazy what's going on outside… and it all happened so fast."

"Crazy," a male voice repeated. "How could they have let it go this far? It's unbelievable. And now *we* have to pay for their mismanagement."

"It's not fair, why can't they just—"

"Shh!" the man whispered. "Good evening, General Roh."

I peeked out from under the stairs, hidden by the large leaves of the plant. General Roh approached the two junior officers, who saluted him. He was only a few feet away from me.

Is this my moment? No… it's too risky, I have to wait until he is alone.

"At ease," General Roh muttered. "Any news from the Capital?"

"Yes, Sir," the man said. "The new orders just came in… we have to increase our delivery quota by fifteen percent."

General Roh sighed, shaking his head.

"Understood… execute the order," he instructed reluctantly. "You know what to do."

"Yes, Sir!"

"Dismissed," General Roh nodded at them and started walking up the stairs. The two officers saluted him again and disappeared into the long corridor.

General Roh was now alone.

This is my chance!

But as I was halfway out from under the stairs, I heard a voice from above that sent shivers down my spine.

"General!" Colonel Wan shouted. "Good I found you… we have a situation."

"What is it, Colonel?"

"It's of a somewhat... *sensitive* nature, Sir... it's about *the Dragons*... would be best to discuss it in private."

"Let's go to my office," General Roh said.

I was left alone listening to the fading echoes of their heavy footsteps as they ascended the stairs.

Shit! What do I do now?

The main entrance door in front of me opened again and a group of guards entered the building and disappeared up the stairs. From what I could hear, they went up two stories and then into the hallway.

The staircase again fell into silence.

This is it!

I quickly took off my shoes - not to repeat the mistake of before - and sprinted up the stairs without making a single sound, listening attentively to make sure no one else was coming onto the staircase.

When I reached the second floor, I heard new voices approaching from the corridor. Here, there was no place to hide - and there was also no turning back - so I jumped three steps at a time up to the third floor, praying they weren't going in the same direction. Fortunately enough, I could hear them heading down toward the main entrance instead.

I listened carefully again, but no other sounds could be heard from upstairs, so without pausing, I continued leaping soundlessly two steps at a time until I reached the fourth and final floor.

I immediately noticed this landing differed from the others, which had offered nothing more than identical plain gray concrete walls. Here, I was greeted by a huge wall-to-wall painting of the Great General standing on the mountain top of his sacred birthplace. His radiant smile - which I always felt was meant directly for me - was beautifully lit up by the descending sun seeping in from the window behind me.

Seeing my *real* Father like that reinforced my courage.

I am a member of the Great General's National Gymnastics Team! Soon, I will again be with my peers. Father - I will not fail you!

To my left, there was a massive oak door, which was closed, unlike the plain metal doors that were kept open on the other floors I had passed. It looked similar to the door leading to Young Il's office in the Ministry of Food Distribution back in the Capital.

There is no doubt - this is the floor of the high-ranking officers! This is where General Roh's office is!

All of a sudden, I heard footsteps from the other side of the oak door. I looked around frantically. There was no other place to hide - and no time to lose - so, quick as the wind, I rushed behind the opening door and prayed it wouldn't smash against my face. As I felt the wind on my face from the massive block of polished wood - which stopped less than an inch from my nose - I almost shrieked. Two officers came out, absorbed in an intense discussion about something I couldn't comprehend, and rushed down the stairs without looking back. Without having time to recompose myself, I took the chance to slip in through the opening before the door closed… unnoticed.

I sighed with relief as I found myself in a long corridor with ten or so plain wooden doors - all of them closed - on each side, facing each other in even intervals. At the end of the corridor, in the middle, was a large dark door, which looked exactly like the one I had just walked through.

That must be it! It has to be!

I started walking down the corridor, slowly. The flickering light of the fluorescent tubes in the ceiling made me dizzy… or maybe it was my nerves. From some rooms, I could hear voices talking on the phone. From others - the clacking of typewriters.

A few rooms were completely silent. The atmosphere was eerie, which was emphasized by the pounding of my heart and the throbbing in my ears.

It's now or never, Areum! But what if Colonel Wan is still there with him in his office? Should I wait?

I swallowed painfully.

No… this is it! This is how I get out of this nightmare!

I increased my pace and sprinted silently the last distance until I reached the massive oak door at the end of the corridor. It had a large bronze plaque at eye level, saying:

Camp Director
Roh Nam Il
General

Sighing with relief, I lifted my hand to knock.

I'm going home! Nothing can stop me now!

But before my knuckles touched the shiny oak surface, the door to the right of me swung open. Looking at me with an expression like he couldn't believe his eyes, was none other than Colonel Wan.

I froze to ice, my fist still in mid-air. My breathing stopped, and it felt like my heart stopped beating as well.

I waited for an explosion of anger… that he would beat me to death right there and then. Instead, something even scarier happened.

Colonel Wan smiled at me.

CHAPTER 20

"Lost, are we?" Colonel Wan said through his disconcerting smile with eyes of a predator savoring his pray before the attack.

"Colonel Wan… good evening, Sir… I… I just needed to talk to General— "

"Is that so?" Colonel Wan's voice was silky-smooth. "Well, I'm afraid the General is an awfully busy man, so right now… I don't think that would be possible."

"But, it's real— "

"*However*…" Colonel Wan interrupted me with the same silk-smooth voice, "it just so happens I might be able to free up some of *my* time for you. So what do you say… how about you and I go somewhere more private and you can tell me all about it?"

Before I had time to react, he grabbed my arm firmly and started pulling me away from General Roh's door.

"Sir… I'm sorry, but I really need to talk to— "

"I afraid you'll have to settle for me," Colonel Wan said harshly. His smile had disappeared, and his eyes were now callous.

In my chest, I felt my heart racing. Large pearls of sweat dripped down from my forehead, burning my eyes.

I'm so close! General Roh is right there on the other side of the door. I've come too close to fail now!

I twisted my body around to knock on General Roh's door with my free hand, but before my knuckles made contact, I was already several feet away as Colonel Wan with enormous force dragged me down the corridor toward the staircase.

I went into a state of panic and lost all self-control.

"GENERAL! GENERAL ROH!" I screamed at the top of my lungs. "I NEED TO TALK TO YOU… PLEASE!"

"Shut up!" Colonel Wan changed his grip and put his hand over my mouth. Several doors on the sides opened with curious faces peering out at us. My panic had reached a level I had never experienced before.

"Mmmmmm… Mmmmmm…" I tried to scream through Colonel Wan's hand, but it was no use. I tried to resist the unstoppable progression down the corridor by pushing my feet against the floorboards, but all that resulted in was my socks being torn to shreds and the soles of my feet painfully burning against the polished surface. I twirled around in Colonel Wan's tight grip, flinging my arms in an attempt to grab a doorway, or a person - *anything* - we passed along the way, but nothing was within reach. Colonel Wan was significantly stronger than me, and as I was relentlessly being dragged towards the stairs, an overwhelming feeling of powerlessness came over me… powerlessness that I hadn't felt going head to head with someone in a physical struggle since…

The face of *Mina* flashed before my eyes.

"Mmmmmmm… Mmmmmmm…" I continued to scream into his hand. The corridor was now full of people, watching at us with open mouths. Everybody seemed to be there - everybody except for the one person I needed.

"Shhhh… Shhhh…" Colonel Wan hushed in my ear. "Everything will be fine. I will take good care of you… you'll see. There, there… shhh…"

As we reached the end of the corridor, Colonel Wan opened the door to the staircase with his free hand, and just as he dragged me through, I managed to get one arm loose. With all my strength I extended my hand and grabbed the side of the doorway with my fingertips.

"You're putting up quite the struggle, little girl," Colonel Wan panted, his voice now strained. He pulled me with his exceptional strength. My arm and my fingers felt like they were about to break, but I didn't let go. I screamed in pain into Colonel Wan's hand, but nothing more than a muffled *ARGMMMMMM…* came out.

"LET GO ALREADY!"

Colonel Wan finally started to lose his patience. He pulled my body again - this time even harder than before - and I thought this time my arm would break. I screamed in pain, but somehow my fingers managed to keep clenching the doorway.

Thank Great General for all those years of training on uneven bars!

But as I felt Colonel Wan getting ready for a final pull, I knew I had lost. This time my arm or my fingers *would* break, and nothing would prevent him from dragging me down into his dungeons.

Why didn't I listen to Jun Ha? How could I have been so stupid?

"What's going on here?"

A dark, authoritative voice suddenly carried through the air from the other end of the corridor. Colonel Wan immediately stopped in his tracks, and I seized the opportunity to renew my grip around the door frame. I exhaled in relief - my fingers wouldn't break… at least not right now.

I tried to look down the corridor, but Colonel Wan's firm hand over my mouth prevented my head from turning. Only with my peripheral vision could I see the blurry outline of someone approaching… someone I hoped and prayed was…

"Nothing to worry about, General Roh," Colonel Wan panted. "This newcomer just hasn't learned her place yet, so I will take it upon myself to educate her."

General Roh's heavy footsteps came closer.

"I see… and why did she come here?"

His voice sounded more curious than angry.

"This little traitor vermin came to see you, actually, General," Colonel Wan laughed with nervous incredulity. "It's one of the kids from the Capital that came yesterday… just as spoiled and arrogant as all the other ones we get from there."

The footsteps stopped right in front of us, but I still couldn't see in that direction.

"But don't worry, General… very soon she will understand *exactly* what her place is."

Colonel Wan unexpectedly pulled my body again, and this time, I lost my grip. With me completely under his control, he started dragging me down the stairs. The massive oak door closed with a bang behind us, leaving my savior on the other side. I tried to scream for him again, but nothing more than unintelligible muffled sounds came out.

"There, little girl," Colonel Wan whispered into my ear in his silky-smooth voice. "Now, it's just the two of us."

This is it… I'm done for! All hope is lost!

I twisted and twirled, fighting to get free, but I had no more strength left in my body.

Then, as we reached the first landing, the massive oak door opened and I again heard the deep voice of General Roh from above.

"Hold on, Colonel Wan… let me see her."

We stopped moving instantly, but the grip around my body and mouth remained firm.

Is my savior here for real this time? Do I dare to hope?

Colonel Wan turned around reluctantly and General Roh finally appeared before my eyes. He examined my face carefully for a while. I could feel the hand over my mouth becoming sweaty. His repugnant breath stung my nose.

"You are Miss Kim, are you not?" General Roh asked.

I was in total shock.

Does he know who I am? He even knows my name?

I still couldn't speak because of Colonel Wan's hand, so I nodded instead.

I could feel Colonel Wan was growing impatient.

"General Roh, can I take this prisoner to the *Center of Truth* now? With all due respect… I have other things to attend to today as well."

"Let her go," General Roh ordered after having examined my face a moment longer. "It's fine… I'll talk to her."

"Excuse me?" Colonel Wan gasped, completely taken aback by this turn of events, but then quickly composed himself with a more respectful tone. "*Sir…* she was here during the orientation this morning… she should know that entering *the Oversight* without permission is a punishable offense. Punishable by *death*!"

"I am well aware of the rules, Colonel… if you remember, I have written most of them myself. But you might also want to remember that as the director of this facility I have the right to talk to whomever I want whenever I want… do you have any objection to that?"

From the corner of my eye, I could see Colonel Wan's face turning deep purple, but he removed his sweaty hand from my mouth and released his grip around my waist and arms. I almost lost my balance as my feet landed on the cold concrete steps and I whimpered from the pain from the friction burn on my soles.

"Follow me, Miss Kim… we can talk in my office. Colonel Wan… now that you have freed up some time, maybe you can work on the problem we discussed earlier?"

"Of course… *Sir*," Colonel Wan replied in a respectful - but to me, clearly venomous - tone.

I started moving towards General Roh who stood at the landing of the stairs in front of the spectacular mural of the smiling Great General, but Colonel Wan grabbed my arm again and whispered with a snake-like hiss into my ear.

"Seems we have to postpone our little chat, Miss Kim, but don't you worry… you and I will have the chance to get to know each other properly… *real soon*."

He let go of his grip and I looked back at his purple face in terror for just a second before hurrying up the stairs to safety. General Roh held up the door for me, which again awkwardly made me feel like when I used to visit my father at the Ministry of Food Distribution.

"Please… my office is at the end of the corridor," he said.

I walked slowly down the same path I had sprinted just a few minutes earlier, which felt like an eternity ago. As my panic started to recede, the pain of my almost broken fingers - which I now noticed were full of splinters - grew in intensity. I extracted the big ones and put them in my pocket not to risk evoking further anger for littering. I could hear General Roh's calm but steady steps against the hard floorboards behind me. The people that had come out to see what was going on returned to their tasks behind closed doors.

As I once more arrived in front of the General's office, I hesitated.

"Please, allow me, Miss Kim," he went around and opened the door for me.

I entered into a large beautiful - but sterile - room with windows on three sides, letting in an abundance of light, which balanced the otherwise dark interior. The floor had dark polished floorboards - there was no carpet - and the walls between the windows were covered by dark bookcases. As my eyes passed over the books in them, I immediately recognized some titles of the Great General that we had at home as well.

But they are probably in the possession of the State Security Department by now…

Through the window on the left side, I could see the beautiful mountain ridge reaching up into the sky, and in front of it, the inconspicuous shape of *Cemetery Hill*. I shuddered. Through the windows in front was a clear view of the vast fields of the camp, and from the last window, I saw the mountain ridge on the opposite side of the camp in between the two other buildings of *the Oversight* complex. I again shuddered thinking of the execution wall and the four poles in *the Bloodyard* right underneath it.

In the middle of the room stood a large desk - also made of dark wood - with an authoritative black leather armchair behind it. In front of it were two plain wooden chairs.

There was no other decoration in the room, but I knew that if I turned around I would see the mandatory picture of the young and serious Great General on the wall. The big desk was almost empty, apart from two neat stacks of paper, a holder with two pens in it on the left side, and a small picture frame that stood diagonally on the right side, facing the leather armchair.

Could that be another picture of the Great General? Is it the one where he's older, with glasses, and smiling?

It felt odd - not even in Young Il's office at the Ministry of Food Distribution had I ever seen anyone putting the Great General's picture on their desk like that.

This man is truly a great patriot. I was right to come here after all!

General Roh went around the desk and sat down in his chair, signaling me to take a seat in one of the chairs in front of him.

As we sat silently in front of each other, I could feel General Roh's healthy eye examining my face. His silvery dead eye, however, felt like it was penetrating my soul. Still, my eyes seemed to be automatically drawn to it. I blinked uncomfortably and quickly looked away.

Did he notice?

I waited for him to start talking, but he didn't say anything. When the uncomfortable silence finally grew unbearable, I opened my mouth.

"Ahem... er... thank you for seeing me... *Sir*... I know I'm not supposed to come here, but— "

"You're the daughter of Kim Sun Hee, am I right?" General Roh asked absentmindedly.

"Eh... yes, Sir... my sister and I are her daughters."

He even knows my mother's name? Why? And why had he looked at her so strangely during orientation? Did he recognize her from the theater... has he seen her perform in the Capital? But she hasn't performed in many years—

"And what's your given name, Miss Kim?"

"Areum, Sir... Kim Areum."

"Areum," he repeated like he was sampling the word in his mouth. "A beautiful name," he smirked.

I tried to smile back, but was too nervous. It also didn't help that I had heard that comment a thousand times before.

I love my name, and I love that it means 'beautiful'... but getting that same remark every single time is tiring. Do people really have such similar minds and poor imagination?

I was suddenly afraid General Roh would see my annoyance, so I quickly pushed that thought out of my mind, nervously observing his reaction from across the desk. He didn't say anything, however - his mind seemed to be preoccupied with something else.

"Sir… I was wondering… have you… have you seen my mother perform?" I asked hesitantly. This was, of course, not why I had come, but the curiosity got the best of me.

"Sorry?"

"I mean… in the theater… have you seen my mother perform in the theater? I was just wondering, because—"

"Oh… she's an actress?" General Roh raised his eyebrows. "Fascinating… but sadly, no… I'm afraid I have never been to the theater… but I'm sure she is splendid."

I felt like I was getting more new questions than answers, but this was not why I was here. I waited a moment to see if General Roh would continue with more questions, but since he didn't, I tried to gain control over our meeting.

"So, thank you again for seeing me," I said. "I needed to talk to you about— "

"And what is your sister's name?" General Roh interrupting me again.

"Nari, Sir."

I felt my cheeks becoming flushed.

"Younger sister?"

"We're twins, actually, Sir. But… she has been sick most of her life, that's why she looks younger than me."

"I see," General Roh said, deep in thought, before going back to observing me in silence.

"So… Sir, the reason I wanted to talk to you— "

"And how about your father… what did he do… before he came here?"

"Eh… my father?" My cheeks were now burning up. "He worked at the Ministry of Food Distribution… Sir."

At the mentioning of Young Il's workplace, General Roh's face darkened.

"At the Ministry of Food Distribution? I see… they do very important work there… *very* important… or at least they *should* be doing…"

I sat like on needles. I had no idea of which direction this conversation was going or how to get it back on track. The panic was creeping back into my body.

"Do you know what they did to Hamhung?" he suddenly asked.

I nervously shook my head. I clearly felt the hatred in his gaze as he asked me, but shortly after, it softened again.

"Well… it doesn't matter," he averted his eyes. "And your mother… she's a theater actress, you say. Is she famous?"

"She… *was* famous. She stopped acting to take care of my sister… almost fourteen years ago."

"Ah… that's a shame," General Roh uttered mechanically, and for some reason, he gazed at the picture frame on his desk with eyes full of sorrow.

There was another moment of excruciating silence. Then General Roh's eyes returned to me. He leaned forward and joined his hands in front of him on the desk.

"So, Areum… tell me why you're here."

Finally!

"Yes, Sir… thank you, Sir! I know I'm not supposed to be here, but it's really important."

"Certainly."

I paused, racing to find the right words.

"This morning… during your speech… you said we must acknowledge our guilt and not claim that we're innocent."

"That's right… without acknowledging your guilt, redemption is not possible."

"But, the thing is… I *am* innocent." I cringed, expecting an outburst, or maybe that he would call back Colonel Wan to drag me off to the *Center of Truth*, but neither of that happened.

General Roh just raised his eyebrows and said, "I see," his calm gaze still firm on my face.

I swallowed.

"You see, Sir… I believe this is all a terrible mistake… I'm not supposed to be here. I understand the principle you explained, that guilt extends over three generations, and that it spreads through love… but you see, Sir… just yesterday, in the Capital, I was accepted into the Great General's National Gymnastics Team." I looked into his face to find any clues to what he was thinking, but none were revealed. "That means… Sir… that since yesterday, I'm no longer a member of my birth family… in all honesty, I haven't been for a long time… and therefore I have also not been susceptible to anything that spreads through *love*… as you were saying…" I felt like I couldn't stop rambling and I was becoming increasingly nervous by the second. I took a deep breath and exhaled. "You see… I'm now a member of our Great General's family… so, I don't know what Young Il, I mean… my *father*… has done, but I'm certain it has nothing to do with me, because I haven't been his daughter for a long time… there has been no *love* for him to be able to spread his poisonous ideas to me…"

General Roh leaned back in his chair, and for the first time I thought I could read the expression on his face. It was not anger. It was a hint of surprise.

"Is that so?" he joined his hands over his lap and peered into my eyes.

"Yes, Sir… that's the truth. Please, Sir… the only thing I'm asking… that I'm *begging* of you… is that you contact the Ministry of Physical Culture and Sports in the Capital… they will confirm everything I have said... they will confirm that I belong to *their* family now."

General Roh leaned forward again and supported his elbows on the desk. I could feel the sweat gathering on my forehead and the palms of my hands. There was a strong pressure over my chest.

"You know," General Roh started at a slow pace, "there are many people in this camp who claim they are innocent. Maybe even most of them... so you are in no way the first person to come to me with a story like this."

I could feel the pressure on my chest intensifying. I could hardly breathe. General Roh continued to look at me with his firm unwavering gaze.

"The thing is... we don't deal with the question of *guilt* here. That question is handled by the State Security Department... and before anyone is sent here to us, those things should have already been settled... and we have to *trust* that the good people at the State Security Department have done their job properly. Everyone doing their small part to make the whole machinery work is the very essence of Juche, which, as you know, is the cornerstone of our society."

My heart sank further down my stomach at the same pace as the sweat was running down my back.

"However," he continued, again leaning back into his armchair, "if what you are saying is true, and you're really not supposed to be here... that would imply that somebody indeed has made a mistake, and that *is* a matter that should be looked into. And Great General knows we need all the talent we can find to prove our excellence in international competitions and to bring honor to Choson."

YES!

I wanted to scream, to cheer, to run around that over-sized desk and hug this man with his silvery ghostlike eye, but instead, I managed to produce a composed and grateful smile.

"Thank you, Sir… in the name of our eternal Father - the Great General - I thank you!" I put my hands over my heart and again remembered that the Great General pin was no longer there.

But that doesn't matter anymore!

General Roh gave me a hint of a smile.

"I'll tell you what… I will personally contact the Ministry of Physical Culture and Sports, and if they confirm your story, I'll talk to my contacts at the State Security Department."

He then pondered for a while before continuing, tapping his chin with his finger.

"I will also take a look into your father's case… I must admit, it's not very common that they send senior people from important ministries like the Ministry for Food Distribution here. I wouldn't get my hopes up, but it's important that we who work here can focus all our attention on reforming the people who have truly strayed from the righteous path. We can't have people who are here by mistake - that would just be a waste of our resources."

I couldn't believe it - this was beyond my wildest expectations. I had been convinced I would get out of here, but I hadn't dared to dream of getting my whole family out as well.

There is no way they will love Nari more than me after this!

"Sir… I can't even begin to tell you how grateful I am… I knew from the minute I first saw you that you are a righteous man and a true patriot."

This time, General Roh gave me a genuine smile.

"Miss Kim… my sole purpose here… the sole purpose of this camp… is to reform traitors… nothing more, and nothing less.

So if we indeed have people who shouldn't be here, I can't fulfill my duty… it's as simple as that."

"You're absolutely right, Sir," my heart sang in my chest.

"Good, then it's settled… I'll get back to you as soon as I've gotten some answers… MRS. GAN!" he screamed so unexpectedly that I jumped in my seat. "You're dismissed, Miss Kim… my secretary will show you out so you won't have any more problems."

I stood up from my chair as an elderly woman with thick glasses showed up at the door.

"Please show this young lady out, Mrs. Gan."

"Yes, Sir," Mrs. Gan said and stepped aside to give me space to pass.

I turned back to General Roh and bowed down reverently.

"Thank you very much again, Sir," I said with my nose almost touching his desk, but his attention was already on something else. I didn't care - all that mattered was that I was getting out of here.

As I slowly straightened my body up again, the picture frame on the desk caught my eye for just an instance.

Wait a minute… what did I just see? Was that…?

I stared at General Roh, who was now busy writing a letter.

"Er…" I started but had no idea what would follow.

General Roh looked up at me, surprised."

"Is… is…?" I stuttered.

"Miss Kim… I said you are dismissed. Please follow Mrs. Gan out. I have a lot of work to do."

My mind screaming for answers, but my survival instinct took over, so I quickly turned around and hurried out of his office. I squeezed in one more *thank you* over my shoulder before Mrs. Gan closed the door.

I didn't have any recollection of walking down the corridor or the stairs, but suddenly I was standing outside the building with my shoes in my hands, and saw Mrs. Gan heading back up the stairs as the door closed in front of me.

The overwhelming mix of emotions that swirled around in my body made me lightheaded and nauseous.

I'm getting out of here!

But still… my mind kept going back to that photograph on General Roh's desk.

I must have made a mistake. There is no other explanation! After all… I only saw that picture for a split second… and from a strange angle.

But despite all my reasoning, deep down I was certain of what I had seen.

It was her! It was!

I closed my eyes and visualized the photograph before my eyes.

But why? And how?… and… and…

My train of thought was interrupted by a guard patrol approaching me and asking what my business was. I quickly lied that I had been called in to help Mrs. Gan, then made a quick bow with an apology and hurried off - back to my very temporary home in the *Orchid Garden*.

CHAPTER 21

I sat in silence back at the house while Nari prepared dinner from the daily ration of cabbage and corn, as well as a couple of portions of rice from our stash in the corner. Nari didn't ask me where I had gone, and I didn't tell her either.

I felt exhausted... and happy... and hopeful... but also worried. If there's one thing gymnastics had taught me, it was never to celebrate a victory before standing on the podium with the medal hanging around your neck. After all - I still didn't know what crimes Young Il had committed. I also couldn't help but wonder how I would react if I were the only one who got released.

Can I leave Nari and the others here to rot while I go and fulfill my destiny of becoming one of the top gymnasts in Choson?

But, on the other hand, there was no point in all of us rotting away in this place. And as soon as I was a renowned gymnast, I could use my influence to get them out. That shouldn't take more than six months, or a maximum of a year.

That's not too long - they can make it. But still... I hope they get out now with me.

Another thought also preoccupied my mind. I couldn't wrap my mind around it… around what I had seen in the picture frame on General Roh's desk.

Had I just imagined it?

No… there was no doubt about what I had seen.

When the rice started to simmer calmly and the familiar sweet fragrance filled the room, Nari looked over at me hesitantly from behind the fire. Then she came over and sat next to me. I noticed her right hand was tightly clenched into a fist.

"I'm sorry about before," she said.

"Don't worry about it… I overreacted too," I said

Nari smiled. Then she put her clenched fist over my lap.

"What have you got there?"

"Well… I saw how upset you got when you had to give up your Great General pin to Corporal Lee this morning," she said. "And… I didn't have mine attached to my shirt, it was in my pocket… so I didn't hand it in… so… if you want… you can have it."

I looked at her startled. Then at her hand. She opened it, and the beaming face of the Great General smiled up at me from her palm.

"You… you risked punishment keeping that… for *me*?"

Nari nodded.

"Well… they were so focused on the people wearing them, so I assumed they wouldn't search us. I was right," she blushed.

I was stunned. I had never seen Nari do anything brave in her entire life, and this even bordered on being bold. I had also never experienced Nari doing something so thoughtful… at least not for me. A strange warm feeling spread through my body.

"Thank you," I said and picked up the warm metal pin from her hand and held it before my eyes. It glimmered comfortingly in the light from the fire.

"You're welcome," Nari smiled before returning to the simmering rice pot. "Just don't let anybody see it."

I nodded.

This is a sign! This proves the Great General is still watching over me. I'm getting out of here... and my family is coming with me!

After I had let the Great General's smile soothe me sufficiently, I attached the pin on my shirt over my heart where it belonged.

Just for tonight... while I'm at home... tomorrow I'll—

I suddenly realized something - I'm not getting out of here tonight, which means I will still be here tomorrow morning. And that means...

"Nari-ah... could you help me memorize the camp rules?"

"Of course," she smiled at me. She checked the food, then took down the frame with the ten Sacred Rules from the wall and sat down next to me, just like she used to do before some important tests on the Great General's speeches in the past which had been too difficult for me to memorize and I didn't have any choice but to swallow my pride and ask for help.

After a couple of hours, mom came home. Her face was pale and her arms trembled. She looked like she would collapse any second. Nari rushed over to hug her.

"Are you alright, mom?"

"I'm fine, dear... just very tired. Could you bring me something to eat? I'm starving."

"Of course, mom."

Nari went over to put some of the now cold rice together with corn and cabbage in a bowl and then handed it to mom, who had sat down with her back resting against the wall.

"Thank you, Nari-ah," mom put it under her nose and whiffed.

At first, a smile spread across her face, but when she looked into her bowl - and then at the pot next to the fire - her face changed.

"Nari-ah… you can't make this much food," she said harshly. "We have to face the fact that we will be here for a *very* long time, and this is the only real food we will get here. We have to make it last… it's really important!"

By the end of the sentence, I could feel how much mom was struggling to keep calm, just like I had seen her so many times before when she was exhausted from having lost too much sleep watching over Nari at the hospital.

"I'm sorry, mom," Nari broke out in tears.

"Shh… it's okay, dear," mom sighed with a guilty expression. "But from tomorrow… only make one quarter of this. We have to learn to eat less. Okay?"

"Okay, mom," Nari wiped her tears.

"Good girl!"

Mom started eating, but her sad eyes lingered on Nari.

"And how are you girls? How was your day?" she asked in a worried tone.

"We're okay," Nari answered quietly. "We went to school. The teacher was nice. Miss Ae. I liked her."

"That's good, Nari-ah… and how… how do you feel? How is your heart?"

"Fine, mom… I feel fine… I haven't had any symptoms."

"That's a relief… I've been worried about you." She put another lump of rice into her mouth. "And… how was it for you, Areum-ah?"

"Fine," I repeated Nari's word without meeting her eyes.

"And how were your classmates… did they seem… friendly?"

"We didn't really talk to anybody," Nari replied. "But after class, there was this boy... Jun Ha... Miss Ae asked him to show us around the camp. He was also nice, but... his stories scared me."

"I know, dear," mom gave her a compassionate look without asking what kind of stories he had told us.

"And how about you, mom... where did they put you to work?" Nari asked.

"They assigned me to the sewing factory... it's not far from the main gate, on the other side of the main road."

Mom talked while she was chewing the rice in her mouth, something we would have been scolded for doing back home. So much had changed in just two days.

"What was it like?" Nari asked.

"Well... the first thing that hit me was the deafening noise of the hammering of over a hundred - maybe even two hundred - sewing machines," mom said. "The room was enormous, and behind every sewing machine sat a woman... in endless rows, filling the whole room... everything from young teenage girls to women my age... no old ladies, though... at least as far as I could see... but the worst thing was not the deafening noise... it was the smell. There was no ventilation, and it was unbearably hot, so the stench of sweat was horrendous. During the first hour, I could hardly breathe... but after a while I stopped noticing it... was like my senses had gotten saturated or something. With the heat and stench and relentless hammering, it's like I went into some kind of haze. And then there were the guards," she rolled her eyes and sighed. "Armed with machine guns, patrolling the rows where we worked... probably twenty or so of them... I don't know what they are afraid of, I mean... what are we going to do... steal cloth?"

Mom fell silent and focused on her food. Nari sat next to her, also silent. I was bursting to ask her about what I had seen earlier in General Roh's office, but I was too afraid. Instead, I chose a safer topic.

"So… what are you sewing there? I guess it can't be uniforms for the prisoners… I mean, it doesn't seem like people here have gotten new clothes in years…"

First then I noticed that mom didn't have the same clothes as this morning.

"Yeah… they gave us adult prisoner uniforms in the morning. But I guess you only get it once you start working," she glanced at our normal - although by now, dirty - attire from the Capital.

"Anyway… we make military uniforms," mom continued with her mouth full of rice. "As far as I could see, that's the only thing we're making - just military uniforms. At first, I thought it was for the guards here, but then I noticed they looked slightly different, and given how many hundreds we must make per day, they must be sending them to units all over the country. I wouldn't be surprised if all the soldiers in Choson are wearing them."

She slurped up the last grains of rice from her bowl and put it down on the ground for Nari to fetch.

"Thank you, dear," she said. "Now I feel better… I'm just tired. And it could be much worse… at least I didn't end up in the mines like some of the other people from our group… poor souls."

CHAPTER 22

I was startled as the door opened again and a dirty and slouching Young Il entered the room. Nari rushed over to hug him.

"Hey," he greeted. "You, okay, Nari-ah?"

"I'm fine, daddy," she said without letting go of him.

I was astonished - and a bit sickened - by how little Nari seemed to care that her father was a traitor.

"Nari-ah... why don't you let your father sit and bring him a bowl of rice," mom said.

Nari reluctantly let him go and went to prepare his food.

Young Il looked at all of us in order with his bulging blood-shot eyes while waiting for the food. I noticed that he had a dirty cloth, covered in blood, wrapped around his hand.

"What happened?" mom gasped as she saw it as well.

"Just a work accident," Young Il hid the blood with his other hand. "It's nothing... happens all the time. As long as you keep your injuries clean and your limbs intact, you're okay... I washed it in the river before coming home."

Nari brought him his bowl, as well as a cup of freshly made barley tea she had prepared for all of us.

"Thank you, Nari-ah," he gave her an affectionate but tired smile, and started eating immediately. "I can't believe I'm eating rice again," he exclaimed incredulously after having swallowed the first bite. His eyes were closed, like he was trying to memorize the sensation of every grain of rice touching his palates. When he again opened his eyes and looked at his wife, his expression immediately changed to worry.

"Sun Hee-ah, I can't believe I forgot to ask you… which work assignment did you get?"

"Sewing factory," mom answered.

Young Il sighed with relief.

"That's good… that's very good. It's one of the safest work assignments you can get. Very few injuries. I'm glad," he gave mom a feeble smile, but her eyes were closed as she rested her head against the wall.

After another bite of rice and cabbage, Young Il threw Nari and me a worried glance.

"And how about you, girls? H-how was school?"

"It was fine," Nari said. "Our teacher, Miss Ae, was really nice."

"That's good," he nodded. "I'm glad you didn't get the other one… Corporal Bun… I hear he's a real monster… it's probably just hearsay, but I heard he once beat one of his students to death because he made a mistake reciting one of the Great General's speeches on Juche. But about this…er… Miss Ae… I haven't heard anything… and that's a good thing."

He continued savoring his food in silence for a while. He then hesitantly looked over at me, clearly remembering our little argument from last night.

"And how about you, Areum-ah? Are you okay?"

"I went to see General Roh today."

Young Il almost choked on the rice he had in his mouth, and both Nari and mom gasped.

"YOU DID WHAT?" mom shrieked, her eyes now wide open.

"Shhh!" Young Il whispered. "Remember… the walls have ears!"

Mom turned to me again with a lower, but equally firm voice.

"Areum, explain yourself!"

I sat up straight and looked at her furiously.

"What's there to explain? I don't belong here! I needed to do… *something*. No one else is doing anything!"

"For Juche's sake, child… don't you understand how dangerous that was?" mom screamed in a whisper, a skill she long since had honed to perfection. "Didn't you listen this morning? *If you enter without permission you will be executed.* Do you even understand how lucky you are to be alive right now?"

Mom's whole body trembled. My body trembled as well.

"I don't care," I glared her in the eyes. "I am a member of the Great General's National Gymnastics Team. I don't belong here, and I *had* to let them know that. That was worth any risk. And you know what… it worked!"

I put my hands on my hips in a gesture of triumph as my mother stood there with her mouth wide open.

"General Roh is going to look into my case," I declared victoriously. "You hear that? He *believed* me! By this time tomorrow, I'll be on a truck back to my team in the Capital. Or maybe they'll send me in a private car… just to show how ashamed they are for making this horrible mistake."

All three of them stared at me, stunned.

"General Roh will… *look into*… your case?" All the anger had left mom's voice. Instead, it was full of fear.

"Yes… General Roh will look into my case. He told me he will verify my story with the Ministry of Physical Culture and

Sports… that I'm here by mistake. He believed me… because I'm *not* the sort of person who belongs here. He could see that."

I had to force myself to control my voice, which was a challenge due to all the adrenaline pumping through my body.

"And… he will look into your case too, *father*… so you're welcome!" I added triumphantly.

"He will *what*?" Young Il gasped in horror.

His reaction took me completely by surprise.

"He told me he could look into your case too… maybe he will find that you are innocent as well."

"Oh no," Young Il whimpered. He pressed his fingers into his temples and stared wildly at the floor. "No, no, no, no, *NO*…"

"Areum," mom looked almost as white as Young Il. "What have you done?"

The feeling of triumph was fading, but I stood firm.

"I… took care of our *problem*… since no one else seemed to do anything about it. And I *succeeded*… like I always do!"

Silence fell over the room. Nari's mouth was still wide open. My heart was pounding through my chest as the unpleasant truth dawned on me.

Nothing has changed… NOTHING! Nothing I ever do for this family is recognized… nothing is appreciated… I could DIE saving this family, and I wouldn't get as much as a thank you!

"Dear," mom put her hand on Young Il's shoulder. "Maybe it'll be okay… what do you think? Is it bad?"

Young Il continued staring at the floor without saying anything, just rubbing his temples. The frantic look in his eyes scared me.

Mom looked back at me and softened her voice.

"Areum-ah… when did General Roh say that he would get back to you?"

"T-tomorrow."

"Okay… then tomorrow we will know, right Young Il-ah?" mom gave her husband a concerned look. "There's nothing we can do about it right now anyway… right, dear?"

"Yeah," Young Il mumble without looking up. "Tomorrow… maybe it'll be fine… maybe… it's okay, Areum-ah."

I heard his words, but his voice clearly stated he didn't believe for a second it would be fine.

Why are they all reacting in this way? I have possibly helped us all to get free… why are they not showering me with hugs and kisses of gratitude?

The answer was of course simple.

I'm not a part of their family… I never have been!

Despite my grief and frustration, the thought from before re-entered my mind, and this time it managed to push all other thoughts aside.

"Mom," I said, "have you met General Roh before?"

"General Roh?" she gave me a surprised look. "No, I don't believe so. Why?"

"Well…" I hesitated, not sure how to proceed. "Well… when I was in his office, there was a picture frame on his desk. And… er… I caught a glimpse of it… and… and…"

My heart was racing.

"And what?" mom asked impatiently.

"And… the picture… the picture in the frame was of… *you.*"

The entire energy and focus of the room instantly directed at me.

"Of *me*?" Sun Hee gasped, her eyes wide open. "What do you mean *'of me'*?"

"Well… just like I said… I bowed down and got a glimpse of it… and it was a picture of you… well… of you, when you were younger… but it was definitely *you.*"

Everybody's eyes were now on mom instead. She looked at Young Il with scared eyes.

"No… that can't be possible… I swear… I have no idea… you… you must have made a mistake… I've never met the man before in my life! Young Il-ah… you must believe me!"

In the silence that followed, mom's face turned scarlet red.

"Areum-ah… are you *absolutely sure* it was your mother you saw?" Young Il asked me calmly.

"Well… *almost* certain. I mean… like I said, I only got a quick glimpse of it… but I would recognize mom anywhere… even from when she was young… like on the posters we have… *had* in our living room."

Mom stood completely still - like a statue - but the turmoil inside her was visible through her eyes.

"Could it be…?" Nari hesitated. "Could it have been from before… when you were an actress? I mean… you were quite famous… maybe he was a fan and got your picture from one of your shows?"

"Well… I don't—" mom started, but I interrupted her.

"That's not it… General Roh asked me all sorts of questions about you, mom… he didn't know you were an actress… he said he's never been to the theater in his life."

Silence again consumed the room.

"Did he have photos of other people around the room?" Young Il asked.

"No," I shook my head. "Just that one… and the normal one of the Great General on the wall."

"It just… it just doesn't make sense," mom shook her head. "It can't be—"

"And it wasn't," Young Il concluded. "Areum made a mistake, that's all… there is no possible way the picture on his desk was of you. Now… let's just drop this topic… there is no point discussing it further."

Everybody looked at me, so I nodded in agreement. But I knew what I had seen - there was no doubt in my mind.

Mom and Nari still looked quite preoccupied, but nobody said anything else.

The discussion was over.

"Okay, family," Young Il said after having finished his barely tea. "We'd better get off to bed. Tomorrow will be another tough day for all of you. The first week is the worst. Nari-ah... thank you for the delicious rice... just keep the portions smaller from now on... we have to make it last."

"I've already told her," mom grunted.

"Good," Young Il smiled at Nari. "Then we'll go to bed. And I just want to tell you again, that even though it's terrible that you're here, I'm glad to have you by my side again."

Nari went over and hugged him, but inside of me, a blazing fire made my blood boil.

"Why *were* you arrested?" I glared at him, and another wave of tension paralyzed the room.

"Areum!" mom reacted immediately. "That's enough from you—"

"We deserve to know!" I didn't let her finish. "He didn't give any answers yesterday... and he still hasn't."

"Areum... that's really—" mom started, but Young Il put a gentle hand on her lap.

"It's okay... you all deserve to know."

He looked down at the floor, his forehead in wrinkles, and sighed.

"They accused me of conspiring with our enemies abroad," he said. "And it's true... I did conduct secret discussions with other countries."

All three of us gasped as his words fertilized the hatred growing inside me.

"But it wasn't to commit treason against the regime… against our people. It was to *help* our people… to *help* our regime… to *help* the Great General. I did what I believed was necessary to prevent a catastrophe."

The agitation in his voice was rising and I started to once again recognize my father deep inside the tormented body before me. But all I could think was - *how dare you take our eternal Father's name in your filthy traitor mouth?*

"You… you… you…" Mom's voice trembled, as did her body. "YOU BASTARD!" she finally shrieked, completely forgetting her volume. "I *told you* not to do that… I *told you* this would happen… YOU BASTARD! YOU IDIOT! How could you do this to us?… To your family… *we* should have been your first priority! YOU SELFISH MORON!"

She sat there gasping for air with her bulging eyes directed at Young Il. He was now just as red as she was. Nari and I looked at each other, dumbfounded.

"You *were* my first priority!" Young Il said firmly. "Don't you see that? I did it all for you! This catastrophe can destroy our entire society… and everybody in it - including our family. I was trying to save *all of us!*"

Both of them sat in silence on the floor, panting and glaring at each other. Nari sobbed softly next to me.

"I… I didn't want to go behind their backs… I didn't… but they just wouldn't listen," Young Il mumbled. "I tried to talk to my father as well before he died… that this might happen… but he didn't listen either… nobody did…"

"What catastrophe?" I glared at him suspiciously.

Young Il gave me a quick glance, but then averted his eyes and looked down at the floor.

"It's better if you don't know… it's safer," he shook his head. "And it doesn't matter anymore… it's coming… it could have been prevented… if they would have listened to reason… but now… it's too late… but being here… we might actually be better off than out there…"

WHAT? Has he lost his mind… like Lucky? This man who sits before us, talking about some kind of doomsday prophesies… this is not my father… this is not the man I thought I knew!

"Okay," I said calmly.

I looked over at Nari and mom. They were both looking at Young Il with scared faces.

They must have realized it too!

Young Il sighed deeply, his eyes still fixed on the floor.

"I have done some terrible things," he said. "Horrible… I'm not going to lie… things I *deserve* to be put here for… but they didn't come for me for *those* things. For *those* things… they called me a hero."

He sighed again and shook his head.

"Dear… maybe it's time for bed," mom put her hand on his back.

He nodded feebly.

"Yeah… let's go to sleep." He lied down on his blanket, but didn't stop talking.

"At least, I still seem to have some friends left back in the Capital," he mumbled. "I was surprised they brought me to this camp, and not to one of the *bad* ones… somebody must have pulled some strings to make that happen… and we got a family house and everything… we might just be able to ride this out… at least we have a chance… just as long as General Roh doesn't…"

His mumbling turned into soft snoring as his body went limp on the quilt in front of the fire. Mom stayed by his side and caressed his hair. Nari continued sobbing by my side. I imagined it must be heart-breaking to see her big strong father in this pitiful state. I also felt sad, but at the same time, I couldn't help but feel a certain sense of justice.

Sitting there by the still fire, I tried to picture in my mind what he meant by '*the bad ones*'.

Are there really camps worse than this one? And is a family house really a benefit? My only family is the one waiting for me back in the Capital… and being forced to share a room with these people felt like an even worse punishment.

"Areum-ah," mom said in a soft voice. "Do you really believe General Roh will set you free?"

Nari also looked at me inquiringly with her red puffy eyes.

"He will," I said confidently. "And I hope he will set you two free as well. But…" I let my eyes fall on Young Il's raising and falling back. "But… I don't think they will let *him* go… I mean, you heard what he said… he did it… he might not think it is bad himself… but he did the crime that he… that *we* were sent here for."

Mom sighed deeply.

"It's… not exactly like that," she said. "There are things that you don't understand, Areum-ah… and many things that I don't know either… but I believe your father is not a traitor… I am convinced he did what he believed was best for the country."

"I'm sure he did," I said. "Nobody thinks what they are doing is bad… not even bad people. But that doesn't make him less of a traitor."

Mom sighed again but didn't say anything else.

"I don't believe he's a traitor," Nari whimpered next to me. "I know he's a good man… he has always been a good man… and a great father… I love him so much…"

"And he loves you too very much, sweetie," mom attempted a smile. "Both of us do."

I lay down on my blanket and pulled my jacket over me for warmth. I took off Nari's Great General pin and held it firmly in my hand as I listened to the dying fire crackling soothingly in my ears. I heard Nari bring her quilt over and put it next to mom, just like she often used to go to their bed at night when we were younger.

My head was still spinning. I replayed every second from start to finish of the time I had spent in General Roh's office, and I got more and more convinced he would be my savior.

But why did he have a picture of my mother on his desk? And if it wasn't mom, why did he know her name? And why had he looked at her like that during orientation?

Then my thoughts left mom and General Roh and circled back to Young Il.

How could I have been so blind? Conspiring with our enemies… how long had this been going on? Did mom known about it? Has she been involved as well?

In the end, there were too many questions - none of which them had any answers - so my overwhelmed mind gave up and drifted off to sleep.

In my dream, I was back in the street with the sun-scorched corpses and the screeching crows soaring in the sky… and from the distance, I heard my father's voice being carried by the wind.

"Hamhung."

"Hamhung."

"Hamhung."

CHAPTER 23

The next morning, we had nothing but corn porridge with a few leftover cabbage leaves for breakfast. Young Il and mom had decided we would only have rice once a day from now on - for dinner.

I didn't feel rested, but I wasn't tired either. It was similar to the sensation I always had before a big competition. Same as I had felt when I woke up in the morning two days ago.

I ate quietly by myself and only listened with half an ear as Young Il gave advice on how to avoid trouble in the camp, as if being here these past two weeks had made him some kind of expert.

"Try to make yourself invisible… keep your heads down, blend in… whenever possible, walk two and two… it's less risk that you'll be assaulted by the guards then… but it's not allowed to be more than two, so if you're three or more you'll attract unwanted attention… guards don't need more of an excuse to beat people up… or even to drag them off to the *Center of Truth*."

Nari nodded and listened attentively, but I was doing my best to block him out. His admittance of guilt last night was still like an open wound in my heart.

And I'm getting out today, so none of this concerns me anyway!

I did, however, review the ten Sacred Rules a couple of times in my head, just in case. I didn't want to stumble and fall before crossing the finishing line.

As my head started to hurt from trying to keep track of all the rules in my head, my old familiar jealousy of Nari and her almost superhuman ability to instantly memorize anything - regardless of its length and complexity - once again sparked to life inside me, but I tried to shake it off.

I finished eating and got ready to go. Nari hurried to wash the utensils and join me out the door.

"Be careful today, girls! Remember what I told you," Young Il shouted after us.

I scoffed.

As the early morning sun peeked over the mountain ridge to the east, the *Orchid Garden* was full of children going to school and adults going to work, although in many cases it was impossible to tell who belonged to which group.

Today felt like it was going to be a warm day.

Today felt like it was going to be a good day.

"Thank you for giving me your pin yesterday," I said to Nari. "It really helped me sleep."

"Of course, Areum-ah," Nari smiled. "I knew it would make you happy."

I didn't have to force myself too hard to return the smile. I felt light at heart.

We walked in silence for a while as more and more people filled the main road, and I hoped the silence would remain until we reached the school. I needed to focus to be prepared for my next meeting with General Roh.

Will he come himself or will he send somebody else to give me the good news?

I hoped he would deliver the news himself. That's the only way I would feel sufficiently vindicated.

"Areum-ah... do you really believe dad is a... *traitor*?" Nari whispered after making sure no one was close enough to hear us.

I sighed and rolled my eyes. The morning peace I had relished was over.

"He told us himself yesterday he had done it, whatever *it* is... and just because *he* doesn't think it was treasonous, it doesn't mean it wasn't. The same is probably true for everybody else in here."

"But this is *dad* we're talking about," Nari whispered emphatically. "We know him... he couldn't have done anything bad."

"Everybody in here is somebody's dad or mom, Nari... and they all probably knew just as little about their criminal activities as we did... and still do."

Nari went silent as we left the *Orchid Garden* behind us and passed through the *Rose Garden*.

"I believe he's innocent," she finally said. "He said that he tried to do something good but that other people didn't like it."

I laughed.

"Come on, Nari... do you really think it works like that? That they would send someone to this hellhole just because of a little disagreement? That's ridiculous."

But then in my heart, I remembered Mina. I remembered *our* little disagreement... and shortly after, she was gone.

"How do you know it's ridiculous?" Nari asked. "How about what that poor woman told us the night we arrived... that her neighbor had informed on her because she wanted her apartment and made up some story about her being a traitor... and I've heard other stories before as well... like there was a teacher at the June 9th Middle School, where our cousin goes, that was taken away for not being able to remember which year the Great General joined the Northeast United Resistance Army… and history wasn't even his subject."

"Just like you said, those are *stories*… made-up stories. That woman the other night, for example… even if it was terrible what happened to her… and it really was… but she was just making up lies trying to save herself. And honestly… I'm pretty sure it takes more than a forgotten date to be sent to a place like this."

"Areum-ah… I don't understand how you can't see what's going on right in fr—?" Nari started, but I was already fed up. I took her arm and pulled her off to the side of the road and looked her seriously into her eyes.

"What *I* don't understand is how you *can't* see… how you can be so ungrateful to our Father - the Great General - for all he has done for you? Haven't we always had food on our table? A place to live? Haven't we always been able to go to school?… Not to mention all your extensive hospital visits and medical treatments? Your operation? The Great General takes care of us - his loyal citizens. And he punishes traitors who want to destroy our society… and if Young Il is here… that means that he *is* a traitor."

"He's *not* a traitor," Nari retorted with a broken but firm voice. "How can you trust the Regime so blindly? If you look around you, you must have seen that things are not as perfect as we have been told. Why are people disappearing without a trace? Remember Mina? And why did the electricity go out almost every night the last couple of years? Why are there no cars on the roads? Why is there less and less food in the stores, forcing people to buy everything in the black markets? Dad has traveled to other countries for his work… and if you would have spent some more time with him he would probably have told you too what it's like over there… that they always have electricity…. that they have more food than you could ever dream of… that there are so many cars you can hardly cross the street… and people are not disappearing without a trace!"

I don't know how loudly we talked, but I noticed that all the people passing on the road stared at us.

I suddenly gasped as I came to a horrible realization.

"Nari… now *you* sound like a traitor."

Nari looked at me silently with her sad eyes wide open.

"You see… that's exactly how the people who sent dad here reason. You are just like them. But now… you are here as well, and it was your beloved *Regime* that sent you here. It's time to see the truth, Areum-ah."

Nari's voice was calm but full of sorrow.

"*My* Regime will soon realize I'm here by mistake and send me home. I was hoping you would be released with me, but… maybe the truth is that you actually belong here."

The adrenaline pumping through my veins made my body tremble. Nari's eyes and mouth opened even wider.

"Areum… I'm your *sister*. How can you say something like that? How can you say something like that about your family?"

"About my *family*?" I scoffed. "You mean the family that had me doing chores for my *poor sick little sister* my whole life? The family who praised everything you did and criticized everything I did? The family that only cared about you, and treated me like I was some unwanted garbage they were stuck with?"

My face was burning, and I noticed that a circle of dirty prisoners had formed around us. I quickly turned around and stormed off towards the school.

"Areum!" Nari called after me but I didn't answer. "Areum! Please stop! Please! I didn't mean to… please believe me, I'm sorry."

Her words reached my ears but were deflected before entering my mind. My whole body was flaming with fire..

They're traitors… all of them! My entire family is a bunch of rotten traitors… and they have ruined my life!

Nari eventually gave up trying to catch up with me and followed behind in silence instead. Once we got to school I quickly walked past the angry shouting of Corporal Bun in the other classroom, apologized to Miss Ae for being late, and then sat down in the same seat as yesterday without looking at Nari, who quietly sat in her seat behind me. Looking around me, however, I quickly realized that the class had not started yet, and the classroom was still filling up with students. I felt stupid for apologizing to Miss Ae for being late, but my mind was too preoccupied by my hatred for my family for that to matter. While waiting, I tried to distract myself by observing my new classmates, but quickly concluded they were too difficult to tell apart.

Suddenly my eyes met with a skinny boy in the first row that was looking back at me with big eyes in an expression that almost looked like disbelief. He had short messy hair, and I was certain I had never seen him before, but… he looked strangely familiar.

As if I would know anyone here… ridiculous!

Looking closer, though, I started questioning my initial assumption.

Is that really a boy? No… those eyes and cheeks are definitely of a girl… it was just the dirty face and short hair that fooled me.

A sudden wave of shame swept over me, and I averted my eyes. But only for a moment. When I looked back in her direction, she had already faced the front. I observed her from the back, but that didn't look familiar at all. To be honest, it looked like she had cut her hair herself - but using something other than scissors. Like most others here she didn't wear shoes, she just had muddy pieces of cloth wrapped around her feet. I tried to remember if I had seen her the day before, but I couldn't recall clearly.

All of a sudden, the girl stood up and again turned around towards me.

What is this… is she coming over to me?

But she wasn't looking at me… she was looking at something behind me.

I started following the line of her eye, but at that very moment, Miss Ae cleared her throat.

"Good morning all… please sit," she said with her now familiar radiant smile. The boyish girl turned around immediately and sat down.

Where have I seen her before?

"Let's start the class," Miss Ae called to order. "Yesterday, I gave you a home assignment to think about how you can apply the principles of Juche to make your lives in here easier and better. This is something we talk about a lot, but I think it's especially important for our newcomers to think about. So why don't we start with… let's see… *Nari!*"

I looked back at Nari, who was blushing two rows behind me.

"I'm sorry, Miss Ae… I thought about it yesterday, but… I really don't know how to apply the principles of Juche to… to a place like *this.*"

"Miss Ae," I said, raising my hand. "Could I answer instead of my sister?"

Nari gave me a surprised look.

"By all means," Miss Ae extended her hands.

"As I see it, the way we can apply Juche to our situation in here, is to not sit around and wait for things to happen or to be given to us… we have to take matters into our own hands to *make* them happen."

"Exactly right… er…" She looked at the class list. "Exactly right, Areum. Keep that in mind, everybody. Life here is hard, especially when you turn fifteen and leave school. The best thing you can do is to not expect things to come to you, you need to take things into your own hands. Right then, next—"

"I'm not sure if I agree," Nari said unexpectedly from the back.

"Sorry?" Miss Ae looked at her, surprised.

"I'm not sure I agree with my sister… I mean… about how to understand the meaning of Juche. As I understand it, the people need to be self-reliant enough to build up this country… but it will only be the best country in the world when the *country* can provide for its *people*. Otherwise, it's not a society… it's just every person for themselves."

Everybody's eyes turned to Miss Ae, who now looked very serious.

"Miss Kim," she crossed her arms. "I see your point… I do… but *that* way of thinking will not help you in here… and I advise you to be very careful with statements like that… they might get you into trouble."

"Yes, Miss Ae," Nari said, flustered.

I looked back and saw her blushing intensely, looking down at the bench in front of her. Facing forward again, I noticed the boyish girl also staring at Nari.

Why does she look so familiar?

After that, Miss Ae drilled us four newcomers on the ten Sacred Rules. She made us say them one by one at first, then we had to recite the whole list top to bottom… and then bottom to top. Whenever we made a mistake or hesitated too long, we had to start from the beginning.

As expected, Nari had every word memorized in exactly the right order and could recite them as fluently as if she had been living by them her whole life. For me, So Won and Min Ji - the other newcomers - it didn't go as smoothly, and Min Ji got so frustrated she banged her desk with her fists at one point. Miss Ae let it slide.

Once Miss Ae was sufficiently satisfied with us, she went back to the topic of Juche, mixed with all kinds of practical advice on how to improve your life in the camp. Then she moved on to History of the Revolution, which she spoke of with noticeably less vigor and passion… for being Miss Ae, that is. For a normal person, it would have been considered quite engaging.

After a while, however, I started to zoom out - like I often did during class back in the Capital - and started thinking about when the news about my release at long last would come from General Roh. I also racked my brain trying to figure out who the boyish girl could be, and why she looked so familiar.

When the bell rang indicating the lunch break, I decided to go and get a closer look at the girl, maybe even talk to her - the curiosity was killing me - but before I had even stood up, Miss Ae waved at me.

"Areum… could you please stay behind for a minute?"

"Er… of course," I said as I saw the mystery girl throwing me a glance before disappearing out the door.

I approached Miss Ae, but she waited for the classroom to be empty before she closed the door and faced me with a smile.

"So, Areum… how are you settling in here?"

"Fine," I lied.

"I can see that." She examined me from top to toe. "You seem to be a very strong girl, both in will and body… and you seem to understand things the way they are."

I nodded. There's never a bad time for flattery.

"But I'm a bit concerned about your sister," she continued. "I'm sure there's no need to tell you this, but… please watch out for her. You're bigger and stronger, but also… she might need some help with dealing with - and *accepting* - this harsh new reality she's in… you have probably already realized it, but only the strong make it here… people like *you*. Your sister is not like that, and if you want her to make it… you must be strong for both of you. Do you understand?"

"I understand," I nodded as my shoulders started tensing up.

"Good." She gave me another one of her radiant smiles. "She is lucky to have you… your whole family is."

"Thank you, Miss Ae," I gave her a sad smile before leaving the room. Sad, because I knew my family would never recognize how lucky they were to have me here, and sad because I might be leaving Nari here alone with no one to protect her.

But this is not my responsibility! It's the responsibility of mom and Young Il… they will have to care for her… to keep her safe!

I came out into the blinding midday sun from the dark school building, squinting, and holding my hand up to shade my eyes. I immediately spotted Nari.

At first, I didn't understand the scene that was playing out in front of me. It looked like Nari was hugging someone… and crying.

As my eyes slowly got accustomed to the bright light, I started recognizing who it was she was hugging. There was no doubt - it was the familiar boyish girl with short messy hair.

What's going on? Who is that girl?

I approached them slowly on unsteady feet. When Nari noticed me, she looked up with a heartfelt smile, all wet from tears.

"Areum, can you believe it… it's Mina. It's *Mina*!"

CHAPTER 24

With my body completely paralyzed by the shock from what I had just heard, I looked at the girl and tried to picture her with long black hair, some makeup instead of dirt, and a little more body fat. Then she smiled at me with her swollen and wet - but still so familiar - eyes and all doubt vanished. It was like my worst nightmare suddenly appeared in the living nightmare that currently was my life.

"I c-can't believe it," I stuttered. "Mina… it's really you… you're really here."

Mina nodded and smiled, her tears making long vertical lines along the dirty dints in her face where the cheeks used to be.

"She has been home with the flu… that's why we didn't see her in class yesterday," Nari beamed.

Mina suddenly let go of Nari and walked over to me, looking me with unwavering eyes. I panicked. I would have taken a step back if I hadn't been paralyzed.

What is she going to do? Does she know?

Mina stood right in front of me for what felt like an eternity, her mesmerizing eyes interlocked with mine. My heart pounded through my chest. Then she opened her arms and threw herself into mine. I was completely taken aback - but just for an instant - then I sighed in relief and put my hands gently on her back as some of my body's tension melted away. Mina still had her strength - I could feel it - but she seemed so frail I was afraid I would injure her if I hugged her too hard… it felt like all that was left of her were bare bones pressing against my body. I had never been hugged by Mina before - us being mortal enemies and all - but I was certain her body didn't used to be like this.

"I'm so glad to see you, Areum-ah," she cried. "Don't get me wrong… it's horrible that you guys also ended up here… but I can't help being glad to see you… my old rival… and my best friend," she beamed looking at Nari, her face now completely wet from tears.

"I… I… I can't believe you're here, Mina," I felt my anxiety level increasing again. "I mean… have you been here this whole time? Since you disappeared? It must have been—"

"Two years," Mina wiped her tears. "It's a bit hard to keep track of time here, but yeah… it was two about years ago when they came to our apartment one night and took us away. My mom and I spent several weeks in a detention center somewhere while they… well… *interrogated* my dad." Another pair of tears fell from Mina's eyes and a slight tremble came over her voice. "I think we were there for one or two weeks, but I can't say for sure… the lights were on day and night. They forced dad to confess to everything… but they were all lies, of course. When they had what they needed, they put us in a truck and brought us here. "

"That's what happened with us too… except our dad was taken away one month before they came for us," Nari said and hugged Mina again. "I have been so worried, you have no idea, Mina… I'm so glad you're still alive."

"I've missed you, Nari!"

"That's really… *terrible*," I made a great effort to display compassion. "But, what… er… what crimes did they charge you with? I mean… what did they charge *your dad* with?"

My panic was again spreading through my body.

"It doesn't matter," Mina wiped away another tear. "They were all made up lies… just like most other people in here… same as it must have been for you, I guess… honestly, I don't even remember."

"So… they just showed up at your door one night?" I continued inquiring. "Did your dad know they were on to him? Do you know why… they started to investigate him?"

Mina gave me an incredulous look and I could feel both my cheeks flaring up.

"They weren't *on to him* because he hadn't *done* anything," she said firmly. "And no… I have no idea why they came for him… and it doesn't matter anymore… now we are here, so we just have to do our best to survive… anyway, people inform on each other for all kinds of crazy reasons… in here I even hear of children informing on their parents… it makes my stomach turn."

I averted my eyes. I felt dizzy and nauseous at the same time.

"So, how are your parents now?" Nari changed the topic. "I missed them too."

A dark cloud came over Mina's face and a new pair of tears blended with the muddy mess on her hollow cheeks.

"My dad became very weak after the weeks of constant… *interrogation*," she sobbed. "And as soon as we got here, they put him to work in the coal mines. Within a year he had developed tuberculosis. He didn't get any medical treatment… and they forced him to continue working just like before… while he was getting weaker by the day. Mom's a doctor, you know… so she treated him as much as she could, but without real medicine, there wasn't much she could do for him… and the other doctor here, the one they call Doctor Death… everybody warned us to stay away from him, so we did… and there was no one else to get help from."

Mina cleared her throat as her trembling voice broke and more teardrops left her eyes.

"Then one day, he just didn't come home from the mines. Nobody told us anything and we had no idea what had happened… finally, we tracked down one of the guys from his work unit, and he confirmed that he just collapsed one day, and about an hour later, he was dead… they left his body in one of the abandoned tunnels, same as they do with everybody else who dies down there."

A steady stream of tears ran down her cheeks, but then she suddenly forced a smile.

"At least I still have mom," she sniffed. "We take care of each other… and now… I have *you*, Nari-ah."

"I'm so sorry, Mina-ah," Nari hugged her again. "I loved your dad… he was a really good man… I can't believe he's gone…"

I swallowed hard, and a strange pain spread in my throat.

"I… I'm really sorry to hear that too," I mumbled, looking down at the ground. Even though I truly felt her pain, my words sounded fake and insincere to my ears.

"Thank you, guys… at least he doesn't have to suffer anymore," Mina wiped her tears. She looked over at me with hesitant eyes. "Areum… I know you and I weren't on the best terms back then… I just want you to know that I'm sorry… about everything I said in the self-criticism sessions… about everything… and I hope we can put all that behind us now. None of that matters anymore… and in here, it's us against them… we must look out for each other to stay strong."

"Of course," I nodded. "That's all in the past. And… I'm sorry as well… I didn't mean to—"

"Areum… don't worry about it," Mina smiled weakly. "From now on, we just look forward."

"Mina… you must come over for dinner tonight," Nari's eyes suddenly lit up. "And your mother too, of course."

"Nari… shouldn't you check that with mom and dad first?" I almost gasped. "I mean… we have the food situation…"

"Oh," Mina rushed to say. "It's okay… we don't have to come to eat… or we can bring our own food, it doesn't matter… but it would be great to come over and meet you all… like old times… my mom would like it too… we talk about you all the time."

"Yes, that would be wonderful," Nari grinned, looking at me. "And don't be ridiculous, Areum… tonight is on us… really, you don't have to bring your own food. It's only *one* night… I'm sure mom and dad will agree. They'll be so happy to see you!"

"B-but… how about the Sacred Rules?" my mind was grasping at straws to prevent the inevitable. "Aren't gatherings of more than two people forbidden… and get you *executed*?"

"That rarely happens," Mina shook her head. "We have people over all the time. We'll just have to be careful. Go when it's dark, sneak in one by one… stuff like that."

"Are you sure it's safe?" Nari asked nervously.

"Absolutely… the rules sound very harsh, but after a while, you learn how things in here *actually* work. Mom has more or less turned into the *real* camp doctor, so some nights we have two or three patients at the same time, and we have never had any problem."

"Okay, let's do it," Nari beamed, nodding at me.

Mina looked over at me for confirmation.

"Sure," I surrendered. "But I'm not as confident as you are about how mom and Young Il will react."

In my heart, however, I felt as if the world had been pulled away from underneath my feet.

What if she somehow finds out the truth? And when will General Roh come and release me?

"Then it's settled," Mina smiled, and the three of us lined up with the other students to get our watery and flavorless lunch rations.

Nari broke the news to mom and Young Il as soon as they returned home. Young Il was delighted - he'd heard about the prisoner doctor but had no idea it was Mina's mother - Mrs. Choy. Mom, on the other hand, was a bit more reserved, giving Young Il a concerned look.

"I'm not sure it's wise to treat them to our food," she said. "We have to make this last… and is it safe to let them see that we have rice? They have been here two years already… who knows how that has changed them?"

"Well… I, of course, agree with you that we shouldn't waste our food," Young Il put his hand on his wife's lap. "But this is nothing short of a miracle… and it's only one night… besides, we have known them forever… we can trust them. And with everything bad going on, we deserve to celebrate that our daughter has been reunited with her best friend."

Mom still looked at him hesitantly.

"But fine," Young Il said. "In order not to waste, let's make the portions extra small tonight. And we'll cover the rice bags with some blankets so they won't see how much we have, okay?"

"Okay… fine," mom conceded reluctantly.

I also had a bad feeling about this, but Nari's unrestrained euphoria gleamed in her dark brown eyes under her crocked glasses as she immediately started preparing the humble feast.

It was already dark when we heard a soft knock on the door. Nari opened it and Mina immediately threw herself into her arms. Her face and hair were now clean so I could recognize her better. Despite her short haircut, she didn't look as boyish anymore - but her clothes and the cloths on her feet were just as dirty as before. After she let go of Nari there was a quiet, but emotional, round of greetings - everybody was aware that the walls had ears.

We sat down and waited in silence. A few minutes later there was another quiet knock on the door. Mina's mother entered with a big smile, whispering greetings to all of us. Mrs. Choy looked almost the same as her daughter - skinny, short, had uneven messy hair, wore dirty rags, and had cloth wrapped around her feet instead of shoes. Her eyes were full of determination. The only real difference was her older facial features and the streaks of gray in her hair.

Without their jackets, it became apparent just how skinny they had become. It was painful to watch.

I guess being the unofficial camp doctor hasn't improved their food situation much…

We sat to eat. Both Mina's and Mrs. Choy's eyes bulged when they saw the pot with fresh steaming rice. I noticed Mrs. Choy covering her mouth and a couple of tears running down her cheeks.

"We're sorry to hear about your loss, In Sook," Young Il said to Mrs. Choy. "Your husband, Ye Jun… he was a good man. I always liked meeting him."

"Thank you," Mrs. Choy said. "We miss him a lot. It's especially hard on Mina."

She stroked Mina's short hair with a pain-filled smile.

Nari served everybody food - rice, corn, and cabbage - and on top, she sprinkled the last of the dried seaweed we had brought with us from the Capital.

Both Mina and Mrs. Choy put their bowls under their noses and closed their eyes as they let the steam carry the aromatic fragrance of the freshly boiled rice into their nostrils. They grabbed their metal chopsticks and looked at Young Il with impatient - almost desperate - eyes.

"Please, dig in!" Young Il smiled.

Mina lifted her bowl to directly under her chin and started gulping down the food.

"Mina-ah... don't eat so fast," Mrs. Choy cautioned her. "Your stomach is not accustomed to this much food... you might get sick... and your stomach will feel fuller if you eat slowly. We have talked about this."

"Yes, mom," Mina lowered her bowl, but it was too late - her face was already distorted by pain.

Nari looked at her worriedly but didn't say anything.

"So... where do you live?" Sun Hee asked. "Are you in one of the barracks?"

"At first, yes... we were split up in two barracks," Mrs. Choy said, "but after people started finding out I'm a doctor - and the guards noticed I was doing a better job than the camp doctor - we were appointed a family house just like this one... it's on the other side of the *Orchid Garden*... and luckily we were allowed to keep it even after Ye Jun... disappeared." She blinked away a couple of tears.

Young Il averted his eyes.

"It's a great tragedy," he said. "But at least the two of you can be together... and it makes life at least a little easier."

"Yes it does," Mrs. Choy wiped her cheeks dry with her sleeve. "But unfortunately, providing medical services doesn't put more food on the table. The prisoners barely have enough to survive themselves, and the guards expect to be treated for free. The most I get is some help gathering herbs up in the mountains… and keeping the family house, of course."

We ate in silence for a while as the tasty food filled both our bodies and our minds.

I observed Mrs. Choy looking around the room, and I noticed her eyes landed on the pile of clothes covering our bags of rice before quickly looking away.

I guess the secret's out…

"So… Mina told me you were taken away at night as well," Mrs. Choy said after she had finished the last grain of rice and put her bowl down on the floor in front of her. "It's a really horrible experience… even though it was two years ago for us, I still have nightmares about it."

"It was horrible," Sun Hee nodded. "But the worst part was that Young Il had disappeared over a month before that, and nobody would tell us where he was… just that he was on a *business trip*. Then, three nights ago, they came to our apartment."

Mrs. Choy threw a concerned look at Nari and then turned back to mom.

"How is she handling it?" she asked. "How is her health?"

"She has chest pains on and off… especially during the truck ride coming here… and after that, she vomited… it was the first time since the surgery… but now she seems to be stable. I just hope it will stay that way… our doctor in the Capital said she needs to eat plenty and preferably drink five cups of green tea every day, for her heart… but I assume neither of that is possible here."

Mrs. Choy shook her head in confirmation.

"We managed to bring some tea - both green and barley - but that won't last long," mom continued. "I guess all we can do is to try to feed her as well as possible… hopefully, it'll be enough to keep her healthy. I'm just worried about what will happen when she turns fifteen and is put to work full days somewhere."

"The most important thing is which work assignment you get," Mrs. Choy said. "The worst fate is for those who get sent to the coal mines, like my poor Ye Jun... there, the question is not *if* you die, but *when*. Personally, I work on the animal farm up by the guards' village - the *Lotus Garden* - keeping the animals healthy, so I had to kind of re-school myself into a veterinarian." She chuckled. "Anyway, it's not so bad there... the guards don't see you at all times, so you can take small breaks without being punished, and there are plenty of places where you can get shade from the burning sun in the summer... the main challenge is keeping your hands off all the food that the animals get."

I suddenly felt repulsed.

"You would actually eat food meant for *animals*?" I gasped.

"Areum!" mom glared at me.

"It's okay, Sun Hee," Mrs. Choy said. "You haven't been here for long... and you have food," she threw another glance at our pile of clothes hiding the rice bags, "but once you experience *real* hunger... I'm embarrassed to say it, but you'll eat *anything* from *anywhere*... even from the pigs' feed box."

That image caused a sudden wave of nausea to sweep over me, and I had to put my bowl down until it had passed.

"And how about the two of you?" Mrs. Choy asked. "Which work assignments did you get?"

"I'm on construction duty," Young Il said. "Been there two weeks now. We're expanding the village to the west... seems like the prison population is growing. Sun Hee started working in the sewing factory."

Mom nodded, annoyed at not being let to speak for herself.

"The sewing factory is also good I hear," Mrs. Choy nodded. "Very few accidents. And the guards are not as mean as in other places."

"Exactly how afraid of the guards should we be?" mom asked unexpectedly. "Looking at the Sacred Rules we had to memorize… we can basically be executed for anything."

Mrs. Choy smiled.

"The rule of thumb is that anything related to escape, food or any kind of disobedience is deadly serious. But then you have to remember that the guards are people like anybody else… the important thing is to learn to distinguish the good ones from the bad ones. You can often go by their looks… so if they look mean, they usually are mean. Stay away from those. A friendly guard, on the other hand, can make your life here much easier."

"The guard that took us to school… Chul… I mean, *Private Gang*… he seems really nice… it's like he doesn't even belong here," Nari said.

"I know him," Mina said. "He is definitely one of the good ones… he has helped us several times."

"Yes, he's good," Mrs. Choy agreed. "Just make sure you don't trust someone too soon… some play nice to gain your trust so they can catch you red-handed later. The same goes for the prisoners, by the way… actually, I would even go so far as to say you should *never* trust another prisoner fully. As you have probably figured out, there are very few guards compared to the prisoner population, so they have created a system where the prisoners themselves are required to act as guards and inform on each other… in that way, the prisoners do the guards' job for them, and the result is that nobody can trust anyone else… anyone could be an informant."

Nari got up to serve everybody a cup of green tea.

Shouldn't we keep that only for her? I thought to myself but didn't say anything.

"The other thing is the daily quotas... everything here is based on them," Mrs. Choy continued. "If one person fails to reach the quota, the whole group is punished. If you're punished, you get less food... which means that the whole group will get less food... and then the group will punish the person who failed... sometimes they even beat him to death. But even if they don't, it usually starts a spiral of increased quotas and cut food rations that'll kill you soon enough anyway." She paused to take a sip of her tea. "It's the workgroup leaders that decide the punishment for the person who failed, and the guards usually look for the cruelest people they can find and put them as leaders of the workgroups, giving them favorable treatment... increased rations and such. Many - if not most - are even worse than the guards. Whatever you do, don't get on their bad side."

Everybody listened to Mrs. Choy with great attention. Nari's face showed the deep horror we all felt. Mina put her arm around Nari's back to comfort her.

Mrs. Choy sighed hesitantly, took another sip of her tea, and continued.

"There's one last thing that you probably should be aware of. If you're lucky, you'll never encounter them... but apart from the group leaders, there is another group of people that works directly for the guards. They call themselves *the Dragons* and the guards use them to do their dirtiest dirty work for them... and in return, they get almost full immunity, extra food rations and other benefits. A word of advice - stay as far away from them as you can. They are crueler than both the guards and the workgroup leaders combined."

"But... how do you know if a person is a member of *the Dragons*?" I asked.

"Well, it's not like they wear a sign or anything... but keep an eye out for people who look healthy and who are not as skinny as the rest... and have better clothes. Chances are they're part of that group."

I tried to remember if I had seen somebody like that, and the first that came to mind was Jun Ha at school, but I quickly dismissed that as a possibility. Jun Ha was one of the nicest boys I had ever met, and also - how could a schoolboy be useful in a gang of ruthless thugs like that?

"That's about all the advice I have accumulated over these two years," Mrs. Choy put her hands on her knees.

"Thank you for sharing that with us, In Sook," Young Il said and sipped his tea.

"Anytime," Mrs. Choy nodded. "Now that we have found each other again, we don't want to lose you... we'll do anything we can to help you stay safe."

Listening to Mrs. Choy's lessons about how to survive in Yodok, my mind became increasingly preoccupied.

Why hadn't General Roh come to set me free? Had he not been able to get in touch with the Ministry of Physical Culture and Sports?

Then and there, I made a decision.

If he doesn't come during school tomorrow, I'll have to go and see him again... there is no other way!

The thought of once more running into Colonel Wan, however, terrified me.

The conversation around me turned more into a discussion about life before the camp and what had happened in Choson and in the Capital, during the two years the Choys had been completely cut off from the outside world. Nari and Mina whispered to each other and giggled in the usual little bubble they created when the adult topics around them became too boring.

I sat in my corner of the room, observing, and pretended to follow the conversation. I couldn't help but notice Mrs. Choy's eyes going to the conspicuous pile of clothes several times during the evening. I saw mom noticing it too, and it made her look tense and uncomfortable. I also felt tense and uncomfortable, but for different reasons.

It was a mistake inviting them here!

Later that night, after the Choys had left, I lay sleepless in my bed, listening to the heavy breathing of Nari and Young Il. Mom seemed to have trouble falling asleep just like me, probably consumed by her own fears and worries.

For me, I had my usual thoughts haunting me during a sleepless eternity, and later, they continued haunting me in my dreams.

How could Mina have ended up here? Will the truth of what I did come out? Will all of them find out my secret? Tomorrow, I need to get out of here! I have to! And if General Roh doesn't come to me, I must go to him… and not even Colonel Wan can stop me!

CHAPTER 25

The next day in school, I barely heard a word of what Miss Ae or my classmates were saying. I didn't even focus on the ill-fated fact that Mina had reappeared in my life at the worst possible moment and in the worst possible place, bringing the secret I had kept buried for so long back to the surface. Instead, I constantly stared at the door, waiting with increasing anxiety for General Roh or somebody else to come and declare my freedom. But the door remained relentlessly shut.

During the lunch break, I stood in front of the school and looked in the direction of *the Oversight* for someone to come. I got my hopes up a couple of times when some officers walked in my direction, but when they reached the main road separating us, they always went off in another direction. When Jun Ha came over and asked if I was okay, I told him I was fine and walked away. I didn't even get shy. Mina and Nari also came over to talk, but I said I was not feeling well and pulled away.

I couldn't understand it - General Roh had said he would get back to me the next day. That was *yesterday*. I needed a way to talk to him immediately after school.

But how?

After school had finished, I caught up with Nari in the hallway.

"Nari… I need to talk to Miss Ae again, so I'll catch up later, okay?"

"Okay, Areum-ah," Nari gave me a suspicious look, but turned back to Mina and they left the building whispering to each other as always.

I waited by the entrance door until Nari was out of sight before going out into the evening sun myself.

My mind raced frantically.

How will I get to General Roh? If I get caught by Colonel Wan again, he will surely drag me down into the dungeons of the Center of Truth and make me disappear for good.

I walked over to the main road, trying not to look like I was up to something suspicious. *The Bloodyard*, enclosed by *the Oversight* buildings, was crowded with guards and officers smoking and talking. I turned right and looked out over the fields with all the gray people still working. The large wooden wheel of the watermill turned slowly in the background.

Then I remembered - Chul said he was overseeing the watermill.

If I find him, he can help me! He told us to come to him if we needed anything.

With my heart racing, I followed the edge of the nascent cornfield until I reached the river and then turned left toward the watermill. There were hundreds of prisoners working in the fields, but there were only a handful of guards. Mrs. Choy was right - the guards really were outnumbered by the prisoners.

I squinted my eyes and tried to recognize Chul's features, but from far away, with all of them dressed the same, it was nearly impossible to tell anyone apart. The only thing I had to go by was that he was slightly smaller and skinnier than the other guards. He also had a more slouching posture.

As I approached the watermill, I noticed I had started drawing unwanted attention, both from the prisoners and the guards in the fields. I felt my heart pound hard in my chest and the sweat pearl on my forehead. But I stayed firm on course to show I walked with a purpose.

The area around the watermill was deserted, so I headed straight for the door and opened it.

"WHO ARE YOU? WHAT DO YOU WANT?" a huge bearded man barked at me from inside the room, scaring me half to death. Chul was nowhere to be seen.

"I'm sorry," I hurried to close the door again.

I could feel all the eyes from the field burning in the back of my head.

What do I do now? Where could he be?

My mind raced. I couldn't get clarity in my thoughts. I remembered when Jun Ha showed us around the camp. I turned around and saw the house over by the main road that he had said was used by the guards supervising all food production.

He must be there!

Ignoring the prying eyes from the fields, I forced myself to take the first determined steps in that direction. The sweat burned my eyes, but I was too afraid to lift my hands to wipe it away.

They saw I didn't have any business at the watermill… if the same happened at the guardhouse, this could quickly turn into a dangerous situation. But if I turn around now, it will look even more suspicious.

There is no turning back!

Halfway to the guardhouse, I caught a movement in the corner of my eye, but I didn't turn my head to look. I was sweating heavily now, and not only from the strong evening sun burning my thick black hair. The guardhouse wasn't far now - it was almost within my reach.

But what if he's not there? What if there instead is an army of guards, just waiting to get their hands on an idling prisoner with no good reason to be there? Or what if it's empty and he's not there at all?

As I reached the first few trees growing around the guardhouse on both sides of the main road, I heard footsteps behind me.

It must be one of the guards from the field… he's coming to question me!

In my panic, I was desperate to run away, but I knew that if I did, I would be down in the *Center of Truth* in the care of Colonel Wan before the sun had set for the day.

The heavy footsteps behind me increased their pace.

I sped up slightly as well, but only slightly - not to make it too obvious. I could hardly see due to the sweat in my eyes. I turned the corner - the door was right there in front of me - but just as I reached out my hand towards it, the door suddenly swung open.

My heart stopped for a split second and my whole body froze.

I'm surrounded! I'm done for! Now they will drag me off to Colonel Wan's dungeon of death!

I finally managed to lift my hand to wipe the sweat from my eyes. After blinking in pain a couple of times, my vision finally cleared, and to my great relief, in the doorway in front of me stood none other than Chul, looking at me with his big childlike eyes full of surprise. I was so relieved my body almost started laughing on its own accord, but at that precise moment, I jumped from shock as a strong hand firmly grabbed my right shoulder.

"Prisoner… what's your business here?"

The youthful - but serious - voice of the guard sounded familiar, but I couldn't place it. Chul's expression became even more surprised and I looked back at him with pleading eyes, begging through them for him to save me.

"It's okay, Sung Ki," Chul finally said with his eyes still searching my face for answers. "This is prisoner Kim... Miss Ae sent her."

Sung Ki's painful grip around my shoulder remained firm.

"To do what exactly?" he asked Chul.

"Well... er... the teachers are complaining that the classes are too big and that we need to get more teachers here... so... er... I promised Miss Ae to report to *the Oversight* if she assessed how much the classes can grow... you know... before they run out of space in the classrooms, and we need to... er... split them up in more groups... you know, with the camp population growing and all... many more children coming... so Miss Ae said that this prisoner... would come over and... er... convey me her assessment."

The grip around my shoulder didn't loosen.

"I don't see any paper," Sung Ki said.

"Miss... Miss Ae asked me to convey it verbally," I panted. "Because of the paper shortage in school."

Chul was pale as a ghost and I saw sweat pearling on his forehead.

"And what was the conclusion then?" Sung Ki inquired suspiciously, tightening his grip even further. I whimpered in pain.

"She... she said that... that she can handle two more pupils in the current classroom... after that, it will be impossible to fit any more... and... and... Corporal Bun has already reached his limit," I twisted my body in agony.

All three of us stood in silence for what felt like an eternity. I looked at Chul, who looked at Sung Ki behind my back. It was as if time almost stood still and only moved in short waves, synchronized with the slow throbbing pain shooting out from my shoulder.

Sung Ki finally released his grip, and for just a moment, I felt an extreme lightness in my body as the blood circulation recommenced.

"Those arrogant teachers," Sung Ki spat on the ground next to me. "Throwing away valuable resources on teaching these worthless traitor children. In my opinion, they should close down that damn school and put the children to proper use. Even a six-year-old can be useful out there in the fields... or in one of the factories. This, what they're doing now," he paused mid-sentence to light a cigarette, "is just a massive waste of time... like teaching pigs to do tricks before the slaughter."

The analogy sent a shiver down my spine and I took the opportunity to distance myself from him by taking a step closer to Chul. As I turned around I remembered where I had heard his voice before. It was the guard - Private On - that had approached Jun Ha during our tour of the camp. The one who had asked him for *information* by the end of the day.

"Couldn't agree more, Sung Ki," Chul sighed, also lighting a cigarette. "But you know... it's the Generals who decide... all we can do is to follow orders." He shrugged his shoulders and exhaled a white cloud of smoke.

"Well... someone should talk some sense into them," Private On gave me a menacing look.

"Hey... if you're feeling brave enough..." Chul laughed nervously.

Private On just shook his head, then nodded goodbye to Chul and headed back towards the fields. After a few steps, he stopped and shouted over his shoulder.

"Since she's here anyway, why don't you put her to work in the fields? Can't have our prisoners wasting valuable time like this."

"I'll see what I can do," Chul shouted back at him as he entered the nearest cornfield, pushing some poor woman who was in his way so she fell to the ground with a shriek.

Once Private On was out of sight, I smiled at Chul with a deep sigh of relief.

"Thank you so much... you saved me!"

"Don't mention it," he blushed and took another drag on his cigarette. "Sung Ki is a nice guy, but he can be a bit hard-headed sometimes... and not only him... you shouldn't walk around alone like that... especially with those clothes... you're not exactly blending in."

"I'll be more careful... I promise."

I suddenly felt a wave of shame sweeping over me.

"So... Areum... why are you *really* here?"

"Yeah... so... you see, I have a problem, and... I didn't know who could help me... and it's very urgent... that's why I came looking for you—"

"For *me*?" Chul raised his eyebrows. "You actually came looking for *me*?"

"Yes... the thing is that... well... General Roh promised to come to see me yesterday, but he didn't... and I need to meet with him, it's extremely important... but prisoners aren't allowed into *the Oversight* without permission, and last time Colonel Wan almost dragged me away to the *Center of Truth*, and—"

"Hold on, hold on," Chul stopped me, waving his arms. "*General Roh* promised to come and see *you*? I don't understand... why would he do that? You must have misunderstood."

"I didn't misunderstand anything" I shook my head. "General Roh promised to review my case... to verify that I really am a member of the Great General's National Gymnastics Team... then he will send me back to the Capital... maybe even with my family..."

Chul looked at me with an expression of growing disbelief.

"Please, Chul... you must believe me... you must help me!"

Chul threw the cigarette butt on the ground and put his hands in his pockets.

"General Roh actually said he would do that? He said those exact words?"

"Yes... he did... just the other day when I was in his office."

Chul let out something in between a scoff and chuckle and shook his head.

"Wow... you know... it's just... I've *never* heard of anything like that before... I mean... that really doesn't sound like General Roh... at least not like I've gotten to know him since I came here last year."

"You have only been here for one year?"

"Yeah... General Roh actually saved my life back in Hamhung... well, both mine and Chang Min's."

"Hamhung?" I almost gasped. "You were in Hamhung? What happened there? And... you were there with Chang Min?"

Why does this city continue to come back and haunt me?

"Yeah... it... it doesn't matter." Chul became visibly uncomfortable and lit another cigarette. "Either way... I have never heard of him releasing anyone before they have served their full sentence. And also... you heard him the other day in the courtyard... they *execute* people who claim they're innocent. That's rule number nine, as you must know by now. They say General Roh came up with that one himself."

I felt a clinch around my heart tightening inside my chest.

"I… I don't even know how long our sentence is…" I mumbled.

"Ask your dad… he must know."

"I… I will." I swallowed painfully. "But… I know what General Roh told me… he *did* promise to help me… please, Chul… will you help me… again? Could you please take me to him?"

Chul let out a nervous laugh, then shook his head and lit another cigarette.

"I mean… I don't know… it just sounds so… *unbelievable*," he said. "And also… I'm not exactly General Roh's favorite person in the world… I don't know why, but I get the feeling he… *hates* me… so I'm not sure if it would help either of us if I take you to him."

"Please, Chul… you're my only hope!"

I locked my pleading watery eyes into his eyes full of hesitation and fear.

"Please, you must help me, Chul… I'm begging you! I promise that's what General Roh told me. I swear! And he will thank you for bringing me… and… and…"

Chul sighed.

"If I take you… you'd better be telling me the truth… us guards can get into serious trouble as well, you know."

"It *is* the truth… I swear it… it *is* the truth."

Chul sighed again and threw his half-smoked cigarette on the ground.

"Okay then… let's go!"

"Thank you, Chul… I can't tell you how much I appreciate it." The tension in my body was instantly released like an explosion. I was so overwhelmed with gratitude that I wanted to hug him, but I knew it would be completely inappropriate… not to mention *dangerous*.

I followed behind Chul along the main road. All the guards in the fields, including Private On, were watching us suspiciously. I bent my head down to show submission. It was an unnatural pose for me.

You're a pretty good liar," Chul said over his shoulder. "That's a skill that can be quite useful in here… as long as you're not caught."

"Thank you… you were not so bad yourself."

Despite my high level of anxiety, I couldn't help but smile.

CHAPTER 26

Just before we reached *the Oversight*, Chul stopped and faced me.

"Are you absolutely sure?" he asked one more time, looking deeply into my eyes.

I nodded.

"Okay, follow me."

I followed him in through the door and up the stairs. Even though I knew I was safe with Chul, my heart pounded fast, and as we walked down the corridor leading to General Roh's office, I could hardly breathe. Some people we passed looked at us suspiciously but didn't say anything.

When we finally stood in front of the General's door, ready to knock, the door to the right suddenly opened and Colonel Wan appeared in the doorway.

Great General, this is exactly the same as happened last time... but this time I have Chul!

Colonel Wan looked at Chul, and then at me, with incredulity.

"What is this?" he asked.

"Good evening, Colonel Wan," Chul saluted him nervously. "I have instructions to bring this prisoner to see General Roh."

After a long moment of intense eye contact, Colonel Wan's face transformed into an ominous smile - the same smile he had before he tried to drag me down to the *Center of Truth* two days ago.

"By all means," Colonel Wan gestured for Chul to knock on the door, but remained in the doorway, smiling.

Chul knocked on the door with a trembling hand. I could see sweat again on his forehead. There was some ruckus from the other side and then General Roh opened the door. I was the first one he saw.

"Miss Kim?" he said, surprised.

He then looked at Colonel Wan, and finally at Chul, at which I noticed his face darkening.

"Private Gang... what is the meaning of this?" he asked impatiently. "Explain yourself!"

"Good evening, Sir," Chul saluted in panic. "I w-was told you wished to see this prisoner."

I could see Colonel Wan's smile widening as he gleefully awaited the General's merciless verdict.

"Private Gang," General Roh furrowed his eyebrows and moving his face mere inches away from Chul's. "If I wished to talk to a prisoner... wouldn't the correct procedure be for *me* to give the order to bring the prisoner up here? To my recollection... I have not done that."

Chul was sweating and blinking rapidly, but he didn't look away.

"Yes, Sir! That would be the correct procedure... I'm deeply sorry, Sir!"

My heart was pounding through my chest.

I have made a huge mistake! I shouldn't have come here! I shouldn't have asked Chul!

I saw Colonel Wan still smiling in the doorway, eagerly waiting for his cue... and this time, there was no doubt in his mind it would come. But after a final disappointed sigh directed at Chul, General Roh straightened up and looked at me.

"It's fine, Miss Kim... I will see you," he opened the door wider for me to pass.

My heart sang - once more had I evaded Colonel Wan's deadly clutches!

The General then turned back to Chul with nothing but disgust written on his face.

"I have warned you about this kind of behavior, Private Gang... it is *not* suitable for a re-education officer... and I swear to the Great General, if it happens again, you *will* be punished... severely! Is that understood?"

"Yes, Sir... I understand, Sir!" Sweat dripped down into Chul's eyes, making him blink even more.

"For your sake, I'd better hope so," General Roh grunted. "Dismissed!"

Chul saluted again, then quickly turned around and half-ran down the corridor on unsteady legs.

I threw a glance at Colonel Wan as I passed him. His smile was gone, and in its place were a pair of furious glaring eyes, silently screaming, '*Just you wait, little girl... this isn't over!*'

I lowered my head and narrowed my shoulders and hurried into General Roh's office, away from Colonel Wan's murderous glare.

"Oh, and Colonel... come to my office after I finish with this," General Roh suddenly remembered. "There is something I need you to do for me."

"Yes, Sir," Colonel Wan replied, failing to hide the venomous tone in his voice, as General Roh closed the door behind us.

He sat down in his leather armchair, muttering something about that boy being such a disappointment - I assumed he was talking about Chul - and I sat down in the chair in front of the *Demon of Yodok* - the man who would set me free.

I took a couple of deep breaths to calm myself, but same as last time, I couldn't read his face, and that made me more nervous. Also, looking at his silvery ghost eye gave me a chill. I hoped he didn't notice.

As General Roh gathered a couple of documents and put them on the side of his desk, I threw a glance at the back of the picture frame that still was on his desk, knowing that my mother's young smiling face was on the other side. I had to forcefully fight back my curiosity.

There can be no distractions… there's only one reason why I'm here!

Once his desk was in order, General Roh joined his hands on top of it and looked at me with stern eyes.

"First of all, Miss Kim… you will never come to see me in this way again. We have rules to follow… and getting one of our *weaker* re-education officers to help you break them, doesn't mean you're not breaking them. Do I make myself clear?"

"Yes, Sir," I said in a fierce internal battle to keep my voice steady. "I'm very sorry, Sir!"

"Good," he said in a cold tone. "So then… this will not take long, Miss Kim." My anxiety reached a previously unprecedented level as General Roh took a file from a pile on his desk and opened it. "I have looked into your case… as well as your father's," he said, and there was a hint of repulsion at the mentioning of Young Il.

I swallowed, and once again an intense pain shot through my swollen throat.

"What I found was that your father's crimes are very severe," he looked up from the file. "Both the ones he confessed to, which are here in this file… but also the ones he has *not* been convicted for, which I learned from my contacts in the Capital."

"Sir?"

My mind was in a state of complete turmoil. I couldn't understand what he was saying… I just knew it was bad.

"I want to thank you, Miss Kim," he leaned back into his armchair without breaking eye contact. "I want to thank you for bringing this to my attention. I'm ashamed to admit I had no idea who I've had right under my nose this past couple of weeks." He shook his head. "Or maybe… that information was *purposely* kept from me, like it sometimes is with Capital hotshots like your father. Either way, it doesn't matter… now, I *do* know who he is… and what he has done."

I struggled to understand as the panic quickly spread throughout my body.

"W-what has he done?" I asked without being sure I wanted to know the answer. This time there was nothing I could do to prevent my voice from trembling.

General Roh leaned over and looked in Young Il's file again.

"Well… in his written confession he admits to *colluding with foreign enemies to undermine the sovereignty of the Democratic People's Republic of Choson*, and for *planning to overthrow the Great General and the Workers Party of Choson together with the illegitimate puppet government in the annexed southern part of our country*." He looked up at me again. "This is all pretty straight forward treasonous behavior… we get people like this from all over the country every single day."

He closed the file and put it back in the pile.

"So that is what he has been convicted for. But that is *nothing* compared to the crimes he has *not* been convicted of… the crimes that ended the lives of millions of our fellow countrymen… the crimes he did to the people of Hamhung."

My heart all but stopped. I opened my mouth, but no sounds came out.

"It truly is beyond me," General Roh continued, "how a traitor of this magnitude ended up in a *re-education* camp, and not in one of the total control camps. I can only gather he must still have friends in high places looking out for him... which actually wouldn't surprise me... a lot of that was going on back when I worked in the Capital as well. Whichever way it is... it's not for me to judge. If our justice system has put him here... then *here* is where he will atone for his crimes."

"I... I... I don't know what to say, Sir," I stuttered. "W-what does this mean?"

"It means you did good bringing this to my attention, Miss Kim. I'm grateful... and that's why I agreed to see you now." His otherwise neutral face gained just a hint of compassion as he continued. "And... I truly am sorry to have to convey to you this unpleasant information about your father, Miss Kim... it brings me no pleasure whatsoever. It's a sad fact that all-too-many sons and daughters of our otherwise wonderful country live large parts of their lives blissfully unaware of the heinous crimes of their mothers and fathers... and it's always a horrible shock when the truth surfaces."

I took a couple of deep breaths in an attempt to regain some control over my mind and body. I could feel the moment - and my life - slipping away.

"Sir... did you manage to get hold of the Ministry of Physical Culture and Sports?"

"No," General Roh answered flatly. "In other circumstances, I might have been able to slightly bend the rules, but with your father being such a high profile traitor as he is, releasing any member of his family is simply not an option... even though I personally would have preferred to see you reach your potential as a national gymnast and bring honor to Choson. But like I said, it's out of my hands."

The room fell into a dead silence. I noticed that my hands were clenching like claws around the sides of the chair, but they didn't feel like my hands. In fact, it felt like I was somewhere outside of my body... like this wasn't really happening to me. I tried to see if I still had control over my mouth. I did - but my voice sounded hollow... like it wasn't mine at all.

"So... you are not sending me back to the Capital?" I heard myself ask.

The plainness of my question made it sound almost absurd.

"Correct, Miss Kim. You will have to stay here for the duration of your sentence with your family. But like I said... you should consider yourself lucky... considering the magnitude of your father's crimes, it's nothing short of a miracle that you're here... and therefore you will have the possibility to re-join society while you're still relatively young. It could have been significantly worse."

I swallowed painfully again as I felt myself slowly re-entering my body.

"H-how long... is our sentence?"

General Roh opened the file again.

"Twenty years," he read. "So you'll be thirty-four when you get out. That is still young... you will still have a big part of your life ahead of you."

"Twenty years..." I mumbled to myself. "Thirty four years old... all because... all because... because of *him*!"

"I understand you're angry... and resentful... towards your father, Miss Kim," General Roh said calmly. "I understand that all-too-well... but a word of advice... try not to end up alone in here... I can assure you that life here when you're alone is *much* harder... just keep that in mind before you do something you'll regret."

I think I nodded, but I couldn't be sure. My mind and body had become one again, and the tense silence of the room pressed me from all sides. I wanted to plead... to cry... to SCREAM... but it was all over... there was nothing more to be said.

"I'm afraid I have to ask you to leave now, Miss Kim... I have a lot of work to do," General Roh closed my father's file and watched me with an uncomfortable expression. "Work hard... fill your quotas... work on your redemption... and when the time comes, re-join society with your family... I wish you the best of luck."

I nodded and stood up from the chair. I felt lightheaded. As I bowed down, General Roh handed me a note.

"Show this in case you are stopped by anyone on your way back," he said. "And... could you please knock on Colonel Wan's door and ask him to come into my office on your way out? Thank you."

He immediately dove into some other documents he had on his desk and didn't pay any attention to me as I went to the door. Before crossing the threshold, I threw one last glance at the back of the picture frame of my mother. In the corridor, I knocked on the door to the left and told a baffled Colonel Wan that General Roh is waiting for him.

The next moment, I was outside the building.

I managed to contain the tears just until I had left *the Bloodyard*, then I collapsed onto the ground behind some bushes, and the floodgates opened. I sat there sobbing uncontrollably, more tears than I knew I had in my body poured down from my face and dripped onto my lap. I took off my shirt and pressed it against my mouth to prevent any sound from coming out as I silently screamed at the top of my lungs.

My life was over.

A violent stream of thoughts swirled around in my head.

How could this happen? I am a professional gymnast in the Great General's National Gymnastics Team. That is my family - not the people I had no choice but to live with my whole life. And how about those monstrous crimes Young Il had committed? Conspiring with our enemies to overthrow the government? Killing millions of people? Was that the same man who had read Nari and me bedtime stories when we were little?

General Roh's words suddenly hit me like a sledgehammer.

'Many sons and daughters live their whole lives blissfully unaware of the heinous crimes of their fathers.'

I had been one of them - blissfully unaware. My only worry in life had been that my parents only cared about Nari… but what did that matter compared to… *compared to THIS!*

The only explanation was that I had never really known Young Il. None of us had.

He deceived us all!

With increasing force, the reality of my situation dawned upon me. My life as I knew it was over. I would never go back to the Capital. I would never again compete in gymnastics. I would never become a national hero and perform before my Father - the Great General. I would never again drink pomegranate liquor by the river with Su Mi. From now on and forever, I would be one thing, and one thing only - the daughter of a traitor and a murderer.

Young Il has destroyed my life… he has destroyed everything!

The hatred I now felt growing in my chest was deeper and stronger than anything I had ever felt before in my life. My tears dried up. I stood up and brushed the dirt off my clothes. I took out the Great General pin from my pocket and squeezed it hard in my hand.

As I walked home past Doctor Death's rundown hospital on my way back to our house, I had only one thought in mind.

Young Il is not my father - he is my *enemy!*

CHAPTER 27

By the time I reached our house, I was completely consumed by rage and fury. I smashed the door open, making Nari, mom, and Young Il almost drop the dinner bowls in their hands. I slammed the door shut behind me and stood there in front of them, panting, with what felt like fire coming out of my eyes. They looked up at me with their mouths and eyes wide open.

"Where have you been?" mom asked nervously.

"I went to see General Roh," I panted.

This time Sun Hee actually dropped her wooden bowl on the ground.

"YOU DID WHAT?" she gasped. "Again? What in the Great General's name were you thinking, Areum? I told you not to—"

"He told me what you did," I glared at Young Il, my voice trembling with fury.

Nari and mom also turned their eyes to him.

"What are you—?" mom started.

"He told me about your crimes," I wheezed through my swollen throat. "He told me *everything*... not only about the crimes you confessed to... but about the other crimes... that you personally have the blood of *millions of people* on your hands."

My breathing was so fast and shallow I didn't feel like I was getting any air. Young Il first looked at me with his mouth open, then looked down at the ground.

"You don't understand, Areum-ah…" he sighed. He sounded tired more than anything else.

"I don't understand what? That you've been a *traitor* this whole time? That you're a *coldblooded murderer*? That you're… you're nothing but a monster… pretending to be our father? WHAT DON'T I UNDERSTAND?"

Nari and mom shifted their eyes away from me and looked at Young Il.

"Dad? What is she talking about?" Nari asked in a whisper.

"She's talking nonsense," mom retorted. "None of that is true. And I *forbid* you to talk to your father like that, Areum!"

"You *forbid* me to talk to him like that?" I scoffed. "But why didn't you forbid *him* from ruining *my life*? And your life? And Nari's life? Or… or… or were you in on it? Did you know about this, mom? D-did you… did you even help him to commit these crimes?"

"ENOUGH!" Sun Hee pounded her fist against the floor. "You will stop this right now, Areum!"

"NO… I WON'T STOP," I screamed. "Not until he admits what he did."

"He didn't do *anything*… he was *framed*," mom squeezed out through her tightly pressed together teeth.

Nari watched the two of us. Her eyes were tearing up.

"Areum-ah," Young Il pleaded softly. "I… I *have* done some horrible things… some things that I wish I could undo. But… it's not as black and white as General Roh makes it out to be. Everything I did, I did… for *Nari*… I needed to… save her life… and the regime would have done something like that anyway… or *worse*… I… I just needed to save my family. And… and… the situation was very dire… difficult decisions had to be made…

so I made them... for all of us... but I still thought there would be time to save them..."

"Dad," Nari sobbed. "W-what are you talking about? Is... is what Areum is talking about... true?"

"*No!*" mom answered firmly. "Your father worked in the Ministry of Food Distribution. It's a difficult job with a lot of responsibility... and sometimes you have to make difficult decisions that are good for the majority, even if it affects some people negatively. Everyone has to do their part for the greater good... that is what the Great General and Juche teaches us... and that does *not* make him a traitor... it's just that you girls don't understand... for so long, his guilt for what he did to save you, Nari, has been eating him up from the inside... and that's why he did this... this... *stupid thing* against the Workers Party lines... which is why they sent him here... but you must understand... he hasn't done anything wrong—"

I scoffed.

"General Roh said he has the blood of *millions of people* on his hands... how is that for *the greater good*? How is that what Juche teaches us?"

"That blood is not on your father's hands!" mom's was scarlet red. "Now you stop with this nonsense, Areum. Your father is the *victim* here... and you are his *daughter*... I demand that you show him respect!"

"I don't believe you, mom," I shook my head. "And why don't I hear it directly from him?"

Young Il looked up at me with sorrowful eyes and sighed deeply.

"Areum-ah... I'm not going to lie to you... I was indeed part of a decision that... that caused a lot of people to die... but you must believe me, I didn't want to be part of it... I wanted to stop it. But I couldn't... there was no other way—"

307

"Young Il… stop talking!" mom commanded. "You don't have to defend carrying out your duties at the Ministry of Food Distribution. You did your job best you could… end of story."

"IT'S *NOT* END OF STORY!" I shrieked. "He just confessed to being part of it… he didn't prevent it—"

"First of all… lower your voice, Areum!" mom snapped. "Second of all… there are things about adult life and adult responsibilities that you just don't understand. But regardless, this discussion ends now. Young Il is your father, and it's your duty as his daughter to respect him… and to believe in him… and to defend him. So sit down, eat your food, and do your daughterly duty!"

The tense silence that filled the room was only interrupted by the soft crackling of the fire.

"I'm *not* his daughter." This time my voice was calm and controlled. "And… I'm not *your* daughter either. And I'm also not your sister," I threw a glance at Nari. "The three of you are not my family… the three of you are the cause of everything bad that has ever happened to me in my life. Nothing more. And now, by dragging me down with you to pay for the crimes you've committed… you've finally managed to ruin my life once and for all."

I glared at the three rotten traitors in front of me with a burning intensity.

"I hate you," I whispered. "I hate you all. Do you hear me? I hate you *all*! You are not my family, and… and… I WILL NEVER TALK TO YOU AGAIN!"

With my heart pounding through my chest I was ready for mom to get up and slap my face and demand respect, but nobody moved. They just stared at me, stunned.

"Areum-ah," Nari broke the silence softly. "I know you're angry, but please… we *are* your family… we *love* you… we *need* you. Please… don't turn away from us!"

I shook my head. Then I took my bowl of rice and my chopsticks and sat in the corner of the room, facing the wall… away from *them*.

"Areum-ah—" mom started, but Young Il interrupted her.

"Let her be," he said quietly. "Just give her time. It's a lot for her to deal with. She'll come around… just give her some time."

No, I won't… not in a million years, I thought to myself.

My mind was made up. I might be forced to live with these traitors here in this hellhole, but no one can force me to talk to them.

And I won't! Never again!

To my surprise, as I was halfway through my bowl of rice and corn, I noticed I actually felt better - it was like a weight had been lifted from my shoulders. Ironically, the feeling was very similar to when I had gotten the results of the gymnastics trials… which felt like an eternity ago. Kyung Sook's broken leg suddenly flashed before my eyes. I thought of the lengths I had gone to - the lengths I had made Su Mi go to - in order to get away from my family… but it had all been for nothing. Everything had been taken away from me.

But at least now I can stop pretending to be part of this family.

CHAPTER 28

At night, I lay on my quilt listening to Young Il's snoring and Sun Hee's deep breathing. I was not surprised they didn't have any problem falling asleep. After all - it had just been yet another one of Areum's tantrums. Nari, however, seemed to be awake. I had the distinct feeling she wanted to talk to me - maybe it was our twin connection letting me know - but I was glad she didn't try.

I was still trying to wrap my head around my situation. I had unknowingly been living with a family of traitors… *for how long? How did I end up here?*

As I lay wide awake with a painful pressure on my chest - my hand clenched around the Great General pin Nari had given me - I remembered that clear summer day back in the Capital three years ago… the day I thought everything was going to change for me… the day I for one fleeting moment had regained hope of being part of this family.

That day, even before she walked through the door, I was happy beyond words. From now on, I wouldn't be alone anymore. From now on, my life would have more purpose than being the one who takes care of the chores. Of course, I was happy for Nari as well. After all - she was my little sister, and it was an incredible relief that she finally, after all these years, was no longer constantly on the brink of death. But I couldn't help but feel the happiest for myself. During the eleven years of fighting for her life, our parents didn't have enough love for both of us - their sick child required all of it. Now, that was about to change. Now, Nari would have to *share*.

For as long as I could remember, the only thing anybody ever talked to me about was how tough it must be for my little sister to live with her heart condition, never knowing if she would make it to our next birthday. Not once did anyone ever ask how tough it was for *me*... how much *I* was struggling... how much *I* was suffering.

With my sister needing all that extra attention and care, not only did I not get any attention - *I* was expected to help my parents take care of *her*... and the house... and all the chores... and the shopping... and even my parents when they didn't have more energy to take care of themselves.

A congenital heart defect is what they called it - the thing that shaped my childhood. I remembered all the doctors she had to go to... all the medicines she had to take... all the nights she cried because she was afraid she wasn't going to wake up the next morning. And all of her fits, or when she spent the whole day in the toilet, vomiting. I remembered my parents trying not to cry in front of her, trying to be strong for her, but most of the time failing and breaking down crying by her bed. And I remembered myself, all alone, with what felt like a huge rock pressing down on my chest so hard I could barely breathe.

Now, I stood in the hallway of our apartment, waiting for Nari to come home from the hospital. The huge rock on my chest was gone. I felt... *hope*.

Suddenly, the door opened. Young Il entered first, and after him - Nari. I hardly recognized my little sister. Her face was different. It looked... *healthy*. And it had an expression I didn't recognize on her. It looked like happiness, disbelief, and wonder, all mixed in one, and as she saw us, tears of joy started running down her cheeks from under her glasses. Dad stood beside her with a glowing smile on his face.

"What did they say?" mom asked, barely able to control herself.

"She's healthy!" dad exclaimed triumphantly. "According to the last test, she has made a complete recovery. The surgery exceeded all expectations. She's completely healthy."

I felt my heart skip a beat and a warm pleasant feeling spreading from my chest throughout my body.

"She will, of course, continue to go for regular check-ups," dad added, "but she doesn't need to take her medicines anymore. The doctors said she'll be able to lead a perfectly normal life from now on."

Mom could not contain herself any longer. Tears poured from her eyes and she shook from top to toe. She rushed to embrace Nari, who was still standing halfway through the doorway.

"My baby! My baby girl!" she cried, tightening her grip around her.

I hesitated, not sure how to react. But not doing anything made me feel even more uneasy, so I took some unsure steps forward. Nari noticed me and extended her arm, so I joined the hug, putting one arm around my mother and one around Nari.

At first, I felt very strange - I couldn't remember the last time I had even touched either of them - but now I was tightly pressed against their skin and clothes, feeling the lingering kimchi smell on their breaths. But it only felt strange for a moment - then it felt like we had been doing it every day of my entire life. With both mom and Nari in my arms, both shivering from tears, and then dad joining in with his long strong arms reaching around all of us, I melted away and disappeared into blissful family love. I felt a weird tension around my mouth and guessed that I must have been smiling.

"Nari... I'm so happy!" I whispered into her ear.

"Thank you, big sister!"

I opened my mouth again, but no more words came out. And it was okay - no more words were needed.

The following days we lived in a state of euphoria. Everybody was so happy and carefree, just talking and laughing and spending time together. We even ate meat with the rice for dinner several days in a row, which was a first for me. The tension that had been constantly present for as long as I could remember had vanished. Slowly, slowly I felt this newfound happiness spreading its roots throughout my body, but at the same time, I couldn't manage to make my heart irreversibly convinced that things had actually changed.

That Saturday, my parents arranged a party in our apartment to celebrate. Family, friends and neighbors were there, of course, but also many of my dad's colleagues from the Ministry of Food Distribution. The tables were filled with plates of different snack foods and expensive-looking bottles of rice wine that I had never seen in our home before. All in honor of Nari and her now healthy heart.

I helped mom carry around the snack trays and bottles to refill drinks, like I had done on the other few occasions when my parents had thrown house parties in our apartment. Everybody commented to me how happy they were that the surgery had gone well and how nice it must be for me to finally have my little sister healthy. I smiled, nodded, thanked them for their kind words, and repeated over and over that I indeed was extremely happy my sister was finally healthy. I also sneaked some snacks from the tray for myself when no one was watching.

After a few hours, when the sound level of the chatter and laugher had reached its peak level, and our kitchen had filled up with empty rice wine bottles, dad tapped his glass, calling everybody's attention. Our guests formed a circle around him and Nari in the middle of the living room. I smiled at Nari, who was blushing from being in the spotlight.

"Everybody… thank you so much for coming today. As you know… thanks to the good grace of our Father - the Great General - the eternal ruler and guardian of Choson and protector of our children and grandchildren long after we are all gone - our beloved daughter Nari has been given a *future*… and I have no doubt her future will shine as bright as the eternal Flame of Juche that guides us all as we relentlessly continue to build the revolution under the wise leadership of the Great General. Our precious Nari has now been given the honor to serve the revolution until the end of her days… which, I hope, will be at a very old age."

There were sporadic chuckles around the room, and dad smiled as well, but the trembling in his voice gave away how deeply moved he was, despite the formalized wording of his speech.

"Nari… you, our beloved daughter, are an exceptionally intelligent and sweet girl… now complete, with a healthy heart… you truly bring us such joy. Without you, I… or we" - he pointed at mom, who stood in the door to the hallway, her face wet from joyous tears - "we could probably not go on living. That is the truth. You mean everything to us. We love you!"

He opened his arms, and Nari, tears running down her cheeks, threw herself into them. The room erupted in applause. Mom then came over and put her arms around both of them, and another wave of applause and cheering - this time even stronger than before - ensued. People around me cried and blew their noses.

I stood on the side, still with the snack tray in my hands, not sure what to do. I felt something strange in my chest. I felt like I needed to go up there and join them, so I looked for a place to put the tray, but before I had time to move, the hug was over and dad raised his glass.

"To our Father - the Great General!" he cheered. "We thank you most humbly for allowing us to continue being a family."

"To our Father - the Great General!" everybody cheered in chorus.

The moment was over, and the circle dispersed back into small groups. As the chatter again filled the room, mom found me and called me into the kitchen to help her serve some more food.

The feeling in my chest had grown and expanded into my head. All sounds and movements around me became muffled and I felt dizzy. I passed dad on my way to the kitchen, but he didn't notice me - he was praising Nari's fantastic intellect to a couple of his colleagues - to Nari's visible discomfort - bragging about how she can recite every text the Great General has ever written by heart.

"You look so pale," mom told me when I entered the kitchen. "You should pinch your cheeks or something... there are many important people out there... people your dad depend on to implement his big plans... everything has to be perfect..."

"Yes, mom," I started mechanically pinching my cheeks. It was painful, but it actually helped to distract me from the pain I was feeling in my heart.

"Here," mom gave me a new tray full of snacks. "Go give them your best smile!" She got an identical tray for herself and rushed out of the kitchen.

For a moment, I stood frozen in the middle of the kitchen. I could hardly breathe. I couldn't completely grasp what had happened and why I was feeling this way. I just stood there with an intense pain in my heart.

"Areum… hurry up… what are you waiting for?" mom shouted at me through the doorway.

My paralysis broke and I began to recover my breath. The pain in my chest also decreased. But instead, thoughts emerged into my head.

How could I have been so naive? How could I have thought that things would change… that I would suddenly take my place next to Nari and be loved equally? How could I have been so stupid?

I hurried out of the kitchen, and with a fake smile plastered on my dying face, I walked - almost ran - around the apartment, forcing my snacks onto anyone I laid eyes on until my tray was empty. I hid the tray behind a sofa and then sneaked off to my bedroom - which tonight served as coat room for the guests - as quickly and discreetly as I could. I felt light-headed, so I hurried to close the door and then crashed onto my bed behind a big pile of summer coats and jackets. I don't know how long I stayed there, maybe hours - I had lost all perception of time. All that existed were the thoughts consuming my mind.

How many times will you let them do this to you, Areum? I asked myself. *How many times will you let them get your hopes up just to crush them again?*

Then and there, behind that tall pile of clothes, I made a decision.

No more! I will never let them get my hopes up again! They will never treat me like they treat Nari… and I'm done trying to gain their love! I'm done trying to be part of this family.

The last thing I remember from that night was the pain in my chest growing tighter and tighter before the exhaustion sent me off to sleep. Like in a dream, I heard people making comments about me as they picked up their coats and jackets and got ready to leave. Then I felt somebody tucking me in once the bed was empty of clothes.

When I woke up the next day, I saw the world with new eyes, and the place I had woken up in was no longer my home. This time I knew - it was time to look for a new family!

That night, three years ago, the exhaustion from sadness and sorrow had put me to sleep. This night, locked up in this moldy house in a faraway prison camp high up in the mountains, anger was keeping me awake.

It was clear now that my so-called father had deceived me all these years, and because of our blood connection, I was forced to stay here and pay for his crimes. My dream of leaving this family for my new one and becoming a star gymnast had crumbled. My destiny was now to rot away in this hell on earth, from where there was no escape. And even if I against all odds survived our twenty-year sentence… what kind of life would I return to if I was branded forever as a traitor? My Regime Loyalty Classification Level would be so low I wouldn't even be able to get a job cleaning toilets.

I pictured my adult self - ten or fifteen years from now - working the fields outside the *Village of the Strayed*, permanently hunched over, more dead than alive. At the next moment, the insane face of Lucky appeared before me in my mind and I shuddered.

As I pressed my eyes together and shook my head to rid myself of those horrible images, my thought from just now revisited my mind.

'My destiny is now to rot away in this hell on earth, from where there is no escape.'

… No escape…

But that's not true… Lucky managed to do it! Jun Ha told us so. That means it is possible… just very difficult!

With resolve, I took out the Great General pin from under my pillow and clenched it in my fist.

When have I ever shied away from things because they are difficult? If a nobody like Lucky could do it and get caught… shouldn't an elite gymnast be able to do it 'without' getting caught? That's not only reasonable… it's even quite probable!

My resolve, however, didn't last long and was shortly replaced by two other all-too-familiar feelings - fear and self-doubt.

Can I really do it? What happens if I fail? Am I willing to be tortured in the Center of Truth and then be tied up to one of the poles in the Bloodyard? And what will happen to my family if I succeed? I mean… I can't take them with me… they don't deserve to come with me. But… am I willing to get them sent to the Center of Truth? I would break rule number one - Do not try to escape, but they would surely be accused of breaking rule number five - Report all and any suspicious behavior. Nobody will believe they didn't know about my plans. I felt like my body and soul were being torn in half. I do hate them, but… could I live with that? With potentially causing their deaths? Especially Nari… because after all, she's just as innocent as me.

I lay there on my rock-hard quilt with my eyes wide open, staring up into the pitch-black ceiling. The enormous pressure on my chest and lungs was back. It was difficult to breathe, and I felt completely alone. I had an overwhelming urge to talk to someone - to talk to Su Mi - but I knew there was no one here who would understand me… that would help me in my struggle.

Stay, and likely die an excruciating death… or try to escape, and likely die an excruciating death - are those really the only options I have to choose from?

With those two equally life-ending alternatives balancing up and down on a giant scale in front of me in the darkness, I finally drifted off to sleep… and again ended up on the corpse-covered street with pitch-black crows soaring above me.

I didn't know how or why, but there was no doubt left in my mind about where this dream was taking me.

It was taking me to Hamhung.

CHAPTER 29

I stayed strong the following morning. I didn't talk to any of my former family members - I didn't even make eye contact - and they kept to their strategy of giving me the time and space I needed. I don't think it mattered too much to Young Il and Sun Hee, but it was tough on Nari - I could tell. But I was too angry to feel guilty about it.

Since today was Sunday, there was no school. Instead, for the first time we had a full day's work ahead of us, and then a mandatory self-criticism session at night. Chul came over early in the morning to take Nari and me to the rice fields. Summer seemed to be coming late this year - or maybe it was because we were so high up - so we had been told the transplantation of the rice seedlings wouldn't start for another couple of weeks. That meant the seedlings remain in the heavily guarded tent full of seedbeds close to the guardhouse, into which only a few trusted prisoners were allowed to enter.

It turned out to be a long and exhausting day, and while I was walking around in the muddy - but still not irrigated - fields with my back bent over removing weeds and rocks, or helping to till the soil, I realized we indeed had been spared the hardest work when our whole school was sent out for the rice sowing day every spring. I guess we really were privileged kids from the Capital, just like everybody here was calling us. But even if I wasn't used to this kind of work, my body was in good shape and adapted quickly. It was worse for Nari, who had spent most of her life in a hospital bed - or her own bed - buried under a book. I could see her panting and sweating on the other side of the field next to Mina, all the time straightening her aching back with a painful expression on her face. Come to think of it, Nari had always been too sick to join in the rice sowing days, so this must have been the first time she ever set foot in an actual rice paddy. Even though I worried if she - and her now supposedly healthy heart - would make it the whole day, a part of me was smiling with glee. That brought shame into the mix of emotions swirling around in my body.

Around midday, it was finally time for the lunch break. I was exhausted and experienced an intense thirst. During the past hour, I had been seriously tempted to scoop up a handful of watery mud and put it in my mouth just to get something humid into my throat, which by now felt like it was full of dry sand. The whole morning I cursed myself for not finishing the cup of barley tea I had with breakfast.

That will never happen again!

As I lined up to get my daily ration of cabbage soup, I suddenly noticed a burning pain in my shoulders. Looking down, I saw they were intensely red from sunburn. For being the end of May it was still not very hot, but my skin was not used to being exposed to the sun for such long periods, and I had made the mistake of putting on a skirt and a short-sleeved shirt this morning - which would have been the normal attire for this kind of weather if I were back in the Capital - but was the most inappropriate choice possible for this kind of work. But I was still glad schoolchildren were not given the normal prisoner uniforms… at least I could keep my dignity for a few more months.

As soon as I got the soup bowl in my hands, I started gulping down the lukewarm liquid, dissipating the dry sand in my throat. It was divine - I could swear that it was the most delicious thing that had ever passed my lips. Even the slimy cabbage slipped down without notice.

After my bowl was finished, I was still dying from thirst. I looked around me with wild eyes to find any other source of water. The river was there in the distance, but there was no way I could make it there and back in time. I looked over at Nari, who was sitting crouching down with her head buried in her arms in the shadow of a tree by the field. Mina, So Won and Min Ji sat next to her, looking at her worriedly.

How is she going to make it six more hours?

In the end, however, I barely had enough energy to worry about myself. I sat down in the shade of another tree, closed my eyes, and started taking deep breaths to gather my strength. I breathed through my nose to avoid drying out my mouth even further.

"Hey!"

The sudden voice startled me and I opened my eyes to see Jun Ha sitting beside me.

"How are you holding up?"

"Not so good," I replied in brutal honesty. "Please tell me they will give us more to drink."

"Usually they only give water rations until summer starts in June… but it is getting hotter, so maybe we'll get lucky."

"I really hope so… I don't think I'll last the whole day otherwise."

"I hear you," he nodded, looking down at the ground. "By the way… I just wanted to thank you for what you did the other day. You're brave… and *strong*!"

"Don't mention it," I chuckled. "I guess I'm your girl when you have crazy people attacking you. You can hire me as your bodyguard... will only cost you a glass of water."

Jun Ha laughed, but just then our group leader - another prisoner with a fierce-looking face - called us back to work. I felt ready to lie down and die on the spot, but somehow I managed to get up on my feet and continued working. More surprisingly - Nari managed to do the same.

About an hour later, Chul appeared with a couple of prisoners carrying a large barrel.

Could it be...? Please let it be...!

The group leader called for a break, and when people started lining up to Chul and the barrel, all doubt was gone - it *was* an extra water ration that had come to save the day.

The wait was eternal, but as I got my tin bowl filled to the brim with fresh cold water, I felt nothing but pure love for Chul... he was my savior. He could read my feelings and smiled at me with his kind face. I immediately put the bowl to my lips and let the elixir of life wash through my body, bringing me back from the dead. I drank half of it in one go but then took the rest back to the shadow of the tree. I wanted to make it last - to savor every drop.

That one cup of water made all the difference and the rest of the afternoon went much easier. It also helped that the sun was now covered by a constant layer of cotton-white clouds, allowing my head and painfully burned shoulders to cool down.

To my relief, the water had the same effect on Nari, and she no longer looked like she would collapse at any moment. My worry did, however, not make me change my decision. Nari came over and tried to talk to me a few times during the afternoon, but I remained firm and walked away from her without saying a single word. I kept my distance, working in a different part of the field, but I continuously threw glances at her to make sure she was alright.

When the sun started to slowly set behind the mountains, Chul came to inform us that the workday would end early and all prisoners must assemble in the courtyard by *the Oversight*, to where I already felt like a frequent visitor. The mandatory Sunday self-criticism session would be postponed until after the courtyard meeting.

I was relieved to finish work early - before my body broke down - but the other prisoners didn't seem equally happy, so I guessed we had another long, boring speech to endure ahead of us. On the way there I made sure to stay closely behind Nari to make sure she was okay.

When we entered the enormous courtyard - or *the Bloodyard*, as I already had gotten used to calling it - I joined the other prisoners in forming a circle facing the concrete wall in the middle. Our workgroup was one of the first to arrive, but soon, the entire prison population was crowding behind and around me.

It turned out to be a long wait, especially since my feet were aching and the pain in my shoulders from the sunburn was pulsating. There were plenty of armed guards, but none of the officers had come yet, so all we had to look at in front of us was the naked wall, the four poles sticking up from the little stage in front of it with two guards leaning against them, smoking and talking. I could feel tension in the crowd. Some people were fidgeting, but most stood in silence with grim expressions on their faces.

By the time I started to feel that my feet couldn't hold me any longer, the crowd to the left of the concrete wall parted to let some more guards through. They were dragging something. At first, I couldn't make out what it was, but when I did - my heart froze to ice. Squirming in futile resistance, two people were being dragged across the ground, one guard on each side holding their arms. Both of them had their hands and legs tied, so they couldn't walk by themselves. Over their heads they had gray cloth bags with stains that I was almost certain was from blood.

What is going on?

As they reached the center of *the Bloodyard*, the guards dragged them up on the little stage, lifted them to their feet, and tied them to the wooden poles with a thick rope, first around the chest, then around the waist. Lastly, they removed the bags from their heads and tied the final rope over their foreheads.

The crowd gasped, and I gasped with them. In front of us was a girl - she couldn't be much older than twenty - and a man in his thirties. I started feeling sick to my stomach from the sight of them. Both of their faces were severely bruised and swollen with dry clots of blood around their lips and eyes. The skin on their bare arms looked uneven, like it had been burnt. On their hands and shoeless feet, I could see some fingers and toes were missing. From the ones remaining, the nails had been pulled out - just like Young Il's. Considering their condition, I was surprised they were still conscious. The man looked decoupled from the situation he was in - his eyes were absent - but the girl was crying and whimpering. I felt her pain in my chest. I wanted to look away - the scene making me nauseous - but I was completely mesmerized.

Is this what I think it is? Are they going to…?

I looked around the crowd for any indication that I was wrong, but found nothing but grim faces looking straight forward or down at the ground in front of them. I felt panic creeping through my paralyzed body.

I don't want to be here! I don't want to see this!

I looked around me for an opening, but the dense crowd of grim-faced prisoners had closed off any escape path. I was stuck. But of course, I knew I couldn't leave either way. At this moment, I didn't care about my anger and resentment against anyone. I looked over at where I last had seen Nari and Mina, but they had disappeared into the crowd. I started looking for other familiar faces in the crowd - Young Il, Sun Hee… or even Miss Ae - but all I could see was a sea of strangers.

The crowd parted once more and General Roh and Colonel Wan emerged in front of the tied-up prisoners together with some other officers. After them came a group of eight guards who lined up right in front of us, facing the prisoners in attention with rifles at their feet. Both Chul and Chang Min were among them. I could tell that Chul shivered slightly. Chang Min looked calm as always, but it was unusual to see him with a serious face and without a cigarette in his mouth.

General Roh took a step forward with a grim look on his face. I noticed him giving Chul a brief disappointed look before letting his gaze sweep over the huge crowd before him. I looked over at Colonel Wan who stood behind General Roh with his usual malicious smile, and as our eyes met for just a split second, his smile expanded. I looked away immediately as a chill down my spine made me shudder. My body tried to mechanically take a step back, but all it resulted in was me stepping on the foot of the person behind me.

General Roh raised his hand and *the Bloodyard* went silent.

"Today is a sad day," he spoke solemnly. "But today is also an important day. Today is a day of learning."

CHAPTER 30

General Roh paused and let his gaze sweep over us.

"You are all here because you are guilty of crimes against our eternal Father - the Great General - and the Regime… because you have strayed from the righteous path, for which you need to be re-educated. That is why *you* are here. That is also why *we* are here… our task is to make sure that once you return to society, you no longer pose a threat and will do no more harm to your fellow countrymen."

His silvery ghost eye swept past me as he made another pause, sending another chill down my spine.

"However, we cannot help you if you can't even follow the very simple rules that are put in place for everybody's benefit… and for your re-education to work. You all know these rules by heart… no one can claim to have broken them due to ignorance."

He took a couple of steps back until he stood right next to the tied-up prisoners.

"These two prisoners broke the rules… *knowingly*. For that, they will pay the ultimate price." He pointed at the absent-looking man. "Prisoner Ku Seung Gi here broke the first and most important rule of all - *Do not try to escape!* For that, he will be executed." He pointed at the sobbing girl one pole away. "Prisoner Ra Namjoo over there was caught stealing food. Doing so she broke rule number three. For that she will be executed."

General Roh took a step forward from the doomed prisoners.

"Now… you must believe me when I say I take no pleasure in doing this… but it is a necessary lesson for the rest of you. We are here for your sake… but if you don't do your part… if you don't follow these simple rules, then we are just wasting our time and effort trying to re-educate you… and there will never be a place for you outside these walls."

General Roh walked over to the other officers on the side of the half-circle and nodded at Colonel Wan, who took the stage. Unlike the grim look of General Roh, he looked like he was enjoying every second of this.

"Indeed… this is a day of learning," he said. "You must learn to follow the Sacred Rules. *All* of them… *all* the time… *without* exception. You may think we're blind… that we're not aware of all the rule breaking that goes on here in our camp… or that we have gone *soft* because you no longer see that many executions, and gather you can get away with it. If that is what you are thinking, I have a message for you - *all that stops today!* There will be no more leniency. There will be no more looking through our fingers. You *will* fill your quotas and you *will* follow the rules. Do those two things and we will get along. Don't… and you will face the consequences."

Colonel Wan walked over to the side of the firing squad. The man, Ku Seung Gi, was still staring at some point in the distance above the crowd, but the girl, Ra Namjoo, started sobbing louder and her pleading for her life transformed from inaudible mumbling into heart-breaking screams, and with the utter silence of the crowd, it was now the only thing that could be heard.

"Please! Please don't do it! Please... I didn't steal... I was set up... you have to believe me! Please... I beg you... PLEASE DON'T DO IT! HELP! HEEELP!"

At first, she was met with nothing but silence, but all of a sudden, I heard an agonizing scream - followed by loud sobbing - from somewhere in the crowd on the other side of *the Bloodyard*. It sounded like it came from a girl. My eyes were immediately drawn to the place from where the sobbing originated, but it stopped before I could see who it was, so my attention went back to Colonel Wan. Without acknowledging the singular outburst from the crowd, he lifted his hand to the firing squad.

"ATTENTION!"

The eight guards straightened up and stomped the ground once with each foot.

"Please... *please*... don't do this!" Namjoo pleaded.

"LOAD!"

The guards picked up their rifles, and I could hear the loud clicking and clanking as they loaded the bullets into the chambers and released the safety. I couldn't be completely sure, but they looked just like the Type 58 Assault Rifles they made us shoot last year on a field trip to the artillery regiment to the south of the Capital. I vividly remembered the pain in my shoulder from the kick - it was like being hit with a sledgehammer. Now, the pain I felt was in my heart from the atrocity that played out before me.

"Please… Hana… don't let them do this… PLEASE, HANA… NOOOO!" Namjoo sobbed.

"AIM!"

I looked over at the guards in the firing squad. Chul's rifle was shaking violently, and I could see his face covered in sweat. I noticed General Roh looking at him as well and shaking his head with an expression of deep-seated resentment. Chang Min, on the other hand, looked dead calm, but he was throwing worried glances at Chul.

Namjoo's pleads became louder and unbearably excruciating. Every syllable was like a drill piercing through my temples.

"Please… you can't do this… I'm a member of *the Dragons*… I'M A MEMBER OF THE DRAGONS…*HANA*… PLEASE, SAVE ME!"

"SHOOT!"

I jumped from shock as the eight rifles fired simultaneously. The bullets - except for one that went astray and hit the concrete wall - severed the ropes holding their heads with precision and penetrated their skulls before letting them lifelessly bounce forward over their now motionless chests. Blood sprayed all over the poles and the bare concrete wall behind them, and their already blood-stained shirts were soaked in the blood gushing from the bloody lumps that used to be their heads.

"NOOOOO!"

Again, I heard the desperate screams from the opposite side of *the Bloodyard*, and this time I could clearly see who it was coming from. A tall girl - about the same age as the girl who had just been shot - emerged to the front and cried uncontrollably as she struggled to break free from the grip of the men holding her back. I had the feeling I had seen her before, but I couldn't place her. To my surprise, I noticed no one dared to look at her. I didn't understand why, but my survival instinct kicked in and I quickly averted my eyes as well. With my peripheral vision I could, however, still distinguish that one of the people holding her back put his hand over her mouth and pulled her back into the crowd, making her sobbing and screaming all but fade away.

As I turned back to the bloody scene in front of me, my whole body shaking violently from the adrenaline, Colonel Wan again raised his hand to the firing squad.

"LOAD!"

"AIM!"

"SHOOT!"

I jumped once more at the deafening noise - even though I was somewhat prepared for it this time - and I felt an acute stab of pain in my ears that then transformed into a persistent high-pitched ringing tone. The second round of shots had cut the ropes holding their chests and penetrated their hearts, making their upper bodies bend forward slightly - almost like in a reverent bow - and soaked the rest of their clothes with dark red blood. Once again, one shot had missed the rope and had hit the man's stomach instead. Looking at Chul's violently trembling rifle, it was not difficult to guess who the shot had come from. General Roh also observed him from the side and shook his head. In a weird way, I couldn't help but feel sorry for him. Sure - he wasn't the one facing the firing squad, but I couldn't even begin to imagine how it would feel to be the one who's forced to pull the trigger.

"LOAD!"

"AIM!"

"SHOOT!"

Another flash of pain penetrated my ears before being replaced by the loud ringing tone. The last round severed the final ropes holding their waists, and the blood-soaked bodies fell to the ground in front of the stage with a thump. I felt tears swelling up and an acute pain in my throat. Again, I heard the crying of the girl on the other side. This time I couldn't prevent myself from throwing a cautious glance in that direction. The other prisoners were not holding her back anymore. Instead, she had fallen to her hands and feet where she continued to cry, her long black hair glued to her face. She covered her mouth with a piece of cloth to muffle her sobbing. None of the guards or officers paid her any attention. I couldn't help but wonder why... I had the feeling this would be something one could be punished for. I wondered what her relationship had been with the poor souls on the ground. Was one of them a brother or a sister... or a maybe a friend?

"ATTENTION!" Colonel Wan commanded, making the eight guards stomp the ground and put their rifles along their right leg. He marched back into the middle of the ring, almost stepping on the bloody corpses on the ground. I was afraid he would do something to the crying girl, but he didn't even dignify her with a look. Peering out over the crowd, he smiled. The whole *Bloodyard* was in complete silence. He then crouched down next to Namjoo's bloody corpse.

"Now," he declared in a strong authoritarian voice. "Imagine this is *you*."

He grabbed Namjoo's head by the hair in her neck and lifted it up from the ground for everybody to behold. The entire *Bloodyard* gasped in horror.

"Take a long and hard look at *her*... and then picture in your minds that this is *you*. I want you to *engrave* that image into your brains... I want you to *etch* it into your retinas... so that from now on, whenever you close your eyes, the only thing you will see is your own mutilated bloody corpse lying here in the mud... I want you to see your own brain substance and your own blood splattered all over the poles and the wall." He said this with his unblinking gaze relentlessly sweeping over us from side to side. "This image is my gift to all of you. Now, you will take this image... and you will keep it with you at all times! So whenever you are facing a temptation to break the rules... to escape... to steal food... to not report a fellow prisoner who is doing so... this image will appear in your mind, and you will make the *right choice*!"

With that he thrust Namjoo's face back into the dirt so hard it bounced, and then stood up. A guard rushed over and handed him a cloth to clean the blood off his hands. The sobbing of the girl on the other side again intensified - I gathered it was the executed girl she was crying for - but she didn't move.

"These two traitors," Colonel Wan continued, pacing along the first row of prisoners in the half circle in my direction, "were caught red handed by our heroic guards. And that... makes me *disappointed*. Why? Because... is it likely that a man planned an elaborate escape, and none of you knew? Is it likely that a girl stole food, and none of you saw? It was surly not the first time she did it. For me, that means that *all of you* were accomplices to these crimes… and *all of you* should be shot as well."

There was a loud chorus of gasps as panic spread through the crowd.

"*However*… no one else will be shot," Colonel Wan continued. "Not *today*… not *this time.*"

He came closer and closer to where I was standing, and finally he stopped directly in front of me. My heart pounded through my chest as I intensely looked down at his shiny black leather shoes.

"This time - and this time *only* - we will show you mercy. The only punishment you will get for this collective betrayal… is that all today's food rations are canceled." Another gasp went through the crowd, but this time it was much more restrained. "But *next* time… many more of you will join these two traitors at the poles."

I could feel his vile breath and glaring eyes burn on the top of my head.

"Understood?"

I had the distinct feeling the question was directed specifically at me.

"UNDERSTOOD, SIR," I shouted in chorus with everybody else.

"Good," Colonel Wan said and stepped back into the middle of the circle. I sighed with relief, but my heart was still pounding ferociously.

"Now… before you leave, I suggest you all thank our eternal Father - the Great General - as well as General Roh, for their great mercy."

General Roh hadn't moved a facial muscle this whole time as he gazed out at us with his healthy and his dead silvery ghost eye.

"THANK YOU, ETERNAL FATHER - THE GREAT GENERAL! THANK YOU, GENERAL ROH!" we all chanted.

"That's more like it!" Colonel Wan smiled. "Now, I suggest that you bring this topic to your meetings of ideological struggle, which will commence in one hour. Report to your meeting leader, they will inform you of your time slot. DISMISSED!"

Upon this command, the crowd instantly started moving away from the execution site, and I gladly let myself be swept away with the flow. I didn't know who my meeting leader was, but I figured one hour was enough time to find out. Right now, I just needed to get as far away from this place of death as possible. With my whole body aching, I looked back over my shoulder just long enough to see Chang Min and some other guards bringing over a wooden cart and carelessly throwing the bloody corpses onto it while casually laughing and joking among themselves. Chul was also there, but he was quiet and stood apart from the rest. His body still trembled, same as mine. Just as I turned away, I saw Chang Min putting his arm over his shoulder, like he was trying to comfort him.

Maybe Chul was right… maybe he does have a good side after all.

When I reached the main road, I saw Nari, Sun Hee and Young Il talking to Mina and Mrs. Choy over by the *School of Juche*.

Are they seriously breaking rule number two - 'Do not gather in groups' - immediately after what we have just witnessed?

As they saw me, they stopped talking and just looked at me. I didn't feel anger anymore - all I could feel inside of me was a strange kind of numbness, like my body had reached its limit of shocking impressions for one day… or even for a lifetime.

I knew that given the situation we're in, it's stupid to hold a grudge against my family… especially against my sister. I took a hesitant step towards them… but then stopped.

I… I just can't… I just can't do it…

I swallowed as I tore my eyes away from Nari's, but not before seeing them filling up with sorrow and tears.

It's better to make a clean break… for all of us. They're not my family anymore. None of them are.

I quickly turned around and followed the crowd back to the *Village of the Strayed*.

I felt hollow inside.

Anyway… Nari is better off with Mina… they have always been more like sisters than we ever have.

Just then, my train of thought was interrupted by a strange scene further down the road. I saw a girl running up to a boy and pushing him hard from behind.

"IT WAS YOU! YOU DID THIS!" she screamed to him at the top of her lungs.

The boy - also in his early twenties, tall and muscular, and with hair that looked like a black lion's mane - stumbled, but didn't lose his balance. The other people with him got ready to attack the girl, but the boy held them back. He casually walked over to her and pushed her to the ground with ease. She didn't get up, just stayed there and continued weeping. Some other prisoners also turned around to look at them, but there were no guards around to break them up.

As I got closer, I recognized her - it was the tall girl who had been crying at the execution.

"You… why?" she sobbed. "After everything I have done for you… you didn't have to…"

"It's over, Hana," he said in a calm but stern voice. "It's over… you're out."

"But why…? Why Namjoo? You didn't have to…"

The boy with the black lion's mane put a cigarette in his mouth and lit it with a flip lighter. It was the first time I had seen a prisoner smoking - let alone having a flip lighter in his possession - I had assumed it was only allowed for the guards.

"Both you and I know that I had to do it," he said calmly. "Go home, Hana... it's over... there is no need for you to get hurt as well."

Without waiting for a response, he signaled to his friends and turned left into one of the side roads. The girl stayed on the ground crying. Nobody, including myself, went over to see if she was alright or to help her up. The other bystanders lost interest and continued on their way home, but I couldn't take my eyes off her. It was just such a mesmerizing contrast to see a big and strong girl sit helplessly on the ground, weeping.

All of a sudden, she raised her head, and our eyes interlocked. Her crying stopped in an instant and my heart dropped to my stomach.

"I-I'm sorry..." I mumbled without any chance of her hearing it, and rushed into one of the side roads. Since there was no turning back, I had to follow the same route back to my house as when I went to visit General Roh for the first time, cutting myself on the leftover barbed wire in the narrow pathways between the barracks and the wall.

As soon as I was safely home and could close the door to the horrible outside world behind me, I collapsed onto my quilt in our still empty room. My insides hurt and I felt like a rug had been pulled away from under my feet.

Did I really just witness two people being brutally slaughtered? Did that actually happen?

There was also something about that crying girl that I couldn't get out of my head. Something about her eyes... something about the way she looked at me.

I still couldn't decide if I had seen her before, but I had the distinct feeling I hadn't seen her for the last time.

CHAPTER 31

The others arrived home not long after me. Only Nari made a shy attempt to greet me, but I didn't answer. I lay down on my quilt facing the wall.

"Areum-ah," I heard Nari's sad voice behind me. "You don't have to talk to me, but... I found out who our meeting leader for the self-criticism session is. It's Corporal Lee... he will come and get us shortly. It's only the two of us... mom and dad are in a different group."

"Okay," I said flatly without turning around.

Of course we got the most arrogant guard in the camp as our leader!

This was, by the way, not an abandonment of my vow never to speak to my family again - but a few temporary exceptions were sometimes needed just to get them off my back.

My thoughts continued in a negative spiral as Nari and Sun Hee prepared dinner, which today was nothing but plain rice, since we - just like Colonel Wan had said after the execution - didn't get our normal corn and cabbage ration. Regardless, the sweet fumes of boiling rice filled the room and made me feel slightly better. But only slightly.

Nari and my parents made small talk in low voices but didn't mention the execution. When the food was ready, Nari served Young Il and Sun Hee, and was about to serve me, but I went over and grabbed the spoon from her hand and served myself with everybody watching me with their eyes wide open. I then handed the spoon back to a shocked Nari and sat back in my corner to eat, facing the wall.

All of a sudden, there were three loud knocks on the door. We all jumped, and the rice I was holding with my chopsticks fell to the floor. Without thinking twice, I picked it up again and put it in my mouth. Normally, it would have gone in the garbage, but here - every grain of rice was essential for survival.

"He's early," Sun Hee went to answer the door. "Hurry up and finish your food, girls."

She had barely touched the handle when the door slammed open, hurting her fingers. She shrieked in pain as she stumbled back into the middle of the room.

Emerging in the doorway from the darkness outside was, however, not Chul - it was General Roh.

We gasped, and Young Il, Sun Hee and Nari rushed to bow to him on the floor. They frantically signaled me to also bow, but I just couldn't bring myself to do it. In any event… I felt we were past such formalities. Having just witnessed him execute two people in cold blood, however, made me perceive him in a different light. Now, I clearly saw the *Demon of Yodok* standing before me. Still… I was not afraid.

I did, however, hurry to hide the Great General pin in my pocket. If they found *that*, there would be no avoiding punishment.

The guards accompanying General Roh closed the door, leaving him alone with us in the gloomy room, barely illuminated by the weak fire. He stood there for a while, observing us, the light from the fire flickering in his ghost eye. I noticed his gaze lingered on Sun Hee, and a hint of sadness struck his otherwise cold face. I remembered the picture frame with my mother's photo on the desk in his office, but again caution trumped my curiosity.

"Pardon my intrusion on this fine evening… I see I interrupted your dinner," he said in a formal voice looking at the bowls of rice on the floor

"Of course not, Sir… no intrusion at all, Sir," Young Il panted, his eyes fixed at the floor as he stood before him on all four "It's a tremendous honor for us that you grace us with your presence, Sir."

"Please… sit up," General Roh ordered.

The three of them reacted immediately, exchanging terrified looks.

It was difficult for me to grasp the situation, but it seemed unusual for a director of a large prison camp to personally make house visits… and my gut told me it didn't bode well.

"Rice," General Roh commented. "What a luxury… something most prisoners here haven't eaten in years… some never." He then looked down at my father, who was careful not to meet his eyes. "But I guess you know all about that, Mr. Kim Young Il."

I saw my father's face turned red, and his body trembled, but he kept his gaze fixed at the floor.

"Your daughter came to see me the other day," General Roh continued. "She's quite the courageous girl, I must say."

"Sir… I'm so sorr—" Young Il started, but General Roh silenced him by lifting his hand.

"I'm *glad* she came to me," he continued. "If she hadn't come and asked me to personally look into your case, Mr. Kim, I would probably never have learned who it is I have here… right in my on camp."

It looked like there was a bittersweet sensation left in his mouth after every word that passed his lips. Nari and Sun Hee stared at Young Il, who shuddered uncontrollably between them. Their eyes then turned to me, and finally back to General Roh.

"Do you know where I'm from... originally?" General Roh asked.

We all looked at each other, not knowing how to react.

"Can you make out my dialect?"

Silence.

"Well... I guess I can't blame you... it has been many years since I left my home town, and... I have to admit, I made quite the effort to lose my accent during my years in the Capital." He chuckled to himself. "So... how about I just tell you." He started pacing in front of us, just like he usually did in *the Bloodyard.* "Originally, I was born in Juche Year twenty-six in the city of Musan, right on the northern border... but I only spent a couple of months there. Back then, Choson was still ruled by our enemies from across the sea, but our modest territory wasn't enough to satisfy their insatiable imperialistic ambitions... so that same year they made an attempt to invade our large neighbor and ally to the north. That became the spark of a long and bloody war... I'm sure I don't have to give you a history lesson on this, you know all of this if you paid attention in school. Anyway... my parents knew it wasn't safe to stay so close to the border... they knew it wouldn't be long before the fighting crossed over to our side... so they sent me off to my grandparents... in Hamhung."

Young Il swallowed loudly.

"That's right," General Roh glared at Young Il. "They sent me to that formerly glorious city on our eastern coast."

His eyes then left my father and were instead set in the unseeable distance far beyond our walls.

"The plan was for them to join me in Hamhung shortly after... they just needed to settle some affairs first, to make sure we had enough money to survive. But the enemy army recruiters crossed into Musan only two days after I had left with my grandmother. My father and all the other able-bodied men were conscripted into their ranks, and the coming years, he was forced to kill countless allies... as well as countless Choson countrymen who were fighting against their tyranny. As for my mother... she, and all the other young women of Musan were taken abroad to serve as pleasure women to keep the enemy soldiers in good spirits... she never came back."

He now turned his sorrowful gaze back to Young Il.

"So, as you can gather from my story... I never went back to Musan again. Instead, I grew up in Hamhung... under the loving care of my grandparents, surrounded by my relatives on my mother's side. They did their best during the years we were still under enemy rule... they brought me to safety in the countryside when the whole city was destroyed amid the Fatherland Liberation War... and once the bloodshed had ended and our Father - the Great General - had finally liberated us, they brought me back home to Hamhung. Together, we joined forces with the other patriots and helped rebuild the city to greatness."

General Roh carefully observed the Young Il's reactions as his story unfolded. Young Il's breathing became increasingly heavy, his eyes fixed on the somber fire before him.

"For many years, Hamhung flourished and thrived. But then came you, Mr. Kim... and I think by now you have guessed why I have come to pay you this visit in person."

When Young Il didn't answer, General Roh squatted down on his knees in front of him and forced his head up with two fingers under his chin. Young Il gasped for air, his face distorted by terror.

"I came here because I wanted to look into the eyes of the man who is ultimately responsible for starving my family to death… the man who is responsible for starving all the innocent people of Hamhung… the man who is responsible for starving the entire province of South Hamgyong."

Young Il didn't avert his eyes, but his teary eyes were blinking rapidly.

"Have you been there?" General Roh asked softly. "Have you walked down the streets paved with starved disfigured corpses? Have you smelled the stench of their rotting sun-scorched flesh? Have you seen the mass graves on the hills surrounding the city? Have you witnessed all the suffering that your handiwork has caused? Have you done that, Mr. Kim?"

Young Il shook his head slightly, and tears were running down his cheeks.

"Of course you haven't," General Roh scoffed. "But *I* have. I have seen and felt all of that… and I'm not exaggerating when I say it will haunt me until I draw my very last breath."

He sighed melancholically, his demonic eyes - both the healthy and the dead one - fixed into my father's.

"I will also never forget finding my grandparents in their bed with plastic bags over their heads… having chosen a swift death instead of letting the starvation slowly and agonizingly eat away at them for weeks until there was no life left in their bodies. I will also never forget finding my cousin's whole family dead in their family home, embracing each other on the floor. Around them was tree bark and saw dust that they had been eating to alleviate their hunger pains… can you imagine what that must have been like, Mr. Kim?"

Young Il sobbed violently as he shook his head again.

"Of course you can't," General Roh shook his head as well. "Because things like that doesn't happen in the Capital… you saw to that, didn't you, Mr. Kim?"

"It's not like that—"

"It's not like *what*?" General Roh cut him off, his voice now stronger and more aggressive.

"We… I… it was just a temporary measure… it wasn't supposed to turn out that way … I… we were just buying time…" Young Il stuttered between his sobs.

"I see," General Roh arched his eyebrows. "Just a '*temporary measure*'… but it *did* turn out that way, didn't it… and it's all because of the decision you made."

He let go of my father's face and stood up.

"But that is, of course, not why you're here… you hotshots don't get punished for those kinds of crimes. You're here because you consorted with our enemies… the same enemies who forced my father to kill his own people and who turned my mother into a prostitute… you consorted with them to overthrow the Regime and our Father - the Great General. Now… I must confess I'm quite surprised that someone of your stature - especially given the crimes you have committed - ended up here with me. Logically, you should have been sent to one of the total control camps, like Camp 14. But… I can only assume you still have people in high places looking out for you… perhaps some of the protégés of your father, Mr. Kim Hyun Woo… the national hero who created the Public Food distribution System… the system that you, his own *son*, later destroyed… ironic, isn't it?" He smirked to himself. "Those protégés are also probably the reason why your arrival here wasn't brought to my attention. But you see, Mr. Kim… I also have friends in high places in the Capital."

Young Il was again bent forward with his hands on the ground and his head hanging down from between his shoulders in an unnatural angle. His now soft sobbing could be heard in the pauses of General Roh's monologue.

General Roh straightened his coat and then suddenly looked at the rest of us like he for a moment had forgotten we were there.

"Anyway... I think I have interrupted your dinner long enough," he cleared his throat. "I just wanted to convey to you in person that now that I know who I have the privilege of accommodating in my humble camp... I will make sure that you get the right level of re-education during your stay. Starting tomorrow, you are reassigned to a different work detail. You will follow the road past the fields until you reach the buildings by the foot of the mountain... I'm sure you won't have any problems finding the way. There you will report to the supervising officer at five o'clock sharp. I assume it superfluous to remind you what would happen if you're late. So Mr. Kim... best of luck to you with your re-education... you're certainly going to need it."

Young Il was still shivering on the floor as General Roh turned to me.

"Miss Kim... I understand that all this is very distressing, but I want to assure you that you did the right thing. In fact... I see great potential for your re-education here. Keep up the good work!"

Without awaiting any reaction from me, he turned to Sun Hee and his features suddenly softened as the sadness returned to his eyes.

"Mrs. Kim... I truly apologize for the intrusion.... please enjoy the rest of your dinner."

"Thank you, Sir," Sun Hee mumbled, throwing him a brief nervous glance.

I noticed his gaze again lingered on her before he finally opened the door and disappeared into the night.

CHAPTER 32

Almost complete silence filled the room - even Young Il's sobbing had faded away.

"W-what… what's beyond the fields?" Nari asked in a trembling voice.

Young Il sat up again. He wasn't crying anymore, but his eyes were red and swollen.

"The coal mines," he said. "That's the only thing that's up there."

Sun Hee broke into tears and hugged her husband from the side.

"Isn't… isn't that where Mina's dad…?"

Nari couldn't bring herself to finish the question, and she didn't need to. Sun Hee nodded without looking up from Young Il's now wet shoulder. Nari didn't gasp - she already knew the answer.

The atmosphere in our little room was tense, but my mind was elsewhere.

"Young Il… what happened in Hamhung?" I abandoned my vow never to speak to my family again… just for this one time.

Young Il swallowed loudly and looked at me with guilty eyes.

"Areum-ah... you must understand... there... there just wasn't enough food... there wasn't enough in our country to feed everybody... and Nari needed the heart surgery... so my superiors gave me an ultimatum... food supply to the Capital had to be guaranteed, and... and I knew that there had been problems with Hamhung and the whole South Hamgyong province... political dissidence... there were signs of them challenging the Great General's supremacy... so, I proposed we send them a message and solve the food supply to the Capital at the same time... so... so..."

"...so you made them starve," I completed his sentence.

Young Il nodded.

"Is... is this true dad?" Nari was completely devastated.

"It... it wasn't supposed to end up like that... it was only supposed to be temporary... we... we were going to solve the food problem... for *all* of Choson... before anyone starved... but... but..."

In the silence of the pause that followed, I suddenly had a realization.

"The streets filled with corpses... I've been dreaming about that... just like General Roh described it... how... how is that possible?"

Young Il looked at me with his forehead in deep wrinkles.

"Oh, Areum-ah... I'm so sorry... I didn't know..." He sighed and exchanged a heavy glance with Sun Hee. "It... it happened about a year ago... when the starvation in Hamhung was a fact, we sent some people from the Ministry to assess the severity... they took a lot of photos... horrible photos... I had the file open in my study... it was careless... one night you woke us up with a scream... we found you in the study looking at the pictures, terrified... it took hours to put you back to sleep... then in the morning, we made you believe it had all been a bad dream, and you seemed fine... we *thought* you were fine... I had no idea it had gotten stuck in your mind and affected you so much, Areum-ah… I'm so sorry!"

"We only did what we thought was best for you, Areum," Sun Hee added in a more stern voice.

I swallowed. It all came back to me now… the horror I had felt that night.

"Y-you… you're responsible for… for *that?*" I stuttered.

"I… I didn't have a choice, Areum-ah," Young Il pleaded. "If I wouldn't have done it, somebody else would have… and I really thought I would be able to stop it in time—"

"You are the son of the creator of the Ministry of Food Distribution," I squeezed through my teeth. "You could have prevented it."

"Your father did everything he could," Sun Hee glared at me with her hand on her husband's back. "It's not fair to blame him for everything that happened."

"We honestly didn't think it would come to that," Young Il said. "When the decision was made, we were certain we would be able to quickly increase the food supply by reaching out to our allies and by maximizing the local harvests… so excluding them from the central distribution was supposed to have only a marginal effect on them. But then the floods came… the worst ones in decades… they wiped out almost all crops, leaving the people with… almost nothing… we pleaded to our so-called *allies,* but they all refused to help us… saying we hadn't paid them in years for all the food and equipment they had sent us, and that our debts to them had reached astronomical proportions…"

"But I don't understand," my head was spinning. "How can there not be enough food? I have never heard anything like that, ever… Choson is the greatest and wealthiest country in the world… where everybody gets three meals a day… while people in other countries are starving."

Both Young Il and Sun Hee looked down at the ground with guilt written on their faces. Nari looked down as well.

"I don't believe you," I shook my head. "You're lying! The truth is that… that you made those people starve… and… and you're too much of a *coward* and a *traitor* to own up to it. General Roh knows what really happened… he knows the truth about you! He knows that you're a… a… a *murderer*! And now I finally know the truth about you as well… about all of you… you're murderers… how could I have not seen it before… you're rotten to the core… you're EVIL—"

The adrenaline rushed through my veins so hard it hurt, and in my fit of rage, I barely noticed Sun Hee standing up until I felt her hand on my cheek as she slapped me so hard I fell to the ground.

"YOU WILL RESPECT YOUR FATHER!" she screamed.

Nari threw herself into Young Il's arms and buried her face.

"I forbid you to utter one more word of this nonsense!" Her voice was now reduced to a strained whisper. "Your father is *not* a murderer… the problem is the *system*! He didn't know it would go so wrong… and he had to do what he did to save Nari… it was the only way… he did it for our *family*."

Sun Hee panted as she towered over me where I lay on the floor, my left cheek burning and pulsating intensely.

"You have always been so blind, Areum… you have never wanted to see… when your father saw what was happening there, he went against the system to save all those people. Do you understand? He was trying to *save* all those people… he should be considered a *hero*, not a traitor… but he should have known better… when you go against the system, you always lose… and that's why they put him here."

She gasped for air and took a moment to compose herself.

"I don't expect you to understand everything… or maybe even to believe us… but I demand that you *respect* your father and that you *respect* your family! Is that clear?"

I didn't answer. After glaring her down for a moment, my hand gently placed over my burning cheek, I turned around and lay down on my quilt, facing the wall. There was nothing more to be said. All of this just proved my decision last night had been the right one.

"I believe you, daddy," I heard Nari whimper from Young Il's arms as Sun Hee re-joined them by the fire. He thanked her with a kiss on her forehead, like he so often did back in the Capital.

A few moments later, there was another knock on the door.

"The self-criticism session!" Sun Hee jumped to her feet, flustered. "I had completely forgotten about that… girls… both of you… you must get ready and go right away." She opened the door and disclosed a glowing red dot outside in the darkness."

"Having ourselves a little family meeting I hear," Corporal Lee said through a cloud of smoke.

Sun Hee's face turned dark red.

"No… Sir… we were just waiting for you… the girls are ready… they're coming now," she rambled.

Corporal Lee only answered with a chuckle and another cloud of smoke that he blew into our house.

Nari and I quickly put on our coats and hurried outside.

At first, I was blinded by the darkness and couldn't see anything, but when the moon peeked out from behind the clouds, I noticed we weren't alone.

"Hey," Mina greeted with a worried look as Nari ran over to hug her.

"Let's go!" Corporal Lee commanded.

We were the only people to be gathered from the *Orchid Garden*, so we proceeded to pick up what I presumed were our classmates from the barracks at the *Rose Garden* before heading over to the enormous *Hall of Ideological Struggle*.

We came into a different room than last time, but it was completely identical, so I couldn't help looking for the bloodstain from poor Jae Eun from the first night.

We sat down in a circle on the floor in the same way as we always did in school. Looking around I noticed Mina sat a few yards away from me, putting Nari again between the two sworn enemies of the battlefield that was the self-criticism sessions.

I guess some things never change...

My eyes met Mina's for a moment and I knew the same thought crossed her mind as well. But then she smiled at me, and it was a friendly smile - not a vicious smile of a sworn enemy. I averted my eyes.

The self-criticism session in itself was not that different from the ones I was used to, except that we now had an armed guard watching over us instead of a teacher. I felt nervous being in a room like this again with Mina, but we were both very cautious in criticizing each other... but not so much that it would anger Corporal Lee.

Due to what we had witnessed today and what Colonel Wan had told us, all of us talked about how we will be more vigilant in the future to catch rule-breakers, and after only about an hour we were finished. Corporal Lee had not been too interested in what we had to say and only yelled at a few people a couple of times to establish dominance.

Nari and I arrived home first and we went to bed immediately without talking - I made sure to not even look in her direction.

Sun Hee and Young Il came home not too long after, and they went to bed immediately as well. For Young Il, a new and harder life awaited him at five o'clock sharp tomorrow morning.

Listening to their breathing and snoring, I had the same relentless thoughts swirling around in my head.

How could I have been so blind? How could I have been living with a monster for so long without knowing it? And… what did any of this have to do with Nari's surgery?

None of it made sense, but by now, I didn't care. All I cared about was feeding my hatred… the hatred for the monsters who had destroyed my life.

Before long I was back in the street of death in Hamhung. Before me, my father was being picked apart by the enormous black crows.

He mouthed, "I'm sorry," before disappearing in a sea of black feathers.

Juche Year 83

-

June

CHAPTER 33

As my first month in Penal Labor Camp No 15 was coming to an end in the final week of June, spring had unquestionably shifted into summer, even though it was a different summer than I was used to back in the Capital. By this time, my teammates in the Great General's National Gymnastics Team were surely having the time of their lives in the secret location of the Gymnastics Village, no doubt preparing for their next major competitions that will bring honor to Choson.

As for me, my existence was the exact opposite. My life had become a routine of school, work, despair, and hopelessness. The worst part, however, was not the pain I got from sitting on the hard school benches for hours on end listening to Miss Ae's - although energetic but still boring - lectures on Juche and the great achievements of our eternal Father - the Great General. It was also not the pain in my back from working several hours hunched over in the fields under the burning sun on Sundays. Neither was it the unbearable tension of the Sunday night self-criticism sessions. It was not even the constant hunger and thirst, although that was a new and overwhelming feeling that I just couldn't get used to. No, the worst part was by far the time I had to spend at home together with my now estranged family.

Nari made some attempts to talk to me during the breaks at school or in the fields, but not at home. Sun Hee tried to force me to speak by yelling at me a couple of times, but I firmly stood my ground. The only one who didn't try to make me talk was Young Il. Maybe he thought it would pass if they gave me some more time. Or maybe, now that the truth was out, he was relieved he could stop pretending to be the man I had purported to be for so many years. Whichever his reason was, I was glad not to have to deal with him as well.

Of course, I couldn't pretend the four of us weren't living together, and I knew I still had to fulfill my responsibilities as a daughter. When they asked me to clean, I cleaned. When they asked me to help prepare and serve the food, I did so. But I didn't utter a single word. My only form of verbal communication was an occasional grunting.

The only relief I got was at school during the breaks, which I most days spent talking to Jun Ha. He had noticed I never sat with Nari and Mina, so he usually came over to keep me company, without pushing me to explain what had happened between us. It felt good having somebody to talk to, and after he had thanked me for saving him from Lucky, my shyness had disappeared and a friendship had formed. He was very kind and helpful, giving all sorts of useful tips on how to survive in the camp. He was also extremely cute. I sometimes imagined how he would look back in the Capital with modern clothes and groomed hair. But to be honest… I kind of liked his hair messy as it was now.

I had become accustomed to going to the river at the end of every day to quench my thirst and wash off the layer of sweat and dirt that had built up during the day, whether it was in the fields or the classroom. It made me feel almost human again. It was also a way for me to spend less time at home.

The other person I often talked to was Chul. He was the supervisor of the watermill, but that job couldn't be too eventful since he often came over and talked to me in the fields on Sundays. Come to think of it, I often met him during our school breaks on weekdays as well. He usually saw me from the main road as he went about some business to *the Oversight* and came over to talk to me. Sometimes I got the feeling he came during that time of the day on purpose just to have an excuse to talk to me. If it was like that, I didn't mind. He was kind and *very* different from the other guards. And remembering his trembling rifle and tormented face during the execution a couple of weeks ago, I still couldn't help feeling sorry for him. Watching those two people die in such a horrible way had been traumatizing for me - that bloody scene had lately replaced the sea of sun-scorched corpses in Hamhung as my nightly torment - but being forced to pull the trigger… it must have been a million times worse.

I also kept in mind Jun Ha's constant advice to make some guard friends, but it was clear that he didn't approve of Chul as my choice. Whenever Chul came over, Jun Ha made sure to distance himself from us but continued to cast sulky glances our way from under the tree or by the wall where he escaped the burning sun. When I ask Jun Ha about it, he just told me to *be careful about him*, and that he *might get me into trouble*, but changed the topic when I asked what kind of trouble or why. In this case, however, I decided to trust my own instincts, and my instincts told me to give Chul the benefit of the doubt.

Another reason for this was that Chul seemed to have a positive effect on Corporal Lee… or *Chang Min,* as Chul always informally called him. Whenever they were together, Chang Min's whole demeanor changed. He was no longer the arrogant and abusive bully I had learned to hate. Instead, the two of them talked and laughed like normal people. And Chang Min always put his muscular arm over Chul's shoulders and messed up his hair as I had often seen big brothers do to younger siblings at school in the Capital. So whenever Chul was close by, I knew Chang Min wouldn't do anything to us. Of course, that didn't stop him from beating up some poor guy for dropping a bucket of water an hour later.

Nari and Mina seemed to be attached by an invisible rope. They sat together in class, spent all the breaks together, ate together, sat next to each other in the self-criticism sessions, and worked side by side in the fields on Sundays. Mina helped Nari fulfill her quotas on those days because of her weak condition, which I was thankful for. In a way, I was grateful Nari had found a way to make this situation more bearable, but still, whenever I saw them together I felt uneasy - even paranoid - especially when I caught them whispering to each other while looking in my direction.

Are they on to me about what I did? Is that what they are talking about?

Also, a couple of nights a week, either Mina came over to our house or Nari went to their house. Whoever went, they always brought food as not to create problems for the other family. Sometimes, Mrs. Choy also came over together with Mina, but Sun Hee tried to discourage it… and always tried to make our bags of rice as inconspicuous as possible.

The Friday that week was the hottest day since we arrived at Yodok. During the lunch break, I sat alone in the shadow of my usual tree outside school, eating the same bland cabbage soup as always. Jun Ha sat with another group of friends, as he did sometimes, and that day, I didn't mind. The heat made me sleepy and uncomfortably sweaty all over… it was a relief not to have to talk to anybody.

In the hazy distance, I suddenly noticed Chul walking down the road from the fields - this was the third day in a row he came to visit me. I sighed, but got up to go behind the school building, where we usually met not to attract unwanted attention - the other prisoners might start suspecting that I'm an informant if I spend too much time with the guards. As soon as I was up on my feet, however, something else caught my attention.

General Roh was crossing *the Bloodyard* with angry determined steps in the direction of the main road, towards... Chul.

What's going on?

When Chul saw me looking at *the Bloodyard*, he looked over his shoulder, and with fear distorting his face, he stopped dead in his tracks. He briefly looked at me with large pleading eyes but then turned back to face General Roh. I took a couple of unsure steps in their direction to be able to see clearer.

What came next happened so fast I hardly had time to react. General Roh walked up to the now trembling Chul without slowing down. Without any warning he hit him right in the nose, knocking him down to the ground. Blood gushed down Chul's mouth and chin and dripped onto his uniform as he squirmed in the dirt. I shrieked, but quickly covered my mouth and hid behind a tree, only leaving my eyes peeking out. General Roh's face was scarlet red and he shook with fury as he towered over the whimpering Chul on the ground.

"YOU PATHETIC DISGRACE... YOU THOUGHT I WOULDN'T FIND OUT?" General Roh screamed at him and kicked him in the stomach. Chul squealed in pain as tears streamed down and mixed with the blood smeared on his face. The whole camp stopped. It was like looking at a live photograph where all the prisoners and guards stood frozen like statues, mesmerized by the scene in the middle of the road.

General Roh panted furiously. I had never seen him lose his temper before. Come to think of it, I had hardly seen him displaying *any* kind of emotion before. Apart from sadness when looking at the picture frame on his desk.

"GET UP!"

He kicked Chul in the stomach again. And then again.

"GET UP! YOU PATHETIC EXCUSE OF A MAN… GET UP!"

He launched another hard kick at Chul, this time hitting his back as Chul desperately tried to shield himself from the attack. General Roh then paused. Chul moved in agony and managed to lift himself on his hands and knees, but just as he tried to gather his strength to stand up, he got another hard kick right to his chest. I heard something crack, and Chul fell back to the ground.

"GET UP, YOU WORTHLESS PIECE OF SHIT! GET UP! YOU THOUGHT YOU COULD GET AWAY WITH IT? YOU THOUGHT I WOULDN'T FIND OUT? I KNOW *EVERYTHING* THAT GOES ON IN MY CAMP… *EVERYTHING!*"

Chul made another attempt to stand up and again managed to get onto his hands and legs. This time General Roh didn't kick him. Instead, he grabbed him by the collar and lifted him so high his feet almost left the ground. Chul screamed in pain, putting his hand over his broken ribs.

Then, to my surprise, General Roh let go of his grip. I was afraid Chul would fall again, and that the beating would continue, but he managed to maintain his balance. General Roh stood right in front of him and stared insanely into his eyes. He was not screaming anymore.

"How could you do this to me, Chul?" he panted. His voice was now so low I had to take a couple of steps closer to hear. "Is this how you repay me for all I have done for you? For saving your life? For bringing you here? For trying to… make a *man* out of you?"

"I'm sorry, Sir," Chul whimpered, still holding his aching ribs. "I… I…"

General Roh turned away from him and sighed deeply. I quickly looked away not to risk meeting his eyes… but only for a second. I noticed Chang Min was standing further up the road. At first, I didn't recognize him because I had never seen him so… *scared* before. His face was completely white, except for puffy red eyes that looked like they were almost crying. He had his hand over his mouth, just like me, and his whole body was visibly trembling.

There was a movement in the corner of my eye, and I turned back to General Roh just in time to see him plant his fist into Chul's stomach. Chul lost all control over his body and was sobbing like a little boy, but General Roh held him so he wouldn't collapse to the ground.

"Pathetic," General Roh spat in pure disgust. "You sicken me. I regret ever taking you in… feeding you… letting you work here… giving you a life. I'm ashamed that you're… that you're…" Instead of finishing his sentence, he just shook his head. "You don't belong here, Chul. You're not worthy of the important work we do here."

"I'm sorry, Sir!" Chul apologized again and braced himself for another blow. But it didn't come. Instead, General Roh grabbed him hard by his neck and pulled his face mere inches away from his own.

"I don't need you to be *sorry*, you pathetic, disgusting vermin. I need you to *change*. Do you understand me? I will give you one more chance. Just one! And I swear by the Great General himself that if you disappoint me again, your life as a guard will be over and I will make you join the *prisoner population* instead. Do you hear me? Maybe that will toughen you up… maybe then you'll start acting like a *man*, instead of… instead of… whatever you are…"

General Roh grabbed Chul's collar again and shoved him hard to the ground. He towered over him extending his right hand index finger.

"*One* more chance, Private. *One* more chance!"

He spat on the ground next to Chul, and without another word he turned around and marched back to *the Oversight*, leaving the whimpering and blood-smeared Chul on the ground holding his broken ribs.

CHAPTER 34

The spell that had turned the prisoners and guards into statues was broken and everybody continued about their business, deliberately ignoring the wounded guard on the ground. Not even the guards went over to help him. Chang Min looked at him with his red sorrowful eyes but didn't dare to go over to him either. I wanted to run over to help him, but I knew it was a bad idea, so I just waited under the tree, silently rooting for him that he would be able to get up on his own accord. It took a couple of tries, but he finally made it. We made eye contact and I nodded in the direction of the school to ask if he could make it to meet me there. I had so many questions. To my surprise he nodded, so I went to the back of the building and waited. It took a while for him to reach me, limping and hunched over, his hand firmly over his ribs.

"Great General… what was that about? You poor thing!"

Chul sat down on the ground, leaning against the wooden wall of the *School of Juche*.

"It… doesn't matter. I just did something I shouldn't have… and he found out about it. I was just stupid… so stupid."

"Doesn't matter?" I gasped. "He almost beat you to death right in the street in front of everybody. In front of the prisoners who are supposed to fear and respect you! What did you do?"

Saying all of this, I remembered Jun Ha's words.

'Stay away from Chul, he will get you into trouble.'

"I... it's nothing." Chul squirmed in pain. "I'm ashamed... it's... it's better you don't know... don't worry, I'll sort it out."

I stopped pushing for answers. Instead, I sat down next to him and we stayed like that for a while before I broke the silence.

"Do you really think he would do that? I mean... do you really think he would turn you into a *prisoner*?"

Chul didn't answer immediately. His eyes were closed and his head rested against the wall.

"Yes," he finally said. "Yes, I do. Honestly... there is absolutely nothing that would surprise me about that man." He then painfully opened his eyes and looked at me. "But I have to appease him... that's what I must do... I have to stop disappointing him, and... I have to become the kind of man he wants me to be. I have to... after all, I owe him my life."

"From back in... Hamhung?"

"Yeah... from back in Hamhung," he again closed his eyes. "Me and Chang Min... he was my senior... we were at the University of Hamhung when... when... things turned bad... *really* bad... at first we tried to manage, but... the whole world just collapsed around us... there was no food to be found anywhere... Chang Min tried to find a way for us to survive... and for a while he did... but then that didn't work either... it was over for us, and we knew it... and just when we had made peace with leaving this world together... *he* showed up, right out of the blue... he brought us here... gave us food and work, but no explanation."

"Just like that?" I asked, baffled. "You didn't know him from before... at all?"

"No... not as far as I can remember," Chul opened his eyes and slowly stood up by leaning against the wall, his face again distorted by pain. "I know my parents used to work in this camp... but that was many years ago... truth to be told, I have no idea why he saved us... but none of that matters anymore. What matters is that I owe him my life... and since I have disappointed him, I will have to atone for it... *somehow*." He pushed away from the wall but kept his hand extended until he found his balance.

"Chul... I can't say I understand what's going on... but, if there's anything I can do to help you, just let me know."

He gave me a surprised look.

"I appreciate it, Areum... but why? I mean... at the end of the day, I'm still a guard... and you're a prisoner... you're much worse off than me. Why would you help me?"

"Because... I care about you. And you're the only nice guard here. I don't want anything to happen to you."

Chul smiled... but only for a moment before the pain again distorted his face.

"Just..." he started. "I don't know what to do. I don't know what *he* wants me to do."

"Maybe you could... ask him?" The idea sounded stupid once I said it, but it made Chul think.

"Maybe," he nodded. "Maybe. Anyway... I'll figure something out. Thank you, Areum!"

"Just do whatever he needs you to do, okay? Get back on his good side."

"I will... thank you."

Chul started limping back towards the main road, supporting himself against the wall with the hand he was not pressing against his broken ribs.

"I think I have to go and see the doctor."

"D-Doctor Death?"

He looked back at me and again smiled through his pain.

"Yes, Doctor Death… but that's a terrible nickname… apart from being drunk all the time, he's supposedly a good doctor."

I waited until he had reached the main road before I went back into the school building. The break had been over for some time, but I knew Miss Ae wouldn't reprimand me for being late.

At least there are two kind people in this camp!

At home, I ate in silence giving the others my back, but I still listened attentively to their conversation, and curiously tried to pick up on any new developments.

Young Il had come home weaker by the day since he started working in the coal mine, always black from top to toe and coughing his lungs out. The new routine was for Nari to prepare a bucket of water from the river and a piece of cloth for him to at least wash his feet, hands, and head before coming inside. Today, I couldn't help turning around and look when I heard both Nari and Sun Hee gasping as Young Il sat down to eat. At first, I didn't see what they had reacted to, but then I noticed a stream of blood running down his forehead. I followed it with my eyes until it reached the tip of his nose, where he wiped it off with his dirty sleeve. I raised my eyes and noticed a large open cut on the top of his head.

"I've told you to be careful," Sun Hee pressed her lips to a thin straight line as Nari rushed to pat the wound with a piece of wet cloth - the cleanest she could find. "Since they don't give you helmets to protect your heads, you have to use what's *inside* your head to protect your head."

"I know, dear," he answered, ashamed like a little boy before his mother. "But the tunnel ceiling is really low and sharp in some places… it's dark as night… and we only get one torch per team…" He filled his mouth with food and stopped talking. At least he still had his appetite.

"Why don't you make the tunnels bigger?" Nari asked.

"We're not allowed to," Young Il answered in between bites. "The coal is not all in one place, so we always have to make new tunnels and go deeper and deeper… there is no time to make proper tunnels."

"H-how deep do they go?"

"*Very* deep," Young Il swallowed his food. "I couldn't tell you how deep, but we have to walk for… I don't know… probably an hour or so through the maze of tunnels before we reach our place to work. That's why we have to start at five in the morning and finish so late. The work is hard… for everyone… but since I'm the newest guy… and you know… being personally targeted by General Roh… I of course get the hardest job of all - pushing coal carts all the way back to the surface. Me and the other new guy. I don't know how long it takes, but by the end of our shift today, we had taken three carts to the surface… it's extremely inefficient, and… honestly, I don't know how long I will last down there. I mean… nobody has died in my team since I started, but in the other teams… every day there has been at least one person less coming out than went in… I think it's just a matter of time…"

Sun Hee and Nari both looked at him in silence with sad expressions on their faces.

"Don't talk like that," Sun Hee whispered tensely.

"I just think we have to be realistic about this situation," Young Il looked at her compassionately. "And, frankly… maybe it would even be for the best… I mean… for *you*… if I'm gone. General Roh is targeting me specifically, and—"

"Stop it!" Sun Hee shrieked. "No! Get that way of thinking out of your head! We can't make it here without you. You're the man of the house. You're the rock that we cling to. We love you... okay?" She crawled over to him, put her hands on his lap, and looked him straight in the eyes. "Okay? I know it's awful. I know that you're suffering... more than any of us. But please... we *need* you! We need you to stay alive... for us. Please!"

Young Il looked at her with sorrowful eyes and removed a strand of hair from her face.

"I will try to be strong for you," he smiled feebly, "but I can't make any promises. Also... there's another thing." He swallowed before continuing. "Colonel Wan came to see us at the mine this morning before the shift started... he said that he will personally oversee the coal extraction from now on."

Sun Hee and Nari gasped.

"Then... he singled me out from the group and told everybody that I was *chosen* to get *special treatment* by General Roh. He gave me a ten percent higher quota than the rest of my team... but everybody still gets punished if I don't fulfill it, so now everybody hates me because I have increased the risk for all of them." He sighed deeply and shook his head. "The sad truth is that if I start missing my quota... you know... they could do anything to me down there, and nobody would know... I just won't resurface at the end of the shift, and the next day I will be replaced by somebody else."

Sun Hee continued looking him straight in the eyes, even though hers were filling up with tears.

"I'm sorry to ask this of you," she pleaded, "but you must endure... for your *family*... just for a little while longer... we will find a solution. We will get you reassigned... somehow. In the meantime, you *must* fulfill your quota... every day... okay?"

"Okay," Young Il nodded, but it was clear there was no conviction behind his promise.

Can she be that naive? How could he ever be reassigned now that he's targeted by General Roh himself? Especially with Colonel Wan there making sure the last days of his life will be a living nightmare?

I lay back down on my quilt, facing the wall.

Maybe she's just trying to find a shred of hope to cling to... anything to keep herself from giving up. Just like I am doing.

In that moment, I realized that my feelings were not as clear and distinct as they had been just a week ago. It was no longer black and white, and I didn't know exactly how I felt about everything that was happening... or how I felt about *him*. What I did know, however, was that after an entire month of silence, it was increasingly difficult to stay angry at the people I shared my life with... especially when seeing them in such agony.

CHAPTER 35

The days were becoming increasingly hotter and the already stuffy classroom was now steamy and smelly. Not even opening the small windows on the side helped much. The thirst was also unbearable, but Miss Ae did the best she could to help us, and in the mornings and afternoons she sent a couple of students to the river with buckets to fetch water for us not to collapse mid-lesson. I could see Nari looking very pale these days, almost like she used to look before she had her surgery… but I knew Mina and Mrs. Choy were looking out for her. It was reassuring to have a skilled doctor so close, even if she didn't have any equipment or medicine at her disposal… only some wild-growing herbs she acquired from her patients or by sneaking up into the mountains herself at night. My feelings of worry for Nari's health made my anger and resentment for her diminish day by day - despite my efforts to fuel it by remembering all the grief she had caused me throughout my entire life - and I stood firm by my decision never to talk to any member of my family again. But sometimes it was difficult. I felt guilty when rubbing the Great General pin in my hand for comfort, which Nari selflessly had put herself at risk to give to me.

Jun Ha kept me company most days, but Chul didn't come around to talk anymore. I assumed he was preoccupied with trying to figure out how to appease General Roh. I saw him from time to time outside *the Oversight* or by the fields, and we greeted each other with a nod, but he didn't smile like he used to. His face looked grim and his whole posture was tense. A few times I overheard some of the guards making fun of him to his face, and I got afraid for him. If he didn't regain the respect of the guards - and General Roh - he would be done for. I couldn't help but wonder what he had done to make General Roh so angry. And even more - how and why General Roh ended up saving both him and Chang Min from starvation in Hamhung?

What was their connection?

I asked Jun Ha if he knew anything about it, but he just told me to leave it alone. At least, now I understood why Chul and Chang Min got along so well despite being so different - they were friends since before.

The last Sunday of June - exactly one month after we had arrived at Yodok - was brutally hot and there was not a cloud to be seen in the sky. I usually didn't sweat much - not even during my most intense gymnastics practices - but this day I felt my clothes damp and glued to my body and salty sweat drops from my forehead dripped down and stung my eyes. My clothes were now quite dirty and had started to tear in some places, but still didn't look as bad as the gray muddy prisoner uniforms that made all the other prisoners indistinguishable. I shuddered thinking about getting one of those on my birthday, which was only a couple of weeks away. Then I would leave Miss Ae's safe sanctuary and be put to work from sunrise to sunset every day... *for twenty years!*

By the time the sun reached its apex in the sky, two middle-aged women had already collapsed and were dragged off to the hospital. Our supervisor came over and ordered some of the men in our work group to bring an extra water ration from the river. It helped a little, but not as much as I had hoped for. Rumors also started circulating that the two collapsed ladies had been dragged off to the *Center of Truth*, and not to Doctor Death… although I wasn't sure which was worse.

During the lunch break, I noticed Chul standing with a group of guards in the shade of some trees by the guardhouse. It was far away, but I got the feeling they were taunting him and laughing. What was even more disconcerting was that they seemed to be looking and pointing in my direction.

Do they know Chul and I are friends? Is that why they are mocking him?

I suddenly felt extremely guilty. By not hiding our friendship well enough, I had selfishly made his already bad situation worse.

The day went on and the excruciating heat didn't abate until long into the evening. After what happened to the two women before lunch, I decided not to work as far away from Nari as I used to. If the sun was almost unbearable for me, I could only imagine how it was for her. Indeed, she looked like she was about to collapse a few times, but Mina intervened before I needed to do anything. I also noticed Mina was working even harder than usual to compensate for Nari's inability to fulfill her own quota. I considered going over to them to offer to help out… but there was still something inside me that didn't let me. Suddenly the guilt for what I had done to Mina resurfaced.

Maybe I should come clean? Maybe she would forgive me now that we are in the same situation?

But I quickly dismissed that idea.

I can't handle more problems right now… maybe later.

As the sun finally started to set behind the mountains after one of the longest and most excruciating days of my life, a sudden cool breeze caressed my face and hair. I almost cried with relief. Shortly after, the group leader blew his whistle, signaling the workday had finished. I had persevered, and so had Nari - with the indispensable help of Mina - and tomorrow we would be back in the stuffy but bearable classroom, where Miss Ae would never punish us for collapsing from the heat.

There was still a group of guards by the trees, and by now, even more of them had gathered. It was unusual to see them in such large groups, but they were probably just hiding from the sun. The newly arrived guards had brought a couple of bottles with them that they all shared, causing my thirst to spike.

Only a little while longer. Only until they have verified our quotas… then I will go to the river and drink to my heart's content!

As the final rays of light seeped over the mountain skyline, our supervisor finally announced that the quotas had been met and we could go home.

Thank the Great General!

I looked over at Nari and saw Mina supporting her as they walked back towards the *Village of the Strayed*. I waited until the coast was clear before I started moving in the direction of the river. Several other people had the same idea, so I made sure to keep my distance, not to draw any unnecessary attention to us.

As soon as I reached my usual spot by the soothing splashing of the watermill, I threw myself down on the grassy bank and plunged my whole head into the water. The feeling was indescribable. I pulled my head up and started drinking. I gulped the sweet water down. I didn't even feel the bitter aftertaste of mud and coal residue that was always present. When I felt like my stomach was going to burst, I rolled over onto my back and rested my head on the soft grass. It was getting darker, so my eyes that had been squinting against the strong sun all day could finally rest. I knew I had to go home so that guards on the way wouldn't question me about why I was out after curfew, but… just one more minute…

I suddenly heard a noise and sat up with a jolt. My heart pounded furiously.

Did I fall asleep?

It was dark now, but I could still distinguish the contours around me in the moonlight. In the direction from where the noise had come from stood a figure. There was no doubt about it - it was a guard.

I panicked.

"I-I'm sorry… I—"

"Hey… d-don't worry… it's me," Chul slurred from the darkness.

"Thank the Great General," I sighed. "You scared me."

Chul didn't say anything - he just stood there, swaying side to side in the light of the emerging full moon.

Something is different about him…

"W-what are you doing here?" I asked nervously.

"I… I needed to see you," Chul slurred barely audibly over the splashing of the watermill. "I saw you c-coming over here… you s-said you would he… help me… I… I need your h-help…"

I looked at him, following his swaying with my eyes.

"Are you… *drunk*?"

I remembered the bottles they were sharing under the trees earlier. I understood now they hadn't contained water.

"General Roh is r-really angry with me," Chul sobbed. "I'm… I'm not m-man enough to be a guard here. I n-need to man up, he says…"

"Okay," I said hesitantly, still not getting up.

"And y-you… you said you would h-help me, right? Y-you would do anything… t-that's what you said… right?"

"Of course," I said, flustered. "Anything… what can I do?"

Chul continued swaying. I couldn't see his face clearly, but I could tell he was crying.

"Please… c-come with me," he said.

I got up from the ground with a growing unease in my heart. I had, of course, been around drunk people before - most often Su Mi - but I always felt uncomfortable when they got so drunk they couldn't walk straight and started slurring nonsense. It's like their personalities change completely.

Suddenly, I noticed a bright red dot in the darkness - *we're not alone* - and I instantly knew who was here with us. I gasped and took a couple of steps back in panic.

"D-don't worry a-about him… h-he's with me," Chul mumbled. "C-come on… we need to go."

I looked at the red dot in the darkness with growing anxiety. Whenever I had seen that red dot before, something bad had happened. Chang Min didn't say anything, but I felt his penetrating eyes on me from the dark.

"C-come on," Chul clumsily grabbed my arm.

My instincts told me to run away - to run *home* - but my friend needed me, so I went along with him, looking nervously over my shoulder at Chang Min's dark contour.

"Where are we going?"

"J-just up there… just a bit u-up the mountainside…"

CHAPTER 36

We walked side by side in silence, and Chang Min followed behind us. Chul was unstable and stumbling. I was ready to catch him at any moment in case he fell. His head was bent forward and he looked straight down at the ground.

"Just a little further," he mumbled.

Once we had left the rice fields behind us, we started moving up the gentle slope at the foot of the mountain. Soon, the prison camp disappeared behind the trees of the increasingly steep slope we were ascending. The comforting splashing of the watermill faded away as well. All I heard now was the cracking of branches and the crunching of dry leaves under our feet… and from behind us, constantly reminding me of Chang Min's presence. My unease grew the further up the slope we got. The fresh scent of the emerging vegetation mixed strangely with the smoke from the burning tobacco behind us.

"Where are we going?" I asked again, but hearing the nervousness in my voice made me feel even more uneasy.

"U-up here… just over there," Chul pointed with an unsteady finger.

We emerged from the trees into a clearing just in front of a steep hillside. To the right was a cliff leading down to the slow flow of the Ipsok River. I went up on the plateau in the middle of the clearing and looked around. From there, I could see the entire camp, veiled in darkness, but softly illuminated by the moonlight from the clear black sky. In the far distance, I saw some tiny spots of yellow light emerging from *the Oversight*, and closer to here was a bright cluster of light, which I gathered was the *Chrysanthemum Garden* - where the officers live.

From up here, the camp looked almost peaceful.

I guess darkness can disguise even a place of horrors like this one…

At first, I thought those were the only sources of electric light around, but then I raised my gaze and noticed a chain of strong bright dots along the skyline of the mountain ridge in even intervals.

The guard towers!

Just then, I felt a couple of hands around my waist. I stiffened like a rock.

"I'm sorry," Chul sobbed in my ear.

He ripped my shirt open and grabbed me again, pulling me down to the ground, putting himself on top of me, holding my arms against the ground above my head. It all happened so fast that my body didn't have time to break its paralysis from the shock and resist.

"What are you doing? Stop it!" I shrieked, my head spinning and flooding with blood. Chul's pungent alcohol breath made me nauseous and prevented me from composing my mind.

"I'm s-sorry," he continued to sob on top of me.

"STOP IT! STOP IT… WHAT ARE YOU DOING?" I screamed again, this time louder. Chul was very light and weak, but somehow I couldn't manage to gather my strength. Maybe after working the whole day in the fields under the scorching sun, I had no more strength left in my body. At the same time, in the corner of my eye, I could see the motionless red dot next to us in the darkness, shielded from the moonlight, observing us.

"You… you said you would d-do anything to help me, r-right? That's what you said… I'm sorry… but t-this is the only way…"

He let go of my arms and started to unbuckle his belt. I took the chance and harnessed my last strength to push him to the side and crawl out from the grip of his legs. My hands slipped on the damp night grass and I felt a sharp rock cut through the skin of my bare chest. I screamed in pain but got up on my hands again.

"NO!" Chul slurred desperately behind me. He grabbed my feet, but it was a loose grip, so I got my right foot free and kicked him right in the face. This time it was Chul screaming in pain. He lay on the ground with his hands over his nose. I noticed something smeared on his face glistening in the moonlight. I must have been blood.

I stood up and closed my shirt over my bleeding chest, but then I remembered the red dot. I looked frantically around me, but it was gone. Then, all of a sudden, an enormous force thrust me back down to the ground.

"Stop fighting!" Chang Min panted as he tried to press my arms against the ground over my head. His breath was also reeking of alcohol.

"GET OFF ME!" I screamed at the top of my lungs. I tried to get my arms free, but Chang Min was too strong and his body was too heavy. But I knew from many years of competing in Taekwondo that brains always beats strength in a fight, so trying to regain control over the situation, I relaxed my arms, surprising Chang Min who in his drunk state almost lost his balance where he sat on top of me. In the brief window, before he regained his bearing, I launched both my knees the hardest I could right into his spine. He screamed in pain, and both my hands became free. I channeled all my strength into my right fist and hit him right in the nose. As he moaning put his hands over his face, I twirled and managed to push him off me to the side, and in the same motion jumped up to my feet.

In the bright moonlight, I saw Chang Min on the ground as he whimpered and held his nose. I looked for Chul - who should have been next to Chang Min on the ground - but he wasn't there. Just as I lifted my eyes, Chul let out a bestial roar to my right. With crazed eyes and his entire face dripping with blood, he swayed towards me with unnatural stumbling steps. I took a step backward but immediately tripped over a rock and fell to the ground, hitting the back of my head on something hard. A split second later Chul was over me again, trying to get control over my arms, blood and saliva dripping down on my face.

"Y-you said you would help m-me. P-please, you must help me!" Chul pleaded in frantic agony.

"GET OFF... YOU'RE CRAZY!" I screamed. "YOU'RE DRUNK! WHAT'S WRONG WITH YOU? GET OFF ME!"

"T-this... this is the o-only way... I'm s-sorry..." Chul panted.

Even though I was in the same position as before, this time I didn't feel defenseless. Chul was significantly smaller and weaker than Chang Min, and his drunken state made his movements slow and clumsy. The shock and fear that initially had paralyzed my body was now replaced with fury. I felt my body being filled with adrenaline in the same way as when I was about to lose an important competition - or *tryouts* - and needed to perform flawlessly. I started using every muscle in my body to create a kind of wave-like motion, and immediately felt that Chul was losing his grip. I used the opportunity to pull my right arm with every bit of strength I had left, and with a primal scream, I managed to break it free.

In the same motion, I again hit Chul on his broken nose - I didn't have much strength in that angle, but I also didn't need it - and I immediately got my other arm free as well. Chul let out an agonized scream and put both hands over his face. I pushed him off me with ease and again jumped onto my feet. To my right, I noticed a movement, and the next second Chang Min was in front of me. With all the adrenaline in my body, I reacted instantly and made a round kick to his face, and he collapsed back down to the ground. Even though I hadn't competed in Taekwondo for a long time, fortunately enough, the movements still came naturally to me. To my left, I saw Chul trying to pull himself up by supporting himself against a tree. I took a step towards him, ready to kick him back down.

"Areum-ah… p-please!" he looked up at me with his blank eyes and his blood and tear-smeared face glistening in the moonlight.

I looked down at him with adrenaline burning my veins.

I thought he was my friend! I thought he was different! But he's just like the rest of them… thinking that we're worthless like vermin… thinking that they can do whatever they want with us!

"Chul… stay down!" I warned him.

"I can't… I'm sorry… I… I can't," he slurred and continued trying to stand up.

"Chul… I'm warning you. You're drunk… you don't know what you're doing… just stop it!"

He was almost completely on his feet now. My face burned and my heart pounded harder. I felt all the anger and all the resentment and humiliation that men had caused me in my life… my father… Colonel Wan… General Roh… and now Chul… all forged into one single overwhelming feeling of hatred… and the object of this hatred was right now this sad little boy - who I until a moment ago had thought was my friend.

I stepped back, centered my balance, and then with a piercing scream, I jumped up high in the air, spun around and kicked him in the face before I landed back on my feet. Chul's body made a half turn. He stumbled a few steps and then fell headfirst down onto the bed of soft grass.

I stood dead still for a while without breathing, ready for a second round. But he didn't move a muscle. I remembered Chang Min and quickly looked over at the place on the ground I had last seen him. He was still there, but his body was moving, so it wouldn't be long before he was back up on his feet.

I looked back at Chul. He was out cold and wasn't moving at all. Then my whole spine froze to ice.

Oh no… what if he's dead? What if I had just killed a guard? I will be the one tied to the poles in front of a firing squad tomorrow. And how about my family? Will they be punished for this as well?

I rushed down on my knees and bent over Chul, scanning frantically to detect any motion, but he lay completely still. I didn't want to touch him - I was afraid to wake him up - so feeling his pulse was out of the question. Instead, I lowered my ear to his mouth to hear if he was breathing. My heart was pounding through my chest.

Nothing.

By the love of the Great General… I have just killed a guard. And tomorrow they will execute me!

My head raced as a thousand scenarios swirled through my mind. None of them ended with me not being shot tomorrow.

What will I do? What will I do? WHAT WILL I DO?

My spiral of panic was all of a sudden disrupted.

What was that? Did I imagine it?

I held my breath not to make a single sound and again lowered my ear. It was now right over his mouth. I could hold my breath but I could not stop my heart from pounding in my ears.

Nothing!

I kept my ear there. Then suddenly—

"Shhhh…"

It was an exhalation. Weak and barely audible - but it was *definitely* an exhalation.

He's alive!

I sank down beside him, panting with relief. I looked closely at his back, and now I could see that it was slightly rising and falling again.

He's not dead… I have not killed a guard… I'm safe!

But then I froze again.

I may not have killed a guard… but I have assaulted two guards!

I remembered the ten Sacred Rules. The punishment for assaulting a guard is exactly the same as for killing one - execution!

I felt light-headed. Not a single clear thought could form in my mind. Except for one.

I have to get out of here. I HAVE TO GET OUT OF HERE!

I jumped to my feet. I was dizzy and my vision was blurred, but I thought I saw Chang Min still on the ground in the same place as before. I started moving. I had to use the sound of the river to regain my orientation and then started stumbling down the hill in the direction that had to be towards the *Village of the Strayed*.

I fell down a couple of times, tripped over rocks or fallen branches - everything was still blurry and dark, and the moonlight didn't break through the dense canopy above me. As I neared the edge of the woods, however, both my head and my vision became clearer as the moonlight broke through and again guided me on my path.

I knew exactly what I needed to do - I needed to get *home*. I needed my *parents*. At this moment I didn't care what crimes they had committed... or how they had ignored me my whole life - now I needed them. I needed them to protect me. To hold me. Whatever happens tomorrow will happen, but right now...

I just need my family!

I ran.

I sprinted through the deserted fields, guided by the moon and a single light in one of the windows of *the Oversight*. I ran so fast that my lungs felt on fire. In my frantic state, I didn't even notice passing a couple of guards who sat on the ground, smoking.

"HEY!" they yelled and got on their feet. "YOU'RE PAST YOUR CURFEW! STOP!"

I didn't slow down - I didn't even look back at them. I just increased my speed and sprinted away from them, tears streaming down my cheeks. I heard them take a couple of running steps towards me and screamed at me to stop, but they gave up almost immediately, and soon I was long gone.

As soon as I reached our house, the exhaustion finally hit me with full force. I panted heavily, struggling to get air into my burning lungs. With my last ounce of energy, I got the door open. Mom and dad were inside. I stumbled in and immediately collapsed on the floor in front of them. I broke out in tears. I cried harder and louder than I had ever cried before in my life.

"Great General... what happened?" mom rushed over to me. "Where have you been? We were looking all over for you." She reached out her arms to hug me, but then remembered the rules of our current relationship and let her arms fall back down to her sides.

"Mom!" I sobbed. "Dad! I'm sorry. I did something terrible. Something really *stupid*. I'm so sorry!"

"What's going on? Are you okay? Are you hurt?" mom asked frantically.

Dad also came over, looking at me with a shocked expression.

"What happened to you? Are you alright? We have been so worried," he said.

I looked up at them and, without hesitation, I threw myself into their arms and continued crying.

"Mom! Dad! I'm sorry! I'm so sorry!"

They were stunned at first but then hugged me back... hard.

"Oh, my poor girl. My poor, sweet little girl. Everything will be alright," mom's voice was breaking up.

"No... it won't," I sobbed. "It won't..."

"Shhh... shhhhh... we're here... mom and dad are here for you, Areum-ah... everything will be fine... shhhhh."

I stayed in my mom's arms while dad heated some cabbage and corn soup for me. He also prepared a cup of green tea. They didn't push me further to tell them what happened. They gave me my space. It felt good being in my mom's arms. With all the bad things that have happened - and still would happen - I somehow felt protected. Hearing the heartbeats from her chest was soothing. I couldn't remember the last time I had been like this.

Maybe I had gotten it all wrong. Maybe my family are the only ones I can count on in this world... maybe I have to put everything behind me and just learn to accept them and love them... regardless of what they have done to me in the past...

At that moment, there was a soft knock on the door. Dad opened and Mina appeared in the doorway. Both mom and dad looked at her with surprise.

"Mina... what are you doing here?" mom asked. "Where is Nari?"

Mina returned the surprised look.

"What do you mean, Mrs. Kim? I came to see her... isn't she here?"

Mom and dad exchanged a scared look. It took a while for me to understand what was going on. I looked around me, and only now did I realize Nari wasn't here.

"She... she said she was going over to *your* house... it must have been over an hour ago... maybe even two," mom had despair in her voice. "Oh, Great General... something must have happened to her... where could she be? We have to go and look for her."

She stood up so abruptly that I fell to the ground. Only when she and dad were putting their coats on did mom remember me.

"Areum... have you seen your sister?"

"No... I haven't seen her." I struggled to get clarity in my memory, which now only contained scenes from the clearing up in the mountain. "I mean... I saw her before... with Mina, after work... but that was the last time."

Mom's eyes were filling up with tears as she stormed to the door, but as soon as she had turned the doorknob, something forcefully pushed the door open from the outside. Something - or someone - fell into the room. We all screamed.

Then I saw the clothes. And the hair. Mom rushed down and removed the hair from her face.

"Nari! Thank Great General it's you... Nari! Can you hear me?"

Mom bent over and hugged Nari's motionless body with all her strength. Her loud sobbing was the only thing that could be heard in the room. Nari's whole body was covered in sweat and dirt. Her face was bruised and swollen, and her clothes were ripped and torn in several places.

"Nari! Nari! Are you okay? Nari! What happened?"

Nari didn't respond, but she suddenly burst her eyes open in an expression of pure horror before breaking into tears. Shortly after, consciousness again left her body and her head thumped against the hard wooden floor. Mina stood next to me with her hand over her mouth and tears in her eyes.

"My sweet baby girl… what happened to you?" dad crouched down and put his arms around her.

"I'll go get my mother… she needs to be looked at by a doctor," Mina headed for the door without asking permission.

"Thank you, Mina… please hurry," dad said.

After the door had closed with a slam, mom looked up at me with her red swollen eyes.

"Areum… what happened to the two of you?"

"I… I don't know," I mumbled barely audibly.

"Areum… listen to me! Was Nari with you? Do you know what happened to her?"

"NO," I screamed. "I don't know what happened! She wasn't with me. I haven't seen her since our work shift ended… that was several hours ago."

The protection and comfort I had just felt was gone. Instead, I felt like I was being interrogated and accused… of *something*.

"Areum… first you come home all dirty and bruised… and shortly after, Nari comes home looking the same… are you telling me that's a coincidence?" mom glared at me.

"I… I'm telling you the truth… I haven't seen her since work finished… I don't know what happened to her… I *swear*!"

I stood there panting as mom and dad helped each other to carry Nari to her quilt.

Suddenly, both of them gasped in horror.

"Oh no… oh no… my sweet baby…" mom sobbed, gently caressing Nari's hair as teardrops fell on her face. "Oh no… Oh no…."

What's going on? What happened?

Dad didn't say anything. He didn't move. He just sat there next to Nari, his face grimmer than I had ever seen it before.

"Mom... dad..." I mumbled. "W-what's going on? What is it?"

There was no answer.

Nari regained consciousness and put her head in mom's lap, her arms around her waist. There she continued her soft and soundless sobbing.

Mom then turned to me again, her face filled with tears, anger, and desperation.

"You're her big sister... you're the *strong* one... you were supposed to *protect* her. You should have protected her! How could you let this happen?"

I stood there with my mouth open, looking at the three of them.

What in the Great General's name happened to her? And... do they think this is my fault?

The saga continues in

PART TWO – THE WEEPING MASSES

Hi there!

*I hope you enjoyed the introduction to the epic
JUCHE SAGA.*

*If you did, I would be immensely grateful if you could
spare just a few minutes of your precious time to help
your fellow book lovers find it by rating it on your
site of preference:*

*It would also be an invaluable help for me.
Ratings and reviews are the only means available for a
struggling indie author like myself to spread the word
about my work that is effective and not
bankruptcy-inducing. Without them, making a living
writing books is simply not possible.*

*A warm and heartfelt thank you for all
your wonderful support!*

Adria Carmichael

4b70516c-29d7-48cb-9ae1-8bef2f034fa9R01